THE TEMPORAL DETE
SERIES

By STEPHEN JOHN

Based on the original internet adve adventures of Jericho Tibbs!" by Ste ...ng as 'William Alexander Stephens.' This b ... contains TWELVE previously unpublished episodes from SERIES 3 of those adventures from 2019.

THIS IS THE THIRD BOOK IN THE SERIES.

ISBN-SBN: 9781739434625

NOTES:

[1] **Front Cover:** the original photograph **is from 'ISTOCK' – 519548561 – 612 x 612 and is used under License by the author.**

[2] For illustration credits, please see page 403 for details.

"Dedicated to my sister Sylvia for her love, loyalty and kindness."

VISIT 'THE TEMPORAL DETECTIVES' WEBSITE:

type: https://temporaldetectives.blogspot.com

SERIES 3 - THE EPISODES:

EPISODE 1: "THE JERUSALEM MIRROR."
START PAGE: 9.

MISSION SUMMARY:
"Dave Fisher and his girlfriend Sally are amazed to discover that a great uncle of Dave's has died and left his rambling old house to his young great nephew. 'Salem House' stands alone in the wilds of Yorkshire, off the beaten track and with few neighbours: But that won't put the young couple off and they move to the old house in June 1974 and find that the old place does, indeed, hold an incredible secret. Jericho Tibbs is now on the case after the pair simply vanished...."

NOTES: This is a special **Extended** Edition.

TRIGGER WARNINGS. ALCOHOL, STRONG LANGUAGE [including racial slurs] SEXUAL REFERENCES [including sexual assault] AND VIOLENCE.

EPISODE 2: "33AD."
START PAGE: 48.

MISSION SUMMARY:
"In the year 33AD, two 'prophets' are battling for the souls of humanity in chaotic Judea; Jesus, the son of a Carpenter from Nazareth and Barabbas, son of a slave trader from Jerusalem are fighting each other for the future of mankind. Barabbas commands the Zealots and wants war against Rome, who occupies his land. Jesus teaches love and forgiveness and putting down the sword. Jericho and his team are dispatched when things start to go wrong with the current Time-Line, and it can be traced back to 33AD."

NOTES: This episode contains Anti-Religious references which may offend certain people!

TRIGGER WARNINGS. ALCOHOL, STRONG LANGUAGE, SEXUAL REFERENCES AND MILD VIOLENCE.

EPISODE 3: "THE PRIEST."
START PAGE: 80.

MISSION SUMMARY:
"In the autumn of 1916, the village of Turning, located in a remote part of Yorkshire, welcomes the new parish priest; Father Peter Meyer, who has been a Padre in the British army and served for two years in Northern France. The young priest quickly proves popular amongst the villagers; especially amongst the many widows and wives of serving soldiers! But what lies behind this priest, who's favourite saying is; God has little to do with religion! But strange happenings in the village bring Jericho on the scene."

NOTES: This is a special **Extended** Edition.

TRIGGER WARNINGS. ALCOHOL, STRONG LANGUAGE, STRONG SEXUAL REFERENCES AND VIOLENCE.

EPISODE 4: "STRANGERS MARKET."
START PAGE: 124.

MISSION SUMMARY:
"Ms. Teresa Green - A Human Agent for Jericho Tibbs in England - during the early 21st Century, passes a strange story onto Jericho which he may be interested in. Apparently, a local London magazine has reported a story about an unknown young man, who is visiting stores and markets in the city purchasing large quantities of Victorian and Edwardian money. Whilst that appears quite innocent - he could be into Numismatics - another story emerges that the same odd fellow has purchased period clothes and has even taken lessons in Victorian and Edwardian etiquette!"

NOTES: This episode contains references to Nazi Germany.

TRIGGER WARNINGS. ALCOHOL, STRONG LANGUAGE, SEXUAL REFERENCES, VIOLENCE & NAZI'S!

EPISODE 5: "NAPOLEON'S CHINESE CABINET OF MAGIC: PART 1."
START PAGE: 155

MISSION SUMMARY:
"Emperor Napoleon receives Ambassadors from the Chinese Emperor and they present him with a very special gift - a magic cabinet! - Napoleon and his staff are cynical about its magic properties until the three Chinese Ambassadors enter the cabinet and simply disappear - for good. But Napoleon is struggling to retain his crown; will he use the gift to change his fortunes?"

NOTES: Part one of a two part mission.

TRIGGER WARNINGS. ALCOHOL, STRONG LANGUAGE, SEXUAL REFERENCES AND MILD VIOLENCE.

EPISODE 6: "NAPOLEON'S CHINESE CABINET OF MAGIC: PART 2."
START PAGE: 184

MISSION SUMMARY:
"Jericho is given a very strange mission by Angel Margret; to discover the truth about claims made by a collected soul that he played Napoleon's double; until he was murdered by the Emperor Napoleon I in May 1821. This, he claims, allowed Napoleon to escape in time. Human Records show that Napoleon's soul is indeed missing! The man: a certain Lucas Boucher was born in August 1769 and died, at the age of 51 - which exactly matches the life span of the Great Emperor. Physically, he did indeed resemble Napoleon. If he's telling the truth; then what happened to Napoleon Bonaparte and where is his soul now?"

NOTES:
[1]This episode was a Seasonal Special [online] and written with humour to the fore!
[2] Part 2 of a two part mission.

TRIGGER WARNINGS. ALCOHOL, STRONG LANGUAGE, SEXUAL REFERENCES AND MILD COMIC VIOLENCE.

EPISODE 7: "XAVIER TABBERT'S HOSPITAL FOR THE DEAD, THE DYING AND THE UNFORGIVEN."
START PAGE: 219.

MISSION SUMMARY:
"Dr. Xavier Tabbert opened his hospital for the chronically sick in the autumn of 1849. It was supposed to be a place of final and peaceful rest for those facing certain death; in modern times it would be referred to as a 'Hospice'. Now in 1999, a team of paranormal students under Professor Alec Sweetman have arrived at the derelict hospital to investigate the many strange happenings that have occurred over the years - are they about to encounter some real evil?"

NOTES: Contains references to poltergeist/Demonic activity.

TRIGGER WARNINGS. **ALCOHOL, STRONG LANGUAGE, SEXUAL REFERENCES, MILD VIOLENCE & HORROR.**

EPISODE 8: "HARBINGER."
START PAGE: 249.

MISSION SUMMARY:
"August1959, three teenage students camping in Dalby Forest, North Yorkshire have suddenly gone missing. The Police have searched the woods which cover 8,000 acres and found nothing. Their little campsite appears to have been abandoned in quite a hurry. The locals believe it's the work of 'HARBINGER' a mythical and dangerous 'Tree-Spirit', a legendary figure in these vast woodlands. But Jericho Tibbs and team 74 are on scene because the student's souls have gone missing from the current human time-line."

NOTES: Contains strong language and scenes of mild BDSM and murder.

TRIGGER WARNINGS. **ALCOHOL, SMOKING, STRONG LANGUAGE, SEXUAL REFERENCES [including BDSM] AND STRONG VIOLENCE.**

EPISODE 9: "UNKNOWN NUMBER."
START PAGE: 289.

MISSION SUMMARY:
"Old Lester Lightfoot hears a disturbance outside the front of his house one night and upon investigation finds that someone has thrown a broken mobile phone into his front garden. It has no battery or Sim card, and Lester tosses it on his hall table to dispose of properly in the morning. but at Midnight the phone starts ringing, and the dead are apparently calling!"

NOTES: This mission is considered quite unique amongst the adventures of Jericho Tibbs. Can you spot why?

TRIGGER WARNINGS. STRONG LANGUAGE, SUICIDE REFERENCES AND MILD VIOLENCE.

EPISODE 10: "SNOOKER, STOCKINGS & DEVILSH DECEIT."
START PAGE: 304.

MISSION SUMMARY:
"Inspector 'Doc' Silas Underhill who heads Team 13 and is Jericho's old Mentor and good friend has visited the Lighthouse with a disturbing story. He has a file which contains a very strange picture and newspaper clipping from England in 1985. Seemingly innocent and just some fun at first, the file contains a picture - apparently of Temporal Constable Alexandra Cappanni - flashing her underwear at the famous final of the World Snooker Championship held that year in Sheffield! But it's the 'man' sitting next to her that sets off alarm bells; it's the 'Dark Prince' himself!"

NOTES: This episode contains references to Demonic activity.

TRIGGER WARNINGS. ALCOHOL, STRONG LANGUAGE, STRONG SEXUAL REFERENCES [including sexual assault] AND MILD VIOLENCE.

EPISODE 11: "1914."
START PAGE: 331.

MISSION SUMMARY:
"The team is heading back to 1914 on the trail of a very dangerous time traveler who is plotting to change world history. It appears that a certain Katerina Potoski has planned to return to 28th June 1914 and the city of Sarajevo. The Archduke Franz Ferdinand Carl Ludwig Joseph Maria of Austria (18 December 1863 – 28 June 1914) was the heir presumptive to the throne of Austria-Hungary. His assassination in Sarajevo on that day, is considered the most immediate cause of World War I. Jericho and his team must prevent the current human timeline from Changing and not for the best!"

NOTES:
[1] It is – partly – based on true events.
[2] This is a special **Extended** Edition.

TRIGGER WARNINGS. ALCOHOL, STRONG LANGUAGE, SEXUAL REFERENCES AND MILD VIOLENCE.

EPISODE 12: "THE CORPSE CHRONICLER OF CANTERBURY CATHEDRAL."
START PAGE: 364.

MISSION SUMMARY:
"The ancient English cathedral of Canterbury is undergoing extensive renovation work for its Nine-hundred-year anniversary, since it was dedicated in 1077 AD. There is great excitement when workman find a medieval room bricked up behind an old wall. But the discovery reveals the remains of a woman - apparently bricked up with her books - whilst still alive! But history has no record of her and her newly found chronicles that could change the current timeline. Mr. Tibbs is sent to investigate."

NOTES: Contains strong language and combat violence.

TRIGGER WARNINGS. ALCOHOL, STRONG LANGUAGE, SEXUAL REFERENCES AND MILD VIOLENCE [including battle violence].

DISCLAIMER FOR ALL WORKS BY THE AUTHOR:

"All incidents and dialogue, and all characters with the exception of some well-known historical figures, are products of the author's imagination and are not to be construed as real. Where real-life historical figures appear, the situations, incidents, and dialogues concerning those persons are entirely fictional and are not intended to depict actual events or to change the entirely fictional nature of the work. In all other respects, any resemblance to actual persons, living or dead, events, or locales is entirely coincidental."

CAUTION:

"SOME OF THESE EPISODES CONTAIN VERY STRONG LANGUAGE, VIOLENCE, HORROR AND SEXUAL REFERENCES. Some are RECOMMENDED suitable for persons aged 15+ years only."

PLEASE REMEMBER: ALL STORIES ARE RATED

OR

AGE 15+ ONLY **AGE 12+ ONLY.**

AVERAGE READING TIMES: between 30 to 45 minutes [approx.]

EPISODE 1: "THE JERUSALEM MIRROR."

MISSION SUMMARY: "Dave Fisher and his girlfriend Sally are amazed to discover that a great uncle of Dave's has died and left his rambling old house to his young great nephew .'Salem House' stands alone in the wilds of Yorkshire, off the beaten track and with few neighbours, the old house is steeped in legend and stories of ghosts and strange happenings. But that won't put the young couple off and they move to the old house in June 1974 and find that the old place does, indeed hide an incredible secret. Jericho Tibbs is now on the case after the pair simply vanished...."

NOTES: This is a special **Extended** Edition.

TRIGGER WARNINGS. ALCOHOL, STRONG LANGUAGE [including racial slurs] SEXUAL REFERENCES [including sexual assault] AND VIOLENCE.

AGE 15+ ONLY. **45 Minutes reading time.**

1. 3rd MAY 1974 - A SOLICITOR CALLS.

Sally eased from the bed and pushed her long blond hair back whilst snatching up her dressing gown from the floor. The door bell sounded again and she muttered; "First bloody time we have a real lay in this week and someone is at the door." She looked back at Dave sprawled under the covers and shook her head. "Christ, you'd sleep through a bloody bomb going off." Sally wrapped her dressing gown around her naked body and headed for the stairs.

She made her way down the stairs, passing the sleeping cat; Amy, on the top stair, which sat up and followed. "I'm coming!" Sally said loudly and reached the door, picking up several pieces of mail from the carpet. She tidied her hair and checked her dressing gown, then unlocked the front door and opened it a few inches. "Hello, can I help you. We're just having a lay in, we both do shift work you see," she said to the middle-aged, well-dressed man standing on their step, clutching a leather briefcase. He smiled; "Does David Edward Fisher live here?" He asked and offered Sally a little white business card.

Sally took the card and read it slowly. "You're a lawyer from York?" She sounded quite surprised and held her dressing gown together quite tightly with the other hand. She didn't really want to flash a bloody solicitor at this time of the morning.

Patrick Well's nodded; "Yes, I'm here to speak to a David Edward Fisher, whose father was Norman David Fisher and Grand-father was Edward John Fisher; all from Sheffield." He rummaged around in his briefcase and pulled some papers out. "I'm here about his Great-Uncle Wesley's will." He smiled and gripped his briefcase.

"I didn't even know he had a Great-Uncle?" She was really surprised by that revelation; David's parents were both dead and he had no brothers or sisters. She slowly pulled the door chain off and opened the door. "You'd better come in and I'll get the idle bugger out of his pit." Sally smiled and gestured for Patrick Well's to go into the living room, whilst she headed back up the stairs and then cursed herself; the bloody man only had to glance up, to see her bare bum. She really should invest in a longer dressing gown, she mused. Sally didn't look back down the stairs to see if he was watching.

She smiled to herself as she reached the bedroom door; still he was a good-looking well-groomed man, at least he probably wouldn't object to seeing a 22-year-old woman's private parts, especially one, most men considered 'pretty'. Well, non-one had complained, when she dances at the 'Blue Star Club' until the early hours of the morning. Her flimsy costume barely covered anything; but the money was good and she really needed money.

She sighed and really didn't want to think about the debt they were in - it gave her enough sleepless days and nights already. Sally stared at the man snoring under the covers and had to smile; David had stood by her throughout the court cases and debt orders, the bailiffs and repossessions. She actually shuddered at the thoughts that crowded quickly into her head and now a bloody solicitor turns up at this time of the morning and she flashes her arse at him!

She shook David strongly and told him about the visitor, telling him to slip on a T-shirt and track bottoms and get downstairs. She would slip on some panties and her long padded house coat and told him to put the bloody kettle on!

Dave was mumbling about he hasn't got any fucking Uncles. He had never heard of a Great-Uncle bleeding Wesley. He stumbled down the stairs into the front room and greeted the solicitor; apologizing for still being in bed, but he had finished nightshift at the local Meat Distribution Depot of Dewhurst the Butchers.

The solicitor waved his apology away with a smile; "I should be the one to apologize Mr. Fisher, I was in the area dealing with a complicated conveyance and I thought I would try my luck." Dave gestured for him to sit and he would put the kettle on. The solicitor continued; "We have written several times and received no replies, so I thought a personal visit would be best." He sat and pulled more papers from his briefcase. "I'll make some tea." Dave muttered and headed for the kitchen, followed by Amy the cat who wanted her breakfast.

Dave switched the kettle on and sighed; "Great-Uncle Wesley?" He had never heard his parents speak of such a man - he couldn't ask them now; they had both passed on five years ago, after suffering a car accident on a dirt road in Spain, whilst on holiday. A tractor had pulled from a field, straight in front of them. Apparently, it took an ambulance nearly a hour to reach the accident site - it was in the foothills of some mountains - They were both dead upon arrival at the local hospital.

He didn't want to be reminded of those dark days and pushed it from his mind as he made tea; yelling to the solicitor how he likes his; milk and two sugars came the reply. Sally appeared in the doorway and whispered; "What the fuck is this all about?" Dave shrugged his shoulders and whispered back; "I've never heard of a bloody Great-Uncle Wesley. He says that they have written to me several times - I've never seen any bloody letters from them."

Sally looked down at the business card and covered her mouth with a hand; "Dave, I'm so sorry. I've seen letters with this Solicitors address on and panicked. I chucked them away. I'm so sorry. I thought they were after me for more money." Dave just shook his head; "Don't worry about it sweetheart; he's here now." He passed her a cup of tea and wandered into the living room with a cup for the solicitor.

Sally stood in the kitchen and sipped her tea; without Dave's steadfast support she really didn't know what would have happened to her. She had lost her flat, her car and even the bloody bank had closed her accounts. She had to leave a couple of steady jobs working in supermarkets because men had turned up at work, threatening her for money, even the Tax man was after his share and Sally found that she was paying a lot of her wages back to the Inland revenue. She struggled with that and finally had to find a job that paid cash in hand; the 'Blue Star Club' did that for her.

Now, four nights a week until the early hours; she danced and served drinks for money in her hand; that had helped greatly. But she really did feel ashamed, that she paraded around the club with a little silver tray and not much else. Her 'uniform' consisted of a little black mini skirt, high heels, frilly white apron, panties and stockings - nothing else - but a black dog collar around her neck with silver lettering showing ' Blue Star Club'. On certain nights she could earn really good tips by completing her duties without any panties on.

Then, there was the chance of earning really serious money by having sex with certain customers at the club. Leon came immediately to mind; he always gave her twenty pounds each time [good money for the era], when she called around his plush apartment in the city on her night off; always when Dave was still on shift. The big African clearly liked small, blond, white girls with ample breasts and he paid well for her company. He wanted her for his full-time mistress and would keep her in comfort, at one of the apartments he owned; if she agreed - she hadn't done so because of what she owed Dave for his unswerving support.

She sighed and then snapped from her thoughts as Dave called her into the living room. She forced a smile and wandered in and sat down. Amy jumped upon her lap and started cleaning herself. Dave grinned broadly and gripped her hand; "You are never going to believe what Patrick has just told me; I've inherited a house near the Yorkshire Moors. Great-Uncle Wesley died without a wife or any children and I'm his nearest blood relative still living. He was my grandfather's youngest brother - I had never heard Grandpa or dad ever talk about him."

Sally couldn't really absorb what Dave was saying for some minutes and then realized this could be the answer to all her problems. She cuddled him, pushing the cat from her lap; "I really won't believe it until I see the place with my own eyes!" She exclaimed and kissed him' much to the amusement of the solicitor who advised the pair to make an appointment with him at his York offices - to receive the keys and sign for the property.

There was also a little cash to come.

"How much cash?" Sally asked straight away and was told that Great-Uncle Wesley had left David about fifteen hundred pounds; after Death Duties had been paid and, of course, some debts owned by his late Great-Uncles estate. Not to mention Solicitors fee's.

So; the happy couple made arrangement to visit 'Salem House; as soon as possible. Sally danced and served drinks that night, with a smile on her face. But Dave worried about his inheritance and what it would mean for the future of the pair. One thought troubled him above the rest; why hadn't his mother, father and grandfather ever spoken about 'Great Uncle Wesley'?

2. 17th JUNE 1974 - SALEM HOUSE - PART 1.

Dave jumped from the old Vauxhall Viva and stared at the old house, a little amazed that he actually owned it. Sally grabbed him around the waist and planted a big kiss on his lips. "I still can't bloody believe its yours." She kissed him again. Dave grinned and held up the keys; "Ours." He said softly and the pair embraced in the overgrown driveway. The removal lorry driver shook his head and stared up at the old house and turned to the other men in the cab; "I wouldn't have this fucking place if it came with gold beds." The younger man nodded and handed around the cigarettes; "I'd fuck his young tart, fantastic pair of tits." He muttered, quietly smoking. They watched as the young couple hugged and celebrated outside the old house.

Paddy the driver stared up at 'Salem House' and stopped smoking, very quietly he spoke to the other two men; "Look up at the attic on the right wing, the big window, can you see it?"

The other two men leaned forward and peered through the windscreen. "I see it." Whispered the younger man; his cigarette falling from his lips onto the cab floor. Terry gripped the dash and swore; "Fucking shit! Do you see her as well?"

All three men watched the figure standing at the dirty window in amazement; "Like something out of an old film." Paddy said softly and Terry agreed; "Like something in an old portrait you see in museums, or those big houses open to the public." Paddy crossed himself and kissed the little crucifix that hung around his neck; "I'd heard all the fucking stories about this shit hole, but never thought I'd see they were true."Terry wiped his face with the back of his hand - he was sweating without actually doing anything - The three exchanged concerned glances and made an unanimous decision; get the stuff into the fucking house as quick as possible and get the fuck out of here. They also decided it would be best - for the young couple - if they said nothing about the figure at the window.

All three men lapsed into a shocked silence as the figure disappeared. Paddy crossed himself again; he had not really prayed in some years; but he did now.

The young couple had unlocked the big double doors and were waving for the removal men to start unloading their possessions. Very reluctantly the men left the cab - all still staring at the upstairs window - and began to shift the boxes and items of furniture from their lorry; in almost silence.

Dave and Sally were so engrossed in their happiness and relief that they had escaped the dingy - and expensive - rented house;

they didn't really notice the change in the removal men's mood. They were impressed with the speed that the men unloaded the lorry and piled their stuff in the house. They didn't even wait for the customary tips - disappearing down the drive without as much as a 'goodbye'.

Sally found a comfortable big bedroom on the first floor, near a bathroom and working toilet, and made up the bed whilst Dave brewed tea in the small kitchen, that had been built on the same floor. He had found that cold tap worked, but the hot tap just made gurgling noises. They guessed correctly, this little suite of rooms, had been occupied by Dave's great uncle Wesley, when he was alive.

It was Dave that pointed out the four locks on the bedroom door and as he looked about, he noticed the strange pattern woven into the old carpet. He studied it for some minutes before realizing that it was a pentagon; what was the significance of that he wondered. Sally called him over to the large Gothic fireplace and both stared at the remains of a bird, burnt in the grate with withered flowers scattered about it. She made Dave clear that revolting mess up straight away.

Dave couldn't open the large window; it had been nailed shut and Sally pulled down the strings of rotted garlic from around the frame and they went in the bin, with the dead bird. "He was one strange old fucker." She said quietly as she cleaned the window frame. Then giggling, she jumped on the bed and bounced up and down upon the large four poster bed, until she looked up and saw the bed's canopy; it was Jesus on the Cross.

"Fucking charming, a religious nut as well as fucking strange and reclusive." She said to Dave, who just chuckled and headed back to the kitchen to see if the electricity meter was on and working. The gas certainly was - he had boiled the kettle on the small two ring stove – which the small kitchen contained.

The electricity only worked in this suite, and he put fifty pence in the meter to start with. They sat on stools in the little kitchen and laughed together; the pair’s relief that most of their problems were behind them now was palatable and obvious. For the first time in quite a while; they were actually happy.

Sally finally did mention about the strange behaviour of the removal men and Dave had to agree; he still had the five pound note, he was going to give them as a tip. He pulled the crumpled note from his pocket as proof. Sally slowly eased it from his fingers with a big smile; "Well, I'll take it as a tip for being your hardworking girlfriend." Dave chuckled and nodded his head; "You're worth every penny." He spoke softly and kissed her again.

Sally released Amy from her cat basket and watched in amazement and surprise that the little creature ran back into her cage and refused to come out. Even food and treats wouldn't make the cat budge. "She just needs time to settle in; it's all new territory to her." Dave smiled and so they left the cage door open with food and water outside. The cat steadfastly remained inside.

They worked for a couple of hours getting the rooms ready; the major disappointment was the little 'Bush' portable TV wouldn't pick a signal up. Dave sighed; "I can't find a aerial socket, old Wesley couldn't have had a TV - strange that, but the solicitor said he was an odd old man." Sally's wireless radio wouldn't pick up a signal either. But her stereo record player worked alright. So they played Beatles records and a couple of singles by the 'Mama's and Papa's' as night gathered in.

After a supper of tinned vegetable soup and bread, they jumped into bed and celebrated their good fortune with passionate love-making. They were both soon asleep; but not for long.

Sally suddenly sat up and took a deep breath; what was that noise? She reached over to the ornate bedside cabinet and grabbed up her watch. She pressed the little button and the LCD display showed: '00.00'. Sally then realized - with some relief and some annoyance - that the grandfather clock in the downstairs hall was chiming Midnight. She glanced at Dave; he was still fast asleep. "A bloody bomb going off wouldn't wake you up." She muttered and flopped back on her pillows, pulling up the sheets again. She counted the chimes as they sounded in the quiet house.

For a second time, she sat straight up and breathed quickly and heavily; the bloody old clock had chimed thirteen times!

She also heard other noises coming from downstairs; it sounded like people having a muffled conversation amongst themselves.

She shook Dave quite violently and whispered that they had intruders in the house. He woke and pulled his trousers and For a second time, she sat straight up and breathed quickly and heavily; the bloody old clock had chimed thirteen times!

She also heard other noises coming from downstairs; it sounded like people having a muffled conversation amongst themselves. She shook Dave quite violently and whispered that they had intruders in the house. He woke and pulled his trousers and shoes on, stopping only to pick up a large, heavy black poker from the fireplace. Sally climbed slowly from the bed and wrapped her long, padded coat around her naked body.

Sally noticed that the cat basket was empty; but the food and water appeared untouched. She scrambled about in a nearby cardboard box and found a torch. They quietly headed from the bedroom into the upper hall; both filled with a mix of fear and trepidation.

3. 24th JUNE 1974 - SALEM HOUSE - PART 2.

Detective Inspector Roy Calms lit a cigarette and eased his large frame from the small car and headed to the uniform constable standing on the door - looking bored with his arms folded. He stood straight and saluted the Inspector. "Your sergeant is on the first floor with a couple more of your boys Sir." He greeted the Inspector who just nodded. A real queer one this; a young couple move into this old relic and simply disappear, he thought; climbing the grand staircase.

Detective Sergeant Greg Chambers finished his cigarette and tossed the butt into the fireplace. He looked about the room and shook his head, speaking to the Detective Constable who was sorting through an open cardboard box on the floor; "Fisher's watch and wallet are still on the dresser and all his clothes still appear to be here. The bloody girl must have been naked - apart from a padded coat she always wore. - Didn't take her purse, watch or shoes either. Bloody strange."

The constable nodded his agreement; "Uniform say that the place was all locked up when they arrived to investigate the missing persons report. They had to break in through a downstairs window, so how the fuck did they get out of the house?" He pulled a large black vibrator from the box and laughed; "Typical tart who danced half naked at that cesspit club and she owns this!" he waved the rubber penis about and switched it on, it didn't work. He laughed again; "She's worn the fucking batteries out and it takes four 'Duracell'."

"She also wasn't averse, to sleeping with some of the customers, so her colleagues tell us." Inspector Calm's stood in the doorway and pulled his note book out. "The man was reliable as a Swiss watch according to his employers - never missed a shift in three years - then suddenly he doesn't turn up with any word – nothing - Right out of character." They all commented about the girl though, little better than a common prostitute. They really didn't know how such a good bloke got involved with a tart like her.

"She was an undercharged bankrupt, had no bank accounts and couldn't get credit anywhere. She was working at that club for 'cash in hand'. Even the bloody tax man was after her. A right one by the sounds of it." The Inspector added, looking around the room.

Sergeant Chambers waved his hand about; "Most of their clothes and personal item are still here, they must have left practically naked and penniless." He pointed to the bedside cabinet and the little black diary laying there.

"That makes good reading Guv, payments from men who fucked her for twenty quid a time." The sergeant picked up the book and handed it to the Inspector. The constable whistled; "Twenty quid a time; she must have been a fucking good shag for that sort of money." The Inspector chuckled and tapped the book; "There are several references to someone called 'Leon'. I wonder if that's our old friend, the pimp and pornographer Leon Devine. I bet we could find a few films with our missing girl starring in them."

Sergeant Chambers folded his arms; "The last people we know, who saw the pair alive, were the three removal men from Baxter's removals. That was on the 17th of this month - no-one has seen them alive since that day. That's where it becomes really interesting; the youngest of the three men; a certain Robert Cornfield has quit his job and moved down south; all on the day he helped move the pair into this dump; and he made sure to leave no forwarding address. Odd co-incidence that."

The Inspector nodded and re-read his notebook; "Interesting

threesome we have here; the driver, Patrick 'Paddy' O'Connor has previous for house breaking and some theft; but it was nearly fifteen years ago when he was much younger. His Driver's mate: Terry Jones has previous for sexual assault on young girls. Nothing is known about young Cornfield."

Detective Constable Matchings looked up from the cardboard box and chuckled; "When I spoke to that pair, they looked paler than a ginger birds arse. Claimed they dropped the gear and got the fuck outta the place because they saw a fucking ghost!" Everyone was amused by that.

Then Detective Constable Harris stuck his head around the door; "Guv, uniform says you're wanted on the radio. The solicitor who dealt with the pair has finally turned up at the nick,"

The Inspector sighed and stared about the small rooms; "The old man who owned the place was found dead - at the foot of the stairs - some three years ago. His death was bloody queer too." the Inspector pushed his notebook away and headed for the door. "How was it queer Guv?" The sergeant asked.

The inspector didn't smile; "No marks upon the body, Doc Roberts believed the old man suffered a massive heart attack and died at the foot of the stairs. A PM confirmed that, but he was found stark naked clutching an old photograph which he had apparently written upon - in crayon - the words 'forgive me'. The picture had been taken about 1880 and showed a very young girl - a child - being abused by some creep. Some straight-laced Victorians really did enjoy child porn. We know he wrote the words because a red crayon was found clutched in his other hand; he must have written the words as he died."

The detective stopped searching the cupboard box and looked up; "How old was the old man Guv?" The Inspector grinned; "I know where you're heading with that Ken, Wesley Fisher was sixty-three years old when he died in 1971 and the photograph was taken in 1879 or 1880 according to the experts who took a look at it. It was shot long before the old man was even born. So why was he asking for forgiveness about something, he couldn't be remotely involved in?"

None of the Detectives present could answer that mystery and so the Inspector shrugged his shoulders and muttered; "Fucking queer all round." The sergeant rubbed his chin; "Shall I pull them removal men in Guv?" The Inspector said no. He wanted them to make voluntary statements for now but instructed the sergeant to issue a 'Person of Interest Notice' to all forces regarding young Cornfield. The Inspector looked about the room and shrugged his shoulders again; "No signs of burglary, no signs of a fight or any disturbance - except that poker and torch lying on top of the stairs - nothing really to go on."

Sergeant Chambers stared out the window and spoke directly to the Inspector; "We could pull in that dirty black bastard Leon and see what he knows about the tart?" The Inspector approved of that idea; "Yeah, sweat him for a few hours and see what jumps out." The Inspector chuckled and walked straight past the two Temporal Detectives standing in the top hall, both consulting their mirrors - he, of course, could not see or hear them - unless they wanted it so.

"Wesley Fisher's soul was collected and processed; he's now a motor mechanic in Mexico City. Nothing untoward was known about him. But he died in 1982 and in France! So who was the stiff that the police were talking about?" Alex tapped her mirror, adding: "But this house has some real questions about it since it was built in 1767. Some of the previous owners have been devil worshippers, rapists and murders - you name something evil and it's happened here - over the centuries." Alex lowered her mirror and stared into the rooms where the other, living, detectives still worked.

"Find out who collected the soul of the dead body found here." Jericho rubbed his chin, something was wrong; if Wesley had been collected somewhere else, who the hell was the dead man? Alex nodded; "I'll get Owen onto it, that's right up his street."

"Here's an interesting thought; Wesley Fisher came from a poor working-class Sheffield family and had no real education or qualifications. In his early life he worked the steel mills for wages - poor wages - yet in his twilight years he could buy a house like this and have serious money in his bank accounts." Jericho gestured towards the grand staircase; "Some of the portraits, just on the bloody staircase could buy a decent house around here, so where did the money come from?"

Alex admitted she didn't know and pushed the mirror into her jacket pocket and watched the Inspector descending the stairs. "I don't think they have a clue about this place." She said quietly, but Jericho smiled; "Why should they? They're still amongst the living." Both looked up as Wilson and Owen appeared at the top of the attic stairs. Wilson gestured for them to join him. "Guess what we found in the attic." He jerked a thumb behind him and added; "A bloody Jerusalem Mirror."

Jericho rubbed his hands together and smiled; "Now that's more like it. We get the call that two souls have vanished - complete with their flesh suits still on - and there's a bloody Jerusalem mirror in the place." They made their way to the attic room and found the old, full-length mirror standing against a dirty wall, next to the window.

"Wonder which time and place it's linked to?" Asked Owen and started to re-read his mirror. Jericho was looking at the back of the mirror with a small torch. "It was made originally in France, at a place called 'la Masion des Tenebres' or that could be the company who manufactured it. The year shown is...." He leaned forward and strained to make out the writing; "In 1646."

"The House of Darkness." Alex sighed; "Charming name, must have had the customers queuing up outside." Owen interrupted everyone and tapped his mirror; "Says here, that one of the owners was a certain Marquis de Sade in 1765, in Paris."

"Now that is one interesting old French pervert - apparently." Wilson chuckled and then something on the floor caught his eye - a simple white rag that was too clean and laundered to have laid on the dusty floor for long. He walked over and picked it up; "A Lace hankie." He muttered and pulled it from his face; "It's being soaked in something very pungent and is still a little overpowering." He offered it to the others. Jericho took a slight sniff and nodded; "Old fashioned knock-out stuff and it's still quite fresh."

Jericho spoke to Owen; "Call into control and tell them we're going to use the mirror." Everyone watched as Jericho simply stepped into the 'glass' and disappeared. They all followed without question and the dirty little attic room was empty - again.

Well, it wasn't quite empty; Amy the cat crept out from beneath a covered stool and ran towards the mirror and jumped through. A dark shadow passed across the dirty floor and the man stood by the mirror; he stared down at his pocket watch and sighed - but he could now hear two of the detectives approaching the attic rooms and without hesitation stepped through - so all Detective Ken Lewis and his colleague found was a dirty room stuffed with old furniture.

There was dust and cobwebs everywhere and so they concluded that no-one had been in the room for years.

They had a quick look around and then left, closing the door behind them. There was silence in the darkness until a weak white light appeared on the mirrors glass and the sound of footsteps could have been heard from the room; had the detectives stayed a little bit longer. But then; the time was now quite different.

The young woman gathered her dress about herself and listened intently at the door, then slowly approached the large window and peered down into the entrance of 'Salem House'. She saw the couple embracing by the ornate front doors and the removal van sitting on the gravel. She watched as the large black car swept into the drive and some people stepped from the car; they looked like Undertakers.

The woman groaned and cussed. "That old bastard; he must really hate me. He must have tipped them off." She whispered and headed for the mirror again.

4. 16th AUGUST, 1767 - LA MASION DES TENEBRES (PARIS).

The carriage threaded slowly through the crowded streets and Alex waved her silk fan across her face - it didn't do much good in this heat. "I didn't think summer in Paris could be this hot." She muttered to Jericho who was wiping his face with a small hankie. He smiled and adjusted his powdered wig, causing little flakes of white chalk to fly about; "I think Owen has overdone the bloody powder on this thing." Alex managed a smile and eased her bosom beneath her thin cloak; "You only have to worry about chalk dust, this bloody corset has pushed my tits up and out so much, I'm practically topless."

Alex was dressed like a lady of the royal Court of King Louis XV, colloquially known as 'the beloved' and the ladies of his court were well known for their outrageous clothes and loose morals. Wilson, who was driving the ornate carriage leaned back and spoke through the small flap, covered with embroidered cloth, to Alex and Jericho; "I think we're here." Owen, who was standing upon the rear step [and gripping the leather straps with both hands] muttered; "Thank God for that, Wilson couldn't drive a greasy stick up a pig's arse."

The carriage stopped outside and a magnificent strapping African male in a stunning red and gold servants uniform, pulled open the door and bowed. Alex accepted his white gloved hand and stepped from the carriage, Jericho followed straightening his sword and blinking in the hot sunshine. He turned to Wilson; "Titus, wait for thirty minutes only." Wilson nodded - then it was Calvary time.

Owen stepped off the carriage and stretched his legs; he stared up at the black fronted building with little windows and bright red roof. The gold plate upon the wall declared; "'la Maison des Tenebres: Fonde 1689." Someone had scrawled beneath in white chalk: 'cher maison de pute'. Owen grinned at that and joined Wilson by the horses, with the water bucket that hung beneath the carriage. "They can have a drink." He said and patted the grey mare nearest to him.

The pair watched Alex and Jericho disappear into the dark building and the big servant resumed his position on the top of the stairs with no expression upon his face. "That's funny, I would have thought, he would have wanted to chat with a fellow African." Wilson murmured, but Owen smiled; "There are hundreds of African servants in Paris at this time, so he probably gets all the chat he could ever want." They both chuckled at that and Owen gave water to the other grey mare of the carriage's team.

Jericho and Alex were shown into a beautifully furnished sitting room by another resplendent African servant, he bowed and gestured towards two bright red upholstered chairs; "Ma'am and Sir, I will inform Madame Bella that you are here." He walked backwards and left the room. Alex slumped upon the chair and loosened her cloak: "In two hundred years, the contents of this room would fetch an absolute fortune, and this is just a bloody brothel." Jericho nodded, and his sharp eyes had already seen the two spy holes set into the wall opposite; disguised as wall decorations of glass. He grunted; "Someone is already watching us; I wonder who that can be?" Alex didn't answer as the door opened and Madame Bella Varden strolled in. She was a tall, skinny woman in her late thirties, wearing thin white gloves with her long [and obviously expensive] gown. Around her neck was a gold chain, a snake and a circle. Jericho sat upright at the sight of her necklace. Then stood and smiled, he bowed and kissed her outstretched hand.

"Madame Bella, may I present my Mistress; Mademoiselle Alexandra." Alex rose and curtsied but said nothing. Madame Bella ran her eyes up and down Alex and smiled; "Monsieur Tibbs, your friend is quite a beauty. Such a woman could earn a fortune here - probably in one night." Jericho also smiled; "Quite so, but I have come on a most urgent matter on behalf of an English friend. I seek the whereabouts of his missing mistress and I know the girl would make for such an establishment like that you command." Madame Bella nodded - her face expressionless; "Please sit." She spoke softly and her African servant placed a chair behind her and she sat with some grace.

"My friend, quite foolishly in my opinion, mistreated the girl and she disappeared into the night. We know she made for France and most certainly to here; Paris I mean. There is a substantial reward for her recovery. Quite substantial." Jericho pulled a small picture from his pocket and offered it to Madame Bella; she took it very slowly and said quietly; "How substantial Monsieur Tibbs?" Jericho leaned forward and whispered into her ear - Alex caught the Madame's expression and smiled to herself; that little amount will put the cat amongst the pigeons; no doubt about that.

Madame Bella produced a beautiful blue fan and waved it about her face. "If your friend has that sort of money to throw after a...well, a....a young whore, then he is a fool. I'm sure that even good-looking harlots are cheap enough in England." She smiled and handed back the picture; Jericho knew she had recognized the likeness and the alarm in her eyes; which most would have missed, didn't go unnoticed by him or Alex.

Jericho chuckled and held up his hands; "I know Madame Bella, I know, but of all people you will understand the vagaries of the heart. He wants her back; it's as simple as that." Madame Bella stared at Alex; "Your young mistress is clearly well trained and obedient. Most girls like her would have endless useless chatter upon their tongues. She says nothing; but observes and hears everything. I am impressed. I would give you ten thousand Francs' right now for her - no questions asked."

Jericho shook his head; "I'm sorry Madame Bella, but it would probably cost me twice that to replace such a gem." Madame Bella smiled at that; "I'm afraid I cannot help you Monsieur Tibbs, I have never seen the girl in the likeness that you have offered. I'm sorry." She rose suddenly from her chair and pulled the rope cord to summon a servant. "Apollo will show you out." The big African re-appeared and gestured towards the door, bowing a little. "This way please." He said and waited for Jericho and Alex to rise and walk to the door.

Jericho turned to Madame Bella, smiled and bowed; "Please consider the reward; should you receive any information about the girl. I am staying with an old friend of my friend; He's called Louis." Madame Bella chuckled with some contempt in her voice; "Paris is a big city Monsieur, with many a Louis hanging about the place, which damn Louis would that be?"

Jericho hesitated in the doorway and smiled; "I am sorry Madame, my old friend's friend stays at Versailles; that's his home now." He took Alex by the hand and the pair left a clearly shocked Madame Bella, who stumbled across the room and slumped into her chair. She watched the pair go and wiped her face; could this pair be for real? The King would certainly have the kind of money mentioned for the English girl. But an old friend of the King? From England? A name popped into her head, The Duke of Buckingham? She groaned quite loudly and shouted for Apollo to come.

That evening, 'la Masion des Tenebres was packed with customers, but Madame Bella sat quietly in her study, sipping wine and staring at fireplace. Her two gentlemen companions also sat in silence, glasses of brandy in their hands.

Madame's maid servant Maria appeared and informed her mistress that Apollo had returned. Everyone sat up as the big African appeared, bowed and removed his hat. Madame Bella gestured for him to speak. "I followed their carriage, and it did indeed travel to Versailles. They entered the Palace through the

King's personal entrance and were met by Le Marquis Du Nantes; the King's Private Secretary. I made some discrete inquiries about the pair, and it appears that Monsieur Tibbs is some kind of envoy for a very important and powerful Englishman. The recovery of the girl seems to be a matter of personal honour for the King now and as you would expect, he cannot take his eyes off Mademoiselle Alexandra."

Madame Bella turned to the men and sighed; "It appears that Roland has fucked up with this one. He made the mistake; he can clear the mess up." She stood and headed for the door. The two men stood and nodded at each other; Madame was not a woman you cross easily. They placed their glasses down and followed her to the attics.

Madame Bella stood in the doorway and consulted her little blue notebook; the girl didn't stand her in too much money and that amount had been paid to Roland for her. She stared down at sally; unconscious and totally naked upon the bed with her hands tied behind her back. She called for Madame Clare, who appeared from a room opposite, wiping her hands. The old woman was a little hunched over and had just a few yellow teeth left in her mouth. She grinned; "That one will be ready for work by tomorrow; she's already seen a few big cocks by my reckoning; her fanny's a little loose, but she's pretty enough for most of the bastards we get here. Besides, she does have a fine pair of milk tits which all men like."

Madame Bella nodded and did not smile; "We may have been compromised by her or rather, by Monsieur Roland, and I have sent a message to him to dispose of her without any links to my mansion." Monsieur Henri coughed and started pulling off his jacket; "Well, we may as well get some of our investment back." Monsieur Phillip agreed and started to remove his jacket. Madame Clare chuckled; "She won't come round for a few hours yet." Both men shrugged their shoulders and Monsieur Henri pulled open his lacey shirt; "I don't mind that, and I know Phillip enjoys a sleeper." The two Madame's both sighed and closed the door on the two men and Sally.

Madame Clare gripped Bella by the arm and spoke softly; "What about the man?" Madame Bella looked quite surprised by the admission that Roland had also acquired a man with the girl. But Bella had no idea what had happened to him. "Knowing Monsieur

Roland I would suspect that he sold him to Monsieur Franklyn." Clare muttered and did grin to herself; Monsieur Franklyn ran the finest Homosexual brothel in Paris, and he always needed straight men for his 'dungeon' - which earns serious money from certain discerning clients.

Madame Bella returned to her customers - deep in thought and instructed Apollo to fetch Monsieur Roland; at once. She collected a glass of brandy and sat in her drawing room alone. But Madame Bella was not alone in the beautiful room and jumped a little, when the large black cat pushed past her feet and disappeared behind a red and gold sofa. She stared at the sofa and wondered where the damn cat came from - they had some in the kitchens - for the rats and mice, but none were allowed upstairs. She hated cats.

Something in her memory was saying that this black cat belonged to Monsieur... She interrupted her thoughts and rose to ring the servant's bell and have the damn thing removed and killed, but never reached the bell pull. Madame Bella lay dead upon the floor with a large, gaping blood-filled wound to her throat, which had been slit wide open.

The figure left the room un-noticed despite the throngs of customers and girls. The cat followed it into the busy street and then into the plain black carriage that awaited them. It disappeared at speed into the gathering gloom of night.

The man stepped from the shadows opposite the grand doors of 'la Maison des Tenebres' and consulted his Italian pocket watch. With a broad smile, he lifted a hand and his handsome, dark red cab trundled towards him. He jumped in and settled down for the thirty-minute ride to Chateau Roi Charles. The big man sitting opposite said nothing and stared out the window - Paris was quite a grand city - but nothing could match the Palace of Versailles - that he was now privileged to attend with his new master. He smiled and adjusted his jacket which concealed both a pistol and dagger. Tomorrow could prove most interesting, he mused.

Apollo returned to the window and admired the countryside passing by. He was a happy man. His master grunted; "Now we need to deal with that bastard Tibbs." Apollo just smiled and thought about Mademoiselle Alexandra.

5. 17th AUGUST 1767 - CHATEAU ROI CHARLES (NEUILLY - SUR - SEINE).

Monsieur Roland watched the large grey crate unloaded from the cart with great care. He pointed towards the doors and told the men to take the grate to the cellar lift. They nodded and disappeared inside. He consulted his fob watch and stared down the driveway; a plain black cab was slowly making its way towards Chateau Roi Charles in the early morning sun.

He turned to Apollo and gestured towards the approaching cab; "By the time he arrives and enters my study, he will be exactly on time." Monsieur Roland chuckled and walked into his Chateau, telling Apollo to show Monsieur Le Chat into his study. He saw Madame Bridget standing by the foot of the main staircase; she bowed slightly but said nothing. He simply nodded and she disappeared towards the cellar stairs entrance; hidden in a grand stateroom cupboard, that stood in a quiet corner of the hallway.

Monsieur Roland eased himself behind his large ornate desk and stared at the open door. If it had been anyone else, he would have simply had the girl strangled and thrown into the Seine and they could go hang. But it was Monsieur Le Chat. A young maid entered and placed a tray of drinks upon a small table by the window, curtsied and left.

Apollo appeared, bowed a little and said simply; "Monsieur Le Chat." He stood to one side and the tall man, dressed in black, stepped slowly into the room, a few feet behind followed a large black cat, wearing a silver collar. Roland indicated to the chair placed in front of his desk. But Monsieur Le Chat shook his head and remained standing. He also refused a drink; the cat now sat at his feet.

"The story spreading around Paris is that Madam Bella was killed by an aggrieved customer who fled the scene. The local magistrate is only too happy to side with that tale." Monsieur Roland stated, smiling and pulled a drawstring bag from his pocket and added; "One hundred gold pieces - good Spanish gold as you requested." He dropped the bag upon the desk and leaned back in his chair. He didn't like to deal with Monsieur Le Chat but in his business, you often had to deal with people like him; regardless of what you thought about them. He needed a drink and stared at the tray by the window.

He almost jumped in surprise as the big cat leapt upon the desk and sniffed at the bag. He watched in utter amazement as the cat turned to its master and squeaked quietly. Monsieur Le Chat actually smiled; "One hundred Spanish gold pieces as agreed and the Girl?" He scooped the bag up and the cat jumped from the desk.

Monsieur Roland wiped his face; "She only arrived minutes before you. I have Bridget cleaning her up and finding a cloak for her. Madame Clare delivered her in the same manner, that I delivered her to them; quite naked." Monsieur Le Chat nodded, his pale face expressionless. "And the young man?" Roland wiped his face again and really did force a smile; "I have sent a message to Monsieur Franklyn but have not received a reply yet."

Monsieur Le Chat almost sighed, but dropped the money bag upon the desk. "That's for the young man's return - alive. Call it expenses." He bowed a little and walked to the door, the cat close behind him. He turned and said quietly; "Send Apollo with the message that you have retrieved him." He stood by the door and watched as Apollo carried the girl, bundled in a dark blue cloak down the steps to his carriage.

Roland rose from his chair and watched the strange man and his cat, disappear from view. Madame Bridget stood by the stairs and crossed herself - twice. "If you ever wished to see Mr. Death himself in person, then I have just witnessed it." She said softly and crossed herself; yet again. Roland wiped his sweaty face and couldn't disagree with her sentiments.

He returned to his study and poured himself a large class of brandy. Delivering the girl to Monsieur Le Chat and not to that man Tibbs had cost him dear. But when Monsieur Le Chat asks you for a 'favour' - you side with him every time - if you value being alive!

He sipped his brandy and watched through the window as the black carriage made it way down the drive. "Why the fuck is that little slut so important to so many powerful men?" He whispered; Roland had heard the stories circulating the dark underworld of Paris. Even the King was involved; apparently. He could understand it - if it was that Mademoiselle Alexandra - the English beauty that had turned the King's Mistresses green with envy. Now that was a female worthy of such endeavours and money. He slumped back in his chair and drank some more brandy; those idiots had really fucked up this time, when they snatched the girl and her dumb boyfriend. Bloody laziness, they thought it would make their mission easy. He stared at the bag of coins upon the desk and wondered if that damn cat actually knew they were all there? Which they were - of course - you didn't cheat Monsieur Le Chat. If you were stupid enough to do so; you may summon the undertaker at the same time. Roland actually shuddered and finished his brandy.

He would now have a irate Monsieur Franklyn to deal with. Fortunately, he was a shrewd businessman and he certainly knew about Monsieur Le Chat's reputation; which should make this a lot easier than it could have been. He gripped his glass and closed his eyes and then they snapped open.

Madame Bridget had appeared in the doorway and curtsied; "That nasty little man of Monsieur Franklyn's has arrived." She walked away and Roland placed down his glass. He hoped that Monsieur Jarden had come with good news. The turnover of young men in Franklyn's dungeon didn't give him much hope for the man. He had been there some weeks, and most didn't survive that long.

Monsieur Jarden bowed a little and sat slowly on the chair; he smiled with a mouthful of yellow teeth. "What have you for me?" Roland asked and clasped both hands on the desk. Monsieur Jarden nodded; "The young man David has been removed and placed in the care of the Sisters of Mercy at St. Maria's Convent. He will heal physically, but..." he tapped his head and didn't smile; "But in his head - he may not." he shrugged his shoulders and stared at the bag upon the desk.

Roland leaned back and ran a hand over his face. "Monsieur Le Chat said alive and nothing more. That is all that matters here." He pushed the bag towards Jarden and said quietly; "Give that to your master as payment for the man and as thanks - personally - from me. It's a hundred Spanish Gold pieces." The look on Monsieur Jarden's face spoke volumes. He carefully picked up the bag and pushed it into his coat pocket.

"All is well between your master and me?" Roland asked and smiled a little. Monsieur Franklyn was another individual he didn't like dealing with; but business was business.

Monsieur Jarden nodded; "My master said that you don't discard a fine watch that has given many years of good service, just because it stops upon occasion. You have it repaired and it continues to serve you well." He rose from the chair and the two men shook hands. Roland noticed with distain, that the little man's hand was cold and clammy - and weak. Monsieur Jarden stopped by the doorway and replaced his hat. "You will inform Monsieur Le Chat about the young man?"

Roland nodded, and Jarden turned and left. That went better than expected. He eased back onto his chair and his attention was drawn to the window. He rose and stared into the driveway. Apollo was greeting a fine carriage and Roland's heart sank. It was accompanied by a King's Officer and a troop of six cavalry.

He watched carefully as Mademoiselle Alexandra and Monsieur Tibbs stepped into the morning sunshine. "Putain de merde!" He exclaimed and returned to his chair, clutching another brandy. He then smiled a little; Monsieur Le Chat was now their problem and lifted his glass in a quiet salute and with some relief. His plan was carefully unfolding, and every little piece was coming together.

6. 22nd AUGUST 1767 - THE PALACE OF VERSAILLES - PART 1.

The King eased down upon his gilded chair and groaned a little; his hemorrhoids were playing up again. He adjusted his fine tunic and stared at Monsieur Tibbs with a little mix of wonderment and fear. The man had not aged a single day since the King last saw him some thirty years ago. But then, that was a privilege of being a messenger of God. "Did it go well?" He asked quietly, gripping the arms of his chair.

"We now know that a certain Monsieur Le Chat has taken possession of the girl and has made arrangements for the recovery of the young man that was taken with her." Jericho bowed a little, standing with hat in hand. The King nodded but did not smile; "Monsieur Le Chat has a sinister, almost supernatural reputation for evil and total ruthlessness that is unequalled in France. He is a very dangerous man Jericho." The King shifted uneasily on his chair, despite the thick cushion placed upon it. Jericho nodded; "We deal with all kinds your majesty." and smiled.

The audience with the King lasted another ten minutes and Jericho left the King's private apartments, walking quickly back to his rooms. Several couriers stood aside as he passed; a couple crossed themselves. Especially old Franco, the king's body servant, he had recognized Jericho from thirty years before, when he was a Hall boy here. He watched Jericho disappear down the magnificent corridor and crossed himself. No doubt his master would confide in him about the reason for such a creature's visit. Franco, of course, didn't know that only Jericho could have a King as a human agent!

The team assembled in Jericho's apartment and enjoyed the hospitality that Versailles offered. The first thing they all agreed upon was finding out who, exactly, was Monsieur Le Chat. Both the King and Monsieur Roland had told them that he was a very clever and dangerous man. The story about the stupid workman - fitting new doors to Monsieur Le Chat's chateau had been told by both; the workman disliked cats and was seen kicking Le Chat's cat up its arse. He was found the following day on a quiet Paris street. He had been butchered; there was no other word for it.

"So he's a murdering psychopath, we've dealt with them before." muttered Owen, who really did like the King's good quality brandy. They had decided that there must be some connection between Le Chat and the young couple - and Salem House. "We need to check the fucker out with our mirrors; Human Records will be able to identify him." Owen added and refilled everyone's glasses. So, the priority was identifying Le Chat and retrieving Sally and Dave from his clutches.

Alex sipped brandy and was reading her mirror with real interest, she looked up and grinned broadly; "Well, we certainly know now who Monsieur Roland really is." She had everyone's attention with that statement. She tapped her mirror; "Monsieur Roland is a certain Sir Malcolm Grieves, whose soul is reported missing - he missed his departure date in February 1871. Guess what he use to own and went missing from in 1870?" Wilson smiled; "Salem House." Alex nodded and continued; "I've just checked Dave Fisher's Great-Uncle Wesley and here's a real turn up for the books; his soul is missing, and he shouldn't even be dead in 1971 [the year the Police Inspector stated that his body had been found in Salem House] he's scheduled for 1982."

"So whose bloody body was found in 1971?" Owen asked and

slumped down on the sofa, clutching his brandy. "Dispatches has no record of a collection on that date or at that place- who ever laid dead at the foot of the stairs wasn't old Great-Uncle Wesley Fisher." Alex said quietly and re-read her mirror.

"Well, either the fucker sold his soul to you-know-who, or he was out of his ordained time." Wilson grunted and relaxed in his chair. Jericho told Owen to check who dealt with the body in 1971; Temporal Detectives would have been called to a body without a soul being found - even if the death was unscheduled.

Owen nodded and started to read his mirror. "Holy shit!" He exclaimed and grinned broadly; "The body belonged to a Monsieur Louis Varden who should have died in 1777 in Paris, at the age of 65. He had a string of sexual offences against women and children. He would have been quarantined for some centuries, but obviously, never turned up at his departure date; his soul is officially missing."

"So it appears that Great Uncle Wesley Fisher is still alive and kicking and he has to be around this time and place; the 'Jerusalem Mirror' is locked here." Jericho said and rubbed his chin.

"There are more time travelers here than you can shake a stick at." Muttered Owen and finished his brandy. Alex sat bolt upright in her chair and clicked her fingers with a broad smile; "Varden was Madame Bella's surname!" Wilson nodded; "That would be stretching co-incidence if the pair are not related." Jericho did the maths in his head; "If Louis should have died in 1777 at the age of 65, he would be 55 at this time and Madam Bella was 31. Either she married an old man, or he was her father or Uncle."

Owen re- read his mirror; "The Collector reported that Madame Bella knew her killer - it was Monsieur Le Chat, with his bloody cat. Madame Bella had three husbands; two died and the third simply disappeared; he was called Louis." Wilson smiled; "Well, that solves who he was. Were the other husbands all older than her?" Owen nodded; "The first one was 61 and she was 18. The second husband was 52 when he married her at 24. The third we know about already."

"Clearly she liked a daddy figure." Alex said and relaxed back in her chair. "Or she had no choice in the matter, like a lot of women during these times."

Jericho actually grinned and nodded his head with some satisfaction. "People, we really need to know who the hell Monsieur Le Chat really is." Everyone agreed with that; but how?

"I have a cunning plan." Was all Jericho said and they gathered around him.

7. 24th AUGUST 1767 - THE PALACE OF VERSAILLES - PART 2.

Alex was a little annoyed; "Your original plan was fantastic but trust the dirty old sod of a King to come up with this." She spoke quietly to Jericho and stroked Mr. Parker with one hand, whilst gripping her light summer cloak about her with the other. Jericho just shrugged his shoulders and smiled; "He is the King and if he wants a 'Tit and Pussy show' - then he gets one." Alex just grunted and started to give Mr. Parker a final brush.

Owen stood behind the table and giggled a little, drawing a stern look from Alex. Wilson folded his arms; "Mr. Parker is a Maine Coon cat - an American breed - the largest breed of domestic cat there is. He will certainly be a sensation in this time and place. Very few people in Europe would have seen one in the flesh." Jericho agreed with that and watched as several other women had arrived with their beloved cats. They were all topless and didn't seem to mind a bit. Owen was certainly enjoying the show - before it even started.

The King would be the judge; with the winning feline receiving a fine silver collar and their owner a night with him. "He's going to be disappointed if Alex wins." Wilson had to grin at Owen's remarks. "Our girl and the damn cat are a winning combination. Pity no-one is taking bets." He said softly, keeping a close eye on the growing crowd in the magnificent Reception Room.

Madame Marie de Rouge [the King's newest and youngest mistress] bounced over and stared at Mr. Parker, whilst Owen stared at her magnificent bosom, adorned with golden nipple caps in the shape of small swans. "My God! Is that really a domestic cat?" She exclaimed and fluttered a silk fan across her face.

Alex grinned and nodded, introducing 'Mr. Parker' to her. The cat bowed and Madame Marie squeaked with joy and ran her hand over his ears. "If he wasn't a bloody cat, I'd swear the bugger was smiling." Wilson said softly to Owen, who wasn't actually looking at the cat because Alex had removed her cloak. He just stared and groaned a little. Now that did make Wilson smile. "Steady lad, just remember that we're here to do a job."

"Their like a blind cobblers thumbs!" Owen muttered and managed to look away. Alex had gold and silver snakes wrapped around her ample breasts and silver rings on each nipple; the circle and the snake - emblems of the Dark Prince's followers. "That will set the cat amongst the pigeons - if you pardon the pun - and will certainly attract our dark friend's followers here." Jericho spoke softly, his eyes darting about the crowd. Then a loud-mouthed servant banged a gold cane upon the floor and announced the arrival of the King.

The King sauntered in with some grace; well. As much as his hemorrhoids allowed him. He made straight for Madam de Rouge, who presented her cat - 'Duveteuse' - to him. He smiled and patted her arm, then saw Alex and Mr. Parker; the smile turned into a broad grin. "You have a wonderful big pussy Mademoiselle Alexandra.... and they are simply magnificent." He gestured to her exposed breasts. "Snakes and circles; very interesting." He added and actually rubbed his hands together!

Alex curtsied and smiled; "Thank you your Majesty. He is such a lovely big cat." The King nodded and the Lord Chamberlain had to remind him twice, that there were several other cats to judge. Quite reluctantly, the King had to move on. Owen tapped Jericho's arm and said quietly; "Look who's turned up."

Standing in the doorway was Monsieur Le Chat and his cat. The conversation in the room slowly died away as people saw who had arrived. The King waved him over and greeted him with some warmth. He introduced the 'English' visitors to Monsieur Le Chat; whilst the two big cats eyed each other up in a very unfriendly manner. Alex had to pat Mr. Parker twice and tell him to behave himself; he didn't listen.

The team sat in Jericho's room - in silence - for a few minutes, then Alex, now suitably covered up - shook her head; "You can't imprison a bloody cat in the Bastille!" Everyone nodded at that and Owen couldn't help himself, he chuckled; "Mr. Parker is probably now famous. The first cat thrown into the bloody Bastille for assaulting the King!" Even Jericho had to smile at that, he turned to Wilson; "What have we got?"

"Actually, no real surprise; Monsieur Le Chat is Great Uncle Wesley Fisher." He lowered his mirror and added; "There is now a real connection with Madame Bella; her old husband was found dead in Salem House and his nephew was taken from there - with his girlfriend. Something must have gone wrong with his little arrangement of jumping between here and there."

Jericho nodded; "He must have lost the ability to jump forward to Salem House and could no longer access the power of the Jerusalem Mirror. But someone else did and snatched his great nephew and the girl." Owen jumped up from his chair and headed for the tray of drinks on a nearby ornate table.

He started to fill glasses and then stopped; "So where does that Monsieur Roland fit in all this?" Alex folded her arms; "Never mind that; how the hell do we get the King to release poor Mr. Parker?" Jericho sighed; "I'll leave that to you Alexandra. I'm sure your charm can easily persuade him to set free our troublesome and feisty colleague." Then smiled broadly; the King was not happy having his elaborate wig knocked off, by the big cat trying to get at Monsieur Le Chat's furry friend.

There had been total confusion and disorder in the Ballroom as the two big cats decided to fight it out - Mr. Parker won and Monsieur Le Chat's cat fled in ignominious defeat - followed by its owner. But the king wasn't impressed and ordered Mr. Parker to the Bastille! Once he had his wig straight. Apparently, his new mistress - Madame de Rouge - won by default. At least the King would be happy with that result.

Jericho finished his drink and gestured towards the door; "While Alexandra gets the King to release our furry friend, we're heading for Monsieur Le Chat's chateau and have words about his nephew and the girl. He of all people must realize the importance of returning the pair to their own time." Alex sighed; "Time to play the bloody tart again." Wilson chuckled at that; "Yes, but you do it so well; it almost comes naturally." The look Alex gave the big man could have frozen peas, without the need for a freezer.

8. STILL THE 24th of AUGUST 1767 - MONSINEUR LE CHAT'S CHATEAU.

Night was falling as the carriage waited in the stone gateway and everyone stared at the house. "Jesus, you could make a horror film here." Wilson lowered the reins and spoke through the small flap to Jericho, who was also staring at the house. Owen had to agree with the big man; "I'm waiting for Dracula or Frankenstein to open the bloody door." Wilson slapped the reins and the carriage rolled down the gravel driveway and stopped outside the dark entrance. They waited for a few minutes, but no servant appeared, and the doors remained closed to 'La Maison de le Nuit'.

Jericho jumped from the carriage and strode up to the big black doors and banged upon them with the hilt of his sword. Wilson and Owen joined him after securing the horses, to the metal railings that formed part of the house's wall. There was no reply from inside. Jericho shouted several times in French, but again - there was no answer and the doors remained shut. That's when Owen pushed at the left door and it crept open. Everyone looked at each other and Jericho again shouted their arrival. Still no answer.

They stood in the grand hallway enveloped in an eerie silence. "The place should be crawling with servants." Muttered Wilson and pulled out his mirror; "Sweet Jesus, there are no living humans recorded here." He added and lowered his mirror. Owen peered through a couple of open doors and rubbed his chin; "Do you know that this place looks like it hasn't had residents for years." There was dust and cobwebs everywhere and some of the furniture looked like it was starting to rot. The air was stale and heavy. "Nice place for a holiday." Wilson said softly and consulted his mirror again.

"La Maison de le Nuit was abandoned by its owners in 1731 after a major fire destroyed the rear of the building. All that remained was the exterior facade and some rooms at the front of the house. It was finally demolished in 1810 and a small villa and vineyard replaced it." Wilson said and Owen gripped his mirror and turned to his companions; "Maybe old Le Chat only uses it for a mail drop?"

"Or Monsieur Roland has fed us a load of bollocks about where Le

Chat resides." Jericho said, a little annoyed with himself at taking what Roland said, at face value. "Why drag us out here?" Wilson asked and then grabbed up his mirror; "We have visitors." The team could see four humans approaching the house from the overgrown forest - two had muskets and two had pistols and swords.

"I don't think they're here to give us a warm French welcome." Muttered Owen and the team moved from the hall into an adjoining room. Wilson and Owen managed to close the door firmly and they stood in semi-darkness, in what was probably, the music room; it contained a derelict pianofortes and a large, string less harp. But it was the beautiful stone fireplace that caught Owens's attention.

"I think we should go into the fireplace." He said and held up his mirror, adding; "There's a time portal there, linked to this very place, but in the year 1980." They could hear raised, unfriendly voices in the hallway and so, the team disappeared into the fireplace.

They found themselves in the utility room cupboard, which was locked. But it didn't take Wilson long to sort that problem. "You were wasted as a cop." Owen muttered as they peered from the little room's door. "We're in the villa that replaced the old chateau, suitably modernised I expect." He added and they walked through the deserted kitchen. They saw Monsieur Le Chat's cat sitting in the doorway of a room off the hallway. It didn't move but squeaked loudly a couple of times. They walked past and saw Le Chat standing by the wood burning stove. He actually smiled.

"I knew you would get away from Malcolm's men [Roland's men] and find the portal. Welcome Jericho, please have a seat gentlemen." His Yorkshire accent was quite noticeable. Jericho dropped on the sofa with Wilson, but Owen stood by the door, clutching his mirror. Jericho got straight to the point.

"You know we must take them back." He said simply and folded his arms; the matter was not up for negotiation. Le Chat nodded; "I know you must. My great nephew is in a bad way. I fear he has lost his sanity for good. But you can return him to 1974 and none of this would have taken place." Le Chat looked and sounded quite grim. He walked to the large window and stared out at the gardens. "The whore can remain back there. That time suits her talents quite well and David will be well rid of her." He sighed and opened the glass drinks cabinet.

"I'm afraid the girl must also return; we must not lose her soul in a time that's not been allocated to her. You know that." Jericho said, but Le Chat just chuckled; "She's outsmarted everyone Jericho. No sooner did I rescue her from Madame Bella and Roland's clutches, than she betrayed me to Monsieur Roland and escaped with him back to Salem House. They will alter your precious Time-line, probably as we are speaking now." He offered brandy all round and downed his own glass in a few sips.

"So Roland has the Jerusalem Mirror now?" Wilson asked, accepting a glass from Le Chat, who smiled; "Sir Malcolm Grieves always had the mirror and in reality, always owned Salem House. I was just a lodger, like Monsieur Varden. That filthy bastard liked little girls, had he stayed with his wife back in France, his crimes would have gained the notice of the King and he would have been hung. But Sir Malcolm protected him because of the business connections with his wife Bella. He was exiled to Salem House in Victorian times and continued his vile practices. He even took up photography to keep his new victims fresh in his mind. I hope no-one ever digs up the woodlands near the house."

"How do they intend to alter the time-line?" Wilson asked. Le Chat sighed; "They will return to the day that Dave and the slut moved into Salem House, Sir Malcolm will pretend to be me and the slut, will act as his new wife. They have carefully crafted a story that they have been abroad. That idiot solicitor believes Sir Malcolm IS me since he has only dealt with Sir Malcolm AS me." He poured himself another glass and stared back out the window. "You know that those imbecilic policemen never asked the solicitor to identify the body found at the foot of the stairs, [Varden] and so it was obviously me."

"What no-one foresaw was that Varden would have a massive heart attack and die, clutching a photograph of him abusing another little victim back in the 1880's. Not one of those stupid police officers realized that the man dead on the floor was the same bastard in the picture!" Le Chat almost spate the words out.

"So, they intend to reclaim Salem House and Dave, with the

other Sally would return to their previous lives - in debt and unhappy?" Owen said quietly and then smiled; "But surely, if the pair [Dave and Sally] was never to have Salem House and the money, then that IS the original time-line?" Jericho nodded at that deduction.

Le Chat slumped in a chair and smiled; "I understand that's it a prime directive of Temporal detectives to prevent two versions of the same person to inhabit the same timeline?" Jericho did not smile; "That's quite true, can I ask how you come to know so much about Temporal Detective duties?" Le Chat softly laughed; "Wouldn't you like to know. But more importantly, you need to return one of the versions of the whore back to 1767." Wilson grunted; "You seem to have forgotten, that if we return the pair to 1974, then nothing would have happened and so - like Owen said - the timeline would be back to its original state." He placed his glass down and did smile.

"That's true; but what will stop Sir Malcolm [Roland] from doing everything again?" Le Chat finished his brandy and fumbled in his pockets. He pulled a faded newspaper cutting from his pocket and unfolded it. He handed the paper to Jericho, who read it with some interest and pushed it into his pocket. "Let's go." Was all Jericho said.

9. 17th JUNE 1974 - SALEM HOUSE - PART 3.

The big black car sat in the lay by and Wilson relaxed in the driver's seat. He turned to Alex and smiled; "You haven't said, how you got old Mr. Parker out of the Bastille?" Alex shrugged her shoulders; "I can't claim that I did. It was Madame Le Rouge we have to thank for that." Owen lowered his mirror; "Madame Le Rouge had Mr. Parker freed?" Alex nodded; "She pleaded with the King that she would be really upset if her 'friend' didn't have her beloved pussy returned and the King agreed - didn't want to upset his new, young mistress I expect." Everyone turned to Jericho, who could be heard to chuckle at that comment. "Tut tut Alexandra." Was all he said.

Jericho grinned and stared down the road; "Yes, I'm sure that is how it happened." Everyone exchanged glances at that. Alex folded her arms; "What do you mean by that?" Jericho didn't answer, but tapped Wilson's arm. The removal van was heading towards them and Salem House. They watched as the van passed by, followed by the old Vauxhall Viva containing Dave and Sally.

Wilson started the car and pulled out, staying well behind the little convoy. Jericho glanced over his shoulder a couple of times; "Owen, give 'Jumbo' a buzz and see how far behind us he is - thanks." Owen checked his mirror and muttered; "The Scottish nutter should come into view about now." Wilson looked in the mirror and saw the van pull in behind them. Alex gave a little wave to Patricia (little Pat) Sabaskinski, the driver, who waved back. "Thank fuck Pat is driving; Jumbo couldn't drive a greasy stick...." Alex gave Owen a gentle slap; "Yes, that's enough. Thank you, we get the point."

Wilson slowed down and waited at the gates; everyone could see the young couple embracing in the driveway. "Do you see her at the attic window?" Wilson said quietly and everyone peered at the old house. "Yes, she's there alright." Owen lowered his mirror and placed it back into his pocket whilst Alex adjusted his tie. "Court appointed officers are always neat and tidy. That's why we all look like bloody undertakers." She grinned as the car and van pulled up behind the removal van. Jericho eased himself out and walked over to Dave and Sally, who stared with a little fear and apprehension, at the team emerging from the car.

Paddy the removal van driver sighed; "I don't think anyone is moving today and our bloody company will have to wait for its fucking money." They watched as the 'Sherriff's Officer' pushed the Court Order into Dave's hand and took possession of Salem House. Dave got a little angry and was shouting that the debts were all Sally's, and his property couldn't be touched. Then he calmed down a little when Wilson walked up. Jericho patiently explained that, if the house was his 'sole' property, why did both he and Sally sign for the house?

Dave hung his head; that bloody Solicitor had told him not to give away part of the house to Sally. But Dave hadn't really listened - he cursed himself and threw down the paper and walked back to his old car and slumped across the wheel. Sally said nothing and walked over the Vauxhall and slowly eased in. Jericho gestured to Wilson and Owen, who entered the house and made for the attic rooms.

Alex walked over and tapped on Dave's driver window; he slowly wound it down. She explained that the house would be sold at auction and the proceeds used to pay off Sally's debts, which were now quite considerable because of the amount of interest accrued over the last couple of years. Dave simply stuck up two fingers and drove away.

The removal van followed the disappointed couple down the drive and everyone turned to the old house as Wilson and Owen appeared with the Jerusalem Mirror, covered with some old bed sheets. "Get it in the van and then we'll search the house thoroughly for anything else that may interest us." Jericho smiled and the two teams disappeared into Salem House.

"If th' glaikit bugger hadn't added her bloody name tae th' deed, thay wid hae bben in th' clear." Jumbo spoke to Alex as they searched the ground floor rooms. She nodded and checked her mirror, for any other nasty little time portals. After a couple of hours, the search was complete and everyone returned to the vehicles.

The team watched as the white van, with Jumbo, Patricia and the Jerusalem Mirror disappeared. Owen passed his hip-flask around; "What did that old piece of paper say?" He asked Jericho, who smiled and pulled the newspaper cutting from his pocket. Owen took it and began to read; " A notable Yorkshire property; Salem House, was today sold at auction for nearly twenty-two thousand pounds by order of the Court. The proceeds' of the sale will clear the previous part-owners debts and stop any further debt order proceedings against her. The new owner is a prominent Yorkshire businessman who plans to renovate the house and turn it into a luxury country hotel." Owen finished and asked Jericho; "Who bought the old place then?"

Jericho chuckled; "A certain Patrick Well's, through a third-party property company that he owns. That Solicitor wasn't really that dumb after all." Alex sighed; "No wonder he didn't object too strongly to Dave putting Sally on the deeds - the sneaky bugger." Jericho accepted the hipflask and gestured towards the house; "It certainly suited our mission - it enabled us to close the portal, return two souls to their correct time and stop a couple of determined time travelers from carrying on their unsavory occupations. Sir Malcolm [Roland] is now trapped in 1767 with no chance to go anywhere or continue his evil trade in human flesh."

"What about Le Chat?" Owen asked and Jericho sighed, but had to smile; "He lives in comfort in 1980 with his bloody cat and can still pop back to 1767 - so he thinks." Wilson rubbed his face and really did grin; "I take it that his little time portal in the cupboard is now closed?" Jericho nodded; "I closed it up before we left. He'll be surprised by that." Owen still looked puzzled; "Why did he tip us off about the sale, that wasn't in his best interests was it?"

Wilson chuckled; "No it wasn't, but since Jericho insisted, we take the girl back - with his great nephew - that was the only way he could stop her benefiting from being with Dave. He must really hate her, but I suspect that he knew Dave would stand by her, but she wouldn't get any of the money this way. I think he's wrong about that too, since her debts are now paid off."

Jericho smiled; "The bonus is that Great Uncle Wesley is trapped in 1980, now his time portal is closed and since he was due to be dispatched [die] in 1982, he's in his own allocated time period and his soul can be collected."

Owen nodded, then turned again to Jericho; "What did you mean, when you said to Alex; 'Yes, I'm sure that is how it happened' earlier?" Jericho chuckled; "Over to you Alexandra. Honesty is always the best policy." Alex pushed back in her seat and folded her arms - she didn't look happy. "Alright, bloody alright. To get Mr. Parker back....I had to...I had to wash the old buggers feet. There, now you know." Wilson looked astounded; "Wash his feet! I mean just wash his feet?" Owen scratched his head; "I know the old King is a strange bugger but wash his feet?"

"Tut Tut Alexandra, half the truth is no truth really." Jericho said and grinned broadly. Alex sighed and threw up her hands in mock despair; "Alright, alright, the truth is, I had to wash his feet whilst stark naked. There, now are you satisfied?" Jericho gave Alex a knowing look and she finally added; "Alright, stark naked except a 'Davey Crockett' hat and red riding boots. That's all I did, and the old pervert pardoned the damn cat!"

There was silence for a few seconds and everyone started to laugh - including Alex. Jericho said quietly; "Honesty is always the best policy; sometimes!"

THE END

EPILOGUE:

"Team 74 managed to recover the two lost souls, prevent an evil flesh peddling time traveler from continuing to operate and closed a very dangerous time portal. The mission was judged a success by Angel Margret; and so, it was!"
SJW.

CHARACTERS:

Miss Sally Irving [Nee Jackson]. Now that all her debts were paid off by the sale of Salem House, Sally left Dave in 1975 and married a John Irving. She remained married to him for some years and had three children. Her husband had to clear her debts a couple of times during their marriage. Finally, she left him in 1992 and moved to Spain and lived with a beach artist until her sudden death in 1997. Her soul was collected and processed.

David Edward Fisher was devastated when Sally left him in 1975 for another man. For some years, he was a drunk and lived on the streets. He died in 1979 and his body wasn't found for some months - he was sheltering in a derelict house in Sheffield - he couldn't be identified and was buried in an unmarked grave. His soul was collected and processed.

Patrick Wells [The Solicitor] became a very prominent lawyer and wealthy businessman in Yorkshire. He lived a life of luxury between his properties in the USA, Spain and England. He died in 2015, whilst on holiday in Jamaica and his soul was collected and processed.

Robert Cornfield [Removal man] continued to work for 'Baxter Removals' until he finished night college classes and obtained a position in prominent firm of solicitors - Well's & Cooper in Yorkshire - as a legal Clark. Unfortunately, he was killed in a motorcycle accident in 1983. His soul was collected and processed.

Terry Jones [Removal man] was convicted of further sexual assaults on young girls in 1978 and sent to prison. He was released in 1994 and worked as a 'Road sweeper' for some years. He died in 1999 of a massive stroke and his soul was collected and processed.

Patrick 'Paddy' O'Connor [Driver & Removal man] was sacked from 'Baxter's Removals' in 1976 for theft of customer's property, which he denied. He made his living driving a bread delivery van for some years. But he is remembered for a couple of books on the supernatural that were quite good but didn't sell well. He died in 2034 at an old people's home in Doncaster. His soul was collected and processed.

Sir Malcolm Grieves [Monsieur Roland] remained trapped in 18th century France, despite trying to find other time portals. He fell into debt and lost his Chateau and servants. He worked as a rat catcher for some years in Paris. His body was found floating in the Seine on Christmas Eve 1775. No soul was collected, and it remains missing to this day.

Wesley Fisher [Monsieur Le Chat] lived out his life in modern France and died in 1982 - as scheduled - his soul was collected and processed; it was quarantined until 2250. His faithful cat died within days of his passing.

Madame Bella Varden [la Maison des Tenebres:] who was murdered by Monsieur Le Chat in 1767, had her soul collected and processed. It was quarantined until 2180.

Monsieur Louis Varden, who died in Salem House in the year 1971, was out of his own time period and no soul was collected. It remains missing to this day.

Detective Inspector Roy Calms [Yorkshire Police] was indicted for corruption in 1984. He was found guilty on several charges and was dismissed from the police service and served four years in Doncaster Prison. He lost his Police pension and struggled to make a living after his release in 1988. He died a broken man in 1991. His soul was collected and processed.

Detective Sergeant Greg Chambers [Yorkshire Police] was tragically killed in a car crash in September 1976. He had no family. His soul was collected and processed.

Leon Casswell Devine [the pornographer] business flourished during the 1980's and he became a great supporter of Prime Minister Margaret Thatcher and legitimized his business. He became very wealthy and successful. He married four times and had six children in all. In 1995, he retired to Jamaica and lived a comfortable life until his death in 2005. His soul was collected and processed.

Apollo - Kama Fanyakka [la Maison des Tenebres] was brutally murdered by a gang in a Paris tavern in 1769. In modern times it would have been described as a 'Hate Crime'. Several patrons of that particular hostelry objected vehemently to Apollo having two white girls with him. He was just unlucky in his choice of drinking establishment. His soul was collected and processed.

Madame Clare Gassmoune [la Maison des Tenebres] died in 1771 of Typhoid and was buried in a mass grave outside the city. Her soul was collected and processed. It was quarantined until 1950.

Madame Bridget Dupont [Monsieur Roland's Housekeeper] found herself unemployed and living on the streets after the fall of Monsieur Roland. She worked as a cheap prostitute for a couple of years and was found dead on a quiet Paris Street in 1774. Her soul was collected and possessed.

Monsieur Henri Jarden [Monsieur Franklyn's messenger] died in his bed of Influenza in 1772. He had no family, and his body was buried in an unmarked grave. His boss, the mysterious Monsieur Franklyn gave him no assistance. His soul was collected and processed - it was quarantined until 2050.

Madame Marie de Rouge [The Kings Mistress] remained the King's Mistress until 1772. After her dismissal from Royal 'Service', she returned to her husband in Normandy and lived out the remainder of her life quietly in the country. Marie and her family did not survive the revolution that swept France in 1789 - they were imprisoned and eventually guillotined in 1790. Her soul was collected and processed.

Franco Cassinni [The Kings Personal Servant] served the King until his death in 1772 from smallpox. His soul was collected and processed.

Monsieur Franklyn -?, this mysterious character was never really identified. He remains unknown to human history. He was never seen or spoken to by temporal detectives. There were several characters who could have fitted his description living at the time. It is believed that the Duty Death Angel [Francis, at the time] knew who he was and dealt with him accordingly. We're not privy to what the Angel's decisions were about Monsieur Franklyn - sorry!

Amy the cat is believed to have lived out her life in France in 1767, after following Dave and Sally through the 'Jerusalem Mirror'. Her eventual fate is unknown. Mr. Parker's enforced stay in the Bastille produced little change to the timeline; The Warden was a great cat fancier and kept the big cat in his apartments with his four cats; all sisters. There is no official explanation how so many half-Maine Coon cats appeared in the French capitol in the late 18th century, but I think we all know now!

SPECIAL APPEARANCE BY King Louis XV of France, as himself.

The King died in 1774 and his soul was collected and processed.

He was succeeded by his Grandson; the ill-fated King Louis XVI who was overthrown during the French revolution and guillotined in 1792. That ended a French Monarchy which had existed for over a thousand years.

The FIRST French republic was declared on 21st September 1792 and paved the way for a certain Napoleon Bonaparte to eventually become Emperor of the French in 1804 - the rest is history!

IMPORTANT NOTE:
"Jericho would like to point out that no animals were injured in this episode; well, except the two bloody big cats, who beat the crap out of each other!"

EPISODE 2: "33AD."

MISSION SUMMARY: "In the year 33AD, two 'prophets' are battling for the souls of humanity in chaotic Judea; Jesus, the son of a Carpenter from Nazareth and Barabbas, son of a slave trader from Jerusalem are fighting each other for the future of mankind. Barabbas commands the Zealots and wants war against Rome, who occupy his land. Jesus teaches love and forgiveness and putting down the sword. Jericho and his team are dispatched when things start to go wrong with the current Timeline, and it can be traced back to 33AD."

NOTES: This episode contains Anti-Religious references which may offend certain people!

TRIGGER WARNINGS. ALCOHOL, STRONG LANGUAGE, SEXUAL REFERENCES AND MILD VIOLENCE.

AGE 15+ ONLY. **30 Minutes reading time.**

1. JERICHO IS SUMMONED BY ANGEL MARGRET.

Jericho sat outside Angel Margret's office and watched the stream of visitor's passing in and out of her doors. He sighed a little and rummaged in his coat pockets and pulled his mirror out; he read for a few minutes until Mr. Colgate [the Angel's private secretary] appeared and gestured for him to enter.

"The Angel will see you now Inspector Tibbs and she asked that you are not disturbed during this meeting. So please switch off your mirror." He announced and the doors slid open, Jericho turned off his mirror and entered.

Angel Margret pointed to the large armchair placed before her desk and leaned back in her chair; "Sit down Jericho; you will need to study your latest mission very carefully and act accordingly." She pushed a brown paper file across to him and rested both hands upon the large ornate desk; totally bare apart from a little gold bell.

Jericho sat down and picked up the file, he noticed immediately the unusual Security Listing stamped across the cover; 'SERAPHIM ONLY'. He hesitated and tapped the cover; "Ma'am I cannot read the contents of such a file, sorry." He replaced the folder upon the desk and nervously stood up. Angel Margret simply smiled; "I have been ordered by 'himself' to ensure, that my best team handle this case." She pointed a long slender finger towards the ceiling; "I did say that my former human operative will have to see the facts for himself and when I proposed you; he did not object and thus you have a special dispensation to view such a document. Now sit down and take a look."

Jericho eased back in the chair and slowly opened the document; he carefully read the summary and his mouth went dry; little wonder that the file carried such a security listing. He swallowed and wiped his face; "He has allowed me to read this?" He asked quite softly. The Angel nodded; "You can imagine the damage to everything created, if the contents of that file was to reach living human's. Currently, it appears to be just conjecture, rumour and conspiracy theory amongst them. But what is happening back there, can change all that. You must succeed in this Jericho; there is no option allowed for failure, do you understand that?" The Angel spoke with real concern in her voice and folded her arms.

Jericho nodded; he really could use a drink now; anything wet. "Brief your team with only what you consider really necessary to achieve the results he demands and expects." The Angel sighed; "Be very, very careful in what you impart about the file to anyone else and that includes the remainder of Team 74." She suddenly stood up and placed both hands back on the desk; Jericho rose quickly and stood, clutching the file. "Commit the contents of that summary to your memory. The file cannot leave this room." "You will be entering the 'Forbidden Era' and you will proceed with the utmost caution whilst on this Mission, you have my authority to change only what is directly required to achieve what himself requires, other than that, you can exercise your usual discretion in any other matters, that arise during the mission." Angel Margret smiled a little; "I would suggest you take what advise you can obtain, from your 'friend' John on these matters."

Jericho nodded and replaced the file upon the desk. He didn't need to re-read it; the summary was burned into his mind, and he bowed a little and headed for the door. Angel Margret called after him as her door slid open; "Watch yourself Jericho, the 'Dark One' is unlikely to miss an opportunity like this, to make mischief out of the situation."

In the quiet corridor outside the Angel's suite of offices, Jericho noticed that his hand trembled a little as he switched on his mirror. He had a feeling that the 'Dark Prince's interference may be the least of his worries on this mission. Mr. Colgate appeared next to him - unsmiling; "Inspector Tibbs, the Angel has arranged for all that you may require, to complete the mission. Costumes, travel papers, discrete extra's, money, local human agents and a knight of God - should you require one - have been provided. Good luck."

Rather unusually, he held out his hand and Jericho shook it slowly. Mr. Colgate gripped his hand firmly and spoke softly; "The Angel has expressed her total confidence and faith in you; to himself. Her staff - myself included - know that you would never betray that faith and so I really do wish you the best." He smiled and walked away.

That little revelation didn't make Jericho any happier about the forthcoming mission, which if he had any sense, he would have refused. But refusal wasn't an option for a Temporal Detective Inspector and so, he activated his mirror and returned to the lighthouse with a heavy heart.

He stood outside the lighthouse on a warm sunny evening on the 6th July, 1901 and watched the three mast sailing ship heading towards the horizon; several seagulls dived and swooped in the light blue sky, in strange silence. He glanced at his small fob watch; 7.35pm - as always. He sighed and headed for the doors deep in thought.

Mr. Harris was waiting - as usual - by the large black doors to take his coat and hat, Jericho slowly walked up to the doors and smiled at him; "Ask everyone to assemble in the study please." Mr. Harris nodded and helped him remove his long frock coat; "James, the Knight of God, has already arrived, Lady Alexandra and Mr. Wilson are entertaining him in there sir." Jericho sighed again and headed for the study, he turned to Mr. Harris; "And where is Mr. Jones?" Harris smiled; "Apparently helping young Ruth with her reading lessons." That did make Jericho smile; "Bloody young love; the poor buggers." He whispered and pushed into the study to greet his very important guest.

They had to wait for a few minutes for Owen; he arrived in a hurry and tried to apologise to everyone, but his apologies were waved aside by Jericho with a smile. Mr. Harris kept up a constant flow of drinks and Jericho called the briefing to order and firstly, pointed out the James [a Knight of God] will be accompanying the team on this particular assignment as an 'Observer' everyone glanced at each other on that statement.

James sipped his drink and said quietly; "Jericho is in charge of this little adventure; I'm along for the ride and to assist if I can." Everyone knew that this was a serious breach of protocol; A Knight of God was only second to an Angel and certainly shouldn't take orders or directions from a mere Temporal Detective Inspector!

"I see a big pile of shite and a big bloody fan." Whispered Wilson to Owen and everyone fell silent as Mr. Harris opened the study door and John wandered in without saying a word and sat in the corner; he accepted a glass of red wine from Mr. Harris and half smiled at everyone. Jericho cleared his throat; "I've asked John to sit in on this one; he knows the era really well." John raised his glass - but said nothing - as usual.

"I've uploaded all details as required to everyone's mirrors and they are quite extensive; I would suggest everyone take some time and read up about the situation. Well, except James of course, he doesn't need a mirror!" Jericho chuckled to himself and then continued; "It all started with a cave in a desolate part of Israel, known in the era; in which we're interested, as Judea.

The year we're interested in is 33AD."

There was a little bit of surprise and Owen just came out with it: "Surely 33AD is part of the forbidden Era; no one is allowed there without 'the BOSSES' express permission......" The look on Jericho's face stopped Owen in mid sentence. "Oh shit!" was all he added - Wilson was right about the big pile of crap and the fan, he thought.

"That's why we have James with us - the light room won't allow us - to jump to the 'Forbidden Era' and the mirrors certainly wouldn't take us there." Alex spoke softly in Wilson's ear and he nodded his agreement. Alex sipped her drink and threw a glance at James; a gorgeous, big strapping young man and then she thought about Wilson - what a quandary - what is a girl to do when faced with this pair; which one does a girl choose? Then a very naughty, but delicious thought flicked through her mind; why not both - together! She actually chuckled and received strange looks from them both. To her surprise, she actually blushed a little, but blamed that on the brandy.

Jericho continued; "It appears in November 2024, a young goat herder was caught in a desert storm and so, pushed his small flock into a nearby cave. Whilst sheltering there he noticed something sticking out the sand and he dug around it with his hands. It was a Roman travel chest, and he knew that people would pay good money for it. He loaded the box onto his donkey and when the storm abated, carried it into the local town and to a man who he knew was a trader in antiquities. That man: Muhammad Kasim purchased the box and then he opened it. The anthology about 'Pandora's box' springs to mind."

Everyone was listening in silence and Jericho sipped his brandy: "The box contained several pieces of parchment in a language that Kassim couldn't understand. He was clever enough to take the box to the local university to have the papers translated. That's when the shit hit the fan - so as to speak." Owen and Wilson exchanged a smile at that comment.

"The language was Roman Latin, and the papers could be dated to 33AD and were the personal writings of a Roman Tax Collector and part time slave trader; Atticus Veris. The papers were correspondence between him and his brother who lived in Rome. Only one of the papers contained references that set the world alight; when the contents were made public some weeks later." Jericho consulted his mirror and continued; "The letter that Atticus sent to his brother in 33AD contained direct, firsthand contact with the Historical persona called Jesus of Nazareth and what he wrote, will cause a bombshell in the Christian world. The ramifications for the current Timeline are enormous and give a huge advantage to the 'Dark Prince'."

Jericho looked quite grim; "Our mission is to return to 33AD and discover if those letters are genuine and if not; make sure they never surface in the future." John held up a hand and Jericho nodded for him to speak; "What if you find they are genuine; what are your orders then?" Wilson whispered to Alex; "Now that's to the point; I've always liked the quiet man, now I know why."

Jericho shrugged his shoulders; "Our orders are the same for both scenarios." Everyone exchanged shocked looks and thought the same; "Cover-up."

"There is a human agent that will assist us and we'll meet them when we arrive in Jerusalem." Jericho added then gestured to James; "Whenever you're ready James." The Knight smiled; "Best we get going." Everyone was gone from the study and Mr. Harris started to clear away the dirty glasses. Ruth appeared and started to help; "Did John really accompany them?" She asked, with surprise in her voice really apparent. Mr. Harris nodded, he made no further comment and the pair returned to the kitchen.

2. JERUSALEM; 33AD - A DIVIDED CITY.

The little group passed unnoticed by the crowds through the old North gate into the city. Owen was leading their donkey and chatting quietly with Wilson; James and Jericho walked together - they were dressed as wealthy merchants of the period and some beggars called out to them for alms.

Alex, who walked behind them, gave the beggars some coin and they immediately began fighting over the money. James sighed and turned back to Alex; "Do not do that again; it will attract the city guard." Jericho agreed with that, and the group hurried away from the scene. John walked slowly behind the group, looking around. Alex joined him, sulking a little over her reprimand from James.

Jericho suddenly stopped for a few seconds and stared into the crowd that were gathering around the troublesome beggars. "I thought I saw someone I know." He muttered to James and did not smile.

Alex noted that the beggars stopped their brawling and stood aside as John walked past; one fell to his knees and tried to grab the hem of John's cloak with withered and crippled hands; "Forgive me Rabbi, please forgive me!" He called out, falling onto the dirt and John placed his hand upon the wretched man's head, then whispered something that Alex couldn't make out. The beggar lay in the dirt for a few seconds and then rose slowly to his knees; the other poor wretches gathered around the man. John caught up with Alex and simply smiled at her; "I think they mistake me for someone else."

Alex nodded, but could hear the shouting and crying behind them; the few words she could make out were cured miracle, Messiah and son of God. Some members of the city guard had arrived and were beating the beggars with sticks and so they shuffled away in some joy, mixed with a little despair. She stared at John, who pushed both hands through his dark hair and smiled at her - again; "As I say, I must look like someone that they know." Alex said nothing and the pair caught up with the remainder of the group. They had not seen the incident and Alex wondered; if they should know about what just apparently happened.

They were stopped, near the entrance to the street 0f carpenters, by a tall young man wrapped in a fine blue coat with a hood that hid his features. He spoke directly to Jericho; "The angel of the Lord has sent you?" Jericho nodded; "That angel is called truth." He replied quietly. The young man threw back the hood and smiled; "Welcome to Jerusalem Mr. Tibbs." Garic was dark skinned with dark hair and eyes; he had rugged features and boasted a small black beard. He gripped Jericho's arm and pulled him close; "We are staying at my father's house on the street of Goldsmith's, near the temple itself." He gestured for the group to follow him, and they made their way quickly through the noisy crowds.

Everyone noticed the large amounts of Roman soldiers about the streets and standing outside government buildings and temples. Garic gestured towards a large group of soldiers formed up outside a fine-looking house; "That's the local magistrate's house, Barabbas has threatened to kill him and so, the Roman Governor is taking no chances." James asked Garic about the man called Barabbas and Garic stopped in his tracks and whispered; "This is not the place for such a discussion my big friend - wait until we arrive at my father's house."

He then saw John walking with Alex; "Who is that man?" He asked Jericho and wiped his face with a trembling hand that all could see. Jericho gripped his arm; "That's an old friend of mine called John; you don't have to concern yourself with him." Garic said nothing more and the group hurried into the small, but apparently comfortable house - in the street of Goldsmith's - directly opposite the entrance to the Great Temple of Jerusalem, which thronged with worshippers, merchants, priests and soldiers.

The house was surprisingly cool and they were greeted by two maid servants bearing trays of wine and figs. Both girls stared long and hard at John as they moved about the visitors, who settled themselves on cushions about a central, low wooden table. Garic smiled broadly and sipped wine from a silver cup; "I bid you welcome to my father's house." He said proudly and dismissed the girls from the room. The smile disappeared and he gestured towards James; "You ask about Barabbas?" James nodded and smiled.

Garic sighed; "The man is a leader of the Zealots who wish to throw off the yoke of Rome - by the sword if necessary. He is quite fanatical in his beliefs and there is a large reward in gold offered by the Roman Governor for his head. He claims the divine gift of Prophecy and wants a holy war in the Lords name." Garic shifted on his cushions and fell silent for a few seconds; "He will plunge Judea into a bath of blood and currently only one man stands in his way; the Prophet Jesus has the ears of the common people, and he preaches a very different way, much to the anger of the Temple elders and priests who secretly support Barabbas. The carpenter's life is in danger every moment, yet it is whispered that he approaches the city, even as we speak." Garic stared again at John and fell silent.

Owen tapped Alex's arm and whispered; "Why does everyone stare at our John with that strange look of fear and almost wonderment?" Alex admitted that she didn't know and remained silent about the incident at the North Gateway. She glanced at John, who sat sipping wine and looking about the room, he had also said nothing about the same incident. What the hell did I witness? Alex wondered and smiled when John caught her staring at him.

"A shekel for your thoughts." He murmured and finished his drink. Jericho leaned forward and spoke directly to Garic; "I need to find a certain Roman Tax Collector who goes by the name of Atticus Veris. Have you any information on him?" Garic nodded slowly and sipped more wine; "He is a strange Roman who arrived with the previous Governor and was given a Tax District that covers Nazareth and other towns. He is also known to trade slaves; but only young pretty females - he pays top prices for the right women and girls. People say that he exports them to Rome, where his brother sells them for small fortunes."

Garic jabbed a finger at Alex and smiled broadly; "You are sitting on a fortune with such a woman!" Jericho nodded - unsmiling; "Do you know where he resides Garic?" The young man leaned back on his cushions, a concerned look upon his face; "He has a fine villa just outside Nazareth and is popular with the current Roman Governor - not a man to mess with Mr. Tibbs."

Alex placed her cup down and folded her arms; "Why do you say he is strange for a Roman?" Owen nodded; "I wondered about that." He muttered and finished his wine. Garic looked quite grim and clasped his hands together and leaned forward, his voice just above a whisper; "There are several stories about the man, some say he is a devil in disguise with strange dark powers. He has been known to simply disappear from the villa without using a door or window. Once, a fierce slave that worked his gardens attacked him with a shovel and Atticus simply raised a hand to him and the man fell dead at his feet!"

Everyone exchanged glances; there was certainly more to this than anyone first thought. Jericho grunted and smiled at James; "Well, I think we best meet this mysterious Roman letter writer." James agreed and everyone rose from the table. That's when a young maid slipped quietly into the room with a look of real fear upon her face and addressed Garic; "Master, the street is full of Roman soldiers searching for two wealthy merchants and their servants. They are searching every house."

Garic said nothing, but turned to Jericho, his face a picture of fear. Jericho griped his arm and smiled; "Go, gather your servants and greet the Romans with smiles and wine. They will not find us here, I promise." Garic wiped his face and with the maid, left the room. James smiled at Jericho and nodded; "Time to visit the tax collector." Everyone could hear the banging upon the doors - the soldiers were here.

Garic was pushed aside by the soldiers who refused wine and figs and searched his house thoroughly. The Centurion, a fat man with an ill-fitting tunic, seemed a little surprised that only Garic and his household staff were on the premises - That didn't go un-noticed by the quick-witted Garic.

Marcus wiped his sweaty face and spoke to Garic quietly; "The Governor himself needs to find two wealthy merchants, new to the city; who have three servants with them. They are a dumb looking boy, a big Nubian and a woman that could rival Venus herself."

Garic also noticed that the Centurion never mentioned the quiet man called 'John'. He wondered about the significance of that omission. The Centurion ordered his men out and they left the villa quietly; Garic saw that, they didn't search any other houses remaining in the street.

He watched them go with mixed feelings; he should have been arrested and dragged off for questioning and probably some torture. They clearly knew he had connections with the strangers to the city; but why had they left him alone?

Garic walked slowly back into the now empty reception room and stared about the place; how the hell did the Roman's find out about Jericho's visit? The answer was clear and dangerous; someone knew about the temporal detectives visit and had betrayed them to the Roman's - but who? He slumped upon some cushions and one of his maids refilled his cup. She hesitated for a few seconds then asked; "Master, how did they just disappear?"

He just smiled and murmured; "They work for God; they can do things like that." The girl gave him a puzzled look and returned to the kitchen - none the wiser. Garic sipped his wine and thought about the man called 'John' - having seen the Rabbi called Jesus of Nazareth; he wondered who the hell was this man called 'John'?

3. ATTICUS VERIS.

The little group stood quietly in the grove of olive trees and stared at the large imposing villa of the Tax Collector Atticus Veris. It was surrounded by a high wall of brick and stone; there was only one entrance and that was guarded by a small group of Roman legionnaires. "He certainly likes his security." Wilson said simply and then added; "Well, we can't just walk up and ask for an appointment - not with the damn Roman's already after us - so what's next on the agenda?" He spoke to Jericho who was deep in conversation with James.

James turned and smiled at Wilson; "If you can't get to see someone; you make damn sure they come to you." The three men all stared at Alex, who folded her arms and shook her head; "No bloody way!" She said with some determination. James smiled broadly; "We won't really sell you - just lend you out for a while." Wilson chuckled; "Like a library book." That comment didn't improve her mood.

But a smiling Jericho spoke quietly to Alex, and she sighed loudly, but agreed - the mission was that important. Owen, who had been trying to pick olives and not paying attention, asked Wilson what was the new plan? Wilson slapped him on the back and half smiled; "Well, baby brother, the answer is simple. We're going to sell Alex!" Owen just stared at him - speechless. The big man chuckled; "Our friend won't resist the chance of buying a female like Alex - he'll scuttle out of his fortress and we can have a cosy chat."

"Blimey, if I had the money; I'd buy Alex!" Owen muttered and everyone just stared at him - especially Alex. He said nothing further and trailed behind the others as they made their way to the nearby road. They stopped suddenly, standing by the roadside was an old man leaning upon a thick staff; he appeared to have a goat on a lead; like a pet dog. He ran some fingers through his white beard and smiled; "I bid you welcome my friends." Bowing slightly; well, as much as his age and back allowed him.

Jericho stared hard at the old man; those sharp unusual blue eyes [for this region] and the smile, made him think. He smiled broadly; "Caphus, you've changed a bit since we last met." and embraced the old man like a loving son to his father. Caphus wiped a little tear from his face and smiled; "It's been many years Jericho; too many years, I think." Jericho gripped his arm and asked quietly; "How did you know I was here, my old friend?" Cephus chuckled; "Your description is all across Judea - and your companions - the Governor really wants to talk to you!"

"That won't make our task any easier." James sighed and then Caphus turned to Alex and smiled; "I take it, you're the honey pot to lure Atticus out of his hole?" Alex just shrugged her shoulders. Jericho rubbed his chin; "Can you help us on this one?" The old man grinned a little; "I can. My Grandson holds auctions of property and slaves at the market. He could easily spread the word about a certain beauty that has come to be sold here - a private auction with only very wealthy patrons invited. Our man Atticus simply could not resist that."

"Come to my villa tonight, Jericho. You will be safe there and enjoy the hospitality that an old friend can offer." Caphus gripped Jericho's arm and added; "You know it well; I haven't moved since you were last here. I'm just older, that's all." Wilson nodded; "It has to be better than wandering around the bloody desert in the middle of the night." So it was agreed to accept the hospitality that Caphus offered. That's when the old man noticed John standing at the rear of the group and gripped his staff. He tried to bow but couldn't make it. "You keep very high company these days Jericho." He stared at John and gestured towards the road.

"This way my lord; I take it that you know he approaches the city, even as we speak." He spoke directly to John, who just nodded. The group set off behind the old man and his goat. Owen whispered to Alex; "Who's approaching the city?" She smiled and glanced at John but spoke to Owen; "Jesus Christ."

"The Jesus Christ?" Owen spluttered quietly and Alex nodded; "Yes, that's the one." he turned to John; "Did you hear that? Jesus bleeding Christ is coming here!" John just grinned and after an hour, they arrived at Caphus's modest villa. As they approached the house, Jericho passed around his hipflask and insisted everyone drink a little toast to their mission - they all did.

Old Caphus kept his word and the team was warmly welcomed into his home with bread, fruit and wine. They sprawled about his modest reception room and chatted, laughed and generally relaxed. Within in the hour, everyone was quiet; sleeping in the position they fell down in. Caphus viewed his work with satisfaction and his two servants stood ready with vases of oil. "Take the girl, wrap her carefully in a cloak and leave her outside - well away from the villa. She is worth a small fortune which is mine now." The two men nodded and carried Alex from the room.

Caphus stared at the sleepers and smiled; "So Mr. Jericho Tibbs, you really did think I would still bow and scrap to you after all these years?" He tipped over a large vase by the window and oil spread across the floor, he stood by the door and waited for his men to return and finish pouring the oil. "You practically abandoned me after all the help I gave you and you just expect me to jump to your whistle again?" He spat the bitter words out; they were directed at Jericho. "A friend tells me that burning is the only way to destroy creatures like you and so be it." He said softly to himself and smiled as his two henchmen finished pouring the oil.

The old man took a small lamp with a flickering flame and threw it upon the floor and fled the room. Outside, the three men watched as the villa was consumed by flames. "Get the wagon and load the girl, we will take her to her new master and collect much gold." Caphus leaned on his staff and smiled - it had been a very satisfying and soon, profitable night.

The wagon disappeared down the dirt road with the men sharing a goatskin of wine. The old man's goat wandered behind, tied with a small piece of rope. They reached the crossroads and stopped; approaching down the road was Atticus Veris and a troop of cavalry - right on time. He greeted Caphus with a raised hand; "You have her?" The old man nodded, and Atticus dismounted and joined the old man by the rear of the wagon. Caphus pulled back the thick curtain; the wagon was empty.

"What fucking trickery is this?" Atticus grabbed him by the hood of his cloak and threw him on the dry dirt. There was silence and Atticus suddenly realised that everyone was still, his men, the horses and even the bloody goat. He pulled out his sword and prodded the old man who appeared like a statue, his mouth open and eyes wide.

Atticus turned slowly and saw the little group standing by the roadside ditch. Jericho stepped forward and spoke quietly; "Atticus Veris?" Atticus nodded - he knew who this creature was and that it had stopped time itself for everyone else. He lowered his sword and pushed it back into the scabbard. "So, you have me creature, what now?" He folded his arms and stared at the Temporal Detectives like they had just crawled from hell itself.

"Creature?" Muttered Owen to Wilson, who just shrugged his shoulders. Jericho looked quite bemused by the 'creature' reference and pointed to Caphus, still prone on the floor and motionless. "I take it that's what the old man calls us?" Atticus nodded; "He told me all about you creatures and your evil ways. How could I possibly fight the spawn of the devil itself?" He was quite startled when everyone started to laugh. Jericho shook his head; "Atticus, we are quite the opposite of that!"

Jericho explained, with some patience, just who they actually worked for. Atticus ran a hand over his face and then stared hard at John; "I've encountered him before, it's the one they call the Rabbi from Nazareth." John sighed; "Everyone gets me mixed up with my big brother." Owen stared at John and gripped hold of Alex's arm; "Did you hear what he just said? Jesus bloody Christ is his big brother!" Alex nodded - somehow not truly surprised by that revelation - after what she witnessed with the beggars earlier.

Wilson turned to James and said quietly; "What the fuck has he been doing, I mean, hiding out with bloody Jericho for years?" James smiled; "Maybe finding a little peace of mind." Wilson grunted and wiped his face; he had been sharing with Jesus Christ's fucking brother all these years!

Jericho turned back to Atticus; "So you actually did meet Jesus of Nazareth?"

Atticus nodded, still staring at John; "I spoke with him and some of his disciples a few months ago. His words ... his words touched me in a strange way; they seem to contain some sort of deep truth; especially about YAHWEH and his inaction with the affairs of men." He turned back to Jericho; "What do you want of me?"

Jericho explained about the letters to his brother and the damning statement about what Jesus had said about God [his father]. Atticus again nodded; "I wrote only what he actually said about him. I took nothing away nor added anything else. I wrote the truth." James and Jericho exchanged a strange glance and Jericho almost smiled; "Thank you for your honesty, Atticus Veris."

That's when James went still and silent, hand raised against the side of his head. Alex whispered to Owen; "He's getting a message - probably from Angel Margret." Owen folded his arms; "I keep forgetting that Knights of God don't need bloody mirrors like we do." James lowered his hand and smiled; "Yes, thank you Atticus. We have to go now, and you will resume your life as before we met. You will remember nothing of this."

The team was gone in an instant and Atticus found himself standing over the crying and babbling Caphius, at the rear of the empty wagon. He kicked the old man in frustration; "What the fuck am I doing here, in the middle of fucking nowhere, with you, you old twat?" Caphus actually didn't know but could see the smoke and flames from his villa filling the night sky. He ran screaming, back towards the burning ruins of his house - well, as best as his age and infirmities allowed him!

Atticus watched as Caphus's henchman followed their master with the wagon - the goat still tethered behind. He spoke to the officer commanding his cavalry troop about what the fuck where they all doing here - in the middle of the night - in the fucking desert. The officer didn't know. "Let's get back to the villa and have some fucking wine." Was all he muttered and mounted the horse; he was having a very strange night indeed.

4. A LITTLE DECEPTION IS ~~BAD~~ GOOD FOR THE SOUL.

"How the hell did you know that old bastard was going to betray and poison us?" Wilson asked as they approached Garic's father's house. Jericho smiled; "I saw him watching us when we entered the North Gate, and I knew he would make contact at some point. I also know him from old and he was a deft hand at poisoning people he didn't like. Hence the antidote in my flask, that I insisted you all drink." James chuckled; "I wondered about the strange taste of that brandy. I thank you my old friend, but human poison - any poison - has no effect on knights of God."

Jericho nodded; "I know, but we all had to drink to keep up the celebrated appearance of the drink. Had I left you out, old Caphus would certainly have been suspicious." James agreed with that. Wilson knocked on the door and smiled at Alex; "Your new master is probably well pissed off that he didn't even get to look over his goods." Alex stuck up a single finger; but smiled.

"I loved the fact, that you let him burn down his own house. That's a nice touch." Wilson said to Jericho, who just smiled. The door slowly opened.

A nervous maid servant showed them in and whispered to Jericho; "The young master has an important visitor Sir." Jericho and James exchanged a glance - caught by Alex and Wilson, "I know; I'm expecting him." Jericho replied. But Owen whispered to Alex; "How the hell does he know these things?" Alex shrugged her shoulders; "Angel Margret wanted her best Inspector for this one and she certainly got that." Owen said nothing more and the group wandered into the reception room and saw Garic sitting with a tall, bearded young man with dark hair and eyes. He looked a great deal like John.

They both rose from their cushions; Jericho and James both bowed, and the other team members quickly followed. Owen whispered to Alex; "Oh fucking Christ - it's him!" Alex smiled; "You certainly got that right." John didn't bow but stepped forward and embraced his brother with real affection. They gripped each other for a few minutes and parted; both smiling. "Here we fucking go." was all Jericho said to the amazement of the others.

Well, the outright screaming, shouting row lasted for a good few minutes as everyone else waited outside in the small hallway. A totally amazed Alex asked Jericho quietly; "Are they always like this?" Jericho nodded and sighed; "Yes, since they both learned to walk and talk. Only their mother could break up their rows. I really wish she was here now to slap some sense into the pair of them." James agreed with that and accepted a cup of wine from Garic, who was doing his best to show hospitality, while the arguments raged in his reception room.

"How long will they keep this up?" Wilson muttered and sipped his wine, with a big grin. James sighed; "Time for action I think Jericho." The pair both turned to Alex and smiled. "Oh no! No bloody way am I going in there to split those two up!" Jericho smiled and pushed her towards the door; "Like their dad, they both have a serious soft spot for beautiful women; especially tough, straight-talking ones." He gently opened the door and shoved Alex through.

The shouting subdued a little, then faded into silence and only Alex's voice could be heard. "Our girl was never one to mince her words; even to a couple of God's." Wilson said - still grinning. Alex opened the door and gestured for everyone to come in - all was quiet between the brothers - for now.

The brothers sat at opposite ends of the room and sipped wine. The silence was palatable and was finally broken by Alex, who waved her wine cup about and quite nonchalantly asked: "Has it been a long time since you two got together?"

The two brothers simultaneously jumped from their cushions and threw their wine cups at each other; the row started with finger pointing and shouting. Everyone was back in the hallway and Jericho sighed; "You just had to open your mouth - didn't you?" He said to Alex and groaned loudly. Alex just folded her arms and was about to reply but thought better of it and remained silent. Garic's maid servant grabbed her master's arm and whispered into his ear.

"She's here. She's here to see John." Garic broke into a huge smile. "Who the fuck is here now?" Asked Owen and then fell silent as the small woman pushed past them, pulling back the hood of her travelling cloak. She was, clearly, still a beautiful woman. Wilson took a swig from his wine cup; she must have been an absolute stunner in her younger days, to still look that good.

Jericho and James both bowed; she smiled at Jericho; "Thank you Jericho for looking out for my boy." Then sighed and pushed open the door to the reception room. "Thank God for that." was all James said. Owen turned to Alex and before he could say anything, Alex nodded; "Yes, that's their poor, long suffering mother." She smiled quite broadly as the row - again – subdued.

Then the room lapsed into silence.

Owen, who was nearest the door, turned to Alex with real surprise on his face and in his voice; "Did I really hear St. Mary, the blessed Queen of Heaven, call the sons of God: a pair of useless bloody twats?" Alex nodded; "Yep, mothers have to do that sometimes, much as she loves the troublesome pair." James and Jericho chuckled, but Wilson laughed outright. Garic just gripped his wine goblet and said nothing - in modern terms - he was suffering a little shock.

Finally, the door creaked open, and Mary smiled at everyone; "Do please come in and enjoy the wine, I must apologise for my boys, they do get carried away discussing politics and religion. I've banned both subjects; for now." Everyone trooped back into the room and Owen whispered to Alex; "Discussion - they call that discussion?" Alex grinned and accepted a refill from a very nervous maid.

The two brother were sitting together: in silence. Their mother eased herself down on a couple of cushions and turned to Jericho; "I hope my boy hasn't been too much trouble Jericho?" He shook his head; "A real pleasure Ma'am. Prince John is always welcome in my house...as his brother would be...and yourself, of course." Mary smiled and accepted a wine cup from a young maid, who was shaking from head to foot. She gripped the young girls hand whispered in her ear. The transformation was electric; the young girl straightened herself up and with a big smile, left the room.

"Now, I know Jericho and I do believe, young man, that you are one of George's Knights?" James nodded and went to stand - she waved him down. "James Ma'am." He said and sat back down - smiling. Owen turned to Wilson; "Who the fuck is George?" Wilson sighed and jerked a thumb upwards; "Himself." was all he said. Owen shook his head in disbelief; "George - fucking hell! - George is his real name?"

Jericho quietly introduced Owen and Wilson to Mary, who smiled at both and asked the pair about their lives - when living - Wilson was, for once, very polite about the details of his demise. There were no profanities in his story, which amazed everyone.

Owen just mumbled about his life in the Monastery and Mary sipped her wine and then said quietly; "Oh no, you're a young man, you should be chasing girls or whoever you fancy, not wasting your time in such a place."

Finally, Jericho introduced Alexandra. Mary did smile and nodded to herself, "I've heard about you Alex - may I call you Alex? - my errant brother-in-law David has quite a thing about you." Owen turned to Wilson and whispered; "Brother-in-law David, that has to be..." Wilson nodded; "Yep, the bloody devil."

Alex sat back on her cushions and clutched her wine cup. "I have met him Ma'am...on a couple of missions, some time ago." her voice just above a whisper. Mary turned to Jericho; "I will ask George to keep an eye on that. David really does like beautiful, intelligent, and strong human females and this one [indicating Alex] ticks every box he has. Keep a close eye on her - yes?" Jericho nodded and swallowed down his wine.

Mary suddenly rose and everyone rose with her. She turned to 'her boys' and said with some authority in her voice; "Come on you two. We're going to have a lovely family dinner and talk politely about things. NO politics or Religion allowed. Thank you again Jericho and it was lovely to meet you all. I will be keeping a special eye on you Alex." The three simply disappeared and the room was totally silent for a few seconds; then trembled with unrestrained laughter.

Garic still sat clutching his goblet - finally he said, "What the fuck just happened?" No-one answered him; they were too busy drinking and laughing. Wilson raised his wine cup and said softly; "Here's to the deception of happy families. Even the bloody holy one's." Everyone agreed with that - except Garic who just raised his glass and repeated; "What the fuck just happened?"

5. THE SHOW MUST GO ON.

"So now, we must mug a Roman courier and steal the bloody mail?" Wilson asked Jericho as they made their way to the city's North gate. Jericho chuckled; "Not the way, I would have phrased it, but your close." The pair stood by the little bakery shop, just yards from the four or five Roman legionaries manning the gateway. The smell of fresh baked bread was gorgeous, and Jericho gave Wilson a few coins from the mission purse. He purchased a couple of sweet rolls, and both stood nibbling, watching for a certain group of Romans to approach.

"Atticus has sent the letters to his brother in Rome. They would have travelled with other messages, parcels and letters from citizens, who could afford to send such things, all the way to Rome." Jericho muttered, really enjoying his little snack. Under his cloak, he discretely consulted his mirror. He gestured down the busy thoroughfare towards a horse and cart; there were another group of about a half dozen Roman soldiers accompanying it. "They're heading for the docks to catch the boat for Rome." He added and finished his snack.

"Is that damn casket on board?" Wilson asked, wiping his mouth. Wine would be good after that excellent little delicacy. Jericho nodded and they watched the cart pass through the gateway; the gate guards just nodded their greeting at the two sitting on the wagon and the other soldiers. Jericho and Wilson casually walked behind the cart and followed it out, onto the dirt road. They could see Owen sitting by the roadside, holding tightly onto 'Freddie's' reins. That damn donkey had been in more missions that they had! But Owen was very fond of the mangy old bugger and always volunteered to look after him. Freddie was one of the best donkey's Supplies had in stock.

On the other side of the road were James and Alex, who was tightly wrapped in a long cloak; to hide her figure and had the hood up. James watched the cart and guards approaching, he smiled at Alex; "Now I know how bloody Dick Turpin felt." She just smiled. James gestured to Jericho and time stopped. Wilson walked forward and through the still soldiers and then pulled the flap back on the wagon. He rummaged amongst the various items until he found a bundle of rough cloth; he pulled it back a little and turned to Jericho; "Got it." and dragged the small travelling chest from the wagon, keeping it wrapped in the cloth.

Owen helped him heave it up on Freddie and the little group was ready to go. They walked slowly back towards the gateway and passed through. James restarted time and they watched, as the Roman cart trundled on; the men totally unaware they had just been robbed!

They made their way back to Garic's house; Jerusalem was swarming with people, some carrying palm leaves and all shouting and talking happily with each other. A couple of young men shouted at them; "You're going the wrong way brothers! He comes into the city!" Jericho just sighed and they reached Garic's house without any incident. Owen stabled the donkey, whilst Wilson discretely carried the bundle of 'cloth' into the house.

Garic ordered wine and food for his guests - again. Jericho and James prised open the casket and began sorting through the correspondence it held.

Wilson picked up one letter and chuckled, reading it slowly. "Anything funny?" James asked. Wilson nodded; "Atticus has written that he can get his hands on a real beauty; one that could fetch a small fortune in Rome. He says that Caphus has told him that, she has a figure like Venus and breasts like cooking pots! Do you think he means our Alex?" They both laughed, but Alex wasn't amused; "Bloody cooking pots?" she muttered, adding; "Bastard." under her breath.

Jericho held up one and nodded; "This is it. Well. He didn't lie. That sounds exactly like what he [Jesus] would say about his father." He lowered the letter and accepted a cup of wine from Garic. That's when James held up another piece of correspondence and didn't look happy. "Atticus states in this one, that people often mistake Jesus' brother for him. Jesus apparently told him to watch out for John; that he'll do anything to thwart his plans for humanity. Can you imagine what this would do to people's ideas about Christ?"

"Good job you stole it then." John stood in the doorway and smiled. He wandered over and slumped down on some cushions; Garic gave him wine and shuffled away. "My dear brother - at this moment in time - is mounted on a bloody donkey and making a grand entrance into the city. He has balls - I'll give him that - but does he really expect dad to interfere? He's off his nut." John sipped his wine and Alex sat opposite him. "What do you mean Sir; Interfere, I mean?"

John smiled; "He thinks that dad will save his dumb arse before they nail him up on that cross. He's trying to force his hand. Make him interfere in human history. That's why, he made that poor sap Judas betray him. The poor bastard really didn't want to; but he made him, and we all know how that ended." John sighed and lay back on the cushions; "Why do you think he [Jesus] shouts; 'why the fuck have you forsaken me?' when hanging on the cross? He really thought dad would interfere; send a couple of Knights or something. That must have come, as a real wake up call."

John actually chuckled. "He always said, if this one failed, he would try again in another few centuries. He's bloody persistent. I'll give him that. Except he will change all sorts of things about how people should behave and confuse everybody; probably cause fighting between the different sects."

John didn't even notice the shocked silence in the room. The whole thing was staged to get his father [the BOSS] to actually interfere in humanity's history! Alex downed her wine and really could use a bloody brandy right now. John shrugged his shoulders; "He really didn't think that all the stuff he preached about would actually catch on. Now that came as a surprise, he was dossed on that mountain of his and wham! Suddenly there's a new religion on the block. But then, I must admit, that was actually my cock up." He sighed and finished his wine.

"Your cock-up Sir?" Wilson asked, pushing both hands through his hair. John nodded; "Yeah, a couple of days after the big event, I dropped by and visited mum; she was still human then, of course. Loads of his [Jesus'] friends and bloody disciples saw me and that was that. He was still sulking on his bloody mountain. I would have given anything to see his face, when he heard about his new religion." John laughed at the thought of that.

"And he did try again; didn't he?" Jericho said, unsmiling. John nodded; "And look how that turned out; he changes his idea's for humanity, like some change their socks!" He had finished his wine and rose up; "I think, I'll disguise myself as an old man and watch the show."

They watched in amazement as John was now, an old man, with a wooden staff. He walked to the door and scratched his flowing white beard; "Based this on that bloody good painting of my Grand Father. The artist was quite good and almost accurate, about how the old bugger looked." He disappeared. Everyone sat quietly and no one said anything. Garic flopped onto some cushions and said softly; "What the fuck just happened?"

6. SOME THOUGHTS.

James burnt the correspondence in the kitchen stove, bit by bit. He gave the little ornate casket to Garic - he could keep or sell it - it didn't matter. The letters no longer existed and would not, now, be found by the shepherd boy. Owen asked if they would join Prince John and watch the 'show' - even if they all knew the ending; nobody wanted too. Alex said softly; "All that happens is he's [Jesus] human form is destroyed. He's still around of course. He can't be killed by humans or anything else in this world. His bloody family made and rules it."

Wilson was sprawled across several cushions, hands behind head and legs crossed. "So that's the cause of the trouble between the brothers; Jesus thinks John deliberately messed up his plan with their father, by appearing after the 'event' and letting everyone believe there had been a physical resurrection. Sweet fuck; what a cosmic cock-up!" No one could disagree with the big man.

Alex sat tapping her wine cup with a finger; she was deep in thought. "Why do they take human females as mates? Why didn't they just create their own females? I mean they made us." She gestured to herself and continued; "Or rather; where are their females?" Everyone sat around and Jericho rubbed his chin; "Alexandra, that is a bloody good question. All their females have been human or born to human mothers. Even our present BOSS has a human mother." [The Dowager Queen Isis was still very popular, in the world that the 'God's' inhabited.]

"If you can come up with an answer to that; you'll be the most clever human that ever lived." James muttered; Alex's question had perplexed him - greatly. Owen sucked his teeth and grinned; "That's because they weren't supposed to breed I expect. Who ever made them - and something or someone must have done - didn't give them females, so that they wouldn't breed another generation. Maybe they were supposed to be 'one off's' and they were clever enough to work around it. I always had a sneaking suspicion that human females were the first thing created, not males - the story of Adam and Eve has it the wrong way round. It's bloody obvious that females came first; if all the Gods were males."

There was real silence in the room, and everyone stared at Owen. "You mean, they're simply a higher species that created an organic Artificial Intelligence for their own pleasure and amusement and that's us?" James leaned back on his cushions and stared at the ceiling. Owen nodded; "Makes sense to me. Humans in the late 21st century created organic robots for heavy labour and some for sexual pleasure. What happens, if they [humans] created one that had an 'artificial' womb and could produce hybrid children? What if we're just their version of them? Except we're a lot more sophisticated and better made. But given time and development; who knows?"

"What about souls?" Alex asked softly; she definitely didn't like where this conversation was going. Owen shrugged his shoulders; "Considering what they are capable of; a little piece of energy that retains a human's persona is not difficult for them. Not difficult by a long shot. Remember; freewill was a supposed 'divine gift' - no other creature possesses it, apparently - so, if they can create that incredible thing, a soul is a piece of cake. More importantly, it exists in their version of 'time', which is a lot different to ours. We're organic; we are born, we live and then die. A straight line. That's how human's measure time. But for them it's never ending, never changes; it's the same 'time' regardless." He almost chuckled; "The theory of relativity means shit to them."

He sighed and finished his wine. "That's the real gift they gave us; [humans] the energy [the soul] that couldn't be destroyed and exists in their time." He added and smiled. He rose from his cushions, scratching his arse. "By taking human females, that they created, they gave themselves the other great gift." Wilson sat up; "And what is that?" He asked quietly. Owen smiled; "The ability to procreate. Something, I think, that was originally denied to them. Clever fuckers aren't they." He made for the stables to check on and feed Freddie.

Wilson grunted; "If brains of Britain has it right and the 'Gods' are masters of all creation; then what the fuck is the duck-billed platypus all about? What, did they get pissed up one Saturday night and say, 'Look, we've got all these bits left over, let's make a fucking duck-billed platypus. That will give those human bastards something to puzzle over!"

He had a room full of people deep in thought and laughing.

7. ROMANS.

Barabbas and his motley crew of 'freedom' fighters thought a night raid would be perfect; he had received information that the so-called Rabbi of Nazareth - and his main rival - was staying at Garic's house and so they turned up just after midnight; armed to the teeth. But they hadn't counted on the power of the humble fig. Jericho had eaten loads of the sweet little things and now was heading - yet again - to the outside toilet in quite a hurry. He sighed as he watched the small mob assembling outside the house.

He stopped time and emerged from the privy, much relieved. He woke everyone up and they went outside and stared at Barabbas and his men. Jericho scratched his chin and smiled; everyone loved his plan and set to work. They all sat watching from the small front window and Jericho used his mirror to restart time. Cups of wine were handed around and everyone settled down to watch. Strangely enough; no one really wanted any more figs or dates.

Barabbas suddenly realised he was waving a palm leaf - the symbol of his rival - as were most of his men; all their swords and daggers had gone, along with their clothes. Nine naked men ran screaming from the small street. They passed a couple of Roman soldiers guarding the crossroads. The Romans watched them dash past with not too much comment.

"Followers of that bloody crazy Rabbi I expect. He's in town you know." One said, scratching his leg, to the other who shrugged his shoulders; "If that's how they protest our occupation of their land - running naked around the streets at night - I don't think old Pontius has much to worry about." The other guard nodded his agreement; a little bored with it all. He wished the Legion had been posted to Germania; those fuckers were always ready for a fight and very rarely turned up naked. It was too bloody cold for a start. He sighed and wished his shift was over.

Owen peered out the window; "Isn't that Atticus and that murdering little fucker Caphus?" Everyone crowded around the small window and Jericho just sighed; "They must have had the same idea. Catch us asleep and steal Alex. She's worth a lot of money to them." Wilson chuckled; "There's about half a dozen of them. All armed to the teeth. What's the plan now?" He asked Jericho who rubbed his chin and grinned, muttering "What's good for the goose...."

The two Roman soldiers guarding the crossroads were leaned against the wall of the local silversmith's and counting the minutes down to their relief. They heard the screaming, and both straightened up; spears at the ready. They watched Atticus and his men rush past them stark naked and disappear into the night. They then watched Caphus staggering past, trailing behind the others. He had a palm leaf hanging out of somewhere quite personal - Alex had enjoyed her little bit of revenge - he nodded to the guards and vanished up the street; groaning.

The two guards sighed; "Why the fuck, couldn't the legion have been posted to bloody Germania?" They went back to counting the minutes to their relief. Their Centurion just stared at the pair, as they made their report on the night's activities. His clerk scribbled down the testimony on his wax tablet with an open mouth. "Naked with palm feathers shoved up their arses; is that what your reporting?" He asked the two smiling guards - glad that their night shift was over - and scratched his chin. He really wished that the fucking legion had been posted to Germania...

The following morning, all was quiet in the street; most people had gone to the trial of the young Rabbi and Garic stood in his reception room staring at the pile of clothes and weapons by the window. He scratched his head and beard. The young maid gave him some wine; he turned to her and whispered: "What the fuck just happened?" She shrugged her shoulders and smiled; "No bloody idea sir and I really don't care." She disappeared back to the kitchen; laughing.

The team decided - unanimously - not to bother watching the rest of the 'show'. They would be leaving today and Owen was a little unhappy; he would have to say goodbye to his favourite donkey - well, until another mission - and Ester, the young housemaid. When Wilson told Alex about Owens's affection for Ester, she just sighed; "He clearly has a thing about housemaids. We may have to have words about that." Wilson nodded; "Good job we don't live in Victorian times; the bloody place would be full of them. We'd never get the little git out on another mission."

They made their way through the quiet streets of the city and out through the great North Gate. A couple of Roman guards on duty watched the little group depart. "Sweet Mars, did you see the tart walking by the donkey? Waving a palm leaf over her face; now, a piece of cake like that would make occupation of this shithole worthwhile." One muttered. The other shook his head; "Nay, she's probably a follower of that crazy Rabbi. She has his symbol; a palm leaf and we all know what they do with them to celebrate their faith."

The other guard grunted and reluctantly agreed; he wouldn't run about the city's streets naked, with a palm leaf stuck up his arse. But, then again, she was a real beauty, with tits like cooking pots and he had certainly done some daft things for women in his time. He gripped his javelin and counted the minutes to his relief.

Pontius Pilate sat in the grand reception room, hands over his face. The bloody Sanhedrin had dumped the case of the young rabbi into his lap. He also had that mad rebel Barabbas in custody. Found with weapons and plans to attack his [Pontius's] palace. Now this! He looked up at the Centurion and said quietly; "So the Rabbi's followers strip naked, shove palm leaves up their bum's and run about the city at night; screaming. Do I have that right?" The Centurion nodded; he really wanted to laugh but restrained himself.

"They carry no weapons and offer no violence to my soldiers or Officials, is that right?" Pontius asked, wiping his face. The Centurion nodded again. His voice betrayed a little restrained laughter; "Do you think it could be some sort of filthy Judean trick my lord?" Then giggled outright. Pontius just stared at him. This Rabbi was clearly far more dangerous than people gave credit to - and he was about to release him and crucify the mad dog Barabbas - until he received the Centurions report.

Pontius rose from his chair and paced the room. If such tactics could make an old soldier like Maximus [the Centurion] laugh and treat the populations like wayward children - by the God's! - The Roman occupation could descend into farce and shit giggles! How could you rule such a people? He groaned loudly; Rome knew how to deal with fighters and warriors, but this?

Pontius shook his head; the Rabbi had to die. The alternative was thousands of naked citizens running about the place with palm leaves stuck up their arse's and his troops laid about in utter hysterics; that caused the great man a daytime nightmare. Caesar would have his balls - and his head - if such a religion spread like plague around the Roman Empire. He sighed and stared at the mob watching him from below, chanting for Barabbas. They were far more stupid than even Rome gave them credit for.

"Crucify the clever bastard." was all he said and picked up the palm leaf that Maximus had presented as evidence and stared at it. Then he realized where the fucking thing may have been. He ordered a bowl of water and washed his hands. The crowds cheered and the rest is history.....

8. MORE TRAVELS IN TIIME.

Atticus watched the little group heading towards the ruins of the village - now deserted and abandoned - with a small smile on his face. He had warned Pontius about these strangers. But the Governor - currently - had his hands full with the zealots and the crazy followers of the young Rabbi. He simply couldn't believe the stories of how they behave. It was a pity history hadn't recorded that little story. He turned to his friend Marcus - the Centurion - and said quietly; "Our Master has great taste in female flesh. She is an absolute Venus; and more." Marcus nodded; "That fool Cephus failed. The Master won't be pleased with him."

They saw the group meet the strangely dressed strangers and watched as everyone simply vanished. - Including Freddie, the donkey - and the ruins returned to their undisturbed state. The two men walked back to their horses; "Are you going to the crucifixions? They say it should be a good turnout because of the young Rabbi. He should attract a good crowd." Marcus asked, wiping his face and neck. Atticus grunted 'no'. He had plans to make and letters to write. The cursed Rabbi could meet his end without his company. He also had matters to settle with Garic. He didn't have the skirts of bloody Jericho Tibbs to hide behind now. But that would have to wait.

Atticus dismissed the servant, who had carried his dinner tray into his private office, dropped the metal bar across the door and sat behind the large ornate marble desk. He pulled the Mesopotamian figurine from his travelling cloaks concealed pocket and placed it on the table. He unlocked the large chest by the door and quickly changed his clothes. He picked up the figurine and whispered the words. He kissed it and was gone.

David Palmer hailed a passing handsome cab; "Whitehall." Was all he said and eased back in his seat. It was a ten-minute run to the Headquarters of Military Intelligence. He stared out into the packed streets of Victorian London and almost smiled. Not half an hour ago, he was in Judea and if concerned, could have watched the supposed crucifixion of the Prophet Jesus Christ. His brother

Antonius, who lived in Rome, had no idea about his younger brother's time travelling habits!

The cab pulled up outside the grand building on the corner of Trafalgar Square. It was part of Admiralty House, and he paid the cab driver and straightened his jacket; it was really warm for an English Summer evening. But not as warm as bloody Judea. He walked up the steps and passed Captain Edgar Roberts - in civilian clothes - coming down the steps. The pair greeted each other. Roberts was on his way to Germany; he would be leaving by steamer that evening. The older man smiled and told David that young Eddy Charms had found a girl that matched the picture. He had, of course, not told the woman, that she would be working for British intelligence.

David Palmer smiled and shook Edgar's hand and made his way to his office. "If she is a close enough resemblance, then the game is on." He whispered to himself and dropped behind his desk. There were several letters awaiting his attention and a couple of handwritten messages. The one from Captain Eddy Charms caught his eye. He read it carefully and smiled. David read the calendar and stepped out of his office; a passing janitor was called over. "What is today's date Patrick?" He asked the man, who chuckled; "Its Tuesday July 7th Mr. Palmer. Been out of touch again?" David nodded and thanked the man, then returned to his office.

He marked the date on his 1891 calendar and realized he had been away for four days. There was a knock at the door, and he shouted; "Enter". It was Eddy Charms, he grinned; "Your back then. Paris must be good; you look like you've got a tan. I have one little peach that you should look at. If I didn't know better; she's the girl in the photograph." He saw the look on David's face and smiled.

"I know the others were bit of a letdown, but this one will turn your head." He turned to go and David called after him; "Well. when can I see the damn woman?"

Eddy looked back and said, "Tonight. We'll have supper at the 'Clarence' [a hotel & pub in Whitehall] bring at least twenty pounds - for a deposit - she won't accept the role without a real deposit." He waved and walked away. David just sighed; the last couple of ladies looked nothing like the damn picture.

David made the pub and restaurant, just a little before seven and sat at his reserved table. He ordered a decent bottle of wine and told the waiter that Mr. Charms would be joining him; with his 'cousin'. The old waiter smiled and walked away; "That pair have more cousins than a bloody Arab has wives." He muttered. David was sipping some wine when Eddy joined him with the lady.

He rose from his seat and dropped his napkin back on the table. Eddy gestured to the immaculately dressed young woman. "David, this is Elizabeth Featherstone; the young and very talented actress, I was telling you about." David really did smile and held out his hand; "It is a real pleasure to meet you Miss Featherstone." Eddy had come through at last; she was a dead ringer for Lady Alexandra Cappanni.

THE END

EPILOGUE:

"This unusual mission could be judged as a success; the letters written by 'Atticus Veris' to his brother in Rome, where destroyed in 33AD and thus, they never surfaced later. The revelation as to who, John the recluse, actually was shocked the Team - except Jericho and James - and they now see the strange man in a very different light. The time travelling 'David Palmer' would become a problem for the Team; especially Jericho and Alexandra."
SJW.

CHARACTERS:

Garic [the Goldsmith's son] had been a human agent of Jericho Tibbs - like his father before him - for many years. He was killed in 36AD during a Roman raid on a party he was attending. The Roman's were after one of the guests, who was a notorious zealot. His soul was collected and processed.

Ester [the maid] was given by her master - Garic's father - in marriage to a Baker called Simon. It was not a happy marriage and Ester had three live children during that marriage. She was widowed in 41AD and avoided re-marrying. She died in 52AD from fever. Her soul was collected and processed.

Caphus was a former human agent of Jericho Tibbs who had turned against him, with real hatred. The old man lived in tents after his Villa was burnt down. His so-called friends offered no help. He died in 35AD alone in the desert. His soul was collected and processed.

Atticus Veris [David Palmer] was a human minion of the Dark Prince and a time traveler. 'David Palmer' was just one of his many identities, he had acquired over his travels through time. Since he was originally 'Atticus Veris' the temporal detectives didn't make too many enquires about the man. He remains a servant of the Dark Prince and his soul remains missing to this day.

Marcus Pullo [The Centurion] was a close friend of Atticus Veris and did his bidding for rewards of gold and slave girls - really young slave girls - he succumbed to 'night fever' during the winter of 37AD. His soul was collected and quarantined until 250AD.

Maximus Testor [the Centurion] was a loyal Roman soldier and officer for the Roman Governor of Judea, at the time. He had seen many campaigns and travelled most of Europe with his Legion. He became a Christian in 39AD and was killed by local zealots in 41AD, who didn't trust the 'New' Christians. His soul was collected and processed.

Barabbas [the zealot] continued to attack the Roman occupation of his land, but his creditability had actually been damaged by his release from Roman custody. His followers wanted a 'martyr' and he was soon killed in fighting between the factions of Jewish patriots. He died in strange circumstances in 34AD. His soul was collected and processed.

Pontius Pilate was dismissed as Governor of Judea, and little is known about his death in 39AD - to historians - but he died by his own hand after a drinking session went wrong. His soul was collected and processed.

Captain Eddy Charms played the spy for some years but was betrayed while undercover in Prussia [part of the German Empire] and was found dead in a small railway station in August 1906. He had never discovered who his friend David actually was. His soul was collected and processed.

Captain Edgar Roberts had worked for Military Intelligence for some years before it was discovered that he was a double agent and selling secrets to German Military Intelligence. To avoid a scandal and much embarrassment to the department he was executed in secret. His body was found floating in the Thames in January 1911. His death was ruled as 'accidental' despite having two bullet holes in his chest! His soul was collected and processed.

The story about the palm leaves and how the 'New Christians' used them was never recorded in the modern Bible. It was thrown out – along with gospels from Judas and Mary Magdalene – at the **First Council of Nicaea**, (325), the first ecumenical council of the Christian church, meeting in ancient Nicaea (now Iznik, Turkey). It was called by the Emperor Constantine I, an un-baptized catechumen (Pagan) who presided over the opening session and took part in the discussions. He basically decided what the Christian message was!!

Miss Elizabeth Featherstone was Alexandra's younger sister and the pair certainly looked alike. People who didn't know them would always mistake them as twins. Her dealings with 'David Palmer' would be disastrous for Alex and Jericho. But that's another story.....

SPECIAL APPEARANCES BY:

Prince John; as himself.

Prince Jesus; as himself.

Queen Mary; as herself.

EPISODE 3: "THE PRIEST."

MISSION SUMMARY: "In the autumn of 1916, the village of Turning, located in a remote part of Yorkshire, welcomes the new parish priest; Father Peter Meyer, who has been a Padre in the British army and served for two years in Northern France. The young priest quickly proves popular amongst the villagers; especially amongst the many widows and wives of serving soldiers! But what lies behind this priest, who's favourite saying is; *God has little to do with religion!* But strange happenings in the village bring Jericho on the scene."

NOTES: This is a special **Extended** Edition.

TRIGGER WARNINGS. ALCOHOL, STRONG LANGUAGE, STRONG SEXUAL REFERENCES AND VIOLENCE.

AGE 15+ ONLY. **45 Minutes reading time.**

1. INTERVIEW WITH THE BISHOP.

Father Peter Meyer could easily be considered 'handsome'; he was over six feet tall with dark curly hair and dark eyes. Thanks to his love of rugby, he had the physical appearance to match his looks; rugged. Despite only being 28 years old, there was a string of disappointed women in his past. Priests of the Holy Roman Church cannot marry.

The Bishop's Secretary, a weedy little man with glasses and an annoying cough, had shown the young priest into the bishop's study. The odd little man coughed [again] into his hankie and smiled; "His Grace will be here shortly Father Meyer." The secretary turned to go, but stopped and glanced back at the young man in uniform, a very handsome young man. He wondered about the rumours and gossip concerning this Priest; the women, the drinking, the defying of church doctrine and why he had been returned to civilian service after two years at the front.

He also wondered about the sense in sending such a priest to North Turning, with all those old legends and stories about the place. But that was not his concern. North Turning had been a hotpot of apparent witchcraft and strange happenings for centuries. It had always required the presence of a 'strong' priest of firm character. This young man certainly didn't fill those requirements. Still, there was a war on; the parish would have to accept what it was given.

"I thought you would be wearing your cassock and not your army uniform?" The little man wiped his face and sweaty hands with his large hankie, then adjusted his glasses. Father Meyer didn't smile; "All my stuff is in storage at the Parish I was at, when drafted into the army padre service in '14. They are sending it onto me at Turning Village." The secretary nodded and said nothing more and motioned the priest to sit, then left the room to organise some tea from the kitchen.

Peter sat quietly smoking; he turned the packet of 'Woodbines' around in his fingers several times. With each little turn, his mind returned to the trenches and the faces of the men with who he had shared the cigarettes with. Each face had a name; each face had a mother, wife or sweetheart. Most of the faces were young and all were now dead.

Father Peter Meyer had defied both Church rules and army discipline on 1st July 1916; he simply could not let his 'boys' go without him and so on that dreadful morning; Father Peter Meyer went 'over the top' carrying a medical kit and extra water bottles.

Every man in the Company that he served with cheered the priest loudly and with much spirit. The very young Lieutenant grinned broadly and slapped Peter's steel helmet with the butt of his pistol: "We can now say, with some honesty, that we go with God!" The sound of whistles drifted down the packed trench and Peter glanced at his watch: 7.30am.

Twenty minutes later, Peter wounded in the leg, was dragging young private Roy Farmer back to the British lines. Farmer had been shot in both legs and chest by machine gun fire. Behind the brave priest lay the rest of 'C Company' - they had not even reached the German wire - never mind the enemy trenches. In fact, Peter had not seen a single German; now 27 men lay dead or wounded in 'No Man's Land' from the 32 that went over the top just twenty minutes ago.

The door opening made him jump slightly and he rose slowly from his comfortable armchair and greeted Bishop Henry Littlewood with a small smile and a handshake. Then he kissed the bishop's ring when offered.

The Bishop, a large man with clumsy tendencies, eased himself behind the large rosewood desk that dominated his study; He quietly drummed his left hand upon the desk and did not smile at Peter. "I'll get straight to the point; the Cardinal is not happy with you Peter and that's why you have been posted to the village of North Turning. Your actions at the front, whilst commendable on many levels, has bought the Church into conflict with His Majesty's Armed Services. That is why you're sitting here; the army has dispensed with your services as a Chaplin."

Peter simply nodded and lit another cigarette; two years in the fucking hell hole of the trenches and his reward is 'exile' to a North Yorkshire backwater. The thought may him smile inside; but he didn't show it.

Bishop Henry clasped his hands together and studied the young man sitting opposite; Army High Command had not been kind to the young Chaplin - he should have been awarded medals - for his actions on that dreadful morning. Despite being wounded, Father Peter had gone back into 'No-Man's Land': twice more and dragged back two more boys who would have surely died. Then he had stayed in the trenches, administering to the wounded and dying, until ordered to the casualty Clearing Station.

A brave and committed young priest, who had put his very life on the line. The bishop sighed; but he also, had his orders - direct from the Cardinal - and he would carry them out - never mind his own feelings about this case. Father Meyer would get what he deserved, that made the bishop smile to himself.

"Just sit out your new assignment for a few years and then we'll think about another parish; a bigger one in the city maybe, when this awful war is over and everyone has settled down." The bishop did smile and looked to the door as his Secretary entered with a tea tray. The pair drank their tea in silence. Father Peter would accept his punishment in the name of God, not the Church; after all, God had little to do with religion. That thought made Peter smile to himself. The interview ended with handshakes and peter left for the railway station in deep thought; but smiling openly now.

Father Peter stood on the platform and watched the crowds; weeping women saying goodbye to more young soldiers and old men shaking hands with their sons and grandsons; with fixed smiles and much sadness. Peter hated this common sight at Railway Stations, and he turned away from it and stared at the war posters that covered the station's walls. Propaganda and total bollocks! He allowed himself a little smile and picked up his battered little suitcase, as the train came to a rolling halt next to him.

A porter pulled open a carriage door for him and smiled; "There you go Father and good luck." Was all the elderly man said and Peter jumped into the packed carriage. He would have to stand; all the seats were taken by soldiers, old men and women with young children. Luckily, the journey to Turning was only about thirty minutes and he gripped the wooden corner of a seat occupied by a tall, skinny and elderly gentleman in a new, bright straw hat. The old man was reading a local paper extolling the 'Victories' of the Somme Battle. That made Peter wince inside and he stared out the window.

The train shuddered a couple of times and pulled slowly from the station. The shrill whistles of the platform staff dragged Peter back to that morning; the smiling young faces, the noise, the screams and shell fire, it flooded his mind, and he gripped the seat with some strength. He closed his eyes tightly and prayed to God for help, any bloody help. Then realised that someone was speaking to him; he snapped open his eyes and saw a pretty young woman smiling at him; her lovely mouth was moving, but he couldn't hear what she was saying because of the shellfire in his head.

He wiped his face with his free hand; he couldn't seem to pull his other hand from the edge of the seat. "Are you coming back or going up to the front Father?" The young woman asked again. Peter nodded and almost smiled; she was a slender, pretty little thing with loads of soft brown hair, curled beneath her hat which was adorned with a single white rose. She laughed - quite beautifully - and said, "Is that yes, you're going home or yes, you're heading for the front?" Peter managed to smile; "Going to my new Parish." was all he said and found that he could release his grip on the seat.

"So, were you there?" She gestured to the headlines on the old man's paper. Peter nodded again. The smile dropped from her face; "My brother David was there, with the Suffolk's. Did you meet anyone from that regiment?" She asked, gripping her little brown leather handbag with both hands. Peter shook his head; "I was with the 3rd Yorkshire. Sorry." His mouth was dry, and he desperately needed a drink.

The young woman nodded, with some sadness in her eyes. "I see; I read about a young priest - like yourself that went out under shellfire and dragged several of our boys in. Did you know him?" Peter managed to swallow, despite his dry throat and mouth. He was staring into those gorgeous, sad brown eyes and couldn't think of any suitable reply. The old man lowered his paper; he had been listening to the brief conversation between the pair. He stared hard at the handsome young Chaplin and nodded to himself. It was him and he knew it.

"Excuse me father, but you ARE Father Peter Meyer; aren't you?" He rested both hands on the newspaper. The priest noticed that several people around them all turned their attention to him, including a couple of soldiers. Peter nodded. The old man eased himself up and held out his thin, almost transparent hand. "Would you do me the honour of shaking my hand father?" He said softly and removed his 'straw boater' with the other. Father Peter gripped his hand and the old man whispered; "God bless you father." A young soldier, squeezed next to him, grabbed the priests arm and said loudly; "Thank fuck for you father. My cousin George was there with the Yorks. You're a fucking legend Father."

"Thank you." Was all he managed to say, as several other passengers stood and wanted to shake his hand. "Went out five times despite a leg wound and dragged his boys to safety. A real fucking hero." The young soldier gripped his hand with real affection, and he whispered close to the father's ear; "All the boys know what those bastard 'brass hats' did to you!"

Peter was really glad to see the station for North Turning appear outside the carriage windows. He made his way from the train, with people slapping his back and gripping his free hand; the other carried his small suitcase. He stood on the platform and found the young woman standing next to him.

"My dad Harold can give you a lift to the Parochial House Father. He'll be here in a few minutes. He run's the Black Oak pub on the Village green." She smiled at him, and he nodded; "Thank you very much Miss; if it's not too much trouble." She grinned; "No trouble Father whatsoever, he'll be honoured to have you ride in his buggy and it's Mrs. Father; my husband Kevin is at the Front; like most young men from the village." She gripped his hand and really did smile - in a strange little way – and Father Meyer could feel soft feminine fingers wrapping about his big hand. God: he loved the touch of her hand.

The young priest knew exactly what the look she gave him meant; he had seen such an expression quite few times before. "You're from the village then?" He asked quietly, making no effort to remove her hand. She nodded; "Oh yes and we can show real hospitality to our brave new priest." Peter felt her squeeze his hand and they both smiled.

"Oh what the hell! What could they do to me now; send me back to the Front?" He whispered to himself and watched the single horse buggy approaching down Railway Lane. "Mrs. Cooper - your housekeeper - is a friend of mine. Her old man Eric is an officer at the Front and has been for almost a year. But she's use to that; he's always been in the army. I've never met him. But she's really going to fuss over you Father." Victoria stared into his eyes and added, very softly; "Like most of us young ladies in the village." Father Meyer simply smiled.

2. NORTH TURNING VILLAGE; YORKSHIRE.

Peter stood by the window stretching and pulled the dark curtain back a little; he had to give the cold glass a little rub before peering out into the darkness of the winter sunrise. There was snow everywhere; he guessed it could be quite deep in places, there had been quite a breeze last night and that would have moved the bloody stuff into every corner of the village. He scratched his bare arse and stared at the bed. "Jesus, it looks like a bomb hit it." He muttered and pushed dark hair out of his face.

He smiled; the two women lay sprawled over the bed, a single sheet thrown across them. They were both naked and he could see Lilly's pale arse with several fading hand marks on its big cheeks, his hand marks. He shook her gently, then gave that inviting arse a gentle slap; "Lil, I really need a cup of tea girl and some scrambled eggs. I have Mass at nine." Lilly shifted and opened her eyes; "My bloody bum still hurts. It's been a long time since I had that done to my arse." Was all she said and pulled herself from the bed. She kissed him slowly on the lips and made for the door; still stark naked. Peter actually chuckled at the awkward way she walked this morning.

Vikki [Victoria] stirred and half sat up on the pillows, her breasts lay bare, and she ran a hand through her hair. "Lilly's gone to make the tea and some breakfast." Peter said and leaned across and kissed her lips. She swung an arm around her neck and smiled; "We must have time for some more surely?" She said softly and kissed him again. He shook his head; "I have Mass at nine and you should never keep your audience waiting; well, not too long anyway." He grinned and headed for the bathroom.

Vikki flopped back on the bed and said softly; "I need a bloody bath." She pushed a hand through her legs and then wiped it, on the sheet that almost covered her. "I need a bloody bath." She repeated. Peter stopped in the doorway and smiled; "Well, don't waste the bloody hot water. Get Lilly to share; she'll probably need one." Vikki just laughed; "You dirty bugger, what do you call that?" She leaned forward, her perk breasts staring at him.

Peter shrugged his shoulders; "Greek. They apparently invented it, so that women didn't have a child every year. It's very popular in all Catholic Countries."

He smiled; "Get use to the idea, your cute, pink little bum will experience it firsthand tonight." Vikki groaned in mock despair; He knew that she would comply with his strange sexual requests with Lilly's help, of course.

"Oh yeah and very popular with men of a certain persuasion. Bloody Oscar Wilde comes to mind. Poor Lilly won't walk straight for days." Vikki grunted and sprawled across the bed and snatched the sheet from her naked body. Then pulled herself up on the pillows and spread open her legs. She grinned; "Sure you don't have time?" Peter just sighed and headed for the bathroom. "You've the bloody stamina of a bull, you could manage it again." She called after him; quite disappointed. She lay back and ran her hands over her firm breasts, still, she thought; Lilly and she could have some fun sharing a bath. That's when she heard Lilly Cooper shouting up the stairs that tea was ready.

Vikki eased from the bed and picked up her bright red dressing gown and wrapped it around herself. She almost giggled; thinking just how well treated Father Meyer was by his Parochial Housekeeper! Then, he was 'well treated' by several young - and not so young - women in the village. Mrs. Joyce Penton, the wife of the village Butcher would be 'popping' in tonight to discuss the minutes of the Parish Council Meeting; held yesterday to arrange the village events for Christmas.

Vikki wandered down the stairs and did laugh to herself. The last time Joyce turned up, Lilly opened the front door, and she pushed past and went straight into the front reception room, where Peter sat reading the paper. She simply stood in the doorway and let her long fur coat drop; she was stark naked - apart from her boots of course - and he fucked her - there and then - on the floor; without saying a word.

Lilly had joined in and the carnal exertions went on for a couple of hours. Vikki was a little jealous that she missed it, when Lilly told her the same night, she shared the priest with her; again. She dropped onto a rough chair and pulled it up against the kitchen table. "His lordship told me I had to share the bath with you. Save hot water and all that." Lilly just nodded and slapped down a china mug full of hot tea in front of her. "Well, there is a bloody war on. My bloody bum still hurts, but he certainly enjoyed it." Lilly grunted and eased herself into the chair opposite - she was wearing her long kitchen apron - and nothing else apart from her little slippers.

Vikki clutched the warm mug with both hands and smiled over the rim at Lilly; "Thanks for that. His lordship has kindly informed me that he's going to ravage my poor bum tonight. Now that's something to look forward to; I don't think." Lilly smiled and sipped her tea; "Yeah, you'll moan about it and play all reluctant, but when he tells you to get you bloody arse in the air and grit your teeth; you'll do it!" Vikki just chuckled and nodded. "Maybe we could persuade him that Mrs. - I'm so bloody high and mighty - Penton would really want it shoved up her bum instead." Lilly did laugh at that; her and Victoria had been friends since Vikki moved to the village, when her father took over the pub in 1913. They were closer than most sisters, especially now they shared the priest.

"Talk of the devil." Vikki muttered as Peter appeared in the doorway. He smiled at the girls and picked up a mug of tea. "The eggs will have to wait, or I will be really late and some git will complain to the Bishop yet again." He took a couple of sips and placed his hat on. Lilly sighed and scratched her large left breast that hung out of her apron; "Don't forget you've Mrs. Penton coming over at four and before that Mrs. Mavis Fellows will be here to parade around in that bloody costume you told her to make."

Father Peter really did grin; "She made it then?" he asked, sipping more tea quickly. Vikki waved a free hand about; "Yes, she does own the dress shop. It's all black with lots of frills. The skirt is so short; you won't even need to lift it up; a Bloody French Maid's outfit; whatever next?"

"She showed Vikki and me yesterday. Copied it from a very naughty French book she had. Apparently, she makes all sorts of outfits for some wealthy clients. She told us that the Countess of Hesby's ladies maid had paid her for two similar costumes last month. One for her ladyship and one for a young footman; can you believe that?" Lilly giggled and sipped her tea.

Peter just shrugged his shoulders; "It's just some harmless fun.

But I'm well pleased that she would go to all that trouble just for me." Lilly shook her head; "Most of the women around here would do a lot more for you, if you fancied them. Just a nod at the right time and most would have their bloody skirts up and drawers down." She almost sighed, only yesterday Mrs. Gordon - the Sub-Postmaster's married daughter - had dropped a big hint to Lilly about the priest. Well, it wasn't so much a big hint. Lottie [Mrs. Charlotte Gordon] had asked Lilly if it was alright, to pop round one night and have the priest; 'bloody service her!' was what she exactly said - but very quietly as Lilly purchased some stamps and a money order - a little shocked to say the least.

That little incident had also confirmed her thoughts - no, fears - that most of the women of the village had guessed what was going on in the Parochial House. It had also confirmed that many of them wanted to join that particular little party; desperately.

Mrs. Gordon had been married fourteen years, with no baby in sight and with her husband [he was known locally as 'gormless' Gordon] at the front, time was running out. Lilly did express her sympathy and understanding; she would speak to the father. Lottie had shyly asked what the priest liked. Lilly thought for a minute and then retraining a big grin said softly; "Black stockings and a nice hat; nothing much else." Mrs. Gordon had nodded and served the other customers with quite a smile on her face. Lilly had walked back to the Parochial House with quite a smile herself.

She and Vikki laughed about it as they shared the bath together, a few minutes after the priest had left for Sunday mass. "I'd swear that our gorgeous young priest would shag anything in a skirt." Lilly splashed water at Vikki, who pushed a sponge around her neck and breasts. "Good job no bloody Scotsmen live in the village then!" Vikki smiled and both women giggled and splashed water over each other. Then Lilly gripped Vikki by the shoulders and pulled her close; their lips came together, and squirming tongues explored each other's mouth. Vikki said softly; "We'll give his lordship a full account of this before he fucks Mrs. Fellows in her stupid outfit." Lilly grinned and ran a hand down Vikki's stomach and between her slightly open legs.

That's when they heard the shot. They almost froze and Lilly whispered; "Did you hear..." She never finished her sentence. A second shot could be clearly heard and both girls scrambled from the bath, grabbing their bath robes. They made their way downstairs, stopping only to pull their boots on. They ran out into the street and saw the priest lying in the thick snow; face upwards. Vikki just stood screaming and clutching her robe about her naked body. Lilly was running towards the still priest. For some reason, she simply could not scream or shout.

Old Mr. Guest had thrown down the circle of Christmas lights that he was about to adorn his shop front with and ran over to the priest. He knelt over him and shouted at Lilly; "Get Doc Piper, Now, for Christ sake!" He was pulling frantically at the priest's clothes. Lilly just stood and stared. He shouted at her again: "For God sake Lilly; get the bloody doctor!" Lilly nodded and ran down the main street, past confused and surprised villagers, emerging from their shops and homes.

She crashed through Doc Piper's front door [no-one locked their doors in the village] now shouting. Luckily, Doc was up and dressed - he would have been going to Sunday Mass - he certainly wouldn't now.

3. "THERE ARE FEW REAL CO-INCIDENCES."- Jericho Tibbs.

The morgue was quite busy for a week before Christmas and the team from the Holy Inquisition sat in the corridor outside the morgue office. The place really did smell of disinfectant and frankly, dead bodies. Owen rubbed his face; "Couldn't they fit a few extractor fans in the bloody ceiling or something?" He moaned to Wilson, who sat reading a local paper. "All bloody war news and nothing about this." He jerked his paper towards the morgue doors. "Not really surprising that." He added and closed up the paper.

Jericho folded his arms and sat back against the cold, painted brick wall. "Our police contact is a certain Inspector Fred Portal; great name that; Portal, considering what we do! He's been told to assist us, given the circumstances surrounding the death."

Wilson smiled at Alex; "Still Alex, it means you can call yourself Doctor Featherstone again. Besides, if anything terrible happens to you; your soul can be collected properly, this being your ordained Time period." He actually chuckled as Alex discretely stuck up a single finger.

She quickly dropped the finger as the morgue doors swung open and a very tall and skinny man stood rubbing his hands. He wore a dirty white coat and had bright check trousers hanging below it. He adjusted his small black bow tie and smiled; "Father Tibbs I presume?" Jericho rose and held out his hand; "You are Doctor Feelgood; the Pathologist?" He asked and they shook hands. Wilson chuckled and whispered to Owen; "Another great name – Feelgood - for a doctor; except he deals only with dead bodies, who wouldn't appreciate the humour." Owen had to smile at that. Jericho introduced his team; Mr. Wilson, an associate of the Church from America, Owen Jones, the Bishop's Assistant and finally; Dr. Alexandra Featherstone from Whitechapel Hospital in London.

Dr. Feelgood really smiled at Alex and shook her hand firmly; "So nice to meet a colleague from the smoke. I understand that you assist the Church in such matters. My granddaughter Alice would love to meet you. She's a second-year medical student in York. A Doctor is all she's ever wanted to be; since very small." He gestured to the doors; "I trust you all have strong stomachs." He looked at Owen as he said that. Jericho nodded; "The team have seen quite a few dead bodies during the time we have worked together on church business." The old pathologist smiled, and they pushed through the doors into the morgue.

For most normal people, the contents of the morgue would have been a ghastly sight, but no-one ran out screaming, fainting or vomiting; which Dr. Feelgood thought was a pretty good start! He took the team over to an open drawer and his assistant - who had bad teeth and very big hands - pulled the tray out. He grinned at Alex; really grinned at her. Dr. Feelgood snatched the sheet up and pulled it right down to the corpse's feet.

"Death was caused by a single insertion of a very fine blade, probably no more than half an inch in width and about six inches in depth or rather, length. Death would have been quite instantaneous. It's what happened before her demise that troubled me; you can see by the marks on the body, what I mean." Dr. Feelgood gestured to the body. Everyone could see the shapes cut into her pale cold flesh; strange symbols and what appeared to be Arabic writing. "They were definitely made before she was murdered. This will interest you Doctor." He indicated for Alex to look closely at the corpse.

"An appendix scar, she had an appendectomy quite recently." Alex nodded her head and the old Doctor smiled; "Quite a new and expensive operation. It may be the big clue to finding her identity as the police detectives would say." Owen rubbed his face and said quietly; "Symbols of Devil worship and the writing is old Arabic; probably Aramaic." The Pathologist nodded his head and spoke to Jericho; "You have quite a team Father, your young man is spot on. I copied some of the symbols and letters and showed them to Gwen at the Library; that's exactly what she said." He threw the sheet back over the young girl and sighed; "I know that this sounds ridiculous in the 20th century, but I believe she was a ritual human sacrifice, probably to the Devil himself. Quite sad really that some people still believe in such nonsense."

"I take it the authorities have put a really big lid on this one?" Jericho asked Doctor Feelgood who just shrugged his shoulders. "Yeah, there's a bloody war on." Muttered Owen; scribbling down the strange symbols in his notebook.

"When was she found sir?" Wilson asked and the old Doctor folded his arms; "Just two days ago, in a ditch just south of North Turning - The day after that other terrible incident - in the same little village." He started to walk to the doors and Wilson asked again; "What other terrible incident was that?" the Pathologist stopped; "You weren't told?" They all shook their heads in silence. He grunted; "I would have thought Inspector Portal would have mentioned that; I mean the victim being a young priest. That's the sort of thing you should know about. Someone shot him - twice - as he walked to early morning Sunday Mass."

Jericho nodded and walked quietly next to the Doctor into the corridor; "I take it he's not one of your customers; yet." Jericho asked and the Pathologist grunted - but smiled - He thrust both hands into his jacket pockets. "Thankfully no, apparently who ever shot him was a lousy shot. They caught him in the right thigh and just below the right elbow. He'll live as long as no infections set in." They all shook hands again and said their goodbyes to the happy old Doctor.

"I think we best have words with Inspector Portal; I believe there are few real co-incidences in this life." Jericho muttered and the team left the old building - and its smells - for the clean crisp air of a snowy Yorkshire morning. They climbed slowly in to the big black Vauxhall car - that Supplies had given them - and Owen held up his Mirror; "Well, we know that the victim was Miss Susan Grimwade from Doncaster, aged nineteen and obviously no soul was collected or we certainly wouldn't be here." Alex made herself comfortable next to Owen in the rear seats. "Pity we can't let her family know what has happened to her; they must be worried sick and it's especially awful at this time of year."

Wilson sat behind the wheel and chuckled; "I've always said our Alex had a soft spot for the living." Jericho tapped his arm and said quietly; "Let's visit inspector Portal and see what he can tell us about people shooting priests on the Sunday before Christmas." Owen leaned over the seat; "You think the two are connected?" Jericho nodded; "Well, we can try and find out if they are." The big car pulled away; there was very little traffic and Owen asked where the team would be staying. Wilson chuckled; "Support has got us a nice little hotel in Hordon - the next village to here - it's called the Black Ram. Now that's a real co-incidence or someone in Supplies likes a joke!"

"Black Ram? Another bloody devil worship reference." Owen muttered and sat back, staring out the windows; "Why is everybody so bloody miserable. Especially with Christmas just around the corner?" He asked no-one in particular. "I doubt there's a family around these parts that haven't lost a son, father, uncle or brother. That's why." Alex said with some sarcasm in her voice. Owen shrugged his shoulders; "I only asked for Christ sake." Was all he replied.

The brief interview the team had with Inspector Fred 'piggy' Portal at the local police station wasn't very helpful. They were shown into his office and the big, overweight man was piled behind his desk, reading various brown files. He wore a dull brown suit that strained at every movement and was eating a foul-smelling egg & onion sandwich. He stared at Alex and sighed; "And what does the broad do for the Holy Inquisition?" He actually sneered; then saw Wilson. He shook his head; "Blacks and bloody women, what the fuck is the world coming too?" He asked himself. He didn't even get out of his seat to greet them.

He made his position clear; to him, they were useless interfering amateurs who probably couldn't detect a gas leak, even if the local gas main ruptured next to them. He chuckled at his own humour - nobody else did - even his own fellow officers. He said the attempted murder of the young priest had 'bugger all' to do with the girls killing. The priest was known to have been shagging loads of local girls and women. Quite obviously, one of the males had taken deep exception to this and took a Kraut hunting rife to him. He grunted and waved to the door; "Now shut that bugger on the way out." The interview was over and Alex was fuming at their treatment.

They returned to the car and Alex calmed down a little; what she called the fat detective wasn't pleasant or lady like. But Wilson sat quietly and gripped the steering wheel; "Why hunting rifle when the place is probably full of 'Lee-Enfield' army rifles? Every soldier home on leave would have one. A German made hunting rifle would be quite unusual around here, during these times. Anything German was avoided like the plague. Even people with German sounding names were set upon, had their shop windows broken. Who would have possession of such a rife in the village?"

Jericho rubbed his face; "Head for the hotel; we'll book in and have something to eat. Then I think a visit to North Turning is on the menu." He turned to Alex and smiled; "When you let the steam out of your drawers, you'll be quite useful with so many females to interview." He smiled and Wilson pulled away. After a few minutes, Owen didn't look over his shoulder, but said quietly; "I think we are being followed my friends. That car pulled away when we left the police station and its sitting - discretely - some way back. But bloody following us nevertheless."

Wilson nodded; "I think your right baby brother. Two big men in hats and coats. Coppers, I think. CID probably." Jericho stared into the wing mirror on his side; "Your right. I think Inspector Portal is not as useless or stupid as he makes out. I think he knows the cases could be connected and he's covering his fat arse." Alex snorted; "Now that's a lot of obnoxious lard to cover for anyone." Everyone chuckled at that.

4. THE BLACK RAM HOTEL.

They sat in the car and just stared. Finally, Owen shook his head and said in some amazement; "Supplies must be having a fucking laugh!" Wilson turned off the engine and looked up at the hotel; "It's probably a lot nicer inside." Alex pushed open the car door; "I don't care, as long as I can get a hot bath and the beds aren't full of bloody lice."

Jericho stepped out and sighed; "Let's get the luggage and see what rooms they have available." Wilson chuckled; "I bag the room with a really big bed; lice can be optional." The team collected their cases from the boot and made their way inside. It didn't improve, in any way. There were some pretty old - and dingy - Christmas decorations about the place. The 'Christmas' tree' looked like it had died years ago. Even the little angle, impaled on the top, looked sad and forlorn.

The small bar had a badly printed sign hanging above it; 'Reception: ring bell if needed'. It was deserted apart from a very ancient looking old man; hidden in his big coat and dark hat. He didn't even look up. Jericho found a little brass bell on the bar and rattled it vigorously. It made no noise whatsoever. He lifted the bell again and looked underneath; there was no hammer.

Owen jerked a thumb towards a little chalk board sitting on the bar; it read: NO SPIRITS. The 'NO' was underlined; twice. He sighed, thinking, thank heaven; they had four bottles of French Brandy scattered about their luggage. Jericho said loudly; "Hello, Service please!" The old man in the corner looked up, he really was old, but still had bright blue eyes. Everyone noticed that. "Go round the back. Lester's probably cleaning the bog." He said in a firm voice that really didn't match his toothless face. Everyone also noticed that the old man was clutching a half-filled whisky glass.

"What do you want?" A little man in a black waistcoat, dirty white shirt and black trousers had popped up behind the bar; that actually made Alex jump a little. Jericho raised his hat; "Good morning, Sir, we have rooms reserved." Lester picked his teeth, and then grimaced; he remembered he had just cleaned the bloody toilet. He wiped his hand down his waistcoat. "You Father Tibbs?" he asked, and Jericho nodded and was about to introduce the others, but Lester stopped him. "I know she's not married to you mate and she certainly wouldn't be married to him." He jabbed a finger at Owen and added; "So it must be the big man at the back." He almost smiled - but didn't.

"No single women are allowed here Father. Me and the Missus run a respectable place. I told that woman of yours, who booked the rooms, that single women are not allowed. She said that the Doctor was married, and her husband was with her. I think she said he was a Yank." Wilson stepped forward - with a real smile on his face - and in his best New York ascent, introduced himself; "Mr. Wilson Featherstone and this lady is my wife, Alex." He patted an astonished Alex on the arm; "As you Brit's say; the little trouble and strife." Old Lester just nodded and rummaged under the bar. "You'll have to share with the boy Father and those two can have the only double we got. Both rooms are at the back; it's nice and quiet. My Missus can knock you up some sandwiches if you want. We only have cheese or bully beef [corn beef], but her home-made pickle should tickle your fancy. It's won prizes." He produced two big keys; each attached to a wooden block the size of half a house brick.

He saw where they are looking and shrugged his shoulders; "It stops buggers going off with the keys in their pockets." Lester indicated to the small staircase, that could be seen through the doorway behind him; "This way. There's no hot water until seven tonight and again at seven in the morning because of the war. So don't shout at me or my missus about that."

In total silence the little group followed him up the creaking staircase. There were three doors at the top of the stairs. One door had a really big sign nailed on it: 'PRIVATE'. The others had big brass letters pined on them; 'A' and 'B'. He slapped a key into Jericho's hand; "That's yours. Two beds." He said and turned to Wilson, handing him a key; "A is yours. It has a nice big bed. Just right for a big man like you and your lovely wife."

He started back down the stairs and then turned; "Oh, if you want dinner tonight, it's at seven o'clock and its Shepherd's Pie with carrots and cabbage. There's no soup or a sweet. There's a bloody war on. Tell me or the missus before six o'clock or you don't get anything. Have a nice stay, as you yanks say." He made his way down the stairs and disappeared. There was total silence on the top landing until Owen finally said; "Well, it's better than sleeping in the bloody car." Alex thumped his arm - quite hard - and dropped her case. She folded her arms; "I'm going to kill that bitch Caroline, in the Operations Centre, she's done this deliberately. I know she has."

Jericho opened the door to his and Owens's room. Everyone stared in. "I've seen bigger telephone boxes." Muttered Owen and threw his case in; it didn't fly far, before landing against the wall opposite. He stared out the window; "There's an outside toilet." He added and ran a hand through his hair.

"Where's the toilet and bathroom for these rooms?" Alex asked, quite concerned. Owen chuckled and leaned under the nearest small bed; he pulled out a dirty white chamber pot. It didn't smell too good, and he pushed it back under the bed; quickly.

Wilson had opened his door with some trepidation. Alex peered over his shoulder; the room was dominated by a large double bed. Wilson stepped in and looked about. There was a small sofa, a small table, two chairs and a small single wardrobe. He peered under the bed and chuckled. "Our one is much bigger and looks quite new." Alex stood in the doorway arms folded; she was not a happy Temporal Detective. Wilson held open his arms and smiled.

Alex stared at him; "What the bloody hell are you doing now?" The big man grinned; "Carry my young bride over the threshold." He ducked just in time, as Alex's case hit the bed and spilled open. Wilson - still grinning - gathered the case up and held up a pair of bright pink French Knickers, right for this time period. "Oh darling, you've packed my favourites." Everyone was laughing, except Alex. She pushed in and snatched her knickers back, giving Wilson a hard slap on the arm. That's when they realised; they were not alone on the top staircase.

The door marked 'PRIVATE' was open and Mavis Bullfinch - Lester's 'Missus' - was standing in the doorway; cigarette in mouth and curlers in her hair. She was a big woman in every sense of the word. She slowly started to smile; especially at Wilson; "Bloody hell girl, you wear them, and he'll never let you alone; you lucky bugger." She laughed and coughed, heaving her huge bosom up with both hands. "If you don't want him, send him over here." She really did smile at that thought. Wilson retreated into the room and pretended to open his case.

Mavis smiled at Alex; "Come on darling, I'll show you where the bathroom is. Normally guests wash up in their bedrooms. You get a big jug of water and a bowl - fresh every morning - but you'll need a bath, eh? So, you can use ours. Never mind old moaning Lester, I'll have words with him." She took Alex down the stairs and through another small doorway; she unlocked yet another door marked 'PRIVATE' and gestured for Alex to enter. It was a beautiful, quite modern bathroom for the times, with a clean toilet and large bath. Mavis grinned and winked, slapping Alex's arm gently."You like big dark men, eh? Don't we bloody all?" She laughed, the cigarette ash dropping down her apron. She tapped the bath; "You need one after keeping a big man like that happy all night. I'll have the glass to the wall tonight. So don't disappoint me!" She laughed and made for the bar. A stunned Alex slowly followed her. "Do you fancy a drop of brandy dear?" Mavis asked, squeezing behind the bar. Alex pointed to the sign. But Mavis just rolled her eyes; "Ignore that darling. It's there to keep the bloody brewery happy. Miserable gits won't send us any. They say our turnover don't justify it, with the war on."

She dished up two huge brandies and sat with Alex at the window table. Her cigarette fell from her mouth and landed exactly in the ashtray. Alex sat in silence and amazement. Mavis pulled out a leather pouch and began to roll another cigarette. "I had a couple of big black fella's when I worked up in Liverpool - before I married Lester - I was a lot thinner and younger then. From France they were....or was it Spain? Never mind that. Jesus, I couldn't walk properly for a couple days after them. So, I know, you'll want a bath and you'll have earn it, I dare say." She laughed and lit her freshly rolled cigarette. "We're like two peas in a pod, eh?" She added and gripped Alex's hand.

Alex could only smile and sip her most welcome brandy. Mavis grinned; "So don't disappoint me our girl. I'll have that glass up to the wall and I know all those wonderful memories will flood back. Don't worry about the bloody bed; it's seen some action I can tell you. You just enjoy yourself and if the bugger still wants more when you're knackered; send him to me!" She slurped her brandy and sucked on her fag. "Put you and your friends down for dinner, shall I?" Alex didn't really know what to say. Mavis patted her hand; "Course I will. There's no other place to eat round here anyway."

Mavis looked up, there was a big, tall man in a new hat standing by the bar, examining the broken bell. She whispered to Alex; "That's Stan Gable - from North Turning - he's in to see Lester. Jesus, you should have heard what he told us, about what that young priest got up to over there. All those bloody women; two or three together - at the same time - would you believe. Must have had the stamina of a bleeding bull." She rose from her seat and slapped 'Stan' on the back. "Do you fancy a quick one darling?" The old man just grinned; "I hope you're talking about a beer Mavis, or I'll be in trouble with bleeding Lester, wouldn't I?" Mavis just laughed and squeezed behind the bar again.

Alex quietly finished her drink and made for the stairs. Mavis shouted after her; "Dinner's at seven darling." Alex managed to shout back; "Yes thanks." and ran up the stairs and straight into Jericho's room. It was empty. She opened the door to her room and found her three colleagues, laid around, drinking brandy from old teacups that they had found. Jericho smiled as she closed the door; "What's up Alexandra, you like you tossed for your dinner and lost."

Wilson offered her a cup and filled it with brandy. Alex took a sip and said quietly; "You'll never guess what just happened to me."

5. THE PAROCHIAL HOUSE.

Wilson was a little surprised - and relieved - that the big car made it through the snow without any mishaps; apart from that old man falling off his bike as they passed on the Turning Road. He pulled up outside the Parochial House and turned the engine off. "What have we got on Father Mayer?" He turned and asked Owen, who was staring at his mirror.

"Would have been a bit of a War hero, went out under fire several times and pulled wounded colleagues back to the British Lines - despite being wounded himself - and was basically shafted by the British High Command for disobeying their orders, not to 'go over the top' on the first day of battle. The Church Authorities then 'exiled' him into North Turning, as a sort of punishment I suppose." Owen scratched his face, adding; "There's not much on Record, only son of German Immigrants who arrived in England in the 1870's. Ordained as a priest in 1913. He worked a hard, working-class Parish in Manchester until he volunteered for the Army Chaplin Service in 1914. Spent two years in the trenches without a scratch; until the opening day of the Battle of the Somme this year."

"Sending him to loads of desperate young women in a remote village, who hadn't seen their men in ages; that's a punishment?" Wilson chuckled and could see the curtains of the front windows moving. "Someone's interested in our arrival." He added.

Jericho pushed his own mirror back into his coat and stared at the big house, standing in the grounds of the Church. It had the old churchyard for a neighbour and fronted the village's main street. He had a real uneasy feeling about the place; he would have sworn that he had seen the house before - but not under snow - but when?

"Let's see what his House-keeper has to say." Jericho finally said and the team left the car and trudged through the snow up to the big, blue door. It was pulled open by a very concerned looking Mrs. Lillian Cooper, who clutched her apron with both hands. Jericho quietly introduced himself and his team. Mrs. Cooper just nodded and showed them into the front reception room. She sat on a high back chair in front of the sofa. Jericho and Alex sat on the sofa, whilst Wilson and Owen found a couple of chairs and sat each side of the sofa.

Jericho smiled and asked Lilly about Father Meyer. Quite unexpectedly, the flood gates opened; it appears that Mrs. Lillian Cooper really did need to talk to someone - anyone - and she mainly directed it towards Alex. An hour later - and two servings of tea - the team made its way back to the car. The snow was falling again, and the flurries were thick and frequent. Wilson started the engine and wiped snow and ice from the windows. Everyone piled into to the car except Jericho; who stood in the snow; staring at the house. Alex had to pull the window down a little and shout to him. He turned and slowly walked to the car.

Wilson pushed open the door and Jericho eased in and wiped snow from his face. Owen leaned over and tapped his shoulder; "What's up?" Jericho sat hand on chin for a few seconds, then turned to Owen; he looked quite grim; "Owen, run the house through records and see what we have on file."

Wilson pulled away with some difficulty, he said to Jericho; "If it keeps snowing like this, we're going to struggle in this bleeding car." Jericho nodded and looked back at the house.

Owen was muttering under his breath, slouched on the big rear seat with Alex. He suddenly sat up "Bloody hell Jericho, how the hell do you, do it?" He exclaimed and held up his mirror; "Listen to this people. The bloody house has been the subject of two temporal Department investigations already. One in 1816 by Dawn Daniels and her team. The place was a bloody witch's

Coven and the nasty fucking group had murdered two young children and sold their souls to the dark side. Then in 1933, Doc Underhill and his team investigated the place for Devil Worship; the priest - a certain Father Clement Gilmore - was murdered and his soul stolen. Guess who, he's bloody sergeant was, only..."

Jericho interrupted him; "It was me. I knew I had seen that house before."

The car only reached the Hordon Crossroads, just yards away and basically gave up the ghost; it couldn't cope with the heavy snow now falling. Wilson switched off the engine and sat back. "Well, that's that." He said and folded his arms. Owen passed his hipflask around, which was most welcome.

Jericho watched the snow hitting the windows and ran a hand over his face. "Father Gilmore was sacrificed by a real evil group of Devil worshippers. They carved messages and symbols to their master, on his body whilst still alive. Then drove a thin sacrificial dagger through his heart, they dumped his body in Banston Woods, just three or four miles from here. We got all of them - except their Black Priest - a man who called himself Eric Harris. But when we run it through Human records; he turned out to be a missing soul from 1706 called Richard Wallis and he hadn't aged a day."

Jericho accepted the flask and took a swig, he continued; "If I remember, Inspector Daniels had reported a Warlock, who attended the Witches Coven back in 1816. His name was Eric Marks; but we guessed it was Richard Wallis. The bastard has been hanging around this village in various disguises for over two hundred years apparently." He handed the flask back; "And everything seems to centre on that bloody house. What his connection with the damn place is, we could never figure. The authorities - at the time - covered the dreadful murder up."

"I wonder what our very un-celibate priest's connection is with all this." Alex mused and took a swig from the hip flask and passed it back to Owen. "Where have we heard the name 'Eric' used around here?" Wilson said quietly and settled back in his seat.

"How many women and girls are on that list and who are their husbands or fathers?" Jericho turned to Alex, who rummaged through her coat pockets and pulled out her little pink notebook. She thumbed through a couple of pages and spoke softly; "Right, we have Mrs. Victoria Helms; her dad Harold runs the 'Black Oak' pub and her husband Kevin is at the Front. Her brother David is also there. Mrs. Joyce Penton; her husband Colin is the village butcher and some thirteen years her senior." She pulled a hankie from a pocket and wiped her mouth.

"We have Mrs. Mavis Fellows- the owner of the dress shop - she's been widowed for some years; her husband was called Reginald. Finally, we have Mrs. Lillian Cooper - the Priest's housekeeper, who husband is currently at the front, he's called Eric...." She stopped reading and looked up. "Another Eric in the village." She added quietly and Jericho asked Owen to look up Eric Cooper.

"Well, that's a definite connection with the house; his bloody wife lives there." Wilson said and stared out the windows. "We're onto fucking something people!" Owen said and tapped his mirror. "There is no trace of Eric John Cooper, for this time and place, according to Human Records." Alex tapped her little notebook on the back of Jericho's seat; "Well, Lillian showed me his picture, its standing on the mantel piece and he's certainly in army uniform."

Wilson nodded; "Maybe we need to run a mirror over that picture; find out who Eric John Cooper really is and if, he's actually at the bloody front and not hiding around here, taking pot shots at priests who can't keep their members under their cassocks." Owen chuckled; "That's great. But what the hell do we do about all this?" He gestured out the windows; the snow was coming down in heavy, thick showers. It had already passed the car's running boards.

Alex groaned, and half opened the door; "All that bloody tea, I need a piss." Owen shook his head; "Now Mrs. Wilson; that's not very lady like." Wilson chuckled and stared back down the road to the house, then turned back to Alex; "Well, we're bleeding stuck here, unless you fancy a three mile walk back to Hordon in all this snow and ice. You best ask your new friend and confidant, if we can stay here." Jericho nodded his agreement at that. Alex sighed and plunged into the snow; it reached her knees. "It's almost up to my bum!" She yelped.

She slowly made her way back to the big house and knocked

loudly; Mrs. Lillian Cooper answered. Alex gestured back to her colleagues; they clearly had a safe haven for the night. Jericho pulled open the car door and stepped out, smiling. "It couldn't have worked out better; now we can have quite a cozy chat with the wife of our possible time travelling devil worshipper. Let's get a mirror over that damn photograph."

Owen slapped Wilson on the back; "Sorry mate, that place is bound to have loads of bedrooms and I bet your new wife will want to have one on her own." He laughed and jumped from the car. "Oh, bollocks!" was all he said as the snow reached his crotch. Wilson didn't reply, but he did smile at Owens's discomfort.

6. OLD PICTURES & THE MAGIC SHED.

Lilly was really glad to have company tonight; especially Alex's. She made them most welcome, and Alex hurried up the staircase to the toilet. But something caught her eye; there were several pictures on the stair wall. Alex carefully read the little plaques attached to each. But nature disturbed her thoughts and she dashed to the bathroom. She would return to the pictures and photographs when she had relieved herself - which was now quite urgent!

Everyone sat in the big reception room and Owen - discretely - warmed his crotch by the fire; much to Wilson's amusement. They all drank tea - again. Lilly disappeared, saying that she would make up the rooms for her stranded guests. She was really happy to have something to do. Jericho found he was looking at a picture of a young man in uniform, on the fireplace's mantle.

Owen ran his mirror over the face; "Yep, that's Richard Wallis; missing from 1706." Jericho stared hard at the photograph and muttered; "I think we're looking at our quarry. I wonder how much Lilly is involved in his evil deeds."

Wilson nodded and pointed to a painting hanging on the wall opposite; it was the Parochial House painted back in 1871. "Look at the left wing of the house, there's a small brick building; like a long, brick shed or something. There's no building there now." Jericho lowered his mirror and joined Wilson. He nodded; "I think it was there, when I visited in 1933. We obviously searched the place. At the time, I think it was Father Gilmore's little workshop; he was a great cycling enthusiast and he fixed bikes there."

Owen rubbed his face; "Excuse me, but how does a building like that be in a painting in 1871 and Jericho's see's it in 1933. But it's not here in 1916?" Wilson folded his arms; "That, baby brother, is a fucking good question." Jericho tapped the picture; "Take a look at the artist?" Wilson and Owen peered closely; "Fuck me, Eric Houseman, another bloody Eric!" Owen muttered and immediately consulted his mirror. He half smiled; "The Parish priest here between 1867 and 1888." He muttered. He stared hard at his mirror; "You'll never believe it; Father Houseman was removed from this parish in 1888 because of 'indiscretions' with his House-Keeper and her sister!"

"That appears to go with this bloody house." Alex said, standing in the doorway - looking much relieved - and gestured behind her. "The pictures running up the staircase wall are very interesting." She held up her mirror "According to Human records, Father Houseman was Richard Wallis, as was Father David Soames in 1904. He was like Father Meyer, an Army Chaplin but in the South African War." Jericho nodded and ran a hand over his face. "Well, he certainly has an attachment to this bloody place, and I wonder why?"

Lilly appeared behind Alex smiling;"I set up the rooms and lit the fires. Father Tibbs is in the big guest room, left, at the top of the stairs and Mr. Jones is the one next door." She straightened her apron and smiled at Alex; "I've put you and your husband next to the bathroom Doctor Featherstone." Alex just stared at her, as Owen actually giggled a little and grinned broadly at Wilson.

"How did you know we're married?" Alex managed to ask, smiling a little. Lilly grinned; "The whole village is talking about it. A nice white Doctor like yourself, married to a big black, American fella, that went around the village like wildfire. They have probably talked about it more than me and Vikki's scandal anyway." Alex still looked puzzled; "But only the Bullfinch's at the 'Black Ram' pub knew and they were only told a few hours ago?"

Lillian just grinned; "Mavis [bullfinch] told Stan Gable all about you and your husband. His wife is Doris, the sub-Post Mistress at Hordon Post Office, she's been on the phone ever since. Which reminds me, I had better ring Mavis and tell her that you'll be staying here." She wandered off again and Alex could only stand and sigh. Owen slapped Wilson on the back; "Hope the bed doesn't creak too much, big man!"

Jericho just chuckled; "Never mind the sleeping arrangements, we need to ask her about that damn magic shed." Wilson tapped his chin; "If there's a bloody phone here, where the hell is it? In this time and era, phones were quite uncommon and nearly always in the hallway; easier to run the wires in. So where is it?" Owen looked puzzled too; "The big man is right. Where's the phone?" Alex grunted and spoke directly to Wilson; "You had better pray that the bedroom has a nice big couch because the bleeding bed is mine." With that she disappeared into the kitchen to find Lilly.

Owen grinned at Wilson; "Never mind big man. I've studied this era and husbands ruled the roost. Just throw Alex over your knee and give her a spanking and demand your conjectural rights. By the laws around here, you have that right; she's not allowed by law to refuse her husband. Wives had to submit; whether they wanted to or not."

Jericho just sighed in some despair; "Firstly, Mr. Marriage guidance Councillor, its conjugal rights and secondly; they're not actually bloody married; or had your sharp mind forgotten that? Fucking conjectural rights, whatever next?"

Owen muttered; "Oh yes, your right." and went up the stairs and studied the wall pictures. Wilson laughed and with Jericho, headed for the garden; they wanted to see if the 'magic shed' was actually still hidden there.

Alex and Lilly sat at the kitchen table and chatted - over yet more tea - the main topic of conversation was Lilly's absent husband. That surprised Lilly: she thought Alex would be more interested in the juicy sex scandal that surrounded her and the other women of the village. Alex found out that the couple had been married since 1912, the same year that Lilly obtained the position of Housekeeper at the Parochial House. The parish Priest at the time was Father John Edwards, an elderly priest coming up to retirement. He had been in position since 1904 after Father Soames had died in the bath. That really caught Alex's attention; Father Soames had suffered a heart attack and died in his bath! The suspected time-traveler had died in 1904.

Alex knew that wasn't right - mirrors NEVER get things wrong and certainly not Human Records - Father Soames was Richard Wallis, now Eric Cooper and he certainly wasn't dead. Was he?

Mind you, if he was a human out of his ordained time and he actually died; then no soul would be collected, and he would be shown as missing; like he was now. The thoughts clouded into Alex's mind, and she sipped her tea. But her attention was drawn back to Lilly offering her fruit cake.

Jericho and Wilson stood in the deep snow and stared at the rectangle of brickwork, old burnt wood and broken roof tiles, scattered around the remains of the shed. "It must have been rebuilt by the time I saw it in 1933. Let's get in before my frozen balls fall off." Jericho muttered and they made their way back into the house and shook snow and ice from their trousers and boots. "Why the fuck didn't we think of that, before freezing our nuts off." moaned Wilson.

Wilson stared out the conservatory window and shook his head; "The snow is getting worse. We would never have made it back to Hordon." Alex stuck her head around the door and smiled; "Lilly's making lunch and have I something to tell you." She closed the door and headed for the big reception room. Jericho and Wilson followed quickly.

"Where's the little pervert?" She asked Wilson, who shrugged his shoulders. "Never mind, this place really does have a reputation for strange goings on. Father Soames apparently died in the bath here in 1904, of a heart attack. His condition had obviously gone undiagnosed. He supposed death is quite impossible; because he's our time traveler and is now married to Lilly!"

She dropped on the sofa and continued; "Eric Cooper apparently moved to the village in 1912 and quickly courted and married Lilly, who had become the old priests, Housekeeper. He retired in 1914 and moved to Australia, to live with his widowed sister. The Parish was vacant until Father Meyer turned up and we know how that turned out. But here's something to chew on, Father Houseman had two children by his House-keeper's sister. After the scandal, she moved to Hordon and married a local farmer, who agreed to raise the children as his own. One of the girls was Lilly. Richard Wallis married his own daughter, when he returned to the village as Eric Cooper!"

Surely her mother recognized him?" Wilson asked, sitting on the sofa with Alex, who shook her head; "Lilly's mum died in 1908. She never met Lilly's husband." Wilson grunted; "So, we after a time travelling, devil worshipping incestuous pervert. Fantastic." Jericho stood by the fireplace and scratched his chin; "How did he fake his death in 1904? I mean, they must have buried him, and his funeral would be quite popular as the Parish priest. How did he get away with that?"

Alex sighed; "Well, if you have some shovels, we could find out. He's buried in the churchyard here." Jericho chuckled; "There's no need for grave robbing, if we can, come face to face with Wallis. Where's Owen?" He walked to the door and looked out - nothing. He pulled out his mirror and buzzed Owen for about a minute before he answered, he could see that Owen was in a dark room with a single small window. He was whispering and looking about. "Where the hell are you?" Jericho asked.

Owen almost smiled and said softly: "It's not so much where I am. I'm still here, in the house. It's when that matters." He looked about again and spoke closely to his mirror very softly; "I'm in the attic, back in 1816 and the place is full of naked witches and a fucking demon I think." Jericho watched, as he moved slowly towards a badly painted door and whispered; "There's a fucking Jerusalem Mirror, fixed to the wall in here. I found it nosing about; it's linked to the house in June 1816. I've put a call in for a Guardian. Oscar's on his way."

His colleagues were already halfway up the stairs before he finished talking.

7. THE GREAT RAID ON NORTH TURNING; 1816.

The team gathered in the old attic room and Jericho checked his mirror; it was June 7th, 1816. A bright sunny day had turned into a warm night with plenty of clear moonlight. He quietly closed the door, after he and Wilson had returned from the stairs, following a little reconnoitre. Wilson chuckled and whispered to Alex; "We saw two young women; both stark naked, carrying a tray, covered in a black cloth, down to the ground floor."

Owen looked up from his mirror, he was squatting on the floor. "In 1816, the Parish priest here was a certain Eric Hobbs; yet another bloody Eric." Jericho didn't smile; "Hobbs is a very old name for a minion of the devil and your right about another Eric."

He pulled an orb from his jacket pocket and watched the little red streaks spinning about its circumference; "A tier two demon. Good, Oscar can handle that." That's when they heard little screams and some real sobbing coming up the stairs. Everyone looked at each other. Alex folded her arms and looked quite concerned; "That's children crying and screaming Jericho. Didn't you say that the bastard's murdered two young girls and that prompted the investigation by Dawn Daniels and her team?" He nodded slowly and remembered the date on his mirror; "For Christ sake, we've arrived before that happened!"

Owen wiped his face; "You mean they're about to murder two little girls?" Jericho nodded; "After the Black Priest or Warlock has raped them." He was quite grim. He glanced at Wilson and the pair nodded; "Fuck it." Was all Wilson said and they made for the door. Jericho pulled it open and almost jumped; Oscar the Guardian was standing there; smiling. He gripped his 'Staff of Mosses' and said, "Hello my friends, I think our black hearted, demon loving witches are about to throw a full-blown blood party and those two poor little girls are the star attraction."

Jericho gripped his old friends shoulder, but turned to the others; "Regretfully, turn your mirrors to stun only." Then added; "Bloody regulations." The team made their way quietly down the stairs. On the second-floor landing, a door opened suddenly, right next to Alex. It was a young witch; naked apart from a devil faced mask. She was gripping a tearful and struggling girl of about seven or eight. The witch opened her mouth to scream for help, but nothing came out because Alex swung a right hook that Muhammad Ali would have been proud of. The witch lay unconscious on the ground; she wouldn't be dancing around the little girl's body now. Alex grabbed the child and held a finger over her lips; "Shhhh, your now with friends. Where's the other girl?"

Owen nudged Wilson; "Your missus is pretty handy. Hope you don't have too many domestic disputes my friend. The money would be on her." Alex cuddled the girl and saw the astonished looks on her colleague's faces; "Didn't have time for the bloody mirror." She explained, then added; "Bloody regulations." The little girl had calmed a lot and pointed a finger to the door opposite. Oscar and Jericho were through the door, before she finished pointing.

The demon; Jesbu was naked apart from a little black and gold loin cloth; he was standing over the other little girl, who was tied and gagged, face down over a chair. The look on his face was priceless as Oscar grinned; "Now try that with me you bastard!" The fight was quick and brutal; the demon ran for it by jumping through the bedroom window and he didn't bother to open it!

Owen and Wilson were already running down the stairs, whilst Jericho freed the child. Alex now had two children gripping her skirts and she cuddled them both like a long-lost mother. Wilson found two naked witches hiding in the kitchens; one waved a thin dagger at him, and he just folded his arms and stared at her. She dropped the knife and the two witches fell to the floor on their knees: screaming and crying. Owen in the hallway slowly opened the small door to the cupboard under the staircase. He grinned; "Sorry mate, but the party's over; for good." The naked man crept out and tried to cover himself with his hands.

Owen pulled the devil headdress off him with some force as Jericho and Oscar appeared. "Alex has called James to wipe the children's memories of all this and then she'll get them home." Jericho stopped speaking and stared at the naked 'Black Priest' cowering on the floor. He waved his mirror over the whimpering man and rubbed his chin; "Well, that's a fucking surprise. Hello Harold Golding; how's Victoria, your daughter doing? You're a long way from the 'Black Oak' pub and exactly a hundred years too early."

"Fuck me, that's not Richard Wallis!" Owen said and examined the devils headdress, then threw it on the floor in contempt. "Not even a real African Voodoo mask." He muttered and was joined by Alex and James - a Knight of God - who jerked a thumb up the stairs. "The children are back with their parents and will wake up tomorrow in their beds and remember nothing whatsoever of all this. Not even a little bad dream." He smiled and peered at the naked man, still groveling on the floor. "That's some pathetic 'Black Priest', one of the worse I have seen in years."

Alex threw a devil's mask onto the floor; "I took that off sleeping beauty upstairs and guess who I found under it?" Jericho just nodded; "Mrs. Victoria Helms, I presume. This fucker's daughter." Alex seemed quite disappointed that she couldn't reveal that; but what did she expect; he was Mister Jericho Tibbs after all. Wilson stuck his head out of the kitchens; he didn't smile; "The masks are off these two ladies - if you can call them that - the one waving the dagger about is our Mrs. Lillian Cooper and the other one I don't know. But she's from around this time; A Mrs. Doris Spooner. Her husband runs the local Bakers."

Jericho sighed and operated his mirror; "I'll call for the clean up team." James peered into the kitchen, both women were sprawled on the floor; clutching each other. "What a right bunch of evil bastards; well done Jericho and well-done team." He said and there was knocking at the door!

Owen stepped over the naked publican and opened the door slowly. He smiled broadly and shook Isabella's hand. "That was bloody quick; Jericho only put the call out." Isabella smiled; "You know us, Owen; you boys and girls yell for a cleanup, and we jump in with our brooms and sweep the garbage away."

Jericho looked up from his mirror; "Right, this one and the girl upstairs are from around here and this time. So is, the older woman in the kitchen. The other woman is from 1888 to 1916. But you can confirm that yourself, of course." Isabella wandered in and smiled at Jericho; "I always take your word for it Jericho." She sighed; "So, they are from here. Well, its 1816 and there's lots of smallpox about. That's do the job nicely, then Angel Margret can deal with their souls." She looked into the kitchen and consulted her mirror; "That one from 1916 can drown in her bath; whilst drunk. That's always a favourite."

Through the front door came two of the biggest, roughest looking men that the team had seen for some time. "Jesus, they're bigger that bloody Wilson." Owen muttered to Alex, adding; "What do we call them?" Alex shrugged her shoulders; "Sir, will probably do." then chuckled.

Jericho pointed up the stairs; "Owen and Alex, get rid of that damn Jerusalem mirror please." The pair nodded and headed for the attic. Wilson stood in the doorway of the kitchen; arms folded; "So what the fuck happened to Richard Wallis?" Jericho ran a hand over his face; "Now that's another bloody good question."

8. DIGGING UP THE PAST OR THE FUTURE?

The team made their way through the snow-covered graveyard. They were followed by Bernie and George; the two big men from the 'clean-up' team of Isabella's; they were carrying shovels and laughing with each other. Owen spotted the grave, near to a wonderful old oak. He gestured to the big men; "This is it Sir." He said to the nearest; Bernie and stood aside. Wilson handed Jericho his hipflask and smiled; "A decent bottle of brandy says that the box is bloody empty."

Jericho accepted the flask and took a sip; "Now, you know I don't bet on certainties." Alex was staring up at the house; she really had a little feeling of sadness, but not sympathy, for Lilly, who currently, was threshing and choking, as she drowns in her bath, after consuming nearly half a bottle of whisky. Owen saw where Alex was looking; "You shouldn't really care Alex, you really shouldn't. Over the centuries that she moved back and forward in time, she must be implicated in at least five ritual murders and two of them were just children. She really doesn't deserve your sympathy." Alex nodded her agreement; but couldn't help feeling a little sadness about Lilly.

Wilson pointed to Alex's wellington's as she stood, dress pulled up - to keep it out of the snow - and grinned; "I have always loved those bright red wellington's of yours. They are very becoming." Owen chuckled; "Come on Wilson; be like most husbands and never compliment your wife on what she wears; it's not the done thing!" He offered Alex his hipflask and could see that the two big men were making short work about the exhumation of Father David Soames or Father Eric Houseman or Richard Wallis or Eric John bleeding Cooper. "Take your bloody pick." He murmured and leaned over the now open grave, to see the elaborate coffin appearing.

Owen glanced up at the house; "The local authorities will conclude that Lilly committed suicide in a fit of depression and remorse, over her part in the sex scandal. There will be lots of gossip and rumour about it for a few years, but then it will be all forgotten; life goes on. The good bit is that Miss Susan Grimwade will never fall prey to Golding and his evil followers and will have the chance of a good life." He accepted his flask back from Alex and took a sip.

"The disappearance of Victoria and her father; Harold Golding will be the talk of this and surrounding villages for some years. But by, say, 1980 they will be forgotten too. The bloody pub Golding ran - the Black Oak - is destroyed by fire in 1963 and where it stands is a bloody car park for the new supermarket built there in 1991. Time covers everything." He finished speaking to the quiet Alex and watched closely as the two big men prised the lid open. They pushed it to one side and Jericho knelt by the open coffin and waved his mirror over the remains inside.

"I told you not to bet against him big man." Owen grinned at the disappointed Wilson who shrugged his shoulders and took a gulp of brandy from his hipflask. "Who the hell is it?" He asked Jericho, who stood up and rubbed his face. "According to my mirror and Human records; it's bloody Father Peter Meyer!" The shock in his voice undisguised. "You are fucking kidding me!" Shouted Owen and he ran his mirror over the remains; it confirmed what Jericho had said!

Alex just stared at the grave and finally said; "How the hell can it be? He's been in the trenches; he only came here in the autumn of this year [1916] and according to everyone, was only wounded by that mad gunman? He's still alive and sitting in a hospital bed in Hordon Cottage hospital!" Everyone stood quietly and finally Jericho said softly to Bernie and George; "Fill it back in please lads." and started to walk back to the house. The rest of the team followed - in silence.

They sat in the large reception room and Jericho picked up the picture of Eric John Cooper, who was in fact; Richard Wallis and Father David Soames. He sighed loudly; "Lilly used an old photograph, which must have been taken before 1904 of Father David Soames. He's in uniform because he was a Chaplin in the South African war, and he died in the bath. Richard Wallis should have been in that coffin. That would make sense, as to why his soul is still missing and why we've heard nothing more of his time travelling adventures. Had he died out of time, his soul would be lost. But I encountered him as young man in 1933. None of this makes sense."

Alex tapped her mirror; "Peter Meyer, the body in the grave, is a missing soul. He should have died in 1900 at the age of sixteen. How did he end up here?"

Wilson leaned back on the sofa; "Do you think we should run an orb over Father Meyer; this stinks of a demon masquerading as a dead man." Owen nodded his agreement with that; "Wilson's right; what if some bloody demon is pretending to be the dead Father Meyer now?" Jericho sighed again; "It still doesn't answer where the hell Richard Wallis is and how the bloody hell did Peter Meyer end up buried in his coffin in 1904, when he would have been only sixteen years old?"

Alex stood up and stared out the window at the graveyard. "We have been distracted by this house and the goings on over the last century and a half that concerned it. We were sent to discover what happened to Miss Susan Grimwade and we've cleared that one up. Jericho was quite right about the house being connected to her killing. But he was sidetracked by Richard Wallis, who he met back in 1933 and yes, he was connected to the house; twice as far as we know. He was the Priest here under various names and he was implicated in the murder of another." She sighed and continued.

"But let's ask ourselves; how was he involved with the original witch Coven here, back in 1816? We know now that Harold Golding and his daughter travelled from that time and set up a new life here - or would have done if we didn't stop them - back in 1816. So, what real evidence have we obtained that Richard Wallis is still around here and actively involved in anything?" She turned back to her colleagues and smiled.

"Peter Meyer died in 1904 aged 16 years old and was buried in the grave intended for Richard Wallis or Father Soames, as he was then. We have two solutions: Father Meyer is currently a demon who has possessed a dead man's identity; we know that is common; remember the demon who masqueraded as that professor back in Edwardian times? [The mission Alex is talking about was; **'The impossible films of Miss Stockyard Canning']**.The second is; what was the connection between this house and the young Peter Meyer and who the hell took over his identity and joined the Priesthood and ultimately, returned to this house in 1916?" Alex sat back down, and her colleagues could only agree with her brilliant summing up.

Jericho slapped his hands together; "Right; let's find out who the current Peter Meyer really is. Let's go and pay a visit to the hospital." That's when they heard the front door open and Jericho immediately operated his mirror and the team was cloaked from human eyes. They heard voices and some man shouting for Lilly. "Shit! She's fucking laying dead in the bath upstairs." whispered Owen to Alex.

They heard footsteps in the kitchens, then up the stairs. Jericho gestured to his team to follow, and he opened the door and peered up the stairs. He stopped time and the team spilled out into the hallway. They could see two men standing on the stairs. One was a young priest, the other, a much older man with a Gladstone bag. Wilson ran his mirror over the pair; "The old man is a Doctor Alec Piper; he's the village Doctor here. The other is..." He stared at his mirror and almost smiled; "Well, our young priest is no demon. He's real name is Peter Dundas and he's from 2004. Another fucking time traveler!"

Alex spoke really quietly; "What's he doing out of hospital so quickly, his arm is still in bandages and his leg is strapped up, yet he's struggling up the stairs with a doctor in tow; on the very day Lilly kills herself and almost the right time to stop it?" Jericho did smile and lowered his mirror; "Peter Dundas lives in this very house in 2004 with his younger brother Robert. He's the Parish Priest here at that time. Now that is no co-incidence!"

Owen tapped his mirror; "According to Human Records, Father Peter Dundas simply vanished from the Human Timeline in 2004 from this very house and crossed over to 1904 in York. He's shown as a missing soul; obviously. There are no connections shown with the dark side, except..." Owen stopped and shook his head in disbelief and said softly: "You'll never guess who the fuck his ancestor is?" Jericho smiled; "Richard Wallis, by any chance?" Owen nodded.

Wilson shook his head; "So Peter Dundas travelled back to 1904 - probably with his ancestors help - and assumed the identity of a young Peter Meyer, who wasn't even in the Priesthood then. We know both Meyer's parents were dead, and he had no siblings, no uncles, or aunts. He was perfect to be replaced by a very similar young man. Dundas's Ancestor [Richard Wallis] probably lured the young Meyer's here and they killed him in the bath, so that the swap could take place. Both would have known about the sex scandal here, coming from the future, if they had done their research. It would have been perfect, except the two women Dundas's became involved with were both bloody witches!"

"That's good big man, but how did they get the authorities to accept a young man's body as Father Soames? Now that's a big stumbling block." Wilson grunted and stared back at the two men on the stairs. Alex folded her arms and sighed; "Wouldn't it be easier just too bloody ask him?" Jericho chuckled at that and released Father Peter Dundas from time isolation; but the doctor remained frozen in time.

9. A TIME TRAVELLERS TALE.

Peter stared down the stairs at the group of people gathered in his hallway and lowered his head. He tapped Doctor Piper and nodded. He gripped his aching leg and slowly eased himself down upon the stair. He looked back up the stairs and shook his head. "She's gone Peter. Her soul was collected some minutes ago." Jericho walked to the foot of the stairs and leaned on the banister.

"It was the bloody snow; I hadn't counted for it being so deep. Old Doc Piper's car only just made it. But I didn't." Peter said and sat with hands over his face for a few seconds. Then he stared back up the stairs.

"Do you know who we are Peter?" Jericho asked and gestured for Alex and Owen to help Peter back down the stairs. "Alex and Owen will help you down and we'll have a little chat in the lounge room." Peter nodded and slumped back on the staircase. "You're Jericho Tibbs; my ancestor Richard told me all about you. I was supposed to avoid you like the plague; just another part of my plan that went tits up." He said sadly.

Owen and Alex took hold under his arms, and he limped down the stairs into the big reception room. Alex was concerned about his leg; there were tiny patches of blood seeping through his trousers. They lowered him gently onto the big sofa and Alex disappeared to fetch her doctor's bag from the upstairs bedroom. Owen handed the young man his hip flask and Peter took a big swig. He thanked Owen and touched his leg, wincing in some discomfort and pain. "I also didn't account for old man Goulding bloody shooting me, for sleeping with his daughter without his say so." He groaned a little and shifted on the sofa.

"How did all this come about Peter?" Jericho sat on the chair opposite the young priest and held his mirror with both hands.

Peter sat in silence for maybe a full minute and then sighed. "My ancestor turned up one day here, I had only been made Parish priest. I knew who he was; Richard was bit of a family legend, and he knew all about the sex scandal here in 1916, during the Great War. He proved who he was and what he was capable of, by taking me back to Victorian Manchester and Tudor York. I was hooked. He then pleaded for me to help him; being blood and all that. So, he brought me back here to 1904. There was a fucking young dead man in the bath!"

Alex returned with her bag and started to fuss over his leg, and he thanked her quietly, Jericho rubbed his face; "How did the boy die in the bath?" He asked and Peter straightened up a little; "My ancestor had accidently killed him during rough homosexual sex in the bath, apparently the boy slipped on the floor and cracked his head open. Well, that what Richard said."

Owen lowered his mirror; "The original Peter Meyer was born in 1884 and worked as a 'Rent Boy'. He was still sixteen when he died in 1904. That means he was four years out of his ordained time period, because he should have died in 1900 of influenza. Richard must have picked the boy up in Victorian Manchester. That's why we didn't know; no soul would have been collected in 1904. Dispatches must have fucked up; no collector was sent and so, no Temporal Detectives were assigned the case of a body without any soul." He offered Peter his flask.

Peter accepted Owens's flask and took another swig. "I helped him. God knows why, but I did. The local Bishop: Henry Littlewood covered the whole thing up, on the strict understanding that Richard fucked off quick and the Church wasn't involved. The local authorities also didn't want the scandal and a lot of the prominent people were all devout Catholics. So the boy's body was placed in the coffin intended for Richard [Father Soames]. It was a sealed funeral; the body was never put on display. Even the bloody local Undertaker's was in on it."

Peter lay back on the sofa and touched his leg; "You've done a good job on that Doc." He smiled at Alex, who just nodded. Peter Dundas was a very good-looking young man and quite charming. Little wonder the desperate village women went after him. "How come you stayed and ended up in that bloody awful war – which you knew was coming - when you could have just gone back to the safety of 2004?" Wilson had to ask, now a little intrigued by what motivated Peter Dundas to stay in Edwardian Times and suffer a horrendous War.

Peter looked up at the ceiling and sighed; "The reason is dead in the bath." Jericho was now intrigued; "Lilly Cooper?" He said quietly and Peter nodded. "She was a girl of sixteen then and really pretty, fantastic sense of humour and a real character. Her mother was the Housekeeper here and had been for some years. I was hooked and I recalled the sex scandal that would engulf her and this house in just a few years time. I decided to do something about it."

Owen chuckled; "So you took over young Peter's identity and became a priest; even though you were already ordained. Well, you could easily pass the Seminary, then. But what about the bishop; he knew you weren't Peter Meyer?"

Peter actually smiled; "Henry had been involved in the homosexual ring that Richard operated. I had actually forgotten that back then [1904] that being a practicing homosexual was a serious crime. So, I easily manipulated him, and he didn't like it. So, when the opportunity arose, he sent me back here. In his strange mind; as a punishment of sorts. I pretended that would be the worse place I could be sent and so he placed me here. I thought I could save young Lilly." He groaned a little and touched his leg. Alex told him to lay as still as possible.

He nodded and continued; "I had no idea that Lilly had become what she had; a witch. She and the other women wouldn't leave me alone and I'm not very proud to say that I succumbed quickly to them. I realise that Victoria was on that train quite deliberately to hook me, and it worked."

Jericho folded his arms; "I'm afraid to say that Victoria and her father were killed in a smallpox outbreak back in 1816. They won't be coming back here; ever." Peter just grunted; "I think Victoria was the real culprit here; along with her father and my bloody ancestor. Lilly had found the picture of Father Soames [Richard] and used it to pretend she was married to an army officer, who was never at home. No-one who saw the picture, realised that it was bloody Father Soames, who had apparently died in 1904. Being a married women, the bishop could appoint her as Housekeeper here; all legitimate and above board."

Peter actually chuckled; "I should have caught on when my ancestor told me the boys name; Peter Meyer. It was the name of the priest involved in the sex scandal back in 1916, I had read about it in confidential documents, in the cardinal's Archive in York. I was one of his assistants for a while in 2001. I didn't bloody realise at the time, that the damn priest would be me!"

Jericho nodded his head; "Peter, how did you ancestor manipulate time? How was he able to travel back and forth through it?" Peter wiped his face and groaned a little; "He had a book, a very old medieval book. The title was in Latin, but translated it said; 'The Devil's Pathways.' He only had to read out loud a certain paragraph on a certain page, whilst clutching an object from the time he wanted to jump to, and he was off. He told me an amusing story; that he held a dinosaur bone and jumped back 66 million years. It nearly killed him. He couldn't breathe the air then. He just made it back."

Wilson leaned forward; "Did he say where he was heading - after his demise - in 1904?" Peter nodded; "He had a real thing about the Norman Invasion of England, and he wanted to see what really happened, so I think he headed back to 1066. Whilst I'm now stuck here; unless he returns for some reason."

Jericho rose from his seat and smiled; "What happened to Father Peter Meyer after the sex scandal here, I mean you read the archives; it must have said what happened to him." Peter wiped his face; again; "Yes, I do and that's what frightens me." He looked back up at the ceiling and sighed again.

"What happened to him Peter?" Jericho repeated his question and Peter stared at the ceiling again. "He left the priesthood and re-enlisted in the army. According to church records, I saw a letter from his Commanding Officer; written in June 1918 that he had been killed. He had no family and so it was sent to Bishop Littlewood. That must have made him very happy."

"Well, you're about to get an offer few humans get; a real second chance." Jericho folded his arms and grinned; "If you stay here and are subsequently killed, your soul will be lost and that's not good. So, you can jump with me back to your own time; 2004 and start your life over from then. All this will just be history, fascinating for local historians and the subject of urban legends. What do you say to that? You can have your life back."

Peter nodded and whispered; "Thank you." Alex patted his arm; "There's also a bonus; you won't have two bullet holes in you either!" Even Peter chuckled at that. Owen and Wilson helped the young man up and Alex said quietly; "Oh and I must just pop to the Operations Centre and have words with *'I'm a laugh a minute'* Caroline." Wilson shook his head; "No right hooks now my dear. I expect my wife to behave herself and not act like a drunken docker on a Saturday night out." He grinned at her, and Owen laughed outright. Jericho just sighed.

THE END

EPILOGUE:

"Despite the loss of some souls, the mission was deemed a success. Two 'Time Portals' had been discovered and closed. 'Richard Wallis' would be the subject of yet another Temporal Investigation; in 1066! Alexandra sorted out her 'little problem' with Caroline in the Operations Centre; well, without too much violence!"
SJW.

CHARACTERS:

Father Peter Dundas returned to life in 2004 and served as Parish Priest at several Church's until his death from cancer in 2037. His funeral was unusual for a catholic Priest; not only, because it was mostly women that were the prominent mourners, but it was also attended, by at least five of his children! His disappearance in 1916 [as Father Peter Meyer] was assigned to the sex scandal that had engulfed him and the subsequent suicide of his House-keeper. His soul was collected and processed. Peter now works as a Collector.

Peter Meyer was just sixteen when he died at North Turning Parochial House in 1904. He had been picked up on the streets of Manchester in 1900 by Father Soames [Richard Wallis etc] Peter was a 'Rent Boy' and died during rough homosexual sex. His soul is still missing.

Bishop Henry Littlewood remained Bishop until his was involved in yet another homosexual scandal [for the times] and was quietly send to South America in 1926. He died of fever in a small township in Brazil in 1929. His soul was collected and processed.

Private Roy Farmer [3rd Yorkshires] was one of the young soldiers that 'Father Peter Meyer' dragged back to the trenches and thereby saved his life - he should have died - but the timeline wasn't affected, because Roy succumbed to his wounds just days later at Casualty Clearing Station No.21. As fate would have it, Jericho Tibbs and his team were there, investigating the very Doctor treating him! [See episode: **'Dr. Alexander Harris and his battle with God'**] Roy's soul was collected and processed; just a little later than expected.

Mrs. Victoria Helms [nee Golding]; died in the smallpox outbreak that swept the local villages in 1816. Many blamed it on the returning soldiers from the Napoleonic Wars and was buried, with many others, in a pit on the outskirts of the village. There are no records available of the people's names that are buried there. She is only remembered, as the daughter who vanished with her father in 1916. Her husband Kevin Helms was killed in February 1917 on the Western Front and never knew about the sex scandal or her time travelling witchcraft. Her soul was collected and placed in quarantine until 2460.

Harold Golding [Publican: Black Oak Tavern - North Turning] also died in the same smallpox outbreak that killed his daughter Victoria in 1816. He was a 'Black Priest' and Warlock for the witches Coven that infested the area. He was known to have murdered at least three young children - as sacrifices to Satan - and so his soul was collected and quarantined until 2800. He has a passing mention in the history of the village, as the local publican, who vanished with his daughter in 1916. The pair remains an intriguing mystery for local historians.

Mrs. Lillian Cooper [nee Houseman] was a practicing witch, who used the Jerusalem Mirror - in the Parochial House's attic - to travel back to 1816 and attend her Witches Coven there. She was the daughter of Richard Wallis [when he was the Parish priest there in 1888 as Father Houseman]. He had abused the young Lillian as Father Soames in the early 20th century; until he had to fake his own death in 1904. Lilly had tried to commit suicide before at Easter 1914 and only just failed. She was an abused child and adult, who fell easily under the influence of the hard core witch that was Victoria Helms/Golding. Her soul was collected and quarantined until 2380.

Mrs. Joyce Penton [Butchers wife - North Turning] had other affairs during her time in the village and was caught by her enraged husband in bed with two Canadian soldiers in March 1918. He beat her so badly, that she died of her injuries just a few days later. Her husband was hanged at York prison for her murder in July 1918. Her soul was collected and processed.

Mrs. Mavis Turner - Previously Mrs. Fellows [Dress shop owner - North Turning] never did get to show Father Peter her 'French Maid' creation, but she treated John Turner [a local farmer] to it and ended up marrying him in 1918. They lived quite happily until her death in 1929. Her soul was collected and processed.

Mrs. Gladys Gordon [Sub-Post Mistress - North Turning] never made her liaison with Father Peter and became a window just after Christmas day 1916. Her husband had been killed on the Western Front. His death, rather surprisingly to most villagers, did affect her deeply. She never remarried and died a childless widow in 1931. She was remembered with great fondness in the village for her kindness to the poor and fatherless children there. Her soul was collected and processed.

Doctor Alec Piper [Village Doctor - North Turning] could never remember why he found himself standing outside the Parochial House, in bitter snow and cold, the day Lilly killed herself in the bath and Father Peter disappeared. He still had no explanation for it, when asked at the time or years later. He retired in 1922 and moved to Blackpool. He died in 1939, on the eve of the Second World War. His soul was collected and processed.

John Guest [Shop keeper - North Turning] is credited with saving Peter's life in the snow that morning; he was old soldier from the Boer war [of 1899-1902] and had applied pressure to the gunshot wounds. He died in 1929 from undiagnosed Type 1 Diabetes and his soul was collected and processed.

Doctor Gerald Feelgood [Pathologist - Hordon Morgue] continued to explore the causes of death for many more people who were brought to Hordon Morgue. He died in 1922 but did manage to see his granddaughter Alice qualify as a doctor. He was terribly proud of her. He even mentioned it the Collector who attended his 'dispatch'. His soul was collected and processed.

Miss Susan Grimwade [Doncaster sacrifice victim] obviously never suffered at the hands of Harold Golding and was quite unaware about the close shave she had with a horrific death. She married a local Railway Clerk in 1921. Susan had four children and died in 1941. Her soul was collected and processed.

Inspector Frederick 'Piggy' Portal [Yorkshire Constabulary] obviously never had Susan's horrific death to investigate and he certainly drew a blank over who shot the Priest, near Christmas 1916. Both the suspect and the victim disappeared that year; never to be seen or heard of again. He retired from the Police Service in 1926 and basically, ate and drank himself to death. He had no real friends and had never married. He was found dead in his dingy flat in Doncaster in 1930. The only people who attended the funeral, was the local vicar - who didn't know him - and the two gravediggers. No one from his old Police Service days bothered to turn up. His soul was collected and processed.

Lester Bullfinch [Publican - Black Ram Hotel - Hordon] lost his licence in 1919 and had to move from the village; he was caught selling liquors and spirits that the brewery had not supplied. He struggled to find work during the great depression [a really big worldwide recession] that followed the First World War He hung himself in 1922 - in a railway station toilet - and his soul was collected and processed.

Mrs. Mavis Bullfinch [Black Ram Hotel - Hordon] had to leave the village with her husband Lester in 1919. She worked lots of different, low paid jobs to keep the pair afloat after Lester struggled to find work, any work. After his death in 1922, she finally ended up in Blackpool, selling sweets and novelties at a seafront stall. She became a very popular and much-loved character around the area and when she died in 1935; her funeral was packed with mourners - including a certain Dr. Featherstone! - Her soul was collected and processed.

Richard Wallis/Eric John Cooper/Father houseman/Father Soames; this mysterious time traveler from 1706 has still not been apprehended but has been reported in other time periods. He became the subject of a second Temporal Investigation by Jericho and Team 74; in 1066. His soul remains missing to this day.

Father John Edwards [Parish Priest, North Turning 1904 to 1914] retired in 1914 and moved to Australia, to live with his widowed sister; Edith. He was quite a popular figure in the local catholic Community in Perth, Western Australia. He died in 1924 and his soul was collected and processed.

Father Robert Gilmore [Parish Priest, North Turning 1917 - 1933] was murdered in a savage black magic ritual in 1933, by Richard Wallis and the matter was investigated by Inspector Doc Underhill and his team. [Which included Jericho at the time; he was Doc's sergeant] They rounded up all the culprits, but Wallis escaped. Father Gilmore's soul was never recovered as his file is marked; LTDA. [Lost to Demonic Activity].

Jesbu [the demon - 1816] returned to his master, after his defeat by Oscar the Guardian in 1816 and was to cross paths with Jericho and his team again. His current whereabouts are unknown.

Mrs. Doris Spooner [Baker's wife, North Turning 1816] was a witch in the North Turning Coven of 1816. She was implicated in the deaths of at least two young children during black magic rituals. She died in the smallpox epidemic that swept the area that year. No soul was collected and is subject of an investigation by Inspector Dawn Daniels and Team 62. There is currently no resolution.

Miss Alice & Miss Emma Walters [child victims of the witches - 1816] woke in their bed and remembered nothing of the incident with the witches - James, a Knight of God - had wiped their memories of the horrific ordeal. Both girls later married and enjoyed quiet lives as farmer's wives and mothers of several children. Alice died in 1831 and Emma in 1848. Both their souls were collected and processed at the relevant times.

EPISODE 4: "STRANGERS MARKET."

MISSION SUMMARY: "Ms. Teresa Green - A Human Agent for Jericho Tibbs in England - during the early 21st Century, passes a strange story onto Jericho which he may be interested in. Apparently, a local London magazine has reported a story about an unknown young man, who is visiting stores and markets in the city purchasing large quantities of Victorian and Edwardian money. Whilst that appears quite innocent - he could be into Numismatics - another story emerges that the same odd fellow has purchased period clothes and has even taken lessons in Victorian and Edwardian etiquette!"

NOTES: This episode contains references to Nazi Germany.

TRIGGER WARNINGS. **ALCOHOL, STRONG LANGUAGE, SEXUAL REFERENCES, VIOLENCE & NAZI'S!**

AGE 12+ ONLY. **30 Minutes reading time.**

1. THE COIN COLLECTOR.

"Well, I'm really surprised how slow it is this morning, hardly worth getting out of bed at 4am for." Ms Teresa Green folded her arms and stared down the street; there were very few people about and it was almost lunchtime. There appeared to be more stall holders than potential customers. She had been speaking to young Ellen, who helped her out on weekends for pocket money;

Ellen was about to sit her exams this summer and hoped to go onto college; she was just sixteen. Teresa, on the other hand, was nearly thirty, small and slim, with dark hair and eyes - many considered her 'quite pretty' - not that she cared about that anymore. She had taken over her late mother's stall in Portobello Road just last year. It sold old clothes, referred to as 'Antique, Retro or Period' to her customers; mainly women looking for dresses that would be unusual and noticeable in these modern times. Her 'Retro' miniskirts [based on the 1960 fashion icons] were good sellers. Sometimes she really wanted to tell some 'ladies' that the skirt they wanted, would not flatter their legs - but she never did - live and let live came to mind; it made them happy.

When she wasn't working her late mother's stall on the weekend, she worked part-time in the local Library. Her late parents had left their only daughter very well provided for and now Teresa could pick and chose what she did and when, she did it. They had left her the house [all paid for] and a substantial bank balance. Her father: Gary, had been a deputy Director of a London Merchant Bank when he died suddenly three years ago; a massive stroke had taken him just months before his planned retirement. Her mother never recovered from his death and kept in poor health thereafter.

She died last year from complications of influenza and Teresa found herself wealthy, but sad and lonely. She had never married or really dated men after Tom Reddigge had destroyed her dreams and her heart. Just weeks before the wedding, she had left the library [where she was working full time in those days] early one afternoon with a slight toothache and returned to the flat they shared; he was in bed with their neighbour's son. The young man fled the scene in his underpants and Tom couldn't really offer any explanation, as he pulled the condom from his limp penis; standing shocked and naked in their bedroom.

That soured their relationship somewhat and they parted - permanently - just days later. She moved back in with her parents and rarely dated anyone after that. Her broken heart was taking time to recover and none of the men she dated really interested her; even sexually. She had her vibrator to relieve matters and some good friends to talk with. But she was desperately lonely now.

She use to laugh about her two cats being her best friends - 'Clare and Susan' - were spoilt like only children and she loved the crazy pair of felines dearly. For many nights they were her only company. Teresa was in a daydream when Ellen tugged her arm and said quietly; "I think old Rosie wants you Tess." She looked over to the stall opposite and saw Rosie gesturing for her to come over. "Well, there's not much going on now. Can you manage Ellen?" Teresa asked and with Ellen's agreement wandered over to old Rosie's stall.

Before she could say anything, Rosie grabbed her arm and pointed down the street; "That's him, the young man in the story. You know, the one in the local paper, I can't believe he's come to my little stall." Teresa looked down the street where Rosie was pointing and just caught a handsome young man, wearing a classic three-piece suit, walking away; brief case in hand.

Teresa grinned; "For heaven's sake Rosie what story in the local rag?" Big Rosie took a deep breath and started to dig amongst the little pile of papers and magazines that she kept for days like this. ""I'll show you Tess, it's him. I know it's him. His description is in the story." Rosie pulled a copy of the local paper out and flicked quickly to a certain page and thrust it under Teresa's nose. "See, it's all about a well dressed - very good looking - young man who is buying old coins. He's bought so many, that coin and antique shops mentioned it to the local Chamber of Commerce, and it was passed onto the paper as a 'human interest' story. That's what they call stories like this."

Tess glanced at the article with very little interest, but she would keep Rosie happy by showing some attention. "So, a young man in a classic suit has been buying old coins, all around the Borough, where's the story in that?" Rosie looked about and turned her back on the street and dropped her voice to a whisper; "Just look at this; they are all genuine; I checked them with the forgery pen." Rosie pulled a wad of twenty-pound notes from her apron pocket.

Teresa stared at the bundle; there must be five hundred pounds there. That did take her back a little, but she recovered and smiled; "Well done Rosie, I wish someone would spend money like that at my stall." Rosie nodded but didn't smile, she pushed the notes back into her apron pocket and waved a hand over her coin and old token stall; "He purchased every Victorian coin I possessed; everyone. Then he bought all my Edwardian coins, but here's the funny thing - just like what the paper says - he only purchased Edwardian coins that where minted before 1905 - he wouldn't accept a single coin after that date - even the rare ones. Now what sort of coin collector is that?"

Teresa admitted it did sound strange; all such collectors would be after rare coins, but this one just wanted everyday Victorian and Edwardian coins minted before 1905; why 1905 she wondered. "He also asked if I had any notes, the old white five-pound notes that were in circulation before 1905. I said I didn't but refereed him to Rubin Cohen's little shop in Newmarket Street. I know that he has some old notes in his antique shop. I bet that's where he's going now." Rosie said quietly, with a look of satisfaction on her face.

Teresa re-read the article with more interest this time. It stated that the young man must have spent thousands on these old coins and notes. But he always insisted that the Edwardian coins were minted before 1905. The Victorian coins could have been produced in any year of Victoria's reign. Then the article went on further to say that the same young man had purchased Edwardian period clothes from a couple of antique shops – again - insisting that they should not have been made before 1905!

Teresa looked up from the paper as Rosie tugged her shoulder and pointed back across to her own stall. The young man was talking to Ellen!

"Thank you Rosie, I'll see you in the 'Wagon & Horses' when we close, if I can." She mumbled and made her way back to her stall - quickly. He was just about to walk away when she introduced herself. Now that she was face to face, Teresa could see that Rosie and the paper hadn't exaggerated his appearance; he was a strikingly handsome man, possibly in his late twenties with deep blue eyes and sandy blond hair. He possessed big, well manicured hands and it was obvious that he knew his way around a gym. Fucking gorgeous! She thought to herself.

He smiled and asked if she possessed any authentic period wear from the early Edwardian era. His voice was firm, and he was clearly educated and well spoken. Teresa had to say no - regretfully - but if he left a contact number, she could put the 'feeler's' out with her associates in the 'Retro' and 'Period' clothes business. She would try and find something that would satisfy his needs. Me for a start; she thought.

He stood and thought for a few seconds and broadly smiled; "You would do that for me? That is most kind." Teresa had a rare thought that actually made her blush a little - she desperately hoped he had not noticed - She would do a little more for him than find some bloody old clothes!

She fumbled in her apron's pocket and pulled a little black note book out and a small pencil - nicked from the local bookmakers when she couldn't find one - and offered to write his number down. He slowly took the book and pencil from her hands, as they touched, Teresa actually trembled a little.

He wrote a number down and said quietly; "Just call that; they'll get a message to me. I particularly need a dress frock coat of the early Edwardian period; say before 1905." He handed the book back and gently lifted her hand and kissed the back of it. "I look forward to hearing from you Miss Green." He smiled again and started to walk away but stopped and spoke over his shoulder with a broad smile; "Oh, tell them it's for Mr. Wells - Harry Wells."

Teresa watched him depart - he walked with grace and strength - not to mention a fabulous arse. She gulped and watched him until he disappeared. Both Ellen and her watched him leave and then started to laugh together.

"Fuck! Now that's some fucking gorgeous bloke!" Ellen exclaimed and started to phone her friend about the young man she just met. Teresa walked behind the stall and ran a hand over her hair. She stared at the hand he kissed and licked her lips; some truly dirty thoughts were jumping around her head and she had not suffered the like for some time - for a very long time.

She quickly pulled open the notebook and stared at the number; it was a local land line number, not a mobile. His home number maybe? She clutched the book closely and allowed herself a big smile. "Harry Wells." She whispered quietly and couldn't stop smiling.

"I think we'll close early Ellen; I need to make some phone calls about a early Edwardian Dress frock coat." She said with real anticipation in her voice. Ellen didn't disagree with that decision and started to pack up the stall. Teresa's delicious dream was interrupted by a strange thought; why was he actually buying coins that most serious collectors wouldn't bother with and why the specific period clothing? She sighed; a handsome, mysterious and clearly wealthy and educated young man had just walked into her life, and all she could think about; was passing the story onto Mr. Jericho Tibbs – well - that's not all she was thinking.

After the stall had been packed up and the goodbyes said to Ellen, Teresa walked to the little private car park at the rear of the shops and sat in her car for some minutes just thinking, mainly about the handsome young man. She sighed and flicked through the contact list on her phone until she came to one marked: 'The Times'. She called the number and finally, after going through the useless 'automated menu', was connected with the Personal Small Adverts' desk and paid for an entry using her credit card.

It was the same advertisement each time:

"In the woodlands of Kent,
the tree's are green,
their colours are only lent,
but visitor's are most welcome,
and some are Heaven sent."

Teresa drove home to Kent House, a little distracted by the events of the day and after feeding her cats, slumped onto the large comfy sofa and watched the news on BBC 1, without any real interest. She must have dozed for a while and lying back on the sofa, stared at the clock above the fireplace; she sat bolt upright; the second hand had stopped.

2. JERICHO DROPS BY.

Jericho and Alex stood by the door and Jericho removed his hat and smiled broadly; "Always nice to drop in on you Teresa, I don't think you've met Alexandra yet." Teresa jumped from the sofa and straightened herself up.

"Jesus Jericho, is she a fashion model or something?" Teresa stared at Alex and admired her lovely clothes and figure; she knew real beauty in other women when she saw it - men would certainly fall at her feet - she grudgingly admitted and offered the pair some tea. Teresa stood in the kitchen waiting for the kettle to boil and could hear Mr. Tibbs explaining to his lovely assistant about Ms. Green and how her father had worked for him since he was a teenager. Teresa had taken over from her father upon his death; Jericho had attended the funeral. It comforted Teresa greatly that she knew her father had moved on. The same feeling of well being had manifested itself when her dear mother passed away. She carried the tea tray into the lounge and found Alex playing with the two crazy cats. "You like cats Alex?" She asked, smiling. Alex nodded; "Jericho's cat, Mr. Parker is a playful bugger when he wants to be; he would love this mad pair."

Jericho chuckled; "Yeah, but you would have to put up with a bucket of kittens." Teresa smiled and said simply; "That would be lovely." They sat drinking tea and Teresa explained about the strange young man collecting Victorian and Edwardian coins; especially that the Edwardian coins couldn't be older than 1905.

Jericho was definitely interested and rubbed his chin; "Any other strange or eccentric behaviour?" Teresa nodded and explained about the young man's desire to purchase Edwardian Period clothing – again - only before 1905.

Now that did really interest Jericho and he consulted his mirror for a certain 'Harry Wells' and rather surprisingly; came up blank for this time period of Human existence. He chuckled to himself; "Bloody H. Wells, he may as well had 'Time Traveler' tattooed on his forehead." Alex accepted a refill from Tess and tapped the cup gently with an elegant finger; "Why before 1905, what's significant about that year? If it was 1914, I could understand that."

Jericho nodded his agreement with that statement. "Well, in 1905 Einstein published his famous papers on Relativity and basically laid the foundations for science to create the Atomic bomb; ending up with the dropping of atomic bombs on Japan in 1945. Many refer to 1905 as the 'Year of miracles'. But if he wanted to stop or change that; then an earlier time in Einstein's life would probably be better." Tess refilled his cup and threw some biscuits crumbs down for her cats. "Wasn't that really important battleship launched in that year, didn't that change the history of warfare?" She spoke quietly and sipped her tea.

"You could be near the point there Tess, the launch of HMS Dreadnought changed navel warfare. Basically, the new ship made every other battleship in the world obsolete. That started a real frenzy in building new, similar warships all around the world." Jericho spoke quietly, placed his cup down and again, consulted his mirror.

Tess explained to Alex that the ship caused an arms race between Britain and Germany that eventually ended up with the First World War. Alex smiled; "But how do you stop a battleship being designed and built - there must have been thousands of people working in that project - who do you take out and when?"

Tess shrugged her shoulders; she didn't know the answer to that. "Maybe it's an event before 1905 that his interested in?" Tess muttered and finished her tea. Jericho looked up from his mirror and smiled; "Perhaps the Wright brothers first flight in 1903? But then he would be buying old American currency!" Everyone chuckled at that. Alex sighed; "Well, we're getting nowhere sitting thinking about this, why not just ask the bugger?"

Tess pulled the telephone number out, she had been given by 'Mr. Wells' and said with a little excitement in her voice; "He wants an Edwardian frock coat and I said I would call him when I found something suitable." Jericho accepted the number and smiled; "Good thinking Tess, I'll have a suitable coat dropped off. I'm sure he'll find a competent Taylor to make any alterations necessary."

Alex nodded; "Tess can arrange a meeting and I can check him against Human Records on my mirror, he won't be too suspicious if she turns up with a female friend in tow. We'll have his real identity then and can investigate him properly." Jericho agreed with that plan and Tessa stroked her cats; she didn't like the idea but said nothing - she really didn't want him having romantic ideas about a beauty like Alex - then cheered up when Jericho told her to call him now and make the meeting happen. "The coat will be from 1903; that should suit his needs nicely." He added and called Supplies on his mirror.

"How much would a coat like that cost now?" Alex asked Tess, who shrugged her shoulders and thought for a few seconds. "We can't make it cheap; he probably knows how much a genuine one would approximately cost; so about three hundred pounds, I think." Jericho looked up, a little amazed at that figure and chuckled; "I think I paid about two pounds for my first one!" Alex grinned; "Yeah, but that was about a million years ago." Everyone laughed at that.

Tess called the number on her mobile, whilst Alex poured more tea all round and relaxed back in her chair. The number rang for a few seconds and to Tess's disappointment - but not shown - a woman answered. Tess explained that she had managed to procure a genuine coat made in 1903. The woman said that she would inform Mr. Well's, who would attend her market stall tomorrow afternoon; at about one o'clock. She didn't even ask the price and the call ended.

"That's excellent Tess, Alex can be your assistant on the stall - a very good cover - I'm sure your young lady assistant won't mind a day off, especially if you still pay her." Jericho was definably happy with the arrangements made to acquire the young man's real identity. But his mood changed slightly as he re-read his mirror. "That's really interesting, according to my mirror, that telephone number didn't exist in this time period - it's simply not listed - anywhere for here and now."

"But surely that's not possible, if it can be called, then it must exist here and now?" Alex asked and took the number Jericho offered. She studied it and placed her cup down. "Doesn't it have too few digits for this time?" Tess was annoyed at herself, that she had missed that significant clue. Jericho grunted and checked his mirror, then sat back and rubbed his chin; "Good spot Alex; that number was listed for London, but not in 2019. It's shown as active between 1957 and 1961 and was allocated to...." He sat upright and looked quite bemused. Jericho tapped his mirror and nodded to himself, then smiled slowly; "It was allocated to British Military Intelligence Department Number Six at their offices in Whitehall; their secret offices at the time."

There was silence for some seconds and Tess looked quite confused; "How the hell did I just ring a number that was only active between 1957 and 1961 on my mobile phone in 2019; nearly sixty years into the past?"

"Now that is a bloody good question." Muttered Jericho and Alex stared at the number; she knew that their mirrors could call between time periods, but surely there was no technology existing in the nineteen fifties and sixties that had that capability?

"I think, we really do need to investigate Mr. Well's. I'll call the team together and bring Angel Margret up to date. This ladies, has now turned into a real mission." Jericho - unsmiling - said quietly and called Wilson on his mirror.

3. Mr. WELL'S? - I PRESUME.

Despite the warm morning sunshine, a sharp breeze had popped up and lowered the temperature all round. Tess pulled on a bright red cardigan and folded her arms; she glanced across at Alex, who clearly didn't feel the drop in temperature. Tess wondered if it was because the lady standing near her had been dead for over two hundred years. She actually shuddered at that and glanced at her little silver wristwatch. "It's almost one." She said softly to Alex, who checked her mirror and watched down the street - it was another quiet morning, turning into a quiet afternoon - and no sign of 'Mr. Well's'.

Alex checked – again - the black frock coat that had been provided by Supplies and replaced it into the clear plastic bag. "That is a beautiful coat, well worth three hundred pounds of anyone's money." She said to Tess, who was staring down the street and nervously tied up her hair; "He's outside the pub." She whispered but didn't point. Alex looked around the pub entrance and caught sight of a good-looking man. Tall and clearly well built, talking to a couple of elderly ladies who were laughing and chatting. "Blimey, you didn't exaggerate Tess; that is one good looking young man by any standard." She whispered, as if anyone could hear the conversation between the women.

It was clear that the old ladies really didn't want their little conversations to end, but Alex watched as 'Mr. Well's' pointed towards their stall and started to walk towards them. He cheerfully waved goodbye to his lady friends and was stopped again, this time by a very pretty young woman dressed like a catwalk model. "He's clearly popular with the girls." Muttered Tess; not hiding the jealousy in her voice. Alex did smile at that. It took a few minutes, but he finally managed to extirpate himself from the woman's persist and obvious attention.

He finally arrived at Tess's stall with a gorgeous smile and an apology for lateness, which the women waved away instantly. Tess, quite reluctantly it should be said, introduced him to her 'Cousin' Alex, who was helping her out today; her assistant having to revise for an important exam. Now her quarry was close up, Alex could really appreciate what a fine, handsome young man 'Mr. Well's' actually was and he was utterly charming and attentive.

Tess chatted away about the coat that Alex produced, and Mr. Well's examined it carefully; "This looks like it was made yesterday!" He exclaimed and ran his big hands over it with great care. Alex stood a little to one side and operated her mirror with great discretion. Harry Well's pulled a brown envelope from his pocket and produced three hundred pounds in denominations of twenty's; they appeared to be all brand new and unused. Alex made a note of that. "You have served me really well ladies, the coat is excellent and well worth the money. I thank you both." He pushed the envelope back into his pocket and Alex thought she saw something in his shirt pocket but couldn't make it out properly.

Alex really did switch on the feminine charm and asked quietly; "You must be a Production Manager for a film company, scouring the county for props; a new period drama is it?" Mr. Well's chuckled; "You're very close in your deductions Alexandra, but we're called Prop Manager's and we find and supply decent props for films and TV. With a period, drama, it's always best to have the real thing. With the drama I'm working on now, I have a small part which requires a proper coat of the period - 1905 - to be exact." He folded the coat over his arm and with another smile; said goodbye and slowly walked away. He seemed to be laughing to himself; Alex thought that was quite strange.

Alex disappeared into the rear of the stall and called Owen on her mirror; "Did Human Records identify our handsome would-be time-traveler?" She smiled broadly as Tess joined her, asking; "Anything yet?" Alex shook her head and Owen said simply; "Best return to the van ladies, as soon as possible." The girls had the stall packed away in record time and headed for the small private car park that Tess normally parked in.

The team was waiting in a plain white Transit van and Wilson pulled open the side door and the girls jumped in, with some impatience. "Well, who the hell is he?" demanded Alex and settled on a rear seat. Owen held up his mirror and sighed; "Now, now ladies. Your gorgeous young man is a certain Mr. Harry Gordon Well's, who lives locally and works at Shepperton Studio's as a Property Buyer for 'Time-Piece' films of London and New York. He is quite genuine; I'm afraid." He grinned, as Alex slumped back in her seat, but Tess grinned broadly; "You mean he actually belongs here? In this time period I mean." Owen did grin; "Oh yes, he's apparently the real deal Tess." The look on her face was priceless and that did make Jericho smile.

Alex was still a little troubled about Mr. Well's and leaned forward - unsmiling - "I thought I caught sight of something in his shirt pocket, a device no bigger than a mobile phone of this time-period. But I don't think it was a phone. I can't be sure what it was." Wilson grunted; "It probably was a phone, Alex. Very few people in this era don't carry one." Alex nodded and then remembered the money or rather the envelope it came in. She tapped Jericho on the shoulder; "Did Supplies give you any money for this mission?"

Owen chuckled; "Careful Boss, I think Alex wants to go shopping." Jericho scratched his chin; "Yes they did." He said quietly. "May I see it please?" Alex held out her hand and Jericho pulled the brown envelope from his pocket and handed it over. "Best count it, when she hands it back." murmured Wilson with quite a smile. Alex pulled open the envelope and showed Tess; "Do you have the money he gave you?" Tess nodded and rummaged in her coat pocket.

Alex held up the money that Supplies had provided Jericho with; a big handful of new twenty-pound notes; all unused. Tess produced the notes that Mr. Well's had given her. - All new twenty-pound notes - unused. "That's some bloody co-incidence. Same envelope and same notes." Owen said and everyone was silent for a few seconds. Alex sighed quite loudly; "The thing in his pocket, I think I know what it was." Everyone turned to her, and she folded her arms; "Our Mr. Well's was carrying a bloody mirror; a temporal detectives bloody mirror!"

Jericho sat up in the front passenger seat and ran both hands through his thick, dark hair. "I do hope we haven't compromised another Team's mission here." He said quietly and pulled out his mirror. Wilson gripped the steering wheel; "This doesn't make sense, if he's on a mission here, then Supplies would have provided anything he needs; including a bloody frock coat." Owen nodded at that deduction, but Alex half smiled; "Not if he was trying to lure someone out...or something like that."Tess sat unsmiling; she really wasn't happy with this particular turn of events; "If he's a Temporal Detective - like yourselves - then he must be...." Alex gripped her arm and said quietly; "Yes, dead like us." She didn't smile. Tess sighed and folded her arms; today wasn't going well for her.

Jericho had put a call through to Operations Control and was waiting to speak to the duty Controller; an old friend of his; Janet Turnkettle. He sat waiting and stared out the passenger window and saw a plain white Transit van sitting at the rear of the private car park - with two people in - they were staring at him.

Jericho ran a hand over his face and groaned; "Unless I'm very much mistaken, Lisa Solomon and Tom Slurburger from Team 52 are sitting opposite us in an identical van - provided by Supplies - and wondering what the hell we're doing here!" His mirror buzzed and he answered it slowly; already knowing what the Controller was about to say.

The conversation was quite brief, and Janet really did laugh. She confirmed that team 52 were on a mission in that time and place - headed by Inspector Harry Hadden - Now that did bring a smile of relief to Jericho, who muttered; "Of all bloody people, I should have recognised a young Harry. What a twat I am." Everyone started to laugh, and Jericho jumped from the van and the team followed, they walked over to their much amused colleagues, who jumped from their van to greet them.

There were handshakes all round and Lisa was introduced to Tess by Alex. There was one topic of conversation: the dashing Inspector of Team 52. Lisa did smile; "Tell me about it, we've only been here a couple of days and he must have been propositioned by half a dozen women and girls, he's like a bloody girl magnet. But is anyone surprised with that gorgeous old-style charm of his. He even opens doors for me and stands up when I enter the bloody room. He's bloody charming and it's real that's how he is around women. For the first time in two hundred years, I've met a real hunk of a man and I'm bloody dead!"

Alex pointed out that everyone was dead – well - except Tess of course. The girls chuckled about that. But Tess wasn't really too happy about it; if she was honest with herself. She had some delicious daydreams about the young man and now, she knew, that's all they would remain; dreams.

Temporal Detective Sergeant Thomas Slurburger slapped Wilson on the back and really did laugh. "I was actually just saying to Lisa, that the big ugly bugger in the identical van opposite looks a lot like bloody Wilson from Team 74." They chatted for some minutes and the happy - but unscheduled - reunion split up, with Jericho asking Tom to tell Harry to pop round to Tess's address and catch up on old times. The conversation in the van was lively as Wilson drove back to Tess's home. The unanimous decision was an Indian take-away and a visit to the local supermarket for brandy.

Alex laughed to herself and pointed out, that when she had met Harry Hadden previously; he was an old man in his late seventies. Little wonder he laughed when walking away; he had certainly recognized her. "He must think we're a right bunch of plonkers." Muttered Owen but cheered up at the prospect of curry and booze. [See episode; **'The ghosts and Miss Jessica Martin'**]

4. HARRY'S MISSION.

"How come your mirrors showed him as genuine and from this time; when he's obviously not?" Tess asked Jericho as she laid warm plates upon the dining table. Jericho tapped his mirror and smiled; "When team members are on an active mission, Control will upload their cover profiles; it's supposed to stop two teams investigating each other; that didn't work today!"

Owen chuckled and pulled the lids off the takeaway containers with some relish. "Does our dashing Inspector like a good curry?" He asked and sniffed at a chicken Madras. Jericho nodded; "Harry loves a good curry and a few beers, his lovely sister Dotty was the same. They were the best human agents I had - in any time period - present company excepted."

Tess really did smile at that compliment from Jericho and fetched her best brandy glasses from the kitchen.

"I've heard you mention Dorothy before, she clearly must have impressed you Jericho." Alex opened the brandy bottle and wiped the glasses Tess had given her. Jericho smiled; "She's a lot like you Alexandra. A real beauty - inside and out - with courage and humour; she really had a superb mind and would have made a first-class detective in the time period she lived; had the silly buggers allowed women to join the police!" Wilson handed around several bottles of cold beer and eased into his dinning chair; "Don't know about you bunch, but that beef Jalfrezi is just begging me to eat it."

That's when the doorbell buzzed and Tess answered; it was Harry. He was shown into the dining room by Tess and given a brandy - immediately - by a smiling Alex. "Thank you, Alexandra." He said quietly and smiled, which gave Alex a few little butterflies in her stomach. Harry Hadden was indeed a handsome young man and utterly charming. He and Jericho embraced like long lost brothers and sat on the sofa together. Alex and Tess started to dish up the meal and Alex simply could not stop herself glancing over towards the young man.

Wilson placed more open beer bottles near each plate and whispered to Alex; "Who's the moth now?" He grinned broadly and piled his plate with the Beef Jalfrezi that had tempted his palate so much. Everyone sat around the table eating and chatting. Harry - with a great deal of amusement in his voice - said he had recognised Alexandra immediately; you don't forget beauty like that, even when your old and dead!

He became quietly serious when Jericho asked about his mission; he explained that a time portal had been detected in this area which was locked to May 5th, 1906, and someone was using it. They had made two trips back and Inspector Longstreet's human agent for this time and place had reported that a young man had been purchasing coins and notes from that period. So, Harry believed, if the time traveler thought he had a rival, he would break cover to discover who else may have discovered the portal.

Harry added that Angel Margret thought he was the best choice for the mission because he obviously knew the Edwardian Era well. Jericho nodded at that and asked where the time portal was. Harry did smile and sipped his brandy; "The old clock tower near the entrance to the East India Docks, which in this era is now really expensive flats and houses. In 1906 it was a thriving dockyard and most importantly, the Edwardian battleship HMS Dreadnought is docked there."

Owen finished his curry; "That ship was really important; it caused the First World War." Harry placed his fork down; "Your almost correct there Owen; the navel arms race that it started really did contribute to the development of the Great War, but there were other factors that actually kicked it off; like the assignation of Austrian Archduke Franz Ferdinand at Sarajevo in 1914. But your right, the ship is really important to the current human timeline."

Harry continued; "We had to make a few assumptions at first; the time jumper must have gone back once and found that he could do little without proper funds and so returned and purchased the relevant money and notes to cover his second trip. He probably took back some gold and silver trinkets to sell and wouldn't need to purchase old coins and notes anymore; there would be plenty of them back there!" Everyone chuckled at that and Wilson grunted; "So if he reads about some young man doing exactly the same as he did, he would certainly want to know, what the new boy on the time travelling block was up to." Everyone agreed that Harry's plan was really good.

"I think it's working, I'm pretty sure that the same young man has followed me on a couple of occasions already. But I had Tom and Lisa follow the follower! That's where Tom and Lisa are now; sitting outside the address we followed him to. We now just have to wait and see if he makes a move." Harry finished his curry and his brandy. Alex gave him a refill with another big smile. Wilson and Jericho exchanged a humorous glance, they were clearly thinking the same thoughts; Alex was smitten, and she really couldn't hide it!

Tess had to ask about the strange telephone number and the woman at the other end. "Why did you use that old number for British Military Intelligence and who was the woman that answered?"

Owen mumbled; "Damn Good question." and accepted a refill of his brandy glass from Alex. Harry chuckled; "Firstly, the woman was Lisa and secondly I thought a real strange number like that would certainly raise the interest of our time traveler; could he resist someone that had contacts apparently going back to the late 1950's and early 1960's?" Tess nodded and sipped her brandy. It had certainly got Jericho interested, who admitted that Harry's plan was a good one. That's when Harry's mirror buzzed and he answered it quickly. He jumped up from the table and smiled; "To quote the great Sherlock Holmes; the games a foot!" He shook everyone's hand and particularly thanked Tess for her hospitality, then operated his mirror; he was gone.

"Well, we best follow him; and leave, I mean." Jericho said and thanked Tess for her superb hospitality; as did the rest of the team and a few minutes later; they were gone. Standing alone in her dining room; Tess realised just how lonely, she had become.

The team walked back to the lighthouse in good spirits and Alex's apparent interest in Inspector Harry Hadden was the major source of amusement. She couldn't really put up any honest arguments, about her colleagues deductions, because they were right!

They sat about the study. Wilson and Jericho chatting about Edwardian times and Wilson was most amused about Jericho's comment - which he always said about the era - that 'civilisation' actually ended in 1914. Owen waved a pack of playing cards about and asked if anyone wanted to play Bridge. Alex was interested and Jericho agreed to play. Wilson grunted and folded his arms; "What about Poker? That's my favourite." Finally, it was agreed, that a few hands of Poker may be interesting; mainly to keep the big man happy!

They gathered around the card table and Owen started to deal, when Mr. Harris appeared in the doorway - he addressed Jericho directly - Mr. Harris explained that 'Little Ivan'; the Messenger, had just delivered this; He held out a brown paper file marked with big red letters: 'Urgent'. Owen chuckled; "How can anything be urgent; we're temporal detectives. We have all the time in the world!"

Jericho accepted the file and broke the seal; he read slowly and didn't smile. Everyone could see the concerned look on his face. "What is it?" Alex asked quietly and Jericho looked up from the file: grim faced. He spoke softly: "The whole team has simply vanished. All their mirrors are off-line, and they are missing. Gone." Jericho lowered the file and stared at the fireplace.

"Who?" Asked Owen and stopped dealing out cards. Jericho sighed; "Harry and his entire team has vanished. We've been tasked to go after them." There was silence for a few seconds and Alex rose from the table; "Well, we had better get going then." She said, with real concern in her voice. The rest of the team followed her to the light room without another word being said.

5. IN THE FOOTSTEPS OF TEAM 52.

Wilson pulled up outside the modest house and wiped his face; the weather couldn't have been better; hot and sunny, with just a gentle breeze. "Supplies have already removed the other van. It was parked outside the Clock Tower with three parking tickets affixed to the windscreen." He said quietly and stared at the silent house. He was already sweating, and it was still only early morning. Owen took a sip of water from the plastic bottle that Alex had handed him. "Nothing is really known about the occupant for this year, A certain Rashid Kamill. Human Records have him born in 1996, so he must be about 23 years old; works as a plumber, apparently for a local Heating Company. No time portals: the house appears clean."

"Well, he must be involved somehow or Harry wouldn't have staked the house out." Jericho muttered and consulted his mirror yet again. Control informed him that there was still no contact with any member of Team 52. "If we draw a blank here, then, it's off to that damn Clock Tower by the old docks." Jericho grunted and the team decamped from the van into the bright sunshine.

The team gathered under the little porch and Alex - rather cheekily - pressed the doorbell. The others stared at her; "The mirrors record no one inside." Owen said and rolled his eyes in mock despair. That's when they heard the barking and Alex just smiled at them. Jericho chuckled; a little basic stuff and they nearly forgot. But Alex hadn't. Wilson peered through the letterbox and started to laugh; "I think you Brits call it a 'Yorkshire terror'." He let Owen have a look, he laughed too. "It's called a Yorkshire Terrier my big yank friend."

Jericho indicated to the door and Wilson pulled his lock pick from a pocket and had the door open in seconds. "You certainly missed your true vocation." Owen muttered as Wilson swung open the door and stepped over the yapping, snarling little dog.

"Well, he's certainly cute." said Alex and tried to pat the dog, which went for her with some ferocity. She stopped and sighed; "Not a friendly little bugger is he." She murmured and followed the team into the living room, which was neat and tidy. The TV was on and they watched as the little dog sat down in front of it. "He must keep the goggle box on to keep the miniature Rottweiler happy." Owen said and with Wilson, headed up the stairs, whilst Alex checked the kitchen. Jericho stood at the bottom of the stairs and consulted his mirror - yet again.

A very amused - and very puzzled - Owen stood at the top of the stairs and gestured for Jericho and Alex to join him. He was really trying hard not to laugh. "The fucking spare bedroom....well, you have to see it for yourself...its fucking unbelievable!" Then laughed outright. Intrigued; Alex and Jericho made their way up the stairs and stood in the bedroom doorway, with a very amused Wilson.

It was a shrine to Adolf Hitler and the Nazi party. There were flags and busts of 'Der Fuhrer', pictures of Nazi soldiers and politicians, maps and a big cabinet of Nazi regalia. Owen checked his mirror again and was even more amazed; "Our Nazi loving friend is originally Pakistani in origin. What the fuck is he doing with all this?" Wilson chuckled and jabbed a finger towards the huge portrait of Hitler on the wall opposite. The painter/artist had placed a halo around Adolf's head!

Jericho just stared around the room in total disbelief; "In all my years, not much has really surprised me, but this has to be the mother of all surprises." Alex folded her arms; "This doesn't make any bloody sense. An English born descendant of a Pakistani family is a Neo-Nazi?" That's when she saw the little white packet on the small, ornate table by the door. She picked it up; "Photographs." She said and opened the packet.

Everyone stood around; there were loads of photographs of Hitler and his cronies, what appears to be Berlin; draped in Nazi flags. There were old cars from the thirties and everyone in the pictures appeared to be dressed for the period, including the wearing of 'Swastika' armbands. "Anyone spot the bloody odd thing out?" She said softly.

Owen picked out a couple of pictures and nodded; "They're all in fucking colour. Very unusual for the time." Alex just sighed and held up two photographs that had really caught her eye. Jericho took the pictures and nodded; "It's our Nazi loving little friend; in Berlin in the late 1930's. But look how he's dressed? That clothing is straight out of the Edwardian era." Wilson stared about the room; "So Harry was right; he was onto something. But how the hell did Rashid end up in Nazi Germany, when the portal is set for 1906?" Alex threw the packet back on the little table and whispered; "It has to be the clock tower next."

But Owen rubbed his face and folded his arms; "Why was the little Nazi prick buying Victorian and Edwardian coins, when he was visiting 1930's fucking Nazi Germany?" No-one had an answer to that intriguing question. "Let's go." Was all Jericho said and they departed for the van.

They were climbing into the van when a nice old lady from next door appeared at her gate, clutching a huge ginger and white cat. She beckoned them over. Jericho and Alex smiled and walked across to her. "Have they found him yet?" She asked, sounding quite concerned. They chatted together for a few minutes and Alex stroked the appreciative cat.

Wilson and Owen sat in the van and watched; "I wonder if the dear old girl knows that her neighbour is a fucking Nazi?" Owen asked and swigged from his plastic bottle of water; he handed it to Wilson, who chuckled; "Who would suspect an English Pakistani is a bloody Nazi? That's like finding one of my brothers in the KKK." Jericho and Alex re-joined them in the van. "It appears our Nazi friend has been missing for about a week. No one has seen or heard from him for days. Nothing; didn't turn up for work or even call his mother, who he's very close to apparently. No sign of him." Jericho told his team.

Alex chuckled; "According to Nan [the old lady] he's a lovely young man, nice and quiet, no noisy parties and he's good to his mum - apparently - and of course; an animal lover." Jericho just sighed; "So was Adolf bloody Hitler."

Owen grunted; "Who's feeding the bloody dog then?" Alex smiled and gestured towards the old lady; "Apparently 'Rommel' and Osborne are the best of friends; they play together." Owen leaned back in his seat; "The cat is called Osborne and the bloody dog is called Rommel?" Alex nodded and sipped her water bottle. "Well, she certainly hasn't poked her nose into that spare bedroom, or she would have a very different opinion about the nice young man next door." Wilson muttered and started the van.

6. THE TOWER.

It took nearly two hours to reach the clock tower; the traffic was horrendous. It took some time to find a parking space and they had to walk nearly fifteen minutes to the tower. "Too many buildings, too many cars, too many people and far too much noise." Jericho was not impressed with the changes since he last visited in 1901. They passed three local lads, sitting on the kerbside drinking cans of beer and smoking dope. Owen just stared at them; coming from a Medieval Monastery in the middle of rural Yorkshire; he was suffering a little 'culture shock'.

They [the lads] swore and stuck up their fingers; asking what the fuck he was looking at? Wilson just stared at them, and they went back to fighting amongst themselves and drinking beer. One made an obscene gesture towards Alex and told her what he wanted to do with her arse. They all laughed about that. She just ignored them.

They found that the tower was now part of a small heritage museum on site. The place was almost empty and the young Indian woman running reception told them the tower was open and that would be fifteen pounds each; to view the bloody thing! Jericho slapped the money down without comment.

Alex asked her about Harry and his team; had she seen them? She shrugged her shoulders and sat back down without saying anything. She was reading a Jeffry Archer novel and wasn't really interested in who went up the tower - as long as they paid. They climbed the stairs, standing aside, so that a party of Japanese tourists could make their way down. They even photographed themselves on the staircase and at the foot of the stairs. Jericho just shook his head; "See what I mean, about when civilisation really ended?" He muttered to Wilson, who just smiled.

They were the only 'tourists' in the clock room and Jericho discretely pulled out his mirror and gestured towards the cage that surrounded the clock mechanism; "It's in there." He said quietly looking about. "The lock won't prove a problem; will it?" Owen asked Wilson, who was already examining it. He shook his head. Jericho suddenly raised his hand and fumbled in his coat jacket pocket; he pulled out his orb and everyone could see the red streaks around its circumference. A powerful demon had passed this way and recently. "Shit!" said Owen and consulted his mirror for reports about the place; from Demon Ingress. Jericho was already contacting control for a Knights assistance - on the hurry up. "We're going no-where until we get assistance." He said quietly and Wilson gestured towards the cages lock; "It's open - someone had already forced the lock."

They heard footsteps coming up the stairs and so the orb and any mirrors were hastily hidden in pockets. They all sighed with some relief; it was James - a Knight of God - and he smiled broadly and shook hands all round. He especially lingered over Alex's handshake; it was well known that he a 'bit of a thing for her' - like most males. James stood hands on hips and did not smile; "It's that sneaky bastard Kiri. He's back." Owen had just received that information via his mirror - but then, Knights of God didn't need mirrors!

"Harry never called for Knight's assistance, but then the traces are quite recent." Jericho said, as he and James chatted together, and Alex was peering through the cage at the clock mechanism. She turned to Wilson; "What's that on the floor, right there by the bare brickwork in the corner?" Wilson knelt down and peered through the bars. "I think it's an old coin. An old English penny I think." He was just able to reach it and showed to it to the team. "Victorian. 1898." Owen lowered his mirror. "Either someone just dropped it or its lain there - unseen - for over a hundred years and I think I know which is the right answer."

"Shall we go?" James gestured to the cage and Wilson pulled it open; they disappeared into the time portal at the very rear of the small room. They all cloaked themselves in anticipation of meeting living humans on the other side, sometime in the middle Edwardian period for the London Docks. They were mistaken about that and several other things.

They had appeared in the dirty, grim backroom of a Berlin music shop, coming out from the old fireplace. The wall's were covered with posters about records and music - all pre-war [the second one]. The shelves had stacks of boxes, filled with gramophone records. There were books about composers and their music stacked in one corner; they looked like they had not been read in sometime. They could all hear the noise coming from outside the small window. Jericho had to wipe the dirty window to see out. There was a big parade going on outside; it was passing the top of the alley that the room looked over. "Fucking Nazi's." Was all Wilson said. It was a Nazi parade with flags, uniforms, and banners. The crowds appeared to be cheering and shouting enthusiastically. Owen held up his mirror, quite grim faced; "Check your mirrors - mine's offline - no signals, nothing." Everyone agreed with him; their mirrors were not working.

Jericho took a deep breath; "Do you realise that if we didn't have James with us; we would be stuck here." Wilson grunted; "That might explain what happened to Harry and Team 52; they're trapped here."

Alex stared out the window and shouted; "What are those bastards doing?" Everyone squeezed around the window. Four Nazi's in uniform had dragged an old man in a black coat and hat into the alley. They were punching and kicking him. Shouting and laughing, they left him laying on the road. He tried to raise himself a couple of times but couldn't. "Come on!" Alex shouted and pulled at the door; it was locked, frustrated she kicked it and went back to the window. The old man lay ominously still in the quiet alley.

That's when they heard the lock being turned on the door.

7. THE OLD MUSIC SHOP.

James actually smiled as the door swung open; he already knew who was on the other side. The old man peered in, clutching the big key with both hands. He turned and spoke to the person who was behind him; "There is no one here my dear. No one." They heard a woman's voice say, "There is Franz, you just watch." Everyone in the room realised that James had uncloaked them - yes, Knights really don't need mirrors!

The old man jumped but didn't seem really surprised by his small back room being suddenly filled with people. Alex rushed to the door and embraced Temporal Detective Lisa Solomon, who looked like she had just won the National lottery's top prize - without having to buy a damn ticket. "They beat up an old man, he's lying..."Alex frantically told her and pushed past the pair.

Lisa gripped her arm; "its ok Alex; Tom and Wolfe are already on their way out there." Alex sighed with relief. Lisa said quietly; "It's bloody common around here. Harry won't let me go out because, well, I really do look Jewish - which isn't strange - considering I was - when alive." She managed to smile, and the pair held each other again.

Lisa then introduced them to old Franz; "He owns this little shop and over the years has seen a few strange people pop out the fireplace. He's not a Nazi supporter; in fact, he detests the bastards and what they're doing to his country. He's being hiding us here. None of the bloody mirrors will work. The portal is one way only and has apparently changed its destination since we checked it last." Owen rubbed his chin; "Who the hell is Wolfe?" He knew that Team 52's trainee was a small Japanese fellow called Suki. Lisa laughed; "His name is Wolfgang; he's Franz's grandson. I call him Wolfe and he seems to like that."

Jericho stared back at the fireplace; "This is just an exit, the portal back in 2019 is a rotating one - a very dangerous aberration - which means it can send its traveler anywhere in time, provided he or she is holding an object from that period. Our little Nazi friend must have had something from this time period on him; something made here. I wonder if he was surprised by the new destination."

Wilson grunted; "If it's one way, how did he get back to place those photographs in his Hitler Shrine?" James smiled; "There must be at least two of them and the second person must have his own control device or be..." Owen had practically read James's mind; "A bloody demon?" He asked. James nodded; "Kiri often uses humans and just abandon's them - the bastard."

The old man gestured down the stairs and mentioned that the coffee pot was on the stove and he had some Schnapps'; if anyone wanted something stronger. Now that did make Owen smile. They could hear the commotion from downstairs and a young boy shouting for his grandfather to come. "Grandpa, its old Mr. Herron, they've beaten him badly." Alex and Lisa ran down the stairs and the old man followed much more slowly; he spoke to Owen, who was behind him; "My days of running anywhere are long gone. The only time I move quickly is for the toilet and when someone opens' a new brandy bottle." He chuckled to himself, and Wilson exchanged an amused glance with Owen, who rubbed his hands together in anticipation.

Jericho and James stood at the top of the stairs and spoke quietly; "There must be a Judas Stone nearby; that's the only thing the 'Dark Side' has that would close down mirrors. If I recall, the last time we encountered Kiri, the bastard had one." James walked slowly down the stairs, with Jericho behind, who did remember his last encounter with Kiri [The Episode: **'Cordless, Cordless & Fraser (Solicitors)'**] When they had been trapped without mirrors. He really was glad that he called James.

It appears Kiri - with some forethought - and secreted a 'Judas Stone' near the time portal exit [the old fireplace] to catch out temporal Detectives on his trail; and it had worked. James always said that; 'He [Kiri] was a sneaky bastard!'

Tom and Wolfe had placed old Mr. Herron in the big office chair that sat behind Franz's desk, which was covered in papers, magazines and vinyl records. He was bleeding about the face and couldn't move the fingers on one hand. Alex examined him and realised he needed an x-ray; the cuts and bruises she could easily deal. with. Mr. Herron thanks her several times but said he couldn't go to hospital. He pointed to the 'Star of David' on his arm. The local hospital wouldn't take him. They didn't treat Jews.

"Little wonder Harry doesn't let you out. The bastards would really have fun with you." Wilson spoke quietly to Lisa; who just nodded with some sadness. Everyone sat around the little shop and drank coffee and brandy; old Franz was a very good host and clearly had acquired some affection for Lisa. He treated and spoke to her like a much-loved granddaughter. He wasn't Jewish, but many of his old friends were. He pointed out, like him, they had served their country, in the trenches of the last war. [The First World War] His disgust with Hitler and the Nazi's was really apparent.

Owen sat on the floor with young Wolfe, drinking coffee, and Owen said to Jericho; "We have a real problem. If the time portal is one way and our little Neo-Nazi friend jumped through it; How did he get the pictures of himself back to 2019? If we can find an answer to that, it would certainly help." Everyone in the team nodded at that conundrum. Alex sipped a very welcome brandy and checked old Mr. Herron again. James almost smiled; "Kiri.

Like I said, certainly has the power to travel where he likes and we've already picked up traces of him." Jericho sighed; "And the bast...bugger would certainly like this little time period of human history." He had moderated his language because young Wolfe was listening with great interest. His grandfather told the boy to refill the kettle and put more coffee on. He left the room with great reluctance. That's when there were several soft knocks on the front door. Owen carefully lifted the 'closed' shutter and peered out. He smiled broadly; "It's Harry and Suki."

He unlocked the door and the pair squeezed in; carrying shopping bags. Everyone greeted them with some warmth; Especially Alex with Harry; that didn't go un-noticed! They had picked up some supplies, another bottle of Cognac, fresh bread, fruit and cheese, with a huge German sausage. Harry handed the food and the change, from the money Franz had given them, over to Franz and patted the old man. He turned to Jericho - unsmiling - and pulled off his jacket. He said quietly; "The place is crawling with bloody demons. My orb was practically blood red." He pulled the 'Swastika' arm band off his discarded jacket; Suki did the same.

Little Suki did not smile; "The bloody Nazi's kept shaking my hands and offering me booze. Apparently, my people are now their Allies." He said that with some real disgust and like Harry, handed his armband back to Franz. They both accepted coffee from Lisa and Harry propped himself on old Franz's desk. "Our strange little, Nazi loving friend won't be going home, and his soul is now in the darkness. He was picked up by the Gestapo and they didn't take kindly to an Indian fellow claiming he was devotee of Adolf. They beat him to death and dumped in body in the local woods. I suspect there are quite a few missing people in there."

"I think that's called Karma." Muttered Wilson and chuckled to himself. But Owen sighed; "Now we'll never know why he was collecting those old notes and coins." Alex sipped her coffee and said quietly; "I suspect that he was heading back to 1905 or around that time and ended up here. Whoever was with him, returned and ditched those photographs at the 'Shrine'. If it's Kiri, then he's probably using the house now for his own ends. He probably has more supporters there, Nazi friends of the dead man. What better proof of his powers, than those photographs? That's bound to recruit the other Neo-Nazi's to his cause."

It appears that young Rashid had travelled through the portal - the first time - and ended up in 1906. It was still standing at that date when Harry and Team 52 had checked it. He must have met up with Kiri in that time period [a demon like him, would know when humans cross through time] and they teamed up.

But for whatever reason; Rashid had used the portal again; this time dressed for the period and with lots of money to use there. Except the 'rotating' gateway had thrown him to Nazi Germany in the thirties. He must have been carrying a strong object from that time. He had no demon with him to affect a return; he was stuck here and that ended badly; he couldn't return because he had fallen into the wrong hands and killed.

8. SOME ORIGINS OF EVIL REVEALLED.

The sounds of a commotion in the street could be heard and Franz lifted the door blind a little, he turned with some real sadness on his old face. "They're smashing old Joseph's windows and looting his shop." Mr. Herron just sighed and wiped his bandaged hand over his face; "I sent Ester to her sisters - thank God." He said and sipped some coffee that Wolfe had given him. Owen stared at the date marked on the calendar behind Franz's desk. "Sweet Jesus; it's the first of September 1939 and Germany has just invaded Poland and started the bloody Second World War!"

Everyone looked at the fragile old man, sitting helplessly on the floor of his old friends shop and all thought the same thing; the 'Final Solution' to Germany's 'Jewish problem' would soon be underway; extermination - mass murder on an industrialized, horrific scale - would now start in earnest. Alex saw Lisa wipe her damp face several times and cuddled her friend. The two women were silent; they didn't have to say anything for the others to understand.

Finally, Jericho turned to Franz and asked him, if had had seen a young Indian fellow appear from the fireplace and disappear down the back stairs. Franz nodded; "Young Wolfgang told me that a little brown man had come from the room with another; a big white fellow and they were laughing and joking together. I never saw them." James had to chuckle; "I'm surprised that you take all this so calmly; I mean all those strange people appearing out of the fireplace and disappearing down your back stairs into the street. Have you ever wondered about that?"

Old Franz smiled; "My Father and grandfather always said they were just visiting and would do us no harm. This shop has been in my family since 1790. The rear parts are all original; the rest has been refurbished over the many years that this shop has stood here. I have seen many such people since I was a child." He shrugged his shoulders and started to rummage in the shopping bags that Harry and Suki had returned with.

Jericho rubbed his face and stared at the old man; there was something very familiar about him. "May I ask Franz, what is your family name?" Franz looked up and smiled; "Leitcher." Jericho and Wilson slowly rose from the floor and then looked at Franz's grandson; "Is young Wolfe named after your father?" Franz seemed a little surprised by that question; "Yes, Wolfgang is a traditional name in our family. My own grandfather was called Wolfgang Franz Leitcher."

Everyone in Team 74 just stared at the gentle old man and remembered their adversary; Wolfgang Leitcher [from two episodes; **'The man who died in the future to save his past'** and **'The Dunmore Witch Trials'**] Jericho asked quietly; "Was your ancestor - the first one in your family - to purchase this shop, was he called Wolfgang Leitcher?" Franz nodded; "Yes, like I said; he bought the shop in 1790. I believe he was some sort of music professor or such like. Probably why music has always been part of my family's life down the generations."

Alex touched the old man's arm: "Are there any strange stories about him; your ancestor, I mean?" Franz nodded; "Family gossip has it, that old Wolfgang was ill - dying apparently - and with his final strength, sought out a healer, who lived in the woods. Well, it is said that he was gone for some time. Then returned home; miraculously cured by the stranger in the woods. But within months; he simply vanished and was never seen or heard of again. But it is just family legend."

Wilson whispered to Jericho; "And we know who the bloody healer in the woods was." Alex folded her arms; "Now that's bloody Karma, his ancestor tries to bump us off and his descendant saves Team 52." Jericho nodded and grunted; "Yes, something about the sins of the father and his children come to mind." James interrupted their quiet discussion; "I think it's time we all went home. I need to close the portal here and the one in the clock tower."

"Hope you got fifteen quid for that one." Owen grunted and finished his brandy.

Everyone said a very warm farewell to their gentle and generous host and his grandson. James closed the portal in the fireplace, then noticed that the door, at the bottom of the rear stairs - that opened onto the back alley - was swinging open. James stared at the fireplace; "Two humans have passed through here whilst we were downstairs. I really need to close that portal in the tower." Then everyone was gone.

Franz stood in the doorway and ruffled his grandson's dark hair; "Don't worry boy, Old great Uncle Wolfgang will soon have it open again for visitors." The pair returned to the shop, they would have to arrange for poor Mr. Herron to get home, after dark and avoiding the Nazi patrols; that were searching the streets for Jews. That's when the shop bell tinkled and old Franz shouted; "Sorry, we're closed." Owen must have left the damn door unlocked when he let in Harry and Suki.

Franz and Wolfgang stood in the quiet shop and looked about; there was nobody there and Mr. Joseph Herron had gone. Franz sighed; "He's probably worried about Ester; they have been married nearly forty years." He smiled and locked the door. He sent young Wolfe to clean up the kitchen and fetch his coat; Franz would walk the boy home. He sat at his desk and pulled the bottom drawer open; he slowly removed the big money box from the back and placed it on his desk.

He slowly lifted the lid and stared at his pile of Victorian Coins and Edwardian notes. He really didn't like lying to those nice young people, but he and Wolfgang had their plan. He lifted one coin; it was an Edwardian half crown and tossed it in his hand. He was a little sorry about the confused young Rashid; but Franz had warned him about dealing with Nazi's - he didn't listen - and now he was in a shallow grave in the woods. But he had added considerably to the old money that the pair was collecting for the 'Great Plan'.

Young Wolfe appeared in the doorway and grinned at his grandfather. "I'm going to be a very rich young man when I go there Grandpa." The old man nodded; "And you will change everything. No Nazi's and Britain on Imperial Germany's side. Your future will be golden Wolfgang." He smiled and dropped the coin back into the box.

THE END

EPILOGUE:

"The mission was deemed a success, despite the mix up earlier between the two teams. A very dangerous time portal had been closed. But the time travelling Leitcher family would prove a pain in the neck for Jericho and Team 74."
SJW.

CHARACTERS:

Teresa Green served as Jericho's human agent for some years. She never married or bore any children. She died in 2032 and her soul was collected and processed. Jericho and Alex attended her funeral. She now works as a Collector but has applied to join the Temporal Detectives Department. She has asked - repeatedly - to be assigned to Inspector Harry Hadden's team...

Tom Reddigge quickly recovered from his breakup with Teresa and over the next few years, dated several women - and young men - he finally married and had two children. But was caught by his young wife with one of his 'boyfriends'; unlike Teresa; she didn't just throw him out. He survived the knife wounds but died of Sepsis some weeks later. His soul was collected and processed.

Ellen Stanton never did get to university; she met a young woman at college and the pair set up home together and had two children. She died in 2054. Her soul was collected and processed.

Rosemary Ellen Cornwallis suffered ill health and had to give up her stall in the market. The diagnosis was not good; the cancer spread quickly, and Rosie died in 2022. Her soul was collected and processed.

Rashid Kamill had died outside his own ordained time period and his soul was lost to the darkness. It was never recovered and remains missing to this day. His dog 'Rommel' was finally adopted by his lovely old neighbour.

Franz Leitcher did not survive the war and was killed a few days after Russian troops entered Berlin. He was sitting in the ruins of his little shop, when a Russian forward patrol discovered him. They didn't even speak to the gentle old man; they simply shot him dead where he sat. His soul was collected and processed.

Wolfgang Henrik Leitcher survived the war and moved to the ancient city of Baden-Baden in 1948. He purchased an old town house that had a strange reputation and in 1951, he simply disappeared from the Human Timeline, in mysterious circumstances. The matter is under investigation by Inspector Jericho Tibbs and Team 74. There is no resolution yet.

Joseph Herron did not survive the Nazi regime [nor did his wife]. He was sent to Treblinka Concentration camp in May 1941 and only lived for a few days. His soul was collected and processed.

EPISODE 5: "NAPOLEON'S CHINESE CABINET OF MAGIC – PART 1."

MISSION SUMMARY: "Emperor Napoleon receives Ambassadors from the Chinese Emperor and they present him with a very special gift - a magic cabinet! - Napoleon and his staff are cynical about its magic properties until the three Chinese Ambassadors enter the cabinet and simply disappear - for good. But Napoleon is struggling to retain his crown; will he use the gift to change his fortunes?"

NOTES: Part one of a two part mission.

TRIGGER WARNINGS. ALCOHOL, STRONG LANGUAGE, SEXUAL REFERENCES AND MILD VIOLENCE.

AGE 12+ ONLY. **30 Minutes reading time.**

1. A GIFT FROM ONE GOD TO ANOTHER.

Captain Jean Pullaire stared at the crate which had been lowered with great care onto the polished wooden floor. He rubbed his chin in puzzlement and spoke quietly to the two footmen standing next to him; "Fetch Colonel Le Grande and inform his Majesty the gift from the Chinese Emperor has arrived and get some labourers to open the damn crate." He turned and smiled at the three strange little men with feathers adorning their small black hats; he had to admit that he had never seen a real Chinese man before and these three resembled exactly the drawings he had viewed in his youth. "I have sent for men to open the crate, Lord Yin." He nodded at the smallest of the trio, who bowed and in prefect French thanked the captain for his assistance.

From around his neck, Lord Yin produced a gold key fixed upon a gold chain and spoke directly to Captain Pullaire; "I need to place this key directly into your God's hand – it was placed directly into mine by my God Emperor Yongyan and must be passed on in the same manner." The little China man bowed yet again and smiled.

Several burly labourers had arrived with removed hats, accompanied by Monsieur Cission; the Emperors Chief Carpenter who viewed the heavy crate with an expert eye. "Use the bloody bars carefully you morons." He said, wiping his face with a clean polishing rag. The old man sighed; not more bloody pieces of expensive wood to maintain – the Palace of Fontainebleau was full of the stuff and now bloody foreigners from the other side of the world were sending their gilded crap!

He stared at the three China amen and blew his nose hard into the polishing cloth; "We'll undress her gently Captain." Monsieur Cission smiled at Pullaire with a mouthful of yellow teeth and wiped snot from his heavy grey moustache, adding; "Will his majesty be present when we open her?"

That question was answered by the regulated stamp of army boots upon the shining wooden floor and through the doors, hurriedly opened by a sweaty Footman, came a dozen of the 'Old Guard'. With precision they took up positions around the room and snapped to attention at the command of their young Lieutenant. Pullaire and Cissions exchanged glances; Lieutenant Vaccaro was not a popular officer or man, who held his Commission directly because of who his father may be: The Emperor.

"I see the little poodle still hasn't found a hat small enough for his tiny brain." Cission whispered to the captain who wagged a disapproving finger at the far too blunt carpenter – but smiled broadly. The Lieutenant's hat was clearly too large and had been the subject of arguments between him and the Quartermaster of the Regiment; without success it appears.

Quartermaster Possini had informed the young man that Officer's supply their own uniform and that naturally; included the hat. But Vaccaro had been unable to find a decent Milliner to furnish such a small hat at a reasonable price – his ungenerous nature added to his unpopular character. So in desperation, he had purchased the hat from a another young Lieutenant who was dying in the local infirmary from wounds received in Prussia – the fact that he gave the young widow a handful of centimes for it, really did his popularity no good. To quote many; 'he was as unpopular as would be finding Wellington in the Emperors bathtub.'

Vaccaro gave Pullaire a clumsy salute and announced that Colonel Le Grande was attending the emperor and they would appear within minutes. Pullaire returned the salute but said nothing. The appearance of Marshal Nay in the chamber signaled the arrival of Napoleon. A large gaggle of Officers and Politian's poured into the small chamber, splitting into little groups and all staring at the strangers who stood quietly by the crate, which was being opened with great care under Cission's direction.

Napoleon sauntered into the room and all conversations stopped. Le Grande spoke directly to him and pointed at the Chinese group; "The small chink is called Lord Yin, he's apparently their Emperors Ambassador, I don't know about the other two, you're Majesty."

The three bowed low as Pullaire whispered to Le Grande; "He speaks perfect French." Le Grande shrugged his shoulders and grunted; "Thank you Pullaire, now get on with it – the emperor is a busy man." Le Grande was not marked out for a career in Diplomacy. But he was a damn good Officer on the field of battle and possessed a characteristic that Napoleon looked for in all his officers; he was lucky.

Le Grande had been shot off his horse on no less than four occasions and walked away with just scratches, and then during one battle, his churning stomach forced him to find a quiet clump of trees to relieve the pain. Squatting down with liquid fire emerging from his bowels, he saw through the trees that the Austrians had left a gap in their right flank to bring up the supply wagons. Clutching his trousers, Le Grande reported the mistake to Marshal Nay. French troops poured through the gap and the Austrians fled the battlefield in disarray. Napoleon had thanked the Captain himself and promoted him to Headquarters' staff with the rank of Colonel.

Napoleon gestured to Lord Yin and the little China man approached bowing quite low: "Your brother Emperor Yongyan sends greetings of love and friendship and hopes you will be pleased with this little gift." He offered the gold key and chain with both hands and Napoleon took it slowly and smiled; "Please inform your Emperor that I will be most pleased to accept any gift from my dear brother and send him my warm regards."

There were little gasps of admiration from the crowd as the final pieces of the dull grey crate were stripped away; revealing a black and silver cabinet decorated with astronomical symbols and gold dragons – it was tall as a man, wide as a double wardrobe and deep as a card table; it was simply magnificent; a real masterpiece.

Napoleon nodded his approval to Lord Yin who spoke quietly to the Emperor, positioning his back to all others; "My Lord, with such a gift that can only be shared amongst God's comes a responsibility – a great responsibility - You must never open or enter the cabinet during the hours of darkness and keep her locked at all times. Please keep that key upon your person, no mere mortal must have access to her; only you."

The Emperor looked quite puzzled by his comments and studied the simple gold key; "What does the cabinet contain my Lord Yin?" He asked and the strange little man smiled and ran his long fingernails through his grey beard; "Darkness and light your majesty."

Lord Yin bowed low, then walked over to the cabinet and opened the doors; a stunning white light shone from the interior making everyone step back, but Napoleon felt himself drawn to it and peered inside, shielding his eyes a little. The interior panels were decorated with glass and silver and Napoleon realised at once; that none of the 'mirrors' showed a reflection.

He turned slowly to Lord Yin and said quietly; "How old is she?" Lord Yin held up his hands and said, "We believe that four such cabinets were created by the God TAI-SUI-XING and given as presents to the early Emperors of the great Chin dynasty; they came into being at the start of human time." He smiled and added; "The interior panels have been re-housed many times over the Centuries, the present construction is only some four hundred years old and so should last; at least that again."

Lord Yin bowed again and gestured to his two silent colleagues, who shuffled gracefully into the cabinet, and both bowed low. He turned to Napoleon and spoke quietly; "We must now return home and report all is well between the great European God and our father who resides in the Heavens - Farewell my Lord and remember that light is darkness to devils and darkness is light to them." Lord Yin stepped into the cabinet of TAI-SUI-XING and slowly closed the doors.

Everyone stood in silence for a few moments until Le Grande tapped gently on the doors and called out; "Lord Yin, what the fuck are you doing?" The emperor smiled and told Le Grande to open the cabinet and help the crazy China men out of his gift.

Everyone was laughing until the doors were opened; the three Chinese men had vanished - completely. There was total silence in the room for some time until Marshal Ney shouted for guards to search the Palace and grounds for the mysterious visitors.

Napoleon and the carpenter Cission examined the cabinet closely and found it solid. He ordered Cission to have it removed to his private study and locked the doors with the gold key; which he hung about his neck. He gripped Cission by the shoulder and said quietly; "I have a task for you my old friend and it must be kept between the two of us." Cission nodded his head; the old carpenter had known the emperor since the days of the Revolution.

But no trace of the three Chinese 'Magicians' were ever found, and no-one was allowed near the gift without Napoleon's express permission - But the Emperor had more pressing matters to contend with; his abdication.

2. A STAR FALLS FROM HEAVEN.

Napoleon quietly unlocked the rear study door and peered out into the corridor; two of his 'Old Guard' was posted at the far end. Napoleon relocked the door and sat down at his large ornate desk and held his head with both hands. He must have sat for some minutes before he heard the gentle tap from the Chinese cabinet. He rose slowly and walked over to it; carefully unlocking the doors and stepping back. The doors opened and she stepped from the cabinet into his study. Lady Helena Covington smiled at her lover, and they embraced for some minutes. "I do love you in dresses of this time; they suit you much better than those damn tents you wear back there." Napoleon kissed the bare cleavage she was showing in her low cut 'Regency' dress. Her breasts had been pushed well up and if she sneezed; her nipples would escape; along with most of her breasts.

Tall and thin with dark Raven hair and soft brown eyes, Lady Helena was considered a beauty at the Royal Court of Queen Victoria in 1864. She had married the wealthy Lord Covington at just eighteen - he was forty-five, fat and failed to bath regally. But he owned a fabulous Chinese cabinet that, it was rumoured, had belonged to Emperor Napoleon I.

Lady Helena had only been married some six weeks and already had enough of her boring, lethargic husband and she avoided his company, as best she could; Covington House had some seventy rooms and she still felt that wasn't enough space to keep away from him. At least he left her alone in the bedroom - he was as impotent as he was smelly.

Then one day she found a fabulous Chinese cabinet hidden in the attic's and wondered why such a stunning piece of furniture wasn't on display in the house's main rooms. Her husband wouldn't explain anything; except that she was to keep away from it and he actually ordered her to do so. The very next morning, after Lord Covington had gone to the City of London, she was back in the attic and trying to open the cabinet. It was locked tight with no key apparent.

It took several days before Helena found that the key was kept in her husband's Library, inside a book about Napoleon and she rushed to the attic and opened the cabinet. She noticed immediately that there was no reflection showing from the mirrors it contained. Some strange force compelled her to step in and close the door. Lady Helena glanced down to the book she was carrying; 'The life and times of Napoleon Bonaparte.' She chuckled to herself and tried to open the door - it was locked.

But she still held the key! She had heard no-one locking her in.

Panicking a little at first, she struggled with the doors until she heard a voice outside; "Please, please help me. I can't get the doors open and strangely enough; there are no dam key-holes inside here." She shouted and heard the door locks being turned; they must have had a key too - but who was it?

She stepped from the cabinet and stared at the man who had rescued her; it was Napoleon Bonaparte, who had been dead some 43 years, but was very much alive. He took her hand and kissed it. He explained about the cabinet and what had happened to her for some minutes, and they drank wine together. A walk in the gardens, of Fontainebleau Palace, put her mind to rest about possibly going insane.

Two hours after arriving in 1814 France, Lady Helena Covington was 'cuckolding' her husband with the French Emperor [who had actually died before she was even born] they enjoyed passionate sex on the floor of the Imperial bedroom which included a sexual activity that was frowned upon by the Church and forbidden in law. Helena couldn't actually believe what Napoleon was doing to her bum and she cried throughout the ordeal - but made no effort to stop him.

He had told his new lover, that clothes from the 'hereafter' were bloody awful and ugly. So he arranged for some dresses of the 'Regency' period to be made for her - with a particularly low cut bodice and she delighted in wearing the tighter, clinging dresses of his time, than the current fashion [of 1864] which she now considered shapeless, awkward and about sexually attractive as wearing a tent.

Now, almost four months into their 'time-travelling' romance, she had arrived to comfort her lover on a very important day - his abdication. But wrapped tightly in brown paper and string was a modest little book; it contained details of Emperor Napoleon's last 100 days as Emperor - including the all important, world changing Battle of Waterloo. It was hidden in Lady Helena's travelling bag. A little present for her lover that didn't detail his death but could change his imminent future. She had, wisely, removed the pages that dealt with his final demise.

"I hate those dresses I'm forced to wear, as you say, it's like wearing a bloody tent my darling." She kissed him quite passionately and he pushed both hands up the back of her dress and gripped her bum. "I still think it strange that you are not even born yet my little dove." Napoleon muttered and they exchanged kisses again; his excited fingers, reluctantly, left her arse and he pulled at the back of her dress. She slowly began to strip off her clothes; "I want you naked." he whispered, and Lady Helena stepped from his arms and pulled her dress down. She was naked apart from her little pink shoes.

"Take me." Was all Lady Helena said - and Napoleon didn't need to be told twice. Their passion was satisfied some hours later and both lay on the bed, staring at each other. The Emperor rose and threw a dressing gown about himself; "I have an unpleasant meeting with my ministers in a few minutes. I will be back in about an hour." Lady Helena grabbed a sheet and half covered herself, she leaned back on two pillows and closed her eyes. The little bedroom clock was chiming one o'clock. She sat upright and stared at the private doorway to the bedroom. The emperor, in uniform, stood smiling at her.

Lady Helena grinned and pulled the sheet from her naked body and lay back, opening her legs. She said nothing and neither did the emperor. They made love for another hour before the emperor, yet again, had to go. She lay breathing heavy for a few minutes and then heard the clock chiming above the fireplace. She stared at it for a few seconds; then realized it must be losing time. It was still only two o'clock, she was a little puzzled by that.

She lay in the bed and watched Napoleon dress and go. She leaned back and sat upright - again. This time surprised; The Emperor was in the doorway; why had he returned so quick? She pushed her hair from her face and smiled a little. He was pulling off his jacket; "I told you I wouldn't be long, my darling." She just stared at him; utterly amazed at his stamina. But laid back on the covers and watched him undress.

That afternoon Napoleon finished his bath and dressed slowly. The meeting with his Marshal's had not ended happily; every single one had demanded he abdicate to prevent the Allied armies swarming into Paris. He had been particularly hurt by the apparent betrayal of Marshall Nay. He stared at the colourful calendar hanging on his dressing room wall; April 11th, 1814. If only he had more time...a little more time, but time was so precious now and trickling through his fingers like beach sand. He had run out of that most vital commodity: time.

Napoleon had dressed without a servant and walked slowly to his study. He sat at his desk and stared at the single, large piece of paper that was the only item upon the large ornate table: The Abdication document. He rested his head on his hands and memories and thoughts clouded into his very troubled mind. He must have sat for some minutes like that and then slowly lifted his head; staring at the Chinese cabinet - the emperor smiled.

3. WHAT COULD BE.

Alex looked quite stunning; even Wilson and Owen had to admit that. She smiled at Jericho and nodded her head; "You really do carry a uniform well. I'm quite pleasantly surprised." She also grinned at Wilson who really did look resplendent in his servant's livery, but he didn't smile; "Why do I always have to play the bloody loyal black servant to his white master?" He groaned - then smiled.

Alex chuckled; "Because you do it so well!" Wilson shook his head and stuck up a single finger, then muttered; "Why can't I, just for once, play the master and Jericho the servant?" Alex patted the big man; "You know it really doesn't bother you - you don't have his enormous ego to please!" Jericho just sighed and finished checking his costume.

Owen looked himself up and down; he really didn't appreciate his young gentleman's outfit of the time. "The bleeding trousers are far too tight; no wonder they were always at war." He muttered and adjusted the crotch of his trousers - again. Wilson slapped his hand away; "Jesus, any excuse to play with yourself." Owen stuck up a single finger and pulled at his trousers yet again.

Everyone chuckled, and Jericho placed his Colonel's hat upon his head; "Now, now children, we ALL look really good in our new play clothes. Let's get going, Supplies have everything ready." He smiled at Alex; "How's your French Madame?" Alex curtsied; "Mon français va bien, à toi?" Jericho just nodded and stared at himself in the mirror; "Not bad. Maybe I should have been a Military man - like my father wanted - and not a bloody lawyer." He said softly to no-one. They all headed for the light room and then had to wait - much to the amusement of Alex - for young

Ruth to appear. She was to be Alex's Lady Maid. No woman of quality would dare travel without one, in the time period that the team was heading for.

Ruth arrived - apologising to everyone - and received a 'wolf whistle' from Owen. She too, looked quite beautiful in his eyes. "I love the clothes of this period!" She exclaimed and joined the team. Jericho just sighed and the little group departed for France in 1814.

The carriage moved quite slowly through the mud of the Fontainebleau Road and rocked steadily. Ruth had her head against Alex's shoulder - she was a little tired - Ruth wasn't use to jumping into the light and like many who weren't accustomed to travelling in that way, felt tiredness sweep over her. Alex patted her hand and smiled at Jericho and Owen, who sat opposite. "A few hours and she'll be fine. In the 20th century they would have called it 'jet-lag'." Owen nodded; "Yep, our young Ruthie has 'Time-lag'."

Wilson leaned through the small window above their heads - he was riding with the driver - and said quietly; "About another twenty minutes." Jericho waved his hand in acknowledgement and turned to Alex; "Napoleon has acquired a new young mistress who is a total mystery to everyone at the Palace. Even Marshall Nay doesn't have a clue who she is. The place has hundreds of servant's and Imperial staff, yet none has caught, as much as a glance of her. How she comes and goes is another mystery, considering the security around the emperor. "

Owen sighed; "We know she exists because Napoleon's boot maker mentions her in a letter to his brother in 1816. He was convinced she was an English spy and he mentioned, but didn't elaborate, about what happened to poor Colonel Durand. So you had better watch yourself Jericho!" He smiled as Ruth roused herself and sat up; "Who's an English spy?" She asked. Owen said quietly; "Napoleon's mysterious mistress." Ruth nodded; "How many did he have - mysterious or not?"

Owen chuckled; "At this time and place, he had about nine." Ruth looked a little amazed and turned to Alex; "How did he find the bloody time to conquer Europe?" That did make Alex chuckle - she didn't know the answer to that.

"And I believe she could be the key to the strange changes that the current time-line is suffering. I've seen the alternative versions of history and they all directly start here at this time and place. The only difference IS the Emperor's new mistress. We need to find and identify her - urgently." Jericho said and checked his mirror for any mission updates.

Alex adjusted her breasts and groaned; "The dresses are gorgeous, but don't suit women with ample breasts." She said to Ruth, who just grinned.

"Yeah, but you won't find a single male complaining about that." Owen muttered and looked out the window, adding; "The palace is bloody gorgeous too." The grand Palace of Fontainebleau had now appeared, and they were approaching - slowly because of the mud. Owen pointed out that mud had affected the outcome at Waterloo and exactly a century later, The Western Front.

Wilson's head appeared and he smiled at Alex, fiddling with her bosom; "If either of those lovely big pups need a new home, I'm your man. By the way, we're entering the Palace through the South gate - apparently Jericho's not important enough - as a mere Colonel - to use the Grand Entrance." He wrapped his dark cloak about his big shoulders and chuckled. Jean Hessaine [the driver and a human agent of Jericho's for this time and place] laughed too.

"Steady there Wilson, I wouldn't mind taking both home myself - with Alex attached of course. She's about the most stunning woman I've ever seen, and I've seen some real crackers here and at Versailles. Old Bony [nickname of Emperor Napoleon] will be drooling in his soup at her, I can definitely tell you that." Jean smiled and slapped the reins; he didn't think much of Jericho's new team members - Owen and Alex - he had thoroughly enjoyed the company of Jericho's old team; Wilson, little Oscar - the crazy dwarf - and Jericho himself.

Jean recalled that the fourth member of Team 74 had been a real strange and moody bastard - he hardly said a word to Jean; or anybody else to be honest. But there was something about the bloody man that drew you to him - like a moth to a flame. Jean grunted; still Alex was a bonus - he would have fucked her at the drop of a hat - even if it damned his soul forever. That delicious thought was disturbed by Wilson pointing ahead, a small troop of cavalry was approaching, slowly through the mud.

"They check everyone and anything that gets within a few miles of old Boney." Jean nodded to Wilson, who leaned through the window again and announced visitors. Jericho was handed an old leather document case by Owen who grinned at the girls; "Best behaviour now ladies; all smiles and bosom's please!"

Alex stuck up a single finger and adjusted her dress - she was almost hanging out of it. "With those beauties staring at him, the young lieutenant won't be too interested in us or our travel papers." Owen chuckled and watched the cavalry troop approach. Jericho flicked through the papers in his old briefcase and smiled to himself. The briefcase had travelled a few miles and many years with him now. He clearly remembered the first day - with the brand-new case under his arm - that he spent at Gray, Ogden & Davis; Solicitors. He was the new junior partner of the famous old law firm. But his thoughts snapped back to here and now.

He smiled at Alex and Ruth; "Remember ladies, that if anyone will have information or knowledge of this mysterious woman, it will be the female staff and ladies of the court. I'm depending on you two and I know you'll come through." Both Alex and Ruth nodded as the carriage rolled to a stop and Wilson jumped down and opened the carriage door. Jericho stepped out and greeted the young Lieutenant, who dismounted with some grace from his sweating mare.

4. FONTAINEBLEAU PALACE.

Colonel Durand slapped his old briefcase down on the small ornate table and stared out the window at the rear grounds of the palace. He spoke in fluent French to his young Secretary; Monsieur Henri Legaurd. "Make sure you stick to old French - all the time - no slip up's. None." He cautioned Owen, who nodded and helped Wilson - now called Titus - to unpack the suitcases. "Alex and Ruth are just around the corner, in a beautiful suite decorated in the Chinese style. She always gets spoilt." Wilson muttered - in old French - and heaved the case upon the dark footlocker, at the bottom of the huge four poster bed.

Owen looked a little puzzled; "It's a strange tradition here that husbands and wives don't share the same rooms - why is that?"

He asked Jericho, who chuckled; "So they could entertain their lovers without embarrassing each other. Fidelity was not a large concern in these decadent days."

"Well, Spoilt or not, she certainly got us noticed, even if we came through the tradesman entrance." Jericho smiled and added; "Apparently the Emperor rarely bothers to stick his head out and have a look at visitors arriving, but he did this morning." Wilson chuckled; "Those two footmen almost had a fist fight over who would carry her bloody bags."

Owen had slumped into a high back chair by the door and consulted his mirror. "Colonel Durand was tasked by General Charles Dulauloy to collate the possible numbers of new recruits that Napoleon could expect from the Northern Departments of France. Currently, history dictates that he arrived on the 13th of April 1814 - two days after the abdication. Still, it didn't matter, the news he carried would not have pleased the emperor."

Jericho sat on the bed and looked around the room; "We'll, we've arrived on the 9th of April with the same unwelcome message; very few recruits available. That won't change anything. But we only have a couple of days to discover how that damn woman changes history. I've seen the results of the possible changes to the current timeline and it's drastic, really drastic: Napoleon wins at Waterloo and Britain is forced to leave most of Europe under his boot."

Wilson pulled a bottle of brandy from the canvas bag he carried over his shoulder and smiled; "Well, a couple of these won't hurt." Owen jumped from his seat and fetched glasses from the ornate cabinet near the writing desk. They all heard the soft knock at the door. Wilson pulled it open and smiled at Alex and Ruth; "Jesus girl, you must have smelt me opening the damn brandy bottle!"

Alex just grinned and swept majestically into the room followed by her 'maid' and plonked herself down on the big bed next to Jericho. She accepted a glass from Owen and Wilson poured her a large one. "Well, we off to a good start, rather unusually - according to Napoleon's Personal secretary - you have been invited to dinner tonight with the emperor." Jericho nodded his approval at that and said softly; "I rather think you have been invited and he had to ask me to attend because I'm your husband." Wilson chuckled at that; "You don't think he has mistress number ten in mind?" Owen offered Ruth a glass of brandy which she declined; "Any lemonade?" She asked and was slightly disappointed that there was none. Jericho lay back on the bed; arms folded and stared at the canopy of the grand bed. "I want you to play up to him Alexandra but keep him at arm's length. He's used to having beautiful women fall at his feet and I think that one who doesn't play the game will really mess with his ego. Forbidden fruit and all that."

Alex smiled; "I certainly won't find it hard to play the faithful and dutiful wife; I did that for my entire life." Then sighed; "Most of the time!" Everyone laughed at that remark. Ruth eased herself down on the chair that Owen had pulled up for her and rubbed her ankles; "I don't like these high shoes; they rub my feet."

She then turned to Alex; "Don't forget your taking coffee and cake with Madame Nay and some ladies of the Court this afternoon. You'll need to change into an afternoon dress; you can't wear your travelling clothes to that." Jericho sat slowly up and smiled broadly; "Now that's what I call a good start. If anyone will know the court gossip about Napoleon's new mistress; it will be the ladies of the court. All girls together and all that." He was well pleased with that turn of events.

Madame Aglae - Duchess of Elchingen [Marshal Nay's wife] watched Alex carefully over the rim of her delicate coffee cup. She certainly could appreciate the real beauty of another woman and Alex - to her - was something special. She smiled; "Your French is quite flawless my dear, but your Italian origins do appear in your voice." The other ladies all murmured their agreement with Madame Algae's deduction. Madame Margaret Du Loupe [Napoleon's current mistress - the official one] placed her cup down and smiled; "I understand that you're from the Italian state of Cappanni?"

Alex nodded; "My father was Count there, but now my brother Phillipe is Count." She sipped her coffee and wondered - strongly - about grabbing another piece of that gorgeous apple pie. She resisted that desire with some reluctance. Madame Margaret tapped her chin; "I am surprised that you are married to a mere Colonel. I mean you're a Lady of noble birth and the Colonel - a fine man, I'm sure - is from a family of bookkeepers or do I have that wrong?"

The other ladies restrained their laughter quietly.

Alex smiled and dabbed her mouth with the lace napkin; "My husband is my best friend and my only lover. Other men would seem....well, inadequate compared to how he pleases me, and he really does please me." There were little gasps of mock shock and Madame Algae chuckled outright. "Oh, my dear, you will have us filled with envy with such a confession." Everyone laughed at that; but in a very ladylike manner!

Ruth sat in the quiet corner of the large stateroom and drank coffee and played cards with the other 'Ladies Maids'. They were all clearly intrigued with her Mistress, Lady Alex. They were all much older than Ruth and really queried how such a young girl could hold such a position. Ruth explained - with some sincerity in her voice - that her mother had been Lady Alex's childhood nanny and when she died, Alex had made her daughter - Ruth - her maid despite her young age, so that she could stay with the family.

"It's good to see such loyalty running both ways." Madame Anna nodded her head and patted Ruth's hand. She was Madame Margaret's maid and knew nearly everything about her mistress's latest catch; the emperor himself. The discussion at the Maid's table was lively and quite coarse at times. Ruth actually found herself going a little red at some of the conversation's content. The other maids thought that was just wonderful and cute.

The little coffee and cake party broke up and the ladies retired to their rooms with their maids in tow, to dress for the Evening Dinner party. Alex and Ruth walked back to their suite in silence. There were staff and servants down every corridor and their discussion had only one topic; The Emperor's imminent abdication.

An unsmiling young footman with a pock marked face opened the door to their rooms and bowed a little. He informed Ruth that Colonel Durand had been summoned by Marshal Nay to give his report on the Northern Departments. Ruth thanked him and both girls waited until he closed the door and left the corridor before speaking. Alex sprawled on the bed and chuckled; "That went well, but we learnt sod all about the new mistress." That's when she saw the smile on Ruth's face and sat up. "Go on, spill the beans; you're bursting to tell me!"

Jericho's meeting with Marshal Nay didn't go well; he was shouted at - several times - as he explained about the lack of potential new soldiers for the emperor's armies. Finally, Nay calmed down and muttered an apology for shooting the messenger. He slapped Jericho on the back and said he would [Jericho that is] enjoy tonight's dinner with the emperor and what a privilege that would be for the lowly Colonel. Jericho just smiled, bowed, and left for his rooms.

He found the team assembled in his rooms and Alex really did smile. He threw the Colonel's hat on the table - along with his old briefcase - and folded his arms. "I take it Alexandra that you have something to tell us?" Alex nodded.

5. THE LADY COMES OUT.

Jericho sat deep in thought, rolling his empty brandy glass about in his fingers. He watched the fire in the grate and waited. Owen slumped on the chair opposite and yawned; "How long does it take one woman to dress another woman for bloody dinner?" That made Jericho smile a little; "Had you lived a bit longer, you would have learnt that men waiting for women to get ready is a time-honoured custom between the sexes. But men must never be late. Ever. Take my word for that." He chuckled at the blank look on young Owens's face.

Ruth opened the bedroom door with a flourish and grinned; "Madame Durand!" She announced with some pride. Jericho and Owen both rose from their chairs as Alex glided into the room and curtsied; she was utterly stunning in a very low-cut French Regency gown of white silk and lace. She wore a fabulous pearl necklace and a small, but exquisite, tiara in her hair that was piled up. Her long white gloves reached her elbows and her tiny white shoes had small, jeweled buckles adoring them. Jericho turned to Owen and said simply; "That's why men wait without any real complaint." Owen nodded his understanding without further comment.

Jericho looked Alex up and down, then placed a hand on his chin: "Alexandra, try not to sneeze, otherwise everyone will enjoy the escape of those." She just smiled demurely; "Apparently it's quite acceptable, at an Imperial ball for that to happen on occasion - almost required social etiquette for this time." Jericho nodded, then peered closer; "Alexandra, you've forgotten your bloody underwear I think." She shrugged her shoulders; "If you look as close as that, at the other women, you'll find they have all suffered the same lapse of memory. It's just something that the beloved Emperor likes, and what he likes, he gets. We poor ladies must obey our Emperor and our husband's commands in such matters."

Jericho muttered; "Obey? Like hell they obey men's orders. Perhaps when hell freezes...." Owen actually groaned a little and received a gentle slap from Wilson; "Steady boy or you might really split those trousers you complain so much about!" Even Ruth chuckled at that. Then blushed a little when she saw the look of disapproval on Owens's face.

Alex pushed her hand through Jericho's arm and grinned; "Shall we go to dinner my darling?" Jericho just smiled and the pair headed for the door, which Wilson opened and nodded to Jericho; "A big Imperial moth is going to head for the flames." He laughed softly and followed the pair, with Ruth and Owen walking behind - chatting quietly. Ruth told Owen what Napoleon's Mistress's maid had told her peers; that the mysterious woman would appear tonight - in disguise - simply because she had heard about the emperors apparent and sudden interest in Alex.

"Hence, the really low-cut bodice. Apparently, if a women is interested in the man, she'll have a little 'nipple slip' when they are together; it's quite acceptable in this Court. A sort of signal that the affair is on." Ruth explained and Owen didn't smile; "Bit of a bloody obvious signal, but I can see why it would work - especially; if Alex falls out of that damn dress in front of him."

Jericho whispered to Alex; "So, the mysterious lady is to make an appearance tonight in disguise, as Lady Guisse of Picardy. She will sit a few seats down from the emperor; to keep up the charade of not knowing each other?" Alex nodded; "Apparently Napoleon had his wife's dressmaker make her gown for tonight. His official mistress's maid believes that something really important will be announced at dinner. All four of his [Napoleon's] most powerful Marshals will be in attendance." Jericho grunted; "Time to unmask our quarry and find out what the hell is going on."

The little group wandered into the Grand Reception Room and was immediately served champagne by liveried footmen [unfortunately for Wilson and Ruth; that didn't include them!] Ruth joined a gaggle of Ladies Maids by the big bay window and Wilson stood a few feet behind his 'master'. He was actually surprised to see three other African personal servants in attendance. They didn't smile.

One of the maids gripped Ruth by the arm and whispered; "I see your mistress has dressed to please him." Ruth just smiled; "Yes, she does love to dress well for her husband." The maid grimaced and released her arm and turned to another maid; "Thirty Franc's that her nipples are out before midnight." The other maid nodded her acceptance.

Alex and Jericho stood quietly by the doorway, sipping their drinks until Alex discretely touched Jericho's arm; "That has to be her." They both watched as the slim, blond woman swept into the room - she wasn't accompanied by a maid and that certainly drew looks from the women of the court. Her gold lace dress was gorgeous, and she gently waved a peacock fan across her face. Jericho nodded to Owen, who discretely operated his mirror.

Lady Helena paused and threw a glance at Alex and then walked on, accepting champagne with a slight smile. She clearly was not happy. Madame Aglae - Duchess of Elchingen turned quietly to her friend and said softly; "I think we have all been fooled. There is no contest between the two, I suspect our Emperor has finally brought his real mysterious mistress to court and cleverly covered it with her husband's presence. Why else would a mere Colonel attend such an important dinner?" The other lady nodded her agreement, and the whispers ran around the assembled Court who exactly, the emperor's new mistress really was.

Napoleon stood in the doorway, until joined by Marshal Nay and then slowly made his entrance. The ladies curtsied and the men bowed; several men in uniform came to attention. A dozen of the emperor's 'Old Guard' followed him and took up positions around the room. Nay introduced him to several officers and Politicians [and their wives] then stopped in front of Colonel Durand, who bowed again. "Well Durand." was all the emperor said and Jericho gestured to Alex; "May I introduce my wife Alexandra, your Majesty." Alex curtsied quite low, and her nipples popped above her bodice; she made no attempt to cover them.

A little, quiet gasp rolled around the room. The lady maid slapped thirty Franc's into her friends hand - well disappointed. Alex modestly held her fan over her breasts and half smiled at the emperor but said nothing. The emperor actually smiled; well, no, it was a grin and he bowed a little; "Madame, your husband is a very, very lucky man and I always reward men of luck." He took her hand and kissed it, pushing the fan up, getting another look at her heaving breasts. "I will have the honour of a dance with you Madame." Alex smiled; "No your Majesty; the honour will be all mine." She curtsied again, revealing more of her ample bosom. Napoleon nodded and stepped a little back, staring at her dress or rather through it. He really did smile and walked away - a little awkwardly, it must be said!

Wilson restrained his smile but muttered to himself; "Straight into the flames."

Owen slowly joined Jericho and Alex and they found a quiet corner. He folded his arms and spoke softly; "Lady Helena Covington, who is from Victorian Times. By her age and knowing her birth date, we can work out that she travelled here from 1864." Wilson nodded and asked; "The big question, of course, is how?"

Owen grinned; "Her husband is Lord Covington and guess what piece of furniture he owns that once belonged to Napoleon?" Wilson sighed; "A Chinese cabinet?" Owen nodded; "A gift from the Chinese Emperor in 1814. The story or legend is that the Chinese ambassadors simply vanished from inside it. But we know that the damn thing contains a time portal. It must be in his study, which is next to his bedroom."

Jericho nodded and smiled; "So we need to get into the study, which is only available from his bedroom. So, a distraction is in order; one which allows us into his bedroom and then the study." He then noticed Alex was struggling with her magnificent breasts; "I need some safety pins." She muttered to Owen.

"And I know how we can do that." Jericho rubbed his chin and glanced across the ballroom to see the emperor talking to 'Lady Guisse of Picardy' - you could have frozen peas with the atmosphere between the two. "He's official mistress will jump at the chance to get back in his favour now and I think we can give her an offer she simply won't refuse." Jericho actually chuckled; Alex will go nuts at this one, he thought.

"We need to get into the emperors study and put that particular time portal out of commission. We can return Lady Helena to her own time, and she won't be able to return, because if the cabinet's time travelling ability is removed here and now, the cabinet won't posses the ability in 1864."

Jericho rubbed his face; "I think the emperor should be diverted by an irate and betrayed husband, whilst another gets to work on the cabinet and Lady Helena. I think it's time to use our very reliable honey-trap." They all looked at Alex, who just sighed; "Playing the bloody tart again." was all she said.

6. THE WRONG RENDERVOUS.

Ruth and Owen slipped from the dining room as the first course was served to the guests, now all seating and enjoying light, polite conversation. Alex and Jericho had been seated just a few chairs down from the emperor himself; that really did cause some quite lively conversation amongst the guests. With Jericho's rank, he should have been at the far end of the table.

Apparently, Napoleon had told his butler to make the changes; but the man was not surprised after seeing the Colonel's wife.

Owen waited in the corridor outside the door to Madame Margaret Du Loupe's rooms; her ladies maid opened it and waved Ruth in, shutting the door firmly on Owen; this was for women only. He stood outside, arms folded and a little bored. Several staff members and servants passed him; none said a word or even acknowledged that he was there. He straightened up as the door opened and Ruth appeared; a little smile of satisfaction on her face.

"Well?" Was all Owen whispered and Ruth slowly nodded, then smiled broadly. She pushed her arm through his and the happy couple headed for the Ball Room; the plan was now in action. They stood by the door and Ruth opened the palm of her hand and said quietly; "I now just have words with Alex, and everything is underway. Oh, and make sure these are fitted correctly; that's really important." She showed Owen her hand, who just rubbed his chin in puzzlement; "Safety pins?" He asked.

Ruth nodded; "I'll fix my lady's bodice so that her nipples don't pop out whilst she's dancing. They've done their job." She grinned. Owen sighed and muttered; "Pity about that. But what about that bloody see-through dress? Do you have anything to fix that?" Ruth shook her head; "There are no strong lights in the ball room; she'll be fine." Owen nodded his head, now he knew why Alex greeted the emperor in front of the fireplace; it was like placing a lamp behind her. "I now realise, what Jericho's been saying about you bloody women and the way you operate is quite true. I shall listen very carefully to him in the future." He grunted; Ruth just shook her head, but still smiled.

The guests were now starting to fill the Ball Room and Alex, with Ruth, disappeared to a side room. Jericho smiled at Owen, who simply nodded; indicating the plan was on. Wilson joined them and informed him that Marshall Nay will make up some excuse, to pull Jericho [Colonel Durand] from the dancing; leaving the field open for his majesty to go after Alex. Jericho really smiled at that; "Good luck to the poor twat." Was all he said - much to Wilson's and Owens's amusement.

"What was the important announcement he made at dinner about?" Wilson quietly asked Jericho - who did not smile - and looked about before answering; "He's not going to resign. His time travelling mistress must have supplied him with information that he believes, can change his destiny. We really must put an end to this - by any means." He glanced back at the doorway; Ruth signaled that Alex was ready and that meant that Madame Margaret Du Loupe was also ready.

The Emperor swept into the ball room; he didn't hide that he was looking for someone and appeared a little disappointed when his official mistress; Madame Du Loupe came up to him. After a few minutes of conversation; the emperor really did smile and kissed her on the cheek. They strode out and danced the first dance together. The 'Lady of Picardy' stood by the fireplace and sipped her drink; the look on her face betrayed a very unhappy woman.

"Now for my walk on part." Jericho muttered and approached the unhappy lady and wondered if she would care to dance. She smiled and took his arm. "He does actually have the charm and looks that women go after." Owen muttered - a little surprised - but Wilson just chuckled; "Come on baby brother; time to perform for our pay." Owen sighed and then rubbed his chin; "Yeah, but we don't actually get bloody paid." He muttered and followed the big man out.

They nodded and smiled at Alex, as she walked gracefully into the ball room and waved away a glass of champagne offered by an attentive footman. She stood arms on hips and stared at the dancers; she did not appear happy. Despite the dancing, everyone had their eyes on Alex, as she strode across the crowded room and walked straight up to her 'husband' and slapped him hard across the face. He staggered and released the 'lady of Guisse, who screamed in shock.

The ball room went silent - apart from a few stunned gasps from the ladies present, oh, and the Count du Moranle, who was known to be quite squeamish - and the pair [Jericho and Alex] had a shouting match in front of everyone. Alex stormed from the ball room, throwing her fan at the feet of the shocked Emperor with Jericho following her, protesting his 'innocence'.

The 'Lady of Guisse' also fled the chamber by a different door. There were just murmurs of shocked conversation about what just happened. The emperor leaned down and picked up Alex's fan. He smiled at Madame Margaret Du Loupe and pushed the fan into his pocket. "Beauty and passion is quite a heady mix." He said to her and indicated that the ball should continue - which it did.

The emperor waved aside demands that the pair should arrested or something. He stood in a quiet corner with just Marshal Nay beside him and pulled the fan from his pocket and read the few lines scrawled on it. He smiled and nodded his head; "Now that is lady worthy of a crown." He muttered and spoke closely in Nay's ear. The Marshall wasn't happy about his instructions; but he would carry them out. Napoleon then nodded at his mistress and the pair began the dancing again, as if nothing had happened.

Marshal Nay danced with his inquisitive wife and whispered to her; "I think this little rendezvous was not made in heaven; but hell." She just smiled and he explained what she had to do. She left the ball some minutes later; her maid trailing behind; totally intrigued.

They were allowed into the emperor's private suite without question and Madame Aglae - Duchess of Elchingen [Marshal Nay's wife] helped her maid uncover the huge bed. She whispered to her loyal maid; "Our beloved Emperor is going to celebrate staying on the throne, in right royal style with a little party of three. He will be the guest of honour of course." The maid smiled and said softly; "Who are the lucky ladies, my lady?" The Duchess grinned; "Well, Madame Du Loupe and that little firebrand; Lady Alexandra, of course!"

The maid chuckled; "I think Colonel Durand will get his wish and don a general's uniform after this." Madame Aglae smiled; "Lady Alexandra is a loving, loyal and obedient wife who will do her husband's bidding. She will open her proud legs and earn that Generals hat on her back; as many women have done!"

They both laughed and straightened the bed clothes. The maid lifted up Napoleon's night shirt, laid out in anticipation of its owner's arrival. Madame Algae took it from her and threw it on the floor. "I don't think his majesty will want that." Both women laughed again and finished what they needed to do and left.

Margaret and Alex walked slowly down the corridor to the emperor's private suite; giggling together in apparent anticipation of what the evening will bring. "He really loved your little performance tonight, to throw the rabid ladies of the court off the scent. Your husband will probably get the Pay Core - no fighting and lots of money. I think he will look quite splendid in his general's uniform and of course, the Title that will go with it. A general will need a title and so will his loyal wife. He will make you a Duchess when you're sadly widowed." Margaret chuckled and the pair swept in the Imperial bedroom.

There was a tray of champagne and wild strawberries placed on the bedroom table. The candles had all been lit and the fire raised into a proper blaze. Madame Du Loupe gripped Alex by the arm and pulled her close, running a finger down her lips; "We'll, enjoy each other first, he really likes that; foreplay that he can enjoy without exerting himself too much." Her finger ran down Alex's chin, then her neck and finally between her breasts; the rest of her fingers on that hand, soon joined it. "Let me undress you first - slowly." She whispered but was interrupted by Napoleon standing in the doorway; jacket unbuttoned and a glass of brandy in his hand.

"Let the party begin." He said softly and placed the brandy glass down on the small table by the door. He pulled off his jacket and threw it down. "You two can play after I've enjoyed my new Lady's arse." He added and really did smile and started to pull at his shirt. He threw it on the floor and scratched his bare belly. "You first my dear." He said softly to Alex with real anticipation in his voice.

7. THAT WASN'T IN THE PLAN!

Napoleon came up behind Alex; he was now shirtless and ran both hands down her back until they reached her bum. He whispered into her ear; "I will take you naked and sitting backwards on a chair with your arse in the air..." He gripped the cheeks of her arse quite firmly as Margret pulled at Alex's dress and loosed the small silver clasps that held her bodice in place. "These are mine for now." She whispered and pulled Alex's heaving breasts out with both hands. She ran her mouth over one and smiled.

Alex was wondering where the hell was Jericho and Wilson; she was feeling really vulnerable now - Napoleon had showed up way too early. Margaret was enjoying her breasts far too much; for it to be just play for the emperor. Where were the boys? She wondered again. What has happened?

That's when; they all heard the noise in the study next door. "Thank heaven for that." Alex whispered to herself; Jericho and Wilson were now on scene - so she thought. The emperor stopped fondling Alex's bum and stared, as the study door swung open. The nearest English translation to what he shouted was; "What the fuck!" Lady Helena Covington stood in the doorway, her face streaked and red from crying, but it was what she held in both hands that really caught everyone's attention. An 186o's revolver and she looked like she would use it.

"You fucking betray me... after I gave you all the information about your future...how to change your bloody failure into victory...then you fuck these whores in preference to me! you fucking bastard!" She clicked the safety off and visibly trembling, took aim. Napoleon pushed Alex to the floor and told her to stay down; Madame Du Loupe was backing away and clutching at her dress with both hands; pleading not to die.

"You wanted to change fucking history! Well, this will do it!" Lady Helena shouted and waved the gun up and down, as if not knowing, who to shoot first, Napoleon or Alexandra. The shot came from the balcony door and slapped into Lady Helena's right shoulder: her pistol went off and fell to the floor. The soldier on guard, on the balcony, had defied orders to keep well away from the glass doors, whilst the emperor entertained his ladies. But simply couldn't resist taking a peek.

Lady Helena fell backwards, screaming in pain and surprise, blood starting to spread over the floor. Alex leapt forward, ripping the hem of her dress off, and set to work on the now quiet woman. "Get my husband for Christ sake!" She yelled and tried to stem the blood, or she would lose the young woman and because she wasn't from this time; her soul.

Jericho and Wilson appeared in the doorway; their plan had gone horribly wrong and Jericho told the Emperor to leave for his own safety. Quite numb from shock, he did so without argument and Madame Du Loupe ran screaming out behind him. Jericho and Alex exchanged a look and Jericho said quietly; "1864 now." He operated his mirror and Alex, with Lady Helena cradled in her arms; disappeared.

Wilson waved the balcony guard away; he was standing with his mouth open and staring at the empty space, where Alex and the girl - he had just shot - once were. Wilson closed the bedroom door and locked it, pulling his mirror from a jacket pocket; "I'll call Owen and Ruth, tell them to get the fuck out of here." Jericho nodded and stared at the study door; "She must have come from there."

There was now shouting outside, and muskets were being slammed against the door. Jericho headed for the study, followed by Wilson, who stopped to scoop up the revolver. They ran into the study and stopped; the doors on the Chinese cabinet were open and Jericho's mirror was buzzing - Alex had got Helena back and she would make it - Wilson slammed the study door, as the bedroom door was finally breached by several soldiers.

"Into the cabinet!" Jericho yelled and they piled in, slamming the doors behind them. The soldiers of Napoleon's 'Old Guard' crashed through the study door and fired their muskets straight at the cabinet. Wood, glass and silver flew about the room and gun smoke filled the place.

Finally, the Corporal forced open the doors, now riddled with musket fire and to his - and his men's - great surprise, found the damn thing empty; except for broken mirrors – apparently - no-one would be jumping through time in that big Chinese box of magic anymore. The Corporal lowered his musket and said to the man nearest him; "You best fetch Marshal Nay. Those bastards have done what the Chinese ambassadors did; vanished into thin air." The soldier nodded and disappeared himself.

Captain Jean Pullaire stared at the cabinet and with a gloved hand, lifted a large piece of glass from the wreckage; he looked at his face in the reflection and dropped it back onto the floor. He turned and saw Colonel Le Grande standing behind him, surveying the damage. "Did anyone ever meet Colonel Durand before he appeared here or more importantly; that wife of his?" He asked the grim looking Colonel. Le Grande shook his head; "He was just a Colonel from a small district; never been in battle, as far as I know."

"Yes, but with a wife like that; a noble lady with such beauty, you would have thought she would have been noticed and gossiped about. But no-one appears to know anything about her. Strange that; especially after the emperor's mysterious new mistress tried to put a pistol ball through his head." Pullaire sighed and the pair walked from the room. That's when Le Grande saw the small brown paper package on the floor. He picked it up; "It's addressed personally to the emperor. I'll give it to Marshal Nay." He muttered and followed Pullaire out.

8. FINAL DAYS AND STRANGE PLANS.

Napoleon sat in Marshal Nay's study and stared at the fireplace; he gripped a glass of brandy. It was all quite in the room, but outside was chaos and noise. Madame Du Loupe sat at his feet and gripped his leg, her head against his knee.

Nay stood in the doorway, arms folded and unsmiling. "There is no trace whatsoever of Durand, his wife or servants. They have vanished completely, along with the so called 'Lady of Guisse'. All that was found, was this package; addressed to you sire." He handed Napoleon the little brown parcel. Napoleon took it without saying a word. "Like those bloody chinks, they got away without anyone seeing them. The palace was crawling with guards - inside and out - yet they simply disappeared." Napoleon dismissed him with a wave of his hand.

Finally Madame Du Loupe whispered; "What's in the package my dear. What has that insane bitch left you?" Napoleon lifted the little parcel and shook his head; "If it's from her, then it's just more lies and fairy stories." He threw the parcel into the flames and watched it burn. "Just lies and falsehoods my dear." He said and sipped his brandy. The real disappointment he felt, was missing out on having Madame Alexandra's arse. He had run his hands over it and it was a real beauty; like the rest of her. He sighed; his abdication was now a certainty - he had run out of time here and his cabinet was destroyed by his overzealous men.

He smiled at the fire burning in the grate; Young Helena had been an obedient and submissive fuck who had tried to help him survive on the throne of France. But he knew all was lost now; the odds were stacked against him. The Allies could mass troops and replacements despite how many victories he won; they were out to destroy him; not France. But in another time and place, with another big war, everything would be different.

But he couldn't understand Colonel Durand - if that's who he really was? - If he was an assassin; as Nay advocates, then why did Durant tell him to go? He had him there with just one guard, who now had an empty musket - nothing to protect him? It didn't make sense. He patted Madame Du Loupe's head; "Let's get some rest my love. I have a busy day tomorrow." He rose and placed the glass down and took one last look at the burning package. What a narrow escape he just had. The woman was clearly insane with passion for him; but obviously matched the Chinese in the skill of magic or was that bloody Durand and his crew?

Napoleon ran a hand over sweaty face; there was something strange about 'Durand' - almost if he knew about Lady Helena and her visits from the 'hereafter' and had appeared to stop him [the emperor] from gaining such knowledge of future events. Napoleon nodded to himself; he had an uneasy feeling that he would meet the mysterious - and clever - fellow again.

The pair made their way to the emperor's private suite; surrounded by his faithful and loyal 'Old Guard'. He stopped and spoke to Colonel Le Grande; he was to inform Marshall Nay, that the emperor would abdicate and accept the Allies offer of exile on Elba. He stopped momentarily outside the door, to the suite of rooms next to his and almost smiled. By the sounds coming from inside, Monsignor Boucher was entertaining another lady of the court. He sighed; something will have to be done about him.

That's when a thought crossed his mind; Monsignor Boucher could do him a final service; a very final service.

Now back at the lighthouse, Jericho stood by the fireplace in his study and watched Alex pour some well-earned brandies for the team. She gave him a glass and smiled, dropping into her favourite armchair by the fire. "If the cabinet was destroyed by musket fire, then Lady Covington - or anyone else - will not be dropping in on Napoleon." She raised her glass, and everyone did the same. "Napoleon." was all she said.

"Well, Lady Helena will have scar on her shoulder for life, but Alex certainly saved her soul. Here's to you girl." Wilson raised his glass, and everyone agreed with him. "I'd love to know how she explained to her old man, how she got shot with a musket ball?" Owen chuckled and sipped his brandy. "It was a good plan; we just didn't count for the wrath of a women scorned or Napoleon being so desperate to have Alex, that he left the ball early and un-noticed. But Lady Helena; now that came out the blue."

Jericho sighed; "I was looking forward to my big outraged and betrayed husband bit with old 'bony', whilst Wilson took care of that bloody cabinet and dragged Lady Covington back to her own time. In a way, our plan did work; Lady Helena is back in her own time and Napoleon won't be able to use the damn cabinet to find out about his future - then change it."

"If she hadn't turned up with big pistol, I may not have been able to sit properly for a few days. That was a close-run thing." Alex sipped her brandy and didn't smile. Jericho took a sip from his glass and rubbed his cheek; "By the way Alexandra; did you have to slap me so hard? We were only play acting you know."

Alex now grinned; "I had to make it look authentic, besides, it was poor old me that had her bum felt up by a horny old man and her breasts fondled by a bisexual nymphomaniac!"

Everyone chuckled at that. Then Owen tapped Wilson on the arm and asked quietly; "What's a nymphomaniac?"

Wilson groaned and said to Alex; "It's about women, so you can bloody tell him!"

But Jericho sat deep in thought, rolling his brandy glass in his hands; he stared at the fire - he was troubled. Ruth and Owen were almost sure; they didn't see the emperor leave the ball so early. Lady Helena had been his mistress for some time before that faithful night; if she had told Napoleon anything important about his future; why didn't he act upon it? The current timeline is unaltered, apart from a few, acceptable minor changes.

Napoleon fails at Waterloo and is exiled; just as history recorded it. Then his suspicious death in 1821. Jericho sighed; a nagging little thought kept pestering him. Why didn't he [Napoleon] try and change his fate in 1814?

THE END?

EPILOGUE:

"This episode continues in ***"Napoleon's Chinese cabinet of magic – Part 2."*** *All the characters appearing in both episodes are listed there."*
SJW.

EPISODE 6: "NAPOLEON'S CHINESE CABINET OF MAGIC – PART 2."

MISSION SUMMARY: "Jericho is given a very strange mission by Angel Margret; to discover the truth about claims made by a collected soul that he played Napoleon's double - until he was murdered by the Emperor Napoleon I in May 1821. This, he claims, allowed Napoleon to escape in time. Human Records show that Napoleon's soul is indeed missing! The man: a certain Lucas Boucher was born in August 1769 and died, at the age of 51 - which exactly matches the life span of the Great Emperor. Physically, he did indeed resemble Napoleon. If he's telling the truth; then what happened to Napoleon Bonaparte and where is his soul now?"

NOTES:
[1]This episode was a Seasonal Special [online] and written with humour to the fore!
[2] Part 2 of a two part mission.

TRIGGER WARNINGS. **ALCOHOL, STRONG LANGUAGE, SEXUAL REFERENCES AND MILD COMIC VIOLENCE.**

AGE 12+ ONLY. **30 Minutes reading time.**

1. THE STORY OF LUCAS BOUCHER.

Jericho sat on the bright marble seat, arms folded and legs stretched out. He sighed with boredom and wondered just how long he had been kept waiting by Angel Margret. He stared down the almost empty corridor and watched Wilson approaching with his casual walk - like he was having a stroll in the local park - until he too, dropped on the seat next to Jericho.

"I suppose I'll have to get use to this; being summoned by Margret for mission briefings." He smiled and folded his arms. Jericho just smiled; "Well, your forthcoming promotion to Inspector means you'll be doing this a lot - sitting outside her office - for what seems an eternity." Wilson took a deep breath; "Yeah, but it's not confirmed yet. The only team currently without a permanent Inspector is 22. They are a good one, but their sergeant isn't exactly going to greet me with open arms, she's been passed over twice already."

Jericho tapped his big friends shoulder and shook his head; "She'll be fine about it. Kate knows that she's still too inexperienced to be given her own team - yet. Besides, she's clever enough to know that the team will be getting a really good Inspector and that is what really matters." Wilson smiled; he knew he could always rely on Jericho's support and full encouragement. But those little nagging doubts about his ability wouldn't leave him alone. He looked up to see Mr. Colgate [the Angels private secretary] in the doorway of the angel's office. He gestured for the pair to enter. They both rose and walked slowly into the office.

Owen moved his castle and sat back; "I suppose he has to cover Jericho all the time now; I mean with his promotion to Inspector in the offering. I shall really miss the big bugger." Alex sighed and moved her Bishop slowly across the board; "Don't lose any sleep that Wilson will suddenly disappear out the door; these things take time. He hasn't actually had the official nod that he's got it yet. It could be ages before he's given a team of his own, normally, new inspectors have to do time as locum's [stand-in's] on other teams. So, he'll be around for a while yet."

Owen stared at the chess board for a few minutes in silence and then said with a wide grin; "Does this mean they'll make you sergeant?" Alex chuckled and rolled her eyes in mock despair; "No bloody way! - I don't think Angel Margret likes me that much. Besides, the Promotions Board for Sergeants has already sat and I wasn't invited. We'll get one of the new sergeants – they will put one of their better one's on Team 74 - simply because Jericho heads the team, and he certainly won't accept one that's not up to scratch. So, I think, I'm here for a while yet." She moved her Queen and grinned; "By the way; that's Check-Mate." Owen groaned; he really hadn't seen that coming.

They both looked up as Jericho and Wilson came through the study door; chatting. "What do they call this Alex? A gaggle of Inspectors or a herd?" Owen chuckled to himself. Alex smiled at the pair, ignoring Owens's comments. "What have we got?" She asked Wilson, who slumped in his favourite armchair and wondered if Jericho would let him take the damn chair - when the time comes! - He gestured to Jericho.

Jericho stood by the fireplace and pulled a brown paper file from his jacket. "This won't make your day Alexandra; we're after Napoleon Bonaparte - again." She threw up her hands and laughed; "What's the dirty old sod up to now?" Wilson smiled; "Murder apparently and illegal time travel." Now that did catch Alex's and Owen's attention. "But his own men shot the shit out of his Chinese cabinet, so how's he moving through time?" Owen asked, stroking Mr. Parker, who had jumped onto his lap and was now playing with the chess pieces.

"That is a good question baby brother. According to a certain look-a-like of the emperor, he apparently laid his hands on another time portal and bumped the poor bloody 'double' off; to cover his escape." Wilson said to Owen, but smiled at Mr. Harris, who opened the study door and announced dinner. "Now this should make for an interesting dinner conversation piece." Muttered Alex and the team headed for the dining room. Owen left Mr. Parker on his seat; pushing chess pieces about the board.

Alex was right; the dinner conversation was lively. Jericho outlined what they had so far: "Most people know and believed that Napoleon died on St. Helena on the 5th of May 1821 aged 51. It was known that he was suffering some sort of serious stomach illness for years. But according to a collected soul; a certain Monsignor Lucas Boucher he didn't. Boucher claims he was Napoleon's double and physically, he really did resemble the emperor. He was used by Napoleon in various situations - like, the double would appear at some big parade or court function and British and Allied spies would report his whereabouts. But he would actually be elsewhere; planning battles and getting up to stuff that the Allies wouldn't hear about. Apparently, the double says he [the double] was so good at impersonating the emperor; even the Emperor's mistress and other lovers fell for it." Wilson grinned at Alex; "We all wondered how Napoleon managed to leave the Ball that night and appear quickly in his bedroom to entertain you and Madame Du Loupe - the double was deputizing for him in the ball room!" Alex muttered; "Cunning old sod - no wonder he conquered most of Europe; he could be in two places at once." Owen rubbed his chin; "What do we know about the time portal?" Jericho sipped his wine and picked up his fork; "What we do know, is that the Timeline was breached by someone travelling from May 5th 1821 to June 1st, 1910, from St. Helena to Paris, France." Owen nodded; "Why 1910; why would that year particularly interest him?"

Jericho shrugged his shoulders - he didn't know; "We've been tasked by Angel Margret to discover if there's any truth in the allegations made by Lucas Boucher and discover what has happened to Napoleon's soul. That's one fact we can accept; his bloody soul is missing, which means, since we have no body, he must have jumped from his own time or been taken by the 'Dark Side'. We need to find out which."

Wilson leaned on the table; "Which means we are going to have to jump back to Paris in 1910 and enjoy the peak of the glamorous, Parisian Edwardian era." He smiled at Alex; "I have no doubt that Costumes will fit you up with some stunning outfits - and of course - some equally stunning hats!" Alex grinned at that; "I'm certainly worth it." Everyone chuckled and continued with their excellent meal of Vegetable casserole.

Jericho rubbed his face; the time portal that Napoleon could be using bothered him. His version [Napoleon's] of the Chinese cabinet had been destroyed and Alex - quick witted and clever, as usual - had checked Covington House for Portals, especially the Chinese Cabinet in the attic - it had gone. Being apparently wrecked back in 1814, it did not exist in 1864 now. That had anchored Lady Covington firmly in her own time.

"Lucas Boucher did say one odd thing to Herbie the Collector; Herbie said that Boucher told him the emperor was unhappy that he had shagged his mistresses {Napoleon's] and some other women, who thought they were sleeping with the Emperor. But

Napoleon never did anything about it because Boucher was so good at his job." Wilson lifted his wine glass and smiled at Alex adding; "Maybe it was the bloody double feeling up your bum and not the great man himself!" Alex grunted and sipped her wine; "Makes no difference; I was still touched up in the line of duty. That never happens to you lot; does it?"

"Strangely enough it doesn't." Muttered Owen with a big grin and set about his meal with some relish. The added with a rueful smile; "Yeah, but Jacqueline would agree with you!"

2. PARIS; FRANCE - 1910.

General Joffre [Conseil supérieur de la guerre] watched the strange man walk down the stairs and disappear into the crowds of Officers, civilians and Politian's that thronged his outer offices. He walked back to his private office deep in thought. Joffre couldn't quite get his head around the man; he clearly knew battle tactics and strategy, yet he had never really heard of Monsignor Lucas Boucher before - only rumours or gossip. The hints he dropped about 'Plan 17' - the French Army Battle plan in case of war with Germany, which was still in the planning stage - were concerning; yet Monsignor Butcher dropped some powerful hints about it and its obvious failings.

Joffre shouted for his Personal Secretary; Colonel Mardue and instructed him to gain background checks on a certain Lucas Boucher. He slumped behind his desk and stared through the big window onto the streets of Paris. He knew that war with Imperial Germany was as certain as death itself; the only question was when?

Monsignor Boucher sat back in his carriage and marveled at the sights and sounds of the city. He was heading back to his modest Chateaux on the outskirts of Paris. But he was a very rich man - rich indeed - because since his exile in 1815; his supporters had been hoarding gold and purchasing the best properties in France. Just one of his bank accounts held nearly a hundred million Francs. After nearly a century, he could buy any person or organisation in France and better still; he was almost anonymous. Only the very rich and powerful knew Lucas Boucher and the power he could exercise.

He pulled a large, gilded book from beneath his seat and flicked through the gilt-edged pages. He stopped at the page; he had stared at numerous times. It was a portrait of a certain Italian Countess who had apparently died in 1801. She had been known as the 'English Countess' and was married to Henri - Count of Cappanni. He ran the back of his hand across the woman's face. She was his little hobby and stealing her from 1801 would be easy. He smiled to himself as he approached the gates of his villa. There were four armed guards waiting and two pulled open the gates. The carriage rolled through, followed by another two carriages that contained his personal bodyguards.

The French Prime Minister was due for dinner this evening and that meal could prove interesting, constructive, and profitable - for both. He glanced down at the newspapers spread across the opposite seat. There were a couple of English ones and 'The Times of London' had contained an obituary that had saddened him a little - just a little - the death of the old Dowager Lady Covington. Still, he had fond memories of their sexual antics.

But the 'English Countess' would not leave his mind. He had few weaknesses, but she had become one of them, ever since, she exposed her breasts to him, and he had seen through that almost transparent dress. It still haunted his dreams. He wanted her and would have her, especially that incredible arse of hers. He had run his hands over it and he wanted it more than anything; except the return of Imperial French dominance of Europe and the new 'Germany' smashed.

Those delicious thoughts were interrupted by the greeting of his personal secretary; Monsignor Beasson and the man, loaded down with 'urgent papers' followed him into the grand house. "At the least the great flooding has disappeared Sir." Beasson tried to make small talk, which Boucher ignored; "Everything laid on for tonight Beasson?" Was all he asked. Beasson nodded; "Monsignor Laurent will see you before the Prime Minister and his lady arrives at seven Sir." Napoleon grunted; "Good." He handed his hat and coat to his Butler and headed for his private study.

Jericho had to smile as he watched the numerous males - and some women - all taking a 'casual and polite'- look at Alexandra. She was standing next to the railings, chatting with her 'maid' Ruth and Jericho's 'valet' - Owen. Wilson lowered his paper and smiled too. "We never do tell Alex, that she really does look like princess; no matter what time period we appear in. The gown is stunning, but what's inside really draws the attention." Jericho nodded his agreement. They were in the 'Jarden du Luxembourg', the park all high-class Parisian's wanted to be seen in - and admired - of course. It was summer 1910 and the weather was good. "Doc Underhill's human agent for this time and place will be here soon. Apparently, she's quite a stunner in her own right and has a clever brain in her head. He speaks highly of Madame Fibroin..." Jericho stopped speaking, as an elegant, well-dressed woman approached Alex, partially hidden by her white parasol. "I think she's here. Doc apparently told her to find the most stunning and well-dressed lady in the park and contact her." Jericho added and rose from the park bench. Wilson folded his paper under his arm and joined him. They casually walked over to the little group.

"Sweet Jesus Jericho! She could be Alex's mother or older sister, they're like two peas in a pod." Wilson sounded quite surprised - because he was - Jericho raised his hat; "Madame Fibroin I presume?" The woman turned and Jericho really had to agree with Wilson's assessment. Standing next to Alex, she really could be her mother or older sister. Madame Fibroin was in her early forties and quite a stunner. She smiled and allowed Jericho to kiss her hand; "Monsignor Underhill did say you were quite the gentleman Inspector Tibbs. You were, indeed, easy to find." She gestured to Alex; "Simply beautiful, so I knew she was the contact."

Wilson removed his hat and smiled at her. She smiled again: "Your colleague is a very handsome man Inspector." She gripped Wilson's arm - just for a few seconds - then released it. The look on her face was obvious to Alex and Ruth. The boys missed it; Well, maybe not Wilson!

Madame Fibroin twirled her parasol and on the arm of Jericho, the pair walked a little ahead of the group, as they strolled the park. "You sure you don't have a French connection in the family? You and she could easily be mistaken for mother and daughter." Ruth whispered to Alex, who was walking on Wilson's arm [Ruth, quite happily, was on Owen's arm]. Alex just smiled; "I don't think so, my mother was from Edinburg!" She admitted.

They walked to the South gateway and joined their carriages waiting there. Madame Fibroin took her leave and departed in a single horse buggy, driven by a tall, immaculacy uniformed

African servant. Wilson helped Alex into their carriage and Owen did the same for Ruth. Jericho sat opposite the girls with Wilson and told the driver to head for Hotel Westminster."Only the best for our Inspector." Alex grinned and adjusted her stunning peacock hat. The feather tickled Owen's nose and he pushed it aside and then went quiet. He nodded to the carriage door; "That little black cab is behind us again; same two people."

Jericho nodded; "Yes, they really do seem interested in us. Anything on your mirror?" Owen sat with his mirror on his lap and chuckled; "Jesus Jericho, the tall man is a Monsignor Jean Dumont - from this era - born in 1866, and guess what he's know for?" Jericho shook his head. Owen turned to the girls; "Careful ladies, don't go near him. He's a known 'white slaver'."

Ruth gave Owen a blank look and Alex had to explain about the sex traffic in white girls and women in this time period. It was notorious; there was serious money available for the right women. Such a supplier as Dumont would sell to French Brothels and individual clients. The police actually did little about it.

Ruth was totally shocked; "Do you mean they just grab girls and sell them for ...for sexual things, like Roman slaves?" Owen nodded and Jericho just sighed; "You'll be fine. Wilson and I will deal with Monsignor Dumont if necessary." Wilson patted Ruth's hand; "Our Jericho is quite a rich and powerful man - apparently - in this time and place. The evil fucker will think long and hard before crossing such a man. You'll be fine."

Jericho rubbed his chin and stared straight at Alex; "I wonder if he's working for a certain person, who really wants to get his hands on our Alexandra?" Wilson sat back and nodded; "Napoleon?" He said quietly and Jericho just smiled.

"Bloody charming. Now I'm the target for sex slavers!" Alex groaned and made herself comfortable in the seat. "Bloody charming." She repeated. Owen looked up from his mirror and ran a hand over his face. "The other gentleman - if you can call him that - is a certain Norman Faulds - an Englishman - currently on the run from Scotland Yard for two murders and several abductions of young girls around London. There's a reward of almost a hundred pounds for him. That's serious money in these times."

Owen chuckled and added; "So it shows that the 'Entente Cordiale' is up and running." Everyone just stared at him, and Wilson shook his head in mock despair. The 'Entente Cordiale' was a treaty between France and Britain; mainly against Germany, signed in 1904. It paved the way for British support of France in 1914.

"Well, he must be protected by someone really powerful, if he's openly riding around Paris with another known evil bastard and the Gendarmes are doing nothing about it." Wilson said and watched the carriage behind them. Jericho glanced at Wilson; they both now had a pretty good idea who that person was; Napoleon.

3. HOTEL WESTMINSTER.

The team walked slowly through the foyer towards the Reception Desk; with Jericho and Wilson unable to hold back big smiles; every eye in the place was on Alex. They reached the desk and the Concierge spoke to Jericho but stared at Alex. "You have the Presidential Suite Monsignor Tibbs. It has rooms for your staff. All your luggage has been taken to your suite." He handed over the keys to Owen. Jericho just nodded and asked if there were any messages. The man reached behind and took several envelopes from the post boxes. "You have several sir." He pushed them to Jericho and tapped the one lying on top and seemed quite impressed. "That was delivered by private messenger from the Palais de l'Élysée, from the private office of the President."

Jericho just smiled and gathered the envelopes up with a casual sweep. He turned to Alex; "I have no doubt that you have been invited to dine and as your husband; I have been invited too." Alex just smiled and said nothing. The little group walked to the lifts. The Concierge turned to his young assistant and said softly; "Why does that not surprise me. He's wife is absolutely stunning, and he is a powerful man of influence in the English Court. Apparently, a close friend of their new King George." The young assistant just nodded but preferred the rich man's Valet.

Owen headed straight for the drinks tray and poured everyone a brandy - except Ruth, who wanted just lemonade - and handed them around. Alex removed her light summer coat and hat. She handed them to Ruth and eased herself down in a plush chair.

the rooms were sumptuous and the height of elegance. "I sometimes think you are right Jericho; civilization did end in 1914." Owen just grunted; "Yeah, civilization for the rich and powerful. The poor bloody working classes didn't think it was so civilized."

Wilson sipped his drink and patted Owens's arm; "Right on my communist baby brother." They all chuckled at that.

Jericho sat on the big sofa and looked through his messages. He held one up with a big smile; "It appears we have been invited to dinner and a ball by a dead man." Wilson took the note and smiled; "Monsignor Lucas Boucher is apparently alive and kicking, nearly ninety years after he died." Jericho sighed; "Our friend Napoleon is wasting no time in letting us know he's alive and living in another time. Strange that."

Owen eased into a chair and rubbed his chin; "Why would he do that? He's knowing who we are, why save us the trouble of hunting him down by inviting you and Alex to bloody dinner and dancing?" Wilson nodded; "That is a good question baby brother." Jericho waved the note towards Alex and said softly; "The answer is probably sitting there." Alex rolled her eyes in mock despair and said nothing, sipping her very welcome brandy.

Jericho waved another note about; "This one is interesting too. It's from Madame Fibroin and she tells us that that Monsignor Lucas Boucher has just visited General Joffre and is dining with the Prime Minister tonight; they will be talking about France's readiness for war with Germany."

Owen sighed; "The plot thickens, can you image the French army in 1914 guided by a military genius? Now that could really change everything." Wilson grunted; "No shit Sherlock." Finished his brandy and headed to the drinks tray for a re-fill. He offered re-fills all round and had his offer accepted by his colleagues.

"For Christ sake, what's he doing here?" Jericho suddenly exclaimed as he read another note. Everyone turned to him, and he held the note up and chuckled; "Bloody McIves is here. He informs us that Boucher is Napoleon Bonaparte and he's been buying people and property all over the place. McIves warns that Napoleon knows we're here and to keep a close eye on Alex. The emperor has been doing research on her and knows her past;

especially in 1801." Now that did surprise Alex; "How the hell could he have found that out?" She asked with real concern in her voice.

Jericho shrugged his shoulders; "He does possess a time portal."

The elegant phone tinkled, and Owen wandered over and picked up the receiver, muttering; "This is the bloody Valet's job I presume." He must have surprised the caller; he answered in perfect French. He listened for a minute and placed the phone down. He smiled; "Guess who's on their way up to our rooms?"

Everyone just shrugged. "Bloody General Joffre and his aide Colonel Mardue; they want to speak to you Jericho. Alone." Jericho nodded; "That's not unexpected actually. I have a feeling that a lot of powerful people know who exactly Monsignor Boucher really is." He stood and straightened his jacket. The remainder of the team headed for their rooms; except Owen who would be required to open the damn door and serve drinks, if required.

There was a soft knock and Owen pulled open the door and bowed slightly. The big man wandered in and shook Jericho's hand, very firmly, as did Colonel Mardue. They accepted brandies from Owen and Jericho waved him away. They all sat and didn't speak until Owen left the room. Everyone was crowded in Alex's bedroom and sat about, waiting. Some fifteen minutes later Jericho knocked on the bedroom door and they re-joined him; he had quite a smile on his face. They gathered around and Jericho informed them of the little meeting's content.

"It appears that the French Secret Service and other intelligence agencies have been watching our Monsignor Boucher for some time. Whilst they are a little amazed - and puzzled - by his striking similarity to the great French Emperor, they are seriously questioning his motives; basically, they don't trust him." Jericho smiled and added; "General Joffre is no fool. He wants' to know - exactly - what are Boucher's plans, and he believes we can assist him. He informed me that Boucher has a real interest in Alex. He actually called it 'obsessive'. Apparently, he [Boucher] has sent agents to Cappanni to check out the so called 'English Countess'. Joffre believes that could be of great assistance to us, as he believes he [Boucher] wants possession of her striking modern look-a-like!"

"Hence the bloody party invitation." Muttered Wilson, adding; "Napoleon knows it's really Alex. But, of course, Joffre believes our Alex is just a look-a-like. He doesn't know about real time travel." Alex sighed and poured herself another brandy; "Typical, I'm being pursued by a horny old Emperor and bloody white slavers!" Everyone chuckled at that, and Jericho rubbed his chin; thinking. "But Napoleon's interest could prove very interesting." He held up yet another note and handed it to Alex, adding; "This one is addressed to you my dear." Alex took it slowly and read it. She didn't smile. "I don't know or even heard of a 'Countess Evelyn Fredericks'. So why would she be inviting me to coffee at her bloody Chateau?"

Owen held up his mirror; "Apparently the Countess is a historical figure in this time and place. She's genuine and is the wife of a bloody German Count; they are visiting Paris at this time." Alex just shrugged her shoulders; "Still don't bloody know her or her husband." She sat down and sipped her new brandy. Jericho gestured to Owen's mirror; "Check him out Owen; see what's known about him." Owen read his mirror for a few minutes and didn't smile; "The bugger is really a spy for Imperial German intelligence. He and his wife - who was English by birth - visited France in 1910, 1912 and early 1914. Travelling around on various holidays, as a cover I suppose."

Jericho smiled; "The plot really does thicken. We have a time travelling Napoleon, French Military Intelligence, white slavers and now German spy's all really interested in our Alex. "Interesting that."

Alex grunted - very un-lady like - and finished her brandy; "I don't call it bloody interesting." She muttered. Jericho walked to the fireplace and burnt all the notes with a match, then crushed the ashes with his boot. "I think I was right. There are lots of powerful people and organizations looking closely at Napoleon and his motives here. Napoleon is one person that Germany would not want to face during a bloody war. Even almost a century after his supposed death."

The team watched - a little puzzled - as Jericho sat at the ornate writing desk by the window and wrote out a couple of notes with his fountain pen. They watched in amazement as he walked back to the fireplace and burnt the notes in it; he didn't crush them with his boots. "Well people; this hotel is also famed for its restaurant. Dinner is at seven, so shall we dress?" Owen was about to ask him about the note burning, when Ruth tapped his arm; "Come on Mr. Valet, the workers have to get their master and mistress ready for dinner." She grinned and Owen followed her into the master bedrooms.

4. SURPRISE ALL ROUND.

Monsignor Dumont and Norman Faulds stood in front of the desk - hats off and silent - while Napoleon sat reading some papers and looked up; "You have followed the lady in question and know her movements?" They both nodded. Napoleon didn't smile; "Do not harm her in any way. If so, much as a hair on her head is disturbed; I will have you torn apart by rabid dogs. Do you understand gentlemen?" They both nodded again, and he waved them away. They stood outside the door and spoke softly with each other; they both knew you didn't fuck with someone like Monsignor Boucher. "But we can always fuck her maid. Right in front of her, to show her we mean business." Norman said, really smiling. Dumont grinned at that; he really did enjoy working with another top class professional and the pair left quietly; by the tradesmen entrance.

The carriage rolled into the impressive driveway and headed for the grand door, where the Butler awaited them. The two ladies were helped from the carriage by two livered footmen. They really did smile; the two women were stunners and dressed like Hartsburg Princess's. The Butler bowed and gestured towards the Chateau's doors. "This way please Madame Tibbs." Alex and her friend followed him in. She whispered to her friend; "This could prove interesting as Jericho is so fond of saying." The other lady just smiled.

They were about to take tea with Countess Evelyn Fredericks and had dressed for the occasion. Outside in the roadway another carriage sat and Dumont and Faulds watched with interest.

"No maid. Just another grand looking tart. Not that it matters." Faulds said, sipping his cognac flask. He offered it to his colleague, but Dumont declined and checked his cosh and pistol. "She's another fucking stunner. Could be worth a small fortune to us. I know someone who'll pay ten thousand Franc's for a girl like that." Dumont muttered and Fauld's whistled; that was serious fucking money. "Five thousand Franc's would suit me nicely.

Would your buyer object if she was knocked about a little. Fucked good and proper by us." He added, now really smiling. Dumont sighed; "If she's a virgin, then he would probably double that." Now Fauld's really did grin; "I don't know if I could resist a twenty thousand Franc fuck." He laughed and checked his pistol and cosh too. They settled back and waited.

Alex and Jackie were shown into the Countesses Morning Room and sat - hats still on - for the countess to appear. Alex whispered to Jackie; "I told Jericho - quite forcibly - that I would simply not put young Ruth at risk. Hence you're back in a dress." She actually giggled as Owen/Jackie just sighed. The countess appeared and sat down; she stared at the pair and slowly smiled.

"Now Alexandra, a little word about our mutual acquaintance; Monsignor Boucher." She opened the conversation, straight to the point and that did catch the pair's interest. The women sipped coffee and nibbled on little cakes and soon the little party was over. Alex and Jacqueline walked back to their carriage. Jackie consulted her mirror as the carriage passed through the grand gateway. Alex was still considering Countess Evelyn's words.

That's when Dumont and Faulds struck, firing a pistol into the air, which made the driver leapt from his seat and simply run off! Dumont pulled the coach door open and stuck a pistol under Jackie's nose; "Out the fucking carriage. Now you bitches!"

Faulds stood behind with handcuffs and bags [to shove over the girls heads] Both Jackie and Alex sighed; Jackie operated her mirror and Dumont flew a couple of feet into the air and fell like a sack of potatoes. He lay twitching on the grass. Fauld's dropped the handcuff's and bags, pulling out his pistol; he too flew a few feet into the air and crashed to earth; lying still on the grass. Alex peered over Jackie's shoulder and sighed; "I suppose we had better call the Gendarmes." Jackie nodded, watching the coachman disappearing in the distance; "I think he was probably part of this." She said quietly and pushed her mirror into her handbag.

Jackie jumped from the carriage and pulled the pistol from the unconscious Dumont and fired two shots in the air. The pair waited for the servants from the Chateau to come running out, through the grand gateway. They didn't wait long. The two young footmen appeared and were absolutely stunned that the two women had overpowered desperate, armed men intent on abducting them!

The evening papers were full of the story and when Alex and Jackie returned to the hotel; both staff and visitors applauded them. They accepted the praise with some modest waves and smiles, but when the people started to crowd around them; they hitched up their skirts and ran for the lifts. "I need a bloody brandy." Muttered Alex and Jackie leaned against the wall of the elevator and sighed; "I never thought we were going to get out of that damn police station." The lift boy was just staring at the pair in disbelief. Jackie gave his young face a pat and winked; "You'll soon learn about women my boy." They left the lift and headed for the 'Presidential Suite'.

Wilson and Jericho were waiting - brandy glasses in hands - and welcomed the 'girls' home. Ruth gave Owen a huge kiss as a sort of 'thank you'. Then commented on what a fabulous woman he made. Jericho explained what the detective Inspector had told him about the pair of 'white slaver's'. They [the police] had been waiting for witnesses to an abduction for some time. Now they have witnesses, victims and the perpetrators in one neat package. "I really didn't think he was going to let us go. That bloody Inspector went over the same thing; a couple of times each."

Owen said and gasped with happiness as he sipped his brandy. Alex lay on the sofa - feet up - and accepted a very welcome glass of brandy from Wilson. She grinned; "He's very good looking and obviously thorough in his job."

"Well get ready for dinner; the hotel has said that the champagne is on them for tonight. You can bring me up to date with the German spies creeping about and what's on offer, over a very good meal." Owen smiled; "Does that mean I'm invited?" Jericho nodded and chuckled; "Yes, Mademoiselle Jacqueline Jones is the toast of Paris - with Alex of course - and we can't really let the people down. They will expect to see the heroic pair together at dinner. We won't disappoint them." Ruth looked quite excited and dragged Owen/Jackie to her feet; "I've got just the dress for you." She turned to Alex; "I've already laid yours out."

The 'girl's' headed for the bedroom to change.

Alex explained the surprising little coffee and cake party; it appears that the Countess Evelyn Fredrick's wasn't all she seemed. "I think she's a double agent and so is her husband. She dropped some really big hints which way they swung; it appears that her husband's mother was English, and they have spent a long time together in Great Britain. They both love France apparently; especially Paris - but then who doesn't? - I really don't know how to take them." Jericho sipped his soup and didn't smile; "What did they want you to do about the situation between France and Germany?" She lowered her voice: "To help Monsignor Boucher gain a post in the military where he can directly influence decisions; especially on the battlefields."

Wilson asked: "How do they expect you to do that?" Alex sighed; "Apparently the President likes beautiful young women." Jericho chuckled; "Now that doesn't surprise me Alex." But Alex really chuckled; "You don't understand. I'm way too old for his tastes; he really likes teenage girls." She jerked a thumb towards Jackie; "According to the Countess; he'll go nuts for our Jackie!" Who groaned and sipped her wine.

Jericho dabbed his mouth with his napkin and thought about the situation with the apparent German double agents. If they wanted Napoleon to guide France's destiny at the crisis hour, then surely they swung towards the Anglo-French alliance? Or did it? The revelation from the so called 'German spies' was quite a surprise. He was about to receive another.

The waiter slipped up to him and whispered in his ear. Jericho rose from the table and threw his napkin on his plate. He didn't look happy; "It appears that Inspector Le Grande is outside the dining room with several gendarmes. They intend to take you and Jackie into protective custody. That means jailing you for your own good; if you believe that." Alex folded her arms; her appetite gone. "And what has prompted the Inspector to come up with this cracker?" Jericho stared towards the door of the restaurant; "Someone walked into the police station and murdered Dumont and Faulds; obviously to prevent them telling anyone about the person who hired them."

Wilson grunted; "Walked into a bloody police station and knocked off two kidnappers; now that takes balls."

Everyone could see the Inspector waiting by the door, hat in hand. There were several uniform officers around him. His sergeant was picking his teeth with a small wooden stick and the Inspector pulled his hat off and handed it back to him. The fat Sergeant just grinned. "Tell him to come back after bloody dinner." was all Alex said and picked up her knife and fork. The Inspector was at the table; his patience apparently gone. "Madame Tibbs and Mademoiselle Jacqueline Jones. I have a court order here to take you into protective custody. You will immediately come with us."

Alex was about to tell him, what he could do with his damn court order, but saw the look on Jericho's face. She rose from her seat and threw her napkin down - she spoke in perfect French, loudly - "So this is French justice Monsignor Inspector. You drag off the poor victims of terrible crimes and jail them, while you let homicidal criminals run around the streets. Is this really French justice?"

Everyone in the restaurant rose as one cheering and clapping. The young Inspector grunted and gestured to his men; "Take them." The fight started almost immediately. A big Frenchman with a huge moustache, grabbed one constable and threw him across a table, shouting; "Viva la France!"

Alex grabbed Jackie by the hand and ran through the kitchen doors; cheered by the Chef's and waiting staff. Two burly constables chased them down the back stairs and both girls dashed into the ladies toilet. The constables hesitated outside; then shrugged their shoulders and crashed through the doors. The place was empty. It didn't have any windows and the only door was the one the constables had come through. They stood scratching their heads; this would take some explaining to the Inspector!

5. ON THE RUN.

The cart trundled down the leafy, narrow lane and Jericho flicked through the pages of the newspaper that the driver had lent him. Alex and Ruth were picking straw from each other's hair and skirts. Jackie was snoring on her side, skirt pulled up to her knees. Ruth giggled and threw straw over Jackie's legs. Wilson sat staring down the road and wiped sweat from his face with some clean straw. "Just out of interest Jericho; now what the fuck do we do?" Jericho looked up from his paper and smiled;

"Well, according to the paper, a general alert has been issued across France for our two girls. Everyone seems to have forgotten they were victims; now they're the equivalent of Ma Baker and her bloody sister. Says two constables and three civilians were injured in the fight and the restaurant was wrecked. The papers are demanding, they're thrown in the Bastille and keys tossed away."

"Bastards." was all Wilson said and sighed loudly. He prodded Jackie with his foot; "Come on sleeping beauty, Rise and Shine." Jackie woke and brushed her dress down. She left her bodice unbuttoned and Wilson tapped her exposed leg; "I just have to ask - again - are those bloody real?" Jackie pulled her bodice tight, and Ruth helped her lace up. "Wouldn't you like to know?" She muttered and asked if anyone had any water. The cart driver turned and gestured to his old canvas sack thrown in the cart.

"There is both wine and water in there Mademoiselle, please help yourself." Jackie did; she was gasping. Alex was leaned back, legs crossed, and arms folded; she spoke directly to Jericho; "Just to echo what Wilson said; what the bloody hell do we do now?"

Jericho smiled and handed the paper to Wilson, he took a deep breath; "Enjoy the fresh country air, there was very little pollution in 1910; anywhere." Alex just sighed; "Well, that really didn't answer any of my concerns, did it?" Jericho laid back and said softly; "Keep your eyes open for a couple of black carriages with closed windows. You'll recognize one of the drivers." He dozed happily in the morning sunshine until Wilson woke him up.

"Your carriages are here, and everyone certainly recognized one of the drivers; it's bloody McIves."Jericho sat up and picked straw from his jacket and trousers. "Let's go people." Was all he said.

McIves sat grinning on the driving seat and Jericho pulled open the door and gestured for the girls to get in. McIves raised his hat and said quietly; "Good morning, ladies, you are famous Alex; you have practically singlehandedly, raised the silent revolutionary spirit of old France." He chuckled and slapped his old floppy hat back on. Alex just shrugged her shoulders and the girls climbed in.

McIves spoke to Jericho and Wilson; "Get in too; the other

carriage already has passengers." Everyone peered at the young driver, who also raised his hat. The carriage door swung open, and five heads appeared; laughing and waving; two men [one a big African] and three women. Jericho just chuckled and squeezed in with the girls. Wilson followed shaking his head; "Bloody McIves."

The carriages set off and McIves leaned down and spoke through the drivers little flap; "Your description is everywhere. We're headed for a nice little house that I own in this time. The examining magistrate desperately wants Alex and Owen ...sorry Jacqueline to give evidence, so they can drag Monsignor Boucher in for questioning. He may have had the two slavers killed and their mouths silenced, but Dumont was no fool; the police Inspector found his little black book with Boucher's name mentioned several times. But the magistrate won't act without the girls. He [Boucher] has pretty powerful friends in this time."

They must have travelled several kilometers before McIves shouted down; "Roadblock ahead. Hang onto to something." The first carriage speeded up and went straight through the roadblock; a couple of Gendarmes fired their pistols in the air. But the young driver didn't stop and McIves turned the carriage off the road and disappeared into the woodland. He stopped and everyone watched the Gendarmes chasing after the first carriage; the passengers hanging out and waving. The team couldn't help it; they laughed outright. McIves certainly knew his way around this forest. Apart from a few stops to let the girls visit a bush or two, he made good time over the bumpy forest trail. Then a bloody wheel fell off!

McIves and Jericho walked the horses, and the team followed them, going deeper in the forest. The sun was starting to set before they reached the Hunting Lodge. Everyone was tired and thirsty. McIves and Jericho stabled the horses and Wilson pushed through the door and everyone was surprised; it was wonderfully furnished with period furniture. Almost instinctively, Alex found the modest bathroom! Jackie found the drinks cabinet - with much happiness - and discovered a couple of very decent bottles of brandy. Ruth quickly followed Alex in the bathroom, smiling. There was only one bedroom and one bed; Alex and Ruth were given that, without having to ask.

Jackie groaned; "Typical, I get all the shit jobs of a woman and none of the perks." Now that did cheer everyone up. Alex patted her arm. "You can snuggle up to Wilson; he won't mind." Wilson stuck up a single finger but said nothing; he just smiled.
They sat around eating toast [the bread was slightly past its best] apples, cheese and cured ham. Jackie boiled some eggs and that was their dinner. They opened a couple of bottlers of wine and settled in for the night. McIves got the fire going and sat on the floor by the door, smoking a small pipe; no one objected because his tobacco smelt delicious. He puffed for a few minutes and said quietly; "They would have discovered by now that the other carriage contained some very talented - and hard up - actors from a show that just folded. The local police are known for pedestrian policing around here. They certainly won't venture out during darkness. But we'll take turns keeping watch."

Jericho nodded his agreement with that.

Wilson had to ask; "What the hell are you doing here McIves?" Jackie whispered to Alex; "Subtly is not the big man's strong point." Despite being tired, Alex had to chuckle at that. McIves just grinned; "Saving your butts of course!" Jericho was subtle and changed the subject; "We need to get back on track; find out what Boucher's plans are and put a stop to them."

McIves puffed his pipe and said casually; "A very talented and pleasant gentlemen will be here tomorrow and take us back into Paris; completely undetected by the police. I doubt if he will even be stopped. I've known him for some time; he's completely trustworthy and clever." He kept grinning and Wilson just had to ask; "How's he going to do that?" McIves sighed and smiled; "My friends, we're about to join a travelling circus!" Wilson just groaned and reached for the brandy bottle.

McIves laughed and then went serious; "You will never guess, for whom they will perform their first Paris show?" Everyone just looked at each other - they didn't know - of course.

McIves smiled and sucked on his pipe; "A certain Monsignor Boucher is throwing a huge costume party for his influential friends and the Circus is part of the entertainments." Now that did catch everyone's imagination and lifted their spirits; except Wilson, who just groaned loudly and shook his head. "Don't put me down to play a bloody clown; that's all." He muttered and everyone laughed, then realized the big man was serious.

6. THE CIRCUS.

The five-carriage convoy entered Paris and was not stopped.

They headed straight for the Boucher Chateau and set up camp in the grounds. Monsignor François Du Pont scratched his fiery red beard and almost smiled, he whispered to McIves; "They can act and dance? Can they?" McIves shrugged his shoulders; "As long as they look the part, they'll do fine." Du Pont grunted; he had seen McIves cross his fingers behind his back. "At least the three girls are pretty enough." He said and wandered off. The team assembled in their 'costumes' and McIves just had to laugh; but he did smile at the girls.

Wilson was now a strong man; dressed in a leopard print costume with a large, feathered bonnet - all he said was - unsmiling; "I look like a total prat." Strangely enough no one disagreed with him. Jericho was dressed as a lion tamer with a large top hat and evil looking whip. There was one slight problem with his act; they had no bloody lions. Monsignor Du Pont gave him three poodles; it wasn't quite the same. "We have to make do with what we get." He muttered to Wilson and patted the dogs; one almost took his hand off.

The girls trooped from the tent that served as their dressing room. Mademoiselle Lucy Du Pont [the daughter] actually smiled; her three new girls certainly looked the part, and they could actually dance. She would do the singing of course.

Even Wilson had to smile. The girls were dressed in quite flimsy costumes - for the time and place - but apparently, that was quite acceptable in Paris at this time. After all, the 'Can Can' dancers performed their routines without any underwear at the 'Moulin Rouge' theatre. No one complained about that apparently! The girls were dressed in very colourful outfits with multi coloured 'stage tights'; very short frilly skirts and bodices that really didn't hide their charms. They were wearing plenty of makeup and Alex admitted that their own mothers probably wouldn't recognize them.

McIves joined Jericho and Wilson - he couldn't refrain from laughing outright - and spoke quietly with the pair; "There's going to be a strong police presence tonight; the bloody Prime Minister and his wife are attending. Monsignor Boucher is not very subtle; he's coming as Napoleon Bonaparte!" They watched the girls rehearsing their routine and Wilson rubbed his chin, then groaned; "That's the routine that the New York Giants cheerleaders perform at matches."

Jericho shrugged; "As long as it keeps everyone happy and distracted; they could dance bloody 'Swan Lake' naked for all I care."

Jericho asked McIves about Monsignor Du Pont; McIves slapped his back. "He wouldn't accept any money, so I gave him the two horses from that bloody broken carriage. He was more than happy with that." The performance would start after the new style 'buffet' dinner was served. A skinny clown [Du Pont's grandson] leapt in front of Wilson and blew bubbles from his backside, laughing to himself. He bowed and Wilson told him to 'fuck off'. That ended his little impromptu performance, and he wandered off; not laughing anymore. McIves and Jericho just sighed.

The girl's rehearsal had attracted most of the police contingent on duty, along with the waiting staff and household servants. They applauded enthusiastically; especially when Alex's big nipples popped out for some fresh air. She pushed them back and Lucy whispered to her; "Do that a couple of times tonight and we'll get loads of bookings!" Alex didn't smile. With night falling on this wonderful summer evening; the circus troop gathered for meals provided by the Chateau's kitchen staff. Two young footmen desperately tried to chat up Alex and Jackie. They went back to their duties unhappy. They had never heard such language from two gorgeous girls like that before.

The performance started after dinner and everyone commented on how wonderful Monsignor Boucher looked, dressed as Napoleon Bonaparte. Jericho was on first with the very uncooperative poodles. They wouldn't jump through hoops or sit on the brightly coloured buckets. In desperation, he cracked his whip in the air a couple of times and the dogs attacked him, ripping his trousers and chewing his hat. He ran away, chased by the angry dogs, and received a standing ovation from the delighted crowd!

Wilson was on next, heaving weights about. The crowd sat in silence. So, the skinny clown leapt on the stage and pretended to lift the weights; falling about the stage. The silent crowd watched and then the young clown made the mistake of bending over right in front of a very unhappy Wilson. He couldn't resist and placed a well-aimed boot up the boys backside and the youth sprawled across the grass. The crowd laughed. He stood up and threw the supposed heavy weights at Wilson, who dodged them and chased him around the makeshift stage, kicking him up the arse. The crowd was roaring with laughter and the pair received enthusiastic applause.

The girls came on and received huge applause; Alex's troublesome nipples made a couple of appearances, and the crowd loved it. They shouted for a couple of encores. Jackie did a high kick and ripped her tights; exposing her lovely little pale bum to everyone; she rushed back to the dressing tent; cheered by the really appreciative audience.

The circus's three clowns did a comedy routine that fell flat. But Monsignor Du Pont was a clever old circus manager and set the bloody poodles on them; the clowns disappeared into the night with a dog hanging from their arses. That was the best applause the three ever had.

The fire eater went down a little better; especially when he set himself alight and Wilson had to jump up and tip a bucket of water on the dumb wretch. He was carried off stage by Wilson; still smiling as he smoldered; he was an old trooper and took such things in his stride.

Rollo the Rocket man was next. The giant cannon was hauled out and he climbed in the muzzle. His nervous assistant lit the fuse and the cannon fired. Rollo was last seen running into the darkness with his arse ablaze and screaming loudly in Bulgarian. He received a huge round of applause, not that he heard it, sitting in the small river crying for his mum.

Lucy finished the performance by singing '"La Marseillaise" – badly - but with lots of enthusiasm and pride. The Prime Minister was seen wiping a tear away; he loved France as much as teenage girls. Everyone applauded with real pride.

McIves stood watching with Monsignor Du Pont, who admitted

that he wanted to hire the team, especially Jericho and Alex. "Best bloody performance in years." He said, scratching his red beard. Jericho appeared panting and grabbed Wilson; they were going to look for Napoleon's time portal. But he had to run away again; the bloody poodles had picked up his scent.

Monsignor Du Pont sighed; "Never seen the dogs take to someone like your man." He walked off, shaking his head and muttering about how unfair circus life could be. He had found one of the best 'circus troops' in years and they wouldn't join the show.

Napoleon stood in his study and scratched his head; three snarling poodles rushed past the French windows. One had a chewed top hat in his mouth and the other two were carrying some very ripped coloured trousers. He grunted and sat down. He slowly read the papers before him. Then a light went on in great man's head, where the hell had he seen such a pair of wonderful big nipples before? He jumped up and shouted for his guards; several men assembled in his study; all armed. "The bloody circus you fools! Tibbs and his bloody team are here! Find them!" He shouted, pulling a pistol from his desk drawer. He led his men out in the darkness.

7. INSPECTOR LE GRANDE'S GREAT RAID.

Inspector Le Grande stood by the gates with his large contingent of Gendarmes and watched through his binoculars, he turned to his fat sergeant; "I don't have a clue what's going on but be careful. There are guard dogs patrolling the place. I've just seen one chewing some poor sod's top hat." The sergeant nodded and picked his nose. The Inspector slapped his hand, then noticed Rollo the Rocket man, staggering back through the woods, clutching his backside and sobbing in Bulgarian.

"Do you hear that sergeant? He must be a bloody Russian Bolshevik - arrest him at once - the place is crawling with bloody Russian revolutionaries!" Two Gendarmes dragged the shouting man away. They didn't understand Bulgarian, so they beat him with their batons and handcuffed him. Rollo wasn't having a good night.

The three sad clowns wandered up and stood staring at the police - who stared back - they had no trousers on, the dogs had got them. Inspector Le Grande shouted; "Arrest those perverts! They're exposing themselves to officers of the law!" The three clowns - protesting loudly - were dragged away to the waiting police wagons. Now a bit calmer, Le Grande continued to watch the Chateau and its grounds. He watched Monsignors Boucher - still dressed as himself - Napoleon - heading for the Circus encampment with several heavily armed men. He turned to the Sergeant: "I didn't think the performance was that bad." He muttered. Then a light went on in the Inspectors head; two women in the dance troop had reminded him of some ladies that he had encountered; but where? He snapped his fingers - of course, those two damn fugitives! - And Boucher was headed there with armed men. "Come on boys! Let's get the bastards!" He also led his men into the darkness.

McIves was sitting on the stone wall of the Chateau, smoking his pipe and watching the events unfold before him. He chuckled to himself; "Jericho my old friend, you sure know how to entertain a fugitive time traveler!" He pulled out his hip flask and took a sip and then settled in to watch. Two young Gendarmes ran past him - trousers in tatters - trying to fend off three snarling poodles with their chewed batons. "Good doggies." Was all McIves said and puffed at his pipe.

There were lots of women screaming, cussing and shouting at the circus encampment. The Gendarmes had raided the tent where the girls had their dressing rooms.

Lucy ran past him, dressed only in her panties and clutching her very ample breasts with both hands; pursued by several policeman; all panting and grinning.

The skinny clown was dragged past by his feet, swearing and shouting, bubbles pouring from his trousers. The two policemen - like Wilson earlier - weren't laughing. McIves chuckled and sucked on his pipe. Then things turned a little serious; he could hear shots being fired. He watched flashes of shotguns going off and several of Napoleon's men ran past him, throwing away their guns and shouting - in French obviously - "Fuck this for a game of bowls!" He sat back and smiled.

The great man [Napoleon] was carried past by four Gendarmes; each gripping a limb and he was shouting - with lots of swear words - "DON'T YOU KNOW WHO THE HELL I FUCKIN AM?" They clearly didn't and beat him with their batons. McIves just shrugged his shoulders and took another sip from his hip flask. Monsignor Du Pont was dragged past, still clutching the tin that held the night's takings. He waved to McIves; "Tell them [the team] I'll pay them double wages...." His voice faded in the darkness.

Inspector Le Grande appeared with the fat panting sergeant in tow. He wasn't happy; "Where the fuck did they go? I saw them run into the props tent and they simply vanished!" He stopped and stared up at the wall; just for a second there, he thought he saw someone sitting up there laughing to himself. He shook his head; he needed a fucking drink.

Jericho and the team stood in Napoleons/Boucher's study and watched the police, and their wagons depart. Jericho scratched his head; "Come on people, mirrors out and let's find that bloody time portal." They split up and started the search. The girls found it; the beautiful chest was hidden in an empty upstairs bedroom. They carefully lifted the lid and saw the non reflective mirrors. Jackie slowly closed the lid and Alex called Jericho and Wilson on her mirror. Ruth commented on just how lovely the chest was but stopped in mid-sentence. They watched in surprise and amazement as the lid was slowly pushed up and a gorgeous Chinese girl stepped out.

She was clearly a 'Geisha' girl; dressed in the traditional costume. She bowed low and handed Alex a piece of paper; written in Chinese Mandarin, of course - and said softly; "Lord Boucher never said it would be an orgy with many beautiful ladies." Alex just smiled, then rubbed her chin; "Surely Geisha girls are from Japan?" The young woman bowed again; "Sorry, but nobody's bloody perfect." Shuffling down the corridor, she disappeared into Boucher's/Napoleon's huge bedroom. They watched her go in silence. Then the lid of the chest opened again, and they watched - still silent - as two medieval women stepped from it; they adjusted their huge, strange hats and smoothed down their dresses. The older one-handed Alex another piece of paper and both curtsied.

Alex gestured towards Boucher's bedroom and didn't smile; they looked suspiciously like mother and daughter. She read the note; they were mother and daughter from 1422!

Jackie said softly; "What the fuck is going on?" The two women, holding their exquisite gowns, walked off down the corridor and into the big bedroom. Alex stood hands on hips and sighed; "Close the bloody portal before even more turn up!" Jackie nodded and operated her mirror. She carefully lifted the lid and smiled with satisfaction; she could now see her own reflection in the mirrors inside.

Ruth had followed the two ladies down and peered through the bedroom door as they entered. She walked back to Alex and Jackie, looking quite puzzled; "The rooms full of women, from all different times apparently." She said and then went a little red. "There are two big African men standing stark naked with feathered bonnets on and they're...." She stopped talking and actually blushed, adding - in a whisper - "They really are big. If you know what I mean." She blushed again. Alex just sighed; "He really is a dirty old Emperor." She muttered; this would take some explaining to Jericho!

Jericho just nodded; "We have to get him back [Napoleon] and return the dirty old bugger back to 1821 to meet his scheduled departure date." They gathered in the empty ballroom; Jericho would call upon the assistance of another team, to shepherd the guests in Napoleon's bedroom back to their own times. Alex really did smile when Jericho announced that Inspector Harry Hadden's team was on way. She really looked forward to meeting the dashing, handsome and charming young Harry again. Jericho and Wilson chuckled at the look on Alex's face. They stopped being happy when they looked at the doorway of the ballroom.

Jericho slowly pulled his orb from his coat pocket and saw that it was blood red; he operated the emergency assistance app on his mirror immediately. Monsignor Laurent stood there, arms folded and unsmiling. Jericho had recognised Janis, the Tier One demon, despite his handsome human disguise. "Hurry the fuck up good knight." He whispered; the demon had started to smile, and it wasn't a pleasant one.

Jericho smiled and held up a hand; "Evening Sir. You missed the circus I'm afraid." He said and shrugged his shoulders. The demon laughed; "Jericho, you have balls of steel. I actually may regret sending you into the darkness." He raised both hands and the team flinched in horrific anticipation of what was about to happen to them.

James casually walked from the French doors that opened onto the magnificent gardens. He nodded at Janis but smiled and spoke to Jericho. "I think you had better go Jericho and find bloody Napoleon. I'll take care of my old adversary Janis." James said softly and transformed; he was now in his silver armour complete with huge sword. Just before they vanished, the team watched the Demon Janis transform into his armour; black of course.

Jackie groaned; she had really wanted to watch the two go to battle. Jericho really admonished her for that; "You really wouldn't want to be around if James got vanquished again." Wilson looked confused by that; "Surely James wins each time?" Jericho just sighed; "I think the score so far, is four to three in James favour. Good doesn't always win you know."

There was only one Knight of God who had a 100% record in these clashes of good and evil; that was 'Arthur' he was colloquially known as 'God's Champion', Arthur had vanished every demon he had encountered. The Dark Side had their 'undefeated Champion' too; he was called - rather unusually for a demon - 'Big Bernie'. Everyone waited in real anticipation of their eventual clash. If betting was possible in the afterlife, then the best odds you could get - for either of the pair - would be 'Evens'.

They stood in the busy street opposite the police station and watched the crowds gathering outside. There were several armed gendarmes [brandishing rifles] guarding the big front doors. "Inspector Le Grande is obviously taking no chances." Jericho muttered and gestured for the team to join him in a little 'Cafe Tabac' for coffee and brandies.

8. THE PARIS POLICE SATION SEIGE.

The little' Cafe Tabac' was packed, but three young men - rather gallantly - gave up their seats to the ladies. Alex and Jackie thanked them and let them kiss their hands. One young man lingered so long over kissing Jackie's hand that she had to wipe it with a napkin. Jericho spoke quietly despite the noise in the little cafe; "Now, how the hell do we get in there?" Everyone just looked at each other and shrugged their shoulders. A very harassed waiter slapped a tray of brandies down and muttered he would bring the coffees - when he could - but smiled at the girls. Jericho gave him a good tip - a very good tip - and he was back almost instantly. He was unhappy again when he asked Jackie out; she told him where to go, in a very un-lady like manner.

Jericho and Wilson stood by the windows and watched as Inspector Le Grande rushed from the police station into several carriages with about a dozen armed men. "Now what the fuck is going on?" Wilson said and rubbed his chin in puzzlement. Jericho smiled and rubbed his hands together; "Great timing. They must have found the notes I wrote and burnt in the fireplace. I knew it would take time to decipher them. Their police scientists must have just read what I wrote."

Wilson nodded and asked; "What the hell did you write on them?" Jericho shrugged his shoulders; "That Boucher and I were about to assassinate the French president and signal the Kaiser [the German Emperor] that he could invade. That's all and it worked." Wilson just groaned.

Jericho whispered to Alex, then turned to both girls; "Off you go. Work your magic and charm; get in that police station. Soon as you find bloody Napoleon call me." The girls sighed - in unison - and headed for the station, now surrounded by an unhappy mob. There were several Bulgarian refugees waving banners - in Bulgarian - that no one could understand. That started a fight with the local natives, who didn't like foreign refugees at the best of times and Alex went straight up to the first young policeman; nervously clutching his rifle and smiled at him. She gestured to Jackie and whispered in his ear. He grinned and escorted them inside.

Wilson rubbed his chin again; "What the hell did she say?" He asked a happy Jericho who downed his brandy in one hit. "Just that they're high-class working girls; summoned by Inspector Le Grande to celebrate the arrest of the traitor Boucher. It's very common to have a piss up and some entertainment when they crack a case open."

Wilson chuckled; "And with the good Inspector racing to the presidents aid; there's no one to question that bloody story. Though Alex won't be happy playing the tart again." He had to smile; Jericho really did amaze him at times. They left the little café and waited in a quiet alley, where no one should notice their disappearance when they received the girls call. Ruth chuckled to herself; the thought of 'Jackie' having to play the tart made her smile.

The young policeman had Jackie against the office door with his probing tongue firmly buried in her mouth and his hands inside her bodice. Alex just smiled and carefully removed the cell keys from the hook behind the door. Jackie finally managed to extradite herself from his grip and throw a mean right hook into his smiling face. He lay on the floor; unconscious, but still grinning.

Jackie brushed down her skirts and pushed her abused bosom back into her bodice. "Let's go." Was all Alex said and they sneaked down the corridor; every available copper was outside dealing with the mob. They found Napoleon sitting in a rough cell, nursing his bruised testicles. He looked up at the girls and groaned; what he said in French wasn't pleasant. Alex operated her mirror and called Jericho.

"The randy little bastard must have cleaned his teeth with bloody garlic." Jackie moaned and wiped her mouth with a dainty hankie; she needed a brandy to take the taste away. The rest of the team appeared, and Jericho took the cell keys from Alex with a big smile; "Well done girls. I knew a true Frenchman couldn't resist two gorgeous and willing tarts. Wilson and Jackie will escort our time travelling emperor back to 1821 and make sure he meets his departure on time." He unlocked the cell and Napoleon stood and almost smiled. "You can smile Jericho Tibbs, but you haven't heard the last of me, I can promise you that." He disappeared with Wilson and Jackie firmly gripping an arm each.

Jericho operated his mirror and the remainder of the team also disappeared. Sitting in the opposite cell was McIves who laughed to himself. Sometimes travelling in time could prove a real laugh and great entertainment. He sighed and disappeared too. The old drunk sitting on the floor next to him rubbed his eyes and sighed; that was the last time he drank bloody cheap Russian vodka. He would stick to Pernod and toilet cleaner in future.

Inspector Le Grande sat in his quiet office and rubbed his backside, where the President's boot had landed. He shuffled the papers about his desk and ran his fingers through his little black beard. With Boucher gone - simply vanished - he was forced to release the circus people. He re-read the report of what happened during the siege of his police station and sighed loudly.

The only good thing to have happened was the demise of Dumont and Faulds. Those two murdering bastards death was the best thing to happen for some years. Women could now walk the streets feeling a lot safer. The sudden and baffling disappearance of Monsignor Laurent from Boucher's villa was also a total mystery. It was now five to three in James favour.

He rose and walked to the small window that overlooked the now quiet streets of Paris, his beloved city. His colleagues in French Intelligence had reported that 'Lord Tibbs' did not exist, and British Intelligence had confirmed that fact. He watched night creeping in and rubbed his backside again. There was more to this strange case than he could fathom. The police Commissioner had thrown his detailed report in the waste basket; right in front of him and shouted for some time. He wouldn't make Chief Inspector now.

Then there was the strange case of the Spanish looking 'Scotsman' who had paid his hotel bill in old Spanish Gold coins. He had also vanished too. Le Grande walked back to his desk and pulled a vodka bottle from the bottom drawer and slowly uncorked it. The only little ray of sunshine in the whole bloody mess was his forthcoming little assignation with the delightful Madame Fibrion. He poured some vodka into his coffee cup and knocked it back in one hit.

Jean-Paul, the regular old drunk had sworn on his mother's grave - if he ever had a mother - that a big olive-skinned male had simply vanished in front of him. After several other people had done so; including three very pretty ladies. Le Grande knew full well who they were. No one would believe the drunks incredible story. But he did.

THE END

EPILOGUE:

"This mission was deemed a success; the Team had prevented changes to the current human timeline at a critical period in its development. They believed that a very dangerous Time Portal had been closed and that a soul had been saved from the darkness. [Lady Covington's soul would have been lost if she had

died out of her own time] But the team had to go after the Wiley Napoleon - yet again! - When he appeared back in France in 1910 with a plan to change France's fortune in the forthcoming World War I. Jericho and his team managed to thwart his plans and return Napoleon to 1821."
SJW.

CHARCTERS:

Captain Jean Pullaire was killed at Waterloo, serving with his cavalry Regiment. He was buried in a mass grave with no record of his name. He is now lost to history. His soul was collected and processed.

Monsieur Cission carried out his master's orders [Napoleon I] with great skill and dedication. He built a fine travelling chest, and the inside of the Chinese cabinet was fitted to the chest. It is understood that the chest was taken by Napoleon into exile. Monsieur Cission took the secret of the switch to his grave. He died in 1826 and his soul was collected and processed. Jericho and Wilson had no idea that the Chinese cabinet no longer was a time portal. They had used their mirrors to escape the musket fire of Napoleon's troops.

Colonel Henri Durand finally appeared at Fontainebleau Palace with his survey and was promptly thrown into prison! He was there for some days until General Charles Dulauloy turned up in person; to vouch for him. Napoleon was - apparently - very disappointed to find that Durand's wife was a sickly creature, who didn't dance or smile much. The Colonel was released, and the story of his incarceration is a family legend to this day. Colonel Durand died in 1831 and his soul was collected and possessed. His wife had preceded him by 9 years.

Lieutenant Vaccaro was killed at Waterloo in 1815. Human Records show that he actually was an illegitimate son of the Great Emperor Napoleon I. He was buried in a mass grave and so remains anonymous to history. His soul was collected and processed.

Colonel Le Grande's luck finally ran out; he had survived the Battle of Waterloo without a scratch. But on the retreat back to Paris, his horse was scared by a barking dog and threw him against a wall. The Colonel suffered head injuries and died a few days later. He was buried hastily in an unmarked grave; the whereabouts are still not discovered to this day. His soul was collected and processed. Inspector Le Grande was his great grandson and had clearly inherited his knack for being lucky; well, for a while at least!

Marshal Nay continued to service France after Napoleon's abdication in 1814. He served the French King Louis XVIII until Napoleon's return and the start of the famous 100 days - ending at Waterloo - Nay had re-joined Napoleon and after the Emperors final defeat, he was executed by firing squad for treason to the new French King in 1815. His final words were: " *Soldiers, when I give the command to fire, fire straight at my heart. Wait for the order. It will be my last to you. I protest against my condemnation. I have fought a hundred battles for France, and not one against her. Soldiers, fire!*" Napoleon always called Nay 'the bravest of the brave' - he was right - as usual. His soul was collected and processed.

Lady Helena Covington ['Lady of Guisse'] didn't have to explain much about her bed rest, suffering from a gunshot wound - to her estranged husband - he simply didn't care. In the summer of 1865, she gave birth to a son. Her husband was pleased he had a legitimate heir, without having to sleep with the woman he hated! Human Records show the boy's father was NOT Napoleon I. Lady Helena died in 1910. Her soul was collected and processed. It was just co-incidence; that Napoleon died on St. Helena, which had the same name of the mistress, who could have altered his destiny and that of the world!

Jean Hessaine was Jericho's Human Agent for this time and place; died in 1827 from 'Consumption'. His soul was collected and processed.

Madame Aglae - Duchess of Elchingen [Marshal Nay's wife] survived her husband and died in 1854. Her soul was collected and processed.

Madame Margaret Du Loupe fell from Napoleon's favour, just weeks after the Fontainebleau incident and his subsequent abdication. She returned to her husband and lived in Normandy until her death in 1833. Her soul was collected and processed.

Lucus Boucher was murdered on Napoleon's orders in 1821 and

his body used to cover Napoleon's escape to 1910. But Napoleon could do nothing about Boucher's soul and so, temporal detectives where soon on the emperor's trail. Boucher's soul was collected and processed.

General Joffre commanded the French Army at the outbreak of the war [1914-1918] until 1916. He is mostly remembered for victory, at the Battle of the Marne in 1914, which is credited with saving France. He died in 1931 and his soul was collected and processed.

Colonel Mardue was the General's aide until 1915, when for some personal reason; his was transferred to an active unit from Staff HQ. He was killed at Verdun in 1916. He had been a professional soldier all his life and had no real family. His soul was collected and processed.

Monsignor Beasson was Boucher/Napoleon's private secretary and knew little of what the emperor was planning. After Boucher/napoleon's disappearance in 1910 he worked for various wealthy men around Paris. He never married and died in 1927. His soul was collected and processed.

Madame Fibroin, the human agent for this time and place continued to use her talents for the Temporal detectives Department over her lifetime. She married three times and had one daughter - Maude - and died in 1942 under the Nazi occupation. She was - of course - a member of the French resistance and was killed in a fight with the Gestapo, when they raided a 'safe House' she was guarding. Her soul was collected and processed. She now works as a Collector and has applied to join the Temporal Detectives; Inspector Doc Underhill has thrown his weight and very worthy reputation behind her application. She awaits the Angels decision.

Monsignor Jean Dumont was shot and killed in his police cell by an assassin paid for by Napoleon/Boucher to prevent him talking. His soul was collected and processed; it was quarantined for 250 Human years because of five murders he had carried out over his time amongst the living.

Norman Faulds was also shot in his police cell, awaiting interview by Inspector Le Grande. His soul was collected and processed. It received 200 human years in quarantine for various murders and killings. On an odd note, a couple of dozen Paris prostitutes sang and danced behind his modest funeral cortege; they were glad to be rid of an evil, sadistic client!

Countess Evelyn Fredericks [unknown to her husband] turned out to be a 'double agent' with her loyalty lying firmly with Great Britain. Her husband didn't survive the war; his biplane was shot down in early 1915 over Ypres, flying for the Imperial German Luftwaffe. She married again - having returned to England - in 1920. She had three children and died in 1937. Her soul was collected and processed.

Inspector Le Grande retired from the police in 1919 and moved to Normandy, where he ran a small farm. He married a much younger woman [there was 17 years between them] in 1922 and had four children; both his two sons joined the Paris police service. He died in 1935 surrounded by his large and loving family; he had succumbed to throat cancer. His soul was collected and processed.

Monsignor François Du Pont continued to run his small travelling circus until 1917, when he died suddenly from a particularly nasty bout of 'flu. His soul was collected and processed.

Mademoiselle Lucy Du Pont took over the circus and continued to manage it until 1924. She met an American journalist that year and the pair quickly married. She lived the remainder of her life in New York and had three children. She died in 1951. Her soul was collected and processed.

Monsignor Laurent [aka 'Janis the demon'] lost yet another battle with James and was cast back to his master - the Dark Prince - but remains a senior minion. Demon Ingress currently reports his whereabouts as Moscow, in the year 1981. Alexander - a Knight of God - and team 34 are on his trail.

SPECIAL APPEARANCE BY Emperor Napoleon Bonaparte I, as himself.

Napoleon Bonaparte died on the 5th May, 1821 at Longwood, Saint Helena. He was 51 years old and had conquered most of Europe during a very short time. He is still regarded as a Military genus by many. His soul was collected and processed. He was given no quarantine for his 'time travelling' adventures.

EPISODE 7: "XAVIER TABBERT'S HOSPITAL FOR THE DEAD, THE DYING AND THE UNFORGIVEN."

MISSION SUMMARY: "Dr. Xavier Tabbert opened his hospital for the chronically sick in the autumn of 1849. It was supposed to be a place of final and peaceful rest for those facing certain death; in modern times it would be referred to as a 'Hospice'. Now in 1999, a team of paranormal students under Professor Alec Sweetman have arrived at the derelict hospital to investigate the many strange happenings that have occurred over the years - are they about to encounter some real evil?"

NOTES: Contains references to poltergeist/Demonic activity.

TRIGGER WARNINGS. ALCOHOL, BAD LANGUAGE, SOME SEXUAL REFERENCES, MILD VIOLENCE & MILD HORROR.

AGE 12+ ONLY. **30 Minutes reading time.**

1. THE FIELD TRIP; DAY ONE.

The University mini bus turned from the road into Tabbert's Lane; "It may get bumpy so hold on!" 'Sibby' shouted [Ms Sylvia Fellows] and the other three occupants gripped seats and arm rests. Sibby kept a tight grip on the wheel and the minibus struggled up the gravel lane; sodden by weeks of rain. "Well, I'm not getting out and bloody pushing." Jen Phillips called out to no one in particular. She drew on her shaking cigarette. She was sitting right next to a large 'NO SMOKING' sign on the window and didn't give a fuck; like she did about most things "You would have thought that old 'Sweetie' [Professor Alec Sweetman] would have bloody warned us about the bloody road." She added and blew little smoke rings about.

Callan Carter just grimaced and waved the smoke away; he was sitting behind Jen and had probably smoked three of her cigarettes with her. "For fuck sake Jen; couldn't you wait to light up when we stop?" He muttered and leaned back in his seat.

'Bloody selfish bitch.' He thought and stared out at the drizzle tumbling down the window. 'Why the fuck did 'iron pants' bother to come on this fucking field trip? She doesn't really belief in any of it.' He kept those thoughts to himself. Jen wasn't shy in expressing her opinion on what people thought about her and didn't care either - apparently - and for the sake of a peaceful trip, Callan would say silent, about what he really thought of her; a self-opinionated, loud mouthed selfish bitch.

Little Morris Maxwell - sitting next to Sibby - smiled; "Should we erect a ring and let them fight it out?" Sibby chuckled and dropped a gear; "No Mouse; she'll bloody kill him." 'Mouse' did laugh quietly at that. He was always called 'Mouse' because he was so small; lots of people told him that he should have been a Jockey; other's weren't so nice; they called him the 'dwarf', 'Midget man' or 'mini man'. He pretended not to care and laugh along with the insensitive bastards; but sometimes the little pain inside wouldn't go away. He glanced at Sibby hanging onto the juddering wheel and sighed; he absolutely adored her. But she wouldn't - of course - look at him twice. All her previous boyfriends were sportsmen or academics or both. Sibby slowed the van and peered through the wet windscreen at the big iron gates. They were heavily padlocked.

The Tabbert hospital for incurables lay shrouded in rain. Sibby stopped the van and said quietly; "For Christ sake, they could make horror movies here." Mouse nodded and tapped her arm; he had seen the figure coming down the path, hunched up in a yellow raincoat with the hood up and walking slowly despite the rain. "Who the fuck is that?" He said softly. Jen tossed her cigarette on the carpets and stubbed it out with her boot. "Fucking Egor of course. He's just woke up Doctor Fucking Frankenstein and told that his new laboratory mice have arrived.

"You had better be careful mouse; you'll be the first under his knife." Jen said, laughing at her own supposed humour. Mouse just smiled; "Yeah, very funny Jen." He really wanted to say something else; but couldn't bring himself to do so.

They watched as the hunched figure began to unlock the three heavy padlocks on the gates, with keys from a big iron key ring. He looked up at the van and its occupants, wiping rain from his face. "Holy fuck! old doctor Frankenstein must have bloody experimented on him." Jen shouted, then laughed adding; "They must have hired the ugly bastard because his mug matches this derelict dump." They could all see the scarred face and twisted lips on the man. He swung open the big gates with little effort and walked towards the van. "Stow any comments please Jen. He must be Gary the caretaker. We don't want to upset the bloody employee's and get thrown off site before we even start." Sibby turned, not smiling at her 'friend'. Jen just shrugged her shoulders.

Gary the caretaker walked up to the driver's side window and tried to smile. It just made his appearance worse. Sibby rolled the window halfway down and did smile at him. "You the party....party...from York University...Profes...Profes..the Sweetman party?" He finally stuttered out. Sibby nodded; realising he was quite a young man; probably in his early twenties. Everyone noticed his stutter. "For fuck sake, course we are. York University is written down both side of the fucking van." Jen muttered quietly; for once.

Sibby explained that the Professor was following in his own car but should be here soon. She introduced herself and briefly, the others in the van. Gary nodded and gestured towards the old hospital; "The East wing....on your...your right...is the only....hab...hab...hab.." He stopped talking and wiped his face; "The only...only part you can use." He stared at the ground and stepped aside as Sibby started the van and thanked him with a big smile.

The van pulled past the man and Jen laughed out loud; "For fuck sake, the place does have its own Egor and what a fucking dummy." Callan just sighed and stared back at figure watching them drive away, up the long driveway towards the old hospital. "Poor bastard, no wonder he lives and works in a place like this." Callan said and mouse agreed with him. Jen just laughed to herself. Sibby stopped outside the 'East Wing' and everyone stared at the building. This part looked alright. Well, the window's still had glass in and the roof above didn't appear to have gaping holes.

"According to Sweetie, this part of the building still has electricity, running water, heating, toilets and showers." Sibby said, leaning back in her seat. "I wonder where the caretaker stays?" Mouse asked.

"Probably got a fucking coffin in the cellars." chuckled Jen and pulled out a cigarette and lighter from her big handbag. No one laughed and Sibby sighed; "We'll get the bags out first and set up the equipment later. We have maps of the place, so, we'll need to look around first. Pick the best places to set up." Mouse agreed with that and pulled on his coat, placing on a bright red woolen hat on his head. That made Jen laugh; "You now look like a fucking gnome." No one laughed at that either. "Come on." Was all Sibby said. The team decamped from the van, grabbing their bags,

Sibby turned and found Gary standing there; she wondered immediately how he got up the drive so fast! He gestured to the big black door and held up a couple of keys. "I'll unlock...unlock for you miss...everything is...on." He stuttered and unlocked the door. Sibby noticed one hand was badly scarred with the little finger missing. The other hand was big and quite normal. She immediately noticed the wedding ring on his finger. Christ, he's married. Then told herself off for being surprised at that.

The little team strolled in and found themselves in some sort of reception area. There was big desk and chairs stacked all round. It looked like a hotel foyer that had definitely seen better days. "There's a kitch...kitchen behind...and toilets." He stopped, staring at the floor again; "And a shower...plenty of...plenty of hot....hot water." He nodded at everyone and left without another word.

"Let’s get settled in. Explore what we have and find a bloody kettle; I'm dying for a cup of tea." Sibby told the others and watched Gary the caretaker disappearing into the rain. Under his awful yellow raincoat, he was quite a big man and definitely only in his twenties. She wondered if they would meet his wife during their stay; she really hoped so. They set up their camp bed in two small rooms off the reception area. Sadly, Sibby would have to share with Jen; "Now that's a real bloody treat." She muttered to herself, throwing her sleeping bag and pillow on her wobbly, old ex-army camp bed. "Smile please." Mouse pointed the camera at her from the doorway and Sibby grinned and bowed a little. "Make sure you film all this. Show the bloody Dean that field trips are not holidays." She told Mouse, who nodded and disappeared, operating his camera with some skill, around the semi dark corridors and rooms.

The team met up for tea in the foyer and ate their packed lunches. They laughed and joked about the old hospital and the stories and legends about the place. Mouse lifted up on his chair and said - with a broad smile - "The boss is here." Sibby dropped her cheese sandwich back in her lunch box and went to the door. She didn't notice the amused look that passed between Callan and Mouse. She watched the professor jump from his old car - a classic Jaguar from the Fifties - collect his bags and walk to the door. He grinned and lifted his bags in greeting. Sibby opened the door and watched him walk up.

Professor Alistair (Alec) Sweetman was a tall, athletic and very handsome man. He was employed to teach History, but the University allowed him to indulge in his hobby - that he was quite passionate about - the study of the paranormal and supernatural. He was thirty-eight years old and had been widowed for five.

His wife Christina dying of breast cancer just a year after their marriage. Sibby watched him come through the door shouting; "Everyone here? Everyone OK?" and dump his bags on the floor. Mouse called back; "Yes boss, including Jen." rolling his eyes in mock despair. Sibby watched her 'boss' carefully; he only had to wag his finger at her again and....she pushed those delicious thoughts and memories away. She would have private words with him, when the occasion arose.

He was dressed like some fashionable young man from the fifties. Three-piece suit, fob watch, classic brown shoes, 'Mackintosh' raincoat and Homburg hat. He openly admitted to being born in the wrong time. He loved the forties and fifties and lived the part; much to the amusement of his students and colleagues. But he was immensely popular with both. He stood hands on hips and looked about. "Well people, we are truly privileged to be here. There have only been two sets of paranormal teams allowed to study this place. So let's do a damn fine job." He removed his hat and joined the group.

Sibby actually shifted her chair to sit next to him. Mouse finished his sandwich and asked the professor; "What did the other team discover? Is there a report available? I didn't think anyone else had been here. I can't find any of their reports."

The professor didn't smile - he sat, hat clasped in his hands - and looked around. He said softly; "They didn't make any reports, I'm afraid." Callan sipped his tea and asked; "Why not boss?" The professor almost smiled; "They didn't make out a report because they simply vanished, they were never seen or heard of again. That was in 1956 and all three simply disappeared from here."

There was absolute silence until Jen said, "Well that's fucking terrific news." She actually felt herself shudder a little; if she had known that wonderful fucking fact; she wouldn't have come. Alec smiled; "Let me settle in and we'll decide on the placement of cameras and microphones. You ok for the thermometers Jen?" She nodded; wishing she was at fucking home watching the TV.

It was quite a subdued team of paranormal investigators that placed their equipment around certain parts of the old hospital that afternoon. There were places they simply couldn't go; parts of the building were closed off because it was dangerous. They settled down and waited the night.

2. FIRST NIGHT.

It was just after seven in the evening and Sibby sat on the chair and watched the monitor; the screen was split into six channels. She adjusted the contrast on Number 4 - for the second time - and returned to her book; 'Pride & Prejudice.' She was covering 6pm to 10pm. Mouse would take the 'witching hours'; ten to two in the morning. The boss had volunteered to take the two to six slot. That allowed the other two to have - hopefully - an undisturbed night of sleep.

She looked up from her book, occasionally glancing at the

flickering screen. She heard something behind her and turned slowly; it sounded like something hitting the floor. There was no one there. Then she noticed the old leather-bound book on the floor; open. She eased from her seat and walked over. Sibby slowly picked the book up and stared at the open page.

"5th July 1956. Three people had signed the visitors book: Mr. John Crabb, Mr. Malcom Sands and Miss Florence Hammond. Leeds University." She read out loud to herself and felt a shiver run up her spine. She knew that was the other team of paranormal investigators - the ones who had vanished here - and she looked around; nothing. "How the hell did it fall off the desk? It must have sat there for years; it's covered in dust. Why fall open at that page?" She was talking to herself for comfort.

She jumped as Alec appeared in the doorway; two cups of tea in his big hands. "Brew time." He said simply and saw the look on her face. He gestured to the chairs in front of the monitor. Sibby took her tea and joined him, explaining about the book. The professor had his notebook out in an instant, scribbling with a well chewed pencil. His tea placed on the dusty floor.

They were deep in conversation when Sibby noticed that the professor - on finishing his notes - reached down for his teacup and found it wasn't there. Nothing was said between the pair, and they carefully and slowly looked around the room.

Sibby actually let out a little yelp; the teacup was on the desk. They both rose from their chairs. Sibby was now shaking a little with the hairs on her arms and neck standing. Alec slowly took her hand and gripped it; he was a picture of calmness. "Keep cool Sibby. I think something is trying to make contact." Sibby could only manage to nod and gripped his big hand tightly; she wouldn't be letting go any time in the immediate future.

They both noticed that the room was ice cold. Sibby could feel her big nipples standing up and visibly showing through her blouse. They both jumped and Sibby let out a scream; they hadn't noticed Mouse come through the door; also holding two cups of tea.

"Christ boss, you and I must have had the same idea. I think we should speak to Gary about the bloody heating in here. It's like a bloody morgue." Sibby sighed and felt the professor release her hand. She wished Mouse hadn't mentioned a bloody 'morgue'. Mouse grinned and held up the cups; "You can have mine. I'll brew another." That's when the cup on the desk flew across the room, smashing on the doorframe by the shocked Mouse's head.

Alec said quietly and with some real authority; "Get the hell out of here. Poltergeist." But he was very calm, and they ran for the door and into the corridor. Alec slammed the door behind them and they stood in silence. He turned to his visibly shaken colleagues and shrugged his shoulders; "Well, we found out one thing about our supernatural visitor." Mouse - between gritted teeth - had to ask; "What's that boss?" Mumbling and rubbing his arms from the cold. Alec smiled a little; "It clearly doesn't like tea."

The three chuckled and Sibby felt a little better. "We now know that there must be substance to the supernatural stories about this place. We've just witnessed it." She said quietly. Alec was listening against the door and nodded; "I can hear a strange noise. I'm not sure but I think it's someone's crying; sobbing actually."

Mouse pressed against the door and went a little pale; "Your bloody right boss. I can hear it too." Sibby stood back, arms folded and wished she was a home in her own bed with Foster [her big tabby cat] laid on the pillows. Alec struggled to concentrate; "I think its saying something. Can you make it out Mouse?" Mouse pulled from the door and wiped his face; he looked terrified. "Yes, I can." He said and stepped well away from the door. Sibby said quietly; "What was it saying?" Mouse stared at both of them and folded his arms and said softly; "Get the fuck out of here."

The professor stood - hands in pockets - looking like he was waiting for a bus, a total picture of calm. He sighed; "Well, all our equipment is in the foyer. So, we must go back in." The others exchanged a nervous glance; both saying the same thing without speaking a word: fuck the equipment.

Callan joined them, yawning; "What's up people?" Then saw the looks on Sibby's and Mouse's faces. "Oh, fucking shit." Was all he said. After a brief discussion, it was decided that Alec and Callan would go in. Sibby fetched two small radios' from her room - not disturbing the sleeping Jen - and returned with them. Both were set to Channel two and the professor tested his. Sibby standing down the corridor gave the thumbs up and answered Alec.

He gave the thumbs up and she re-joined them.

Alec hesitated with his hand on the door handle. He turned and smiled; "Should I knock? It may appreciate the courtesy." Everyone chuckled; the boss was certainly the man to have in a tight situation. He slowly turned the handle and pushed slowly into the room. He noticed immediately the warmth in the room and sighed with a little relief; turning to the others, he said softly; "I think it's gone." They shuffled into the room and looked about. Sibby raised her hand and pointed to the old reception desk or rather the small door behind it marked; 'KEEP OUT. AUTHORISED STAFF ONLY', she knew full well that the door had been shut and locked. She whispered to Mouse; "Do you know where that goes?" Mouse nodded and really didn't smile; "To the bloody cellars."

Callan said what they were all thinking; "Is it an invitation? But to where or what?" Alec gestured to the bags by the window; "There are torches in there. It would be quite rude not to accept." Everyone looked at each other - again - with the same thought. 'Who the hell is going with the boss?'

Everyone jumped again as someone knocked on the front door. They all stared at the door and jumped yet again; "Well, are you going to bloody answer it?" Jen wandered in - wearing her 'Thomas the tank engine' pajama's - and walked over and pulled it open. She spoke briefly and turned to Alec; "You ain't going to believe this boss. It's another bloody professor and his team from Edinburgh University. They're in the same game as us!" She stood aside and the visitors wandered in, burdened down with baggage and equipment.

The tall young man in the old raincoat held out his hand to Alec; "Jerry Tibbs. Edinburgh University: I normally teach history, but my little hobby is chasing the unknown. This is my team."

Alec shook his hand - with some disbelief - another bloody team of paranormal investigators! "Mr. Prouse [a member of the Board of Trustee's for the old hospital] said that another group was already here. Which surprised me as we had this place booked a couple of months ago." Jerry spoke quietly looking around the foyer and nodded, addressing his team; "This is the last place that the team in '56 were seen alive. The caretaker at the time; a Mr. Ray Evan's reported that they were about to explore the cellars."

Alec's team all looked at each other - except Jen - she hadn't been present, she had been snoring in her bed. "Just in the fucking nick of time." Callan said and meant it.

Alec and Jerry sat and chatted while their teams talked quietly with each other. It was decided [by the two 'mad' professors'] to share the project. They had travelled all the way from bloody Scotland after all. Alex would bunk in with girls and the boys would bed down in the corridor between the rooms. "We'll be snug as bugs in a rug." exclaimed Owen. Sibby did stare at him closely; he did appear to have the traces of nail polish on one hand. Each to their own she thought. She took an immediate liking to Alex and helped her with her kit. She was amazed at her bed. Alex pulled a couple of levers and the bloody thing unfolded and inflated into a very comfortable looking cot.

But it was Owen that really cheered everyone up; he pulled a couple of decent looking bottles of brandy from his old bag and held them up; "Brandy anyone?" He was nearly killed in the rush!

They sat about the old foyer and talked. Callan and Mouse really couldn't stop staring at Alex in her short skirt and business suit. Callan whispered; "That is one fucking gorgeous piece of skirt." Mouse, normally quiet about such matters, just had to agree. It was clear that the new girl liked the look of Professor Alec and that ruffled Sibby's feathers a little; but she wasn't surprised. Nearly every girl on campus fancied him, including her.

Callan, Mouse and Wilson discussed both team's equipment and Callan was impressed with the big man's knowledge of the technology. Mouse showed off his new 'Sonny' cam-recorder which could play the video back through a small screen attached. He showed the pair the film he had shot earlier. He replayed Sibby making up her bed and nearly dropped the bloody thing on the floor in shock.

All three watched - Mouse & Callan a little horrified - as Sibby waved and bowed. The man standing on the other side of her camp bed was smiling too. A big fellow in an ill-fitting, old-fashioned, three-piece suit. He folded his arms and walked away. Mouse jumped up shouting and Alec calmed him down enough for him to run the video, through the big monitor. Everyone watched in absolute silence. Alec's team didn't notice the look passing between the other team. Jericho whispered; "Doctor Tabbert I presume." Wilson nodded; "Must have a time portal hidden around the place." Alex sighed; "He's got some balls appearing like that, must be checking out the new arrivals at this dreadful place." Owen was staring at his hand - cursing himself a little - having noticed the nail polish remains on his fingers.

Alec couldn't hide his delight at the capture of the 'spectre' on film. Jericho pulled his team into the corridor where their beds were and spoke softly, consulting his mirror; "There are three earth bound spirits in this place. If one can cause books and cups to move; they could prove dangerous to living humans. If it can harness telekinetic powers; then it's dangerous."

Wilson scratched his chin; "Shall I put in a call for a Guardian?" Jericho nodded; "It's time to put an end to their little games around here, especially the good doctor who should have died in 1861." Then Owen grunted; "How the fuck didn't Mouse, or Sibby see him? I mean he's a living human - a time traveler - how come the camera picked him up, but they couldn't see him at the time?" Jericho rubbed his chin and said quietly; "That Owen, is a bloody good question."

The two teams settled down for the remainder of the night. Owen joined Sibby at the monitor and pair chatted; Sibby really liked the quiet young man, who clearly had a sharp mind. Nothing happened and they were relieved By Mouse and Wilson. Sibby had to smile at the difference - physically - between the pair. But they certainly seemed to be getting on. Mouse didn't surprise her; he got on with anyone, even the bastards that took the piss out of the little fellow.

She wandered off to find Alex. They could have a good gossip about the two 'mad professors' as Callan called them. She also wanted to know more about the clearly effeminate young Owen. What was his story? She wondered.

3. THE FIELD TRIP; DAY TWO.

Everyone was pleasantly surprised by Alex and Sibby; they had knocked up a decent breakfast of porridge, bacon, eggs and beans on the small paraffin camping stove in the kitchen. Everyone was also surprised how well the two women were getting on; well, except Jen who only noticed the food. When Callan chided her about not helping the other girls; she just stuffed her face with a egg sandwich and muttered; "I'm a fucking lousy cook." No one disbelieved her. There was aloud rapping on the front door and Owen opened it and was surprised. A very pretty young woman stood there, clutching a casserole pot. Owen immediately took it from her and invited her in. Sibby looked delighted and quickly went to the door with Alex. "You must be Gary's wife. Lovely to meet you." She said as Charlotte told Owen that it could be easily reheated; it was vegetable casserole.

She didn't smile; "No I'm not Gary's wife; I'm his long-suffering sister. Someone has to look after him. My boyfriend Leon and he get on really well. They're both keen horse riders." Sibby apologized, but that was waved away. The three women sat and talked. It appears that Gary was a veteran of the Afghan war. Charlotte [Lottie to her friends] explained that Gary's team had been caught by some Afghan fighters and two men were wounded. Gary had gone out to get them. He dragged one back under enemy fire and then returned to fetch the other man. But a homemade bomb had got them. He was badly wounded and rushed to a nearby Army Surgeon who saved his life. But he was scarred. The bomb and ripped up his face and tore off a finger. It had also damaged the nerves in his back and legs. But he had survived to come home to his wife and family.

That's when Lottie's attitude changed at the mention of his wife. "Caroline was beautiful on the outside [she gestured to Alex] a lot like you. But inside she was a festering bag of maggots. The very week Gary was discharged from the hospital she told him that she couldn't stand the thought of looking at him or letting him touch her. She packed her bags and fucked off. I believe she hooked up with some ponce that breeds really expensive dogs for a living." She spat the words out, adding with a small smile; "Appropriate that. Living with a pack of dogs. She's in good company."

Lotte told the girls that Gary struggled to find a job. Prospective employers took one look at him and said the position was closed. But the Corps of Commissioners had found him this job;

apparently no one else would take it.

Both Sibby and Alex were actually moved by the story; a very brave young man reduced to hiding away in a derelict hospital because the world really didn't want to face or want him. Lotte left, promising to bring back with some mash for the casserole near supper time. She was going to throw some chicken in, but didn't know if anyone was vegetarian. Everyone thanked her for her unexpected generosity. Alec's team now saw 'Egor' in a very different light - except Jen of course - who said simply; "So he's a brave ugly bugger." Sibby turned to her and said - with some restraint in her voice - "Just shut up Jen. Just shut up and keep you bloody filthy comments to yourself. No one wants to hear them." Now that did really surprise everyone else. Sibby normally tolerated Jen's nasty comments, but she didn't this time. Jen just shrugged and - wisely - didn't say anything else.

Later that afternoon, Jericho, Alec, Wilson and Callan disappeared down into the cellars. Sibby and Alex manned the small radio, drinking coffee and chatting quietly together. Jen apparently excluded from joining the other girls on 'radio watch' grabbed a reluctant Mouse and went exploring the safe parts of the old hospital. Mouse collected a radio from Sibby and followed, shaking his head in real despair.

The team in the cellars reported back nothing of interest. But near lunch time a quiet sounding Jen was calling on her radio; well she was almost whispering actually. Finally, Mouse must have taken the radio from her. He spoke quite normally to Sibby; they had found several shallow graves, which looked a lot newer than the others, in the large cemetery that had serviced the hospital. The cemetery was located at the rear of the old stables block. Their call was interrupted by Alec who said they were on the way back and everyone stay put.

Both teams walked around the derelict cemetery. There were graves dating back to the 1850's, right through to the 1920's, when the hospital was closed down. Most of the small headstones were unreadable; they could make out the odd date or name, but little else. "They must have used cheap stone to save money and they haven't weathered well." Alec explained, but he couldn't explain the apparent 'modern' ones; buried at the rear of the cemetery, near the old stable block. There was some sort of memorial, but it was already too worn to be read properly. They could make out part of the date; 19--.

Wilson whispered to Jericho; "That's not weathered. It's been deliberately defaced." Jericho nodded; he had already spotted that - but why? - What the fuck was going on?

"How the fuck were there burials after the bloody place closed. It had apparently been shut since the early 20's?" Mouse asked, filming the unusual graves. Alec tried his mobile phone -again - and still had no signal. Sibby wondered if the caretaker had a phone in the lodge. Alec nodded; he would contact Mr. Prouse on it and ask, if he knew the story of the 'modern' burials. They all walked back to the old hospital, talking quietly amongst themselves.

Alec's team disappeared inside, leaving Jericho and team 74 standing in the grounds. They were all staring at the young boy in ragged clothes and bare feet by the front doors of the building. Owen lifted his mirror and spoke quietly: "Charles Jobson; died aged 13 in 1882. His soul is listed as missing. He's one of the three earth bound spirits hiding here."

The boy was about to turn and go when Alex called out to him; "Charles or is it Charley? Which do you prefer?" She asked him. He wiped his nose on his jumper and said, "My mum always calls me Charles." He muttered and almost smiled at her. Alex walked slowly up to him and smiled; "Well Charles, my friends and I are here to help you. You don't have to be frightened of us." The boy smiled; "I ain't frightened. Gabriele looks after me." That's when Herbie the Collector appeared. Jericho had summoned him with his mirror. Herbie was one of the best collector's, when it came to reluctant souls. He normally was able to 'scoop' them up. He and Alex stood talking to Charles.

Jericho, Wilson and Owen went back to the foyer and left it to them. "Herbie should really join the department. He's a real good man with the unhappy dead." Owen said and Wilson couldn't disagree; "So the other bugger, that can throw things about must be this 'Gabriele' he spoke about."

Owen nodded and re-read his mirror and sighed; "There's no patient called 'Gabriele' that died here or listed as staff member who died here." Wilson nodded; "So who the fuck is he?"

They found only Sibby sitting at the monitor. She explained that the others were checking the equipment for the coming night. She told them that Alec had taken the group to the West Wing to set up detection equipment. There had been several reports of strange happening in the West Wing over the years; including a very unhappy young Victorian woman who could be heard sobbing. But the most interesting incident had happened during the Second World War. Army engineers had arrived to survey the old place for possible military use; but encountered an evil gargoyle that threw stuff about and chased them away. One young soldier had actually fired his service revolver at it and watched - horrified - as the bullets passed through it!

Needless to say; that the army never moved in. Sibby concluded her story and smiled at Owen, who sat with her. Wilson and Jericho wandered off. They knew that Doctor Tabbert's time portal must be in the building somewhere. They could now use their mirrors freely, with the other group not around.

They were joined by a smiling Alex; she told them that Herbie had worked his magic and the boy had gone with him. She also told them that 'Charles' had died of Type 1 Diabetes in 1882. It was incurable then and always resulted in death. Charles was from a poor family and that's why he was placed here. The hospital would bury the boy in its cemetery and the family could avoid a funeral bill they simply couldn't afford. He unfortunately, wouldn't talk about 'Gabriele' - except to say - he was a very unhappy man. "Most poltergeists usually are unhappy ex-humans." muttered Wilson.

Charles had admitted liking the other 'spirit' but - again - didn't talk about it; except to say that it was also unhappy. Wilson grunted; "We could have two bloody poltergeists about the place." Jericho nodded and they headed off, on their search for the time portal and the other two missing souls.

The rear of the extensive building was the oldest - and originally part of the old manor house that stood here - and so they started there. Wilson found it. It was a carved medieval doorway on the ground floor. "Locked to 1472, June 3rd. Tabbert must have found it soon after the bloody place was built around the old Manor House. Shall we go and pay a visit?" He smiled at Jericho and Alex. Jericho nodded and the team stepped through the brickwork and where gone.

Gary stepped from the curtains at the far end of the corridor and walked up to the doorway and wasn't happy. "The good doctor will not be impressed." He muttered and stepped through. The corridor was now empty.

4. DOCTOR TABBERT; I PRESUME?

They were in a medieval Chapel; the carved doorway had originally been the entrance. It was a hot summer day, and the sky was blue and cloudless. Jericho gestured to the Manor House and pointed out that it was quite beautiful. "If it was still standing now [1999] it would be worth a small fortune. But the bloody Victorians knocked it down and built the bloody hospital."

Alex consulted her mirror and spoke quietly; "Currently [1472] the place is the family home of Sir Reginald Culpepper, his wife Margaret, daughter Elizabeth and son; John. He's a Knight of King Edward IV. The bloody War of the Roses was going on at this time."

"So where is our time travelling doctor hanging out?" Wilson asked and they walked up the old house. Outside the front door was a young boy - sweeping - and he just stared at them, apparently unfazed by their modern appearance. But he did look hard at Alex's long legs, then at Wilson; he had never seen a man with skin that colour. He leaned on his broom and grinned; he already had teeth missing. He jerked the broom towards a house some distance down the dusty road; "Your friend is there. He's knows your coming. He gave me an apple to tell you." He pulled it from his ragged shirt and held it up. Then quickly placed it back.

Jericho nodded and thanked him, saying to the others; "Expecting us?" They walked down to the modest little cottage and Wilson banged on the door.

It was opened by a young girl who was lacing up her bodice and pulling down her skirts. She didn't smile or say anything but strode past them and headed for the Manor House. The team all looked at each other and Jericho shouted in; "Doctor Tabbert I presume?" The doctor was sitting at a rough table writing in a small notebook; he looked up and smiled; "I wondered how quickly you would find the portal. Please come in. That was young Lizzie; she's in early pregnancy. The baby's father is dead

- killed in the bloody wars around here - but Lady Margaret is looking after her. The girl's mother was one of her maids. Loyalty runs deep in this time." He gestured to the equally rough chairs and added; "Please sit."

The team sat and looked about the cottage; it was stacked with books and bottles, bushes of herbs and a small bubbling cauldron. "In these times I'm called an 'Apothecary'. A man of medicine and science; as you can imagine, I have quite a few patients." The doctor smiled and loosened the medieval long coat; he was feeling the summer heat. Underneath he was wearing his Victorian suit. He closed his little notebook and pushed it into his pocket. He leaned back in the chair and clasped his hands in front of him; "I have no doubt you're on the trail of the missing paranormal investigators that are swarming about my old hospital?"

Jericho nodded - he didn't smile - and said slowly; "Them and a certain time travelling doctor who should have passed over in 1861." The doctor smiled; "Very commendable, I'm sure. You can snatch the investigators - they actually don't know they are dead and should pass over - but the doctor is far too busy to desert his patients in any time period." Jericho just nodded; "Quite so doctor, but our boss - Angel Margret - has her own ideas about that."

Wilson asked the Doctor about the paranormal investigators who were around the hospital in 1956. The doctor sat back and ran a hand over his chin; "Oh yes. Those three." He muttered and leaned forward. "They must have been carrying something from the late medieval period - like I do - and they all disappeared through the portal." He held up a large Medieval Crucifix. "Must have come as quite a surprise." He chuckled. "Do you know what become of them?" Alex asked.

Doctor Tabbert nodded. "The older man - Crabb - I think. Didn't last long; he just couldn't handle the dark ages and went a little mad. He was last seen begging near the castle. But I think he didn't survive the harsh winter, living in the wilds."

Alex nodded and asked about the other two. The Doctor sighed; "The woman survived; she managed to get the local magistrate - an old widower - to marry her. She died some years ago; no children." He stared down at his hands and shook his head; "The young man was a bloody fool; he was a communist and an Atheist and practically preached it. The Church Inquisition got him. Screamed and struggled all the way to the flames. The idiot couldn't actually believe he was to be burnt alive for saying what he thinks." Their conversations with the doctor were interrupted. The door swung open and Gary stepped in; he had a very large piece of wood clenched in both hands. The team slowly rose from their seats and the doctor sighed, waving at Gary. "It's alright Gabriele, they are just leaving." The team all looked at each other and Alex whispered; "Of course; Gary is a modern version of the name Gabriele. He's our bloody poltergeist!"

Gary lowered the stick and Doctor Tabbert said quietly; "As I said, loyalty runs deep around this parts. I gave Gabriele a job and a home in 1840, when the ungrateful British Government tossed him away like garbage. He was a very brave man, serving his country and paid a terrible price for that. But you do know his story?" Alex nodded; "So Professor Sweetman's team think he was injured in the Afghan war that took place in the 1990's, not realizing it was the bloody 1840's!" She then thought about his sister; how did she end up a ghost at the hospital?

Doctor Tabbert stood and shook his coat. "His sister worked at the hospital and looked after her brother, after the departure of his very unfaithful wife. She died in 1847, but couldn't bring herself to leave her brother, who she had cared for with so much love and attention." He gestured towards the door; "Goodbye my friends. Please do take those wretched paranormal investigators with you." He smiled and folded his arms.

Jericho just sighed loudly and operated his mirror; time stood still. He walked to the door and stared at Gary/Gabriele and said softly; "You deserve a better fate than this. You need to jump and start a new life."

Alex jumped a little as Oscar appeared in the doorway - smiling and gripping his Staff of Moses - he was a Guardian of God and had the power to compel reluctant and unwilling souls to the light. Little Oscar was a good friend of the team, and they welcomed him with some affection. He gave Alex a big kiss and said, "What's up Jericho? I got the call you had a poltergeist running about?"

Jericho chuckled and pointed at Gary; "That's your man, he's all yours. The other is just a reluctant soul that needs to jump, whether he wants to or not." Oscar smiled and slapped his Staff onto his shoulder, "Sooner said than done." He was gone and so was Gary and the good doctor. Jericho consulted his mirror and smiled broadly; "Oscar is always on top of these things. He's already closed the time portal. Now that's what I call service from the Guardians Department." They all chuckled and Jericho operated his mirror, and the cottage was empty. The small boy climbed down from the barrel under the window and scratched his lice ridden crotch. He thought the dwarf [Oscar] was funny, but he really liked Alex's long legs. He walked slowly back to the Manor House, tossing the apple in the air.

They walked down the corridor, heading back to the foyer, and Wilson stopped; "How did he appear in Sibby's room and get caught on Mouse's film, yet Mouse and Sibby didn't see him? He was a living human - just a time traveler - how the hell didn't they see him?" Jericho stood hands on hips and looked about the corridor; "I have a feeling the answer lies in those graves." Alex and Wilson just looked at each other; what was Jericho thinking now?

Alex volunteered to tell Lottie about her brother and the doctor. "Hopefully, she can now jump to another life. Her duty of love to her brother is now finally over." She said and left them. Both Jericho and Wilson agreed with that. They walked to the burnt-out East Wing and found Mouse and Callan there; filming. Jericho asked where Professor Sweetman was. "He's back with Sibby and Jen; they're setting up an external night camera on those graves. The professor thinks they could yield some interesting stuff." Jericho nodded and tapped Wilson's arm; "I think the good professor is right." He whispered and the pair headed back to the foyer.

5. SECOND NIGHT.

Sibby and Jen were watching the monitor as night was falling fast. They both wondered why Lottie hadn't appeared with the bloody mash she promised. Owen and Alex sat by the old desk and sipped their coffees. Alex had bought Owen up to date with the story of the caretaker and his loyal sister. Owen nodded and rubbed his chin; "So Gary actually died in 1845, probably from the injuries he suffered. He and Lottie must be buried in the old cemetery, but their graves are now lost with the headstones so unreadable." Alex sighed and finished her coffee; "She was actually quite happy to see Herbie the Collector. I think she really wanted all this to end."

Owen sipped his coffee and nodded his agreement with that. Callan and Mouse were catching up on some sleep, but Alex wondered where the gorgeous professor had disappeared too. Owen collected her cup and shouted to the other girls; "Any one wants a refill?" They both smiled and held up their cups. He collected them and headed for the kitchen. Alex leaned back in her chair and stared about the foyer. She turned and picked up the Visitors Book from the desk and blew off some dust and slowly flicked through the yellowing pages. She stopped and read the entry made by the paranormal investigators in 1956. They certainly discovered something, and it had killed them - for good - they were in the darkness; lost souls. There were few other entries; all workmen, building Inspectors and visitors from various members of the Board of Trustee's.

There was an entry from the fire inspection team, who dealt with the fire earlier this year. Alex looked at the date; 13th May 1999. But the entry just before the fire was also for this very year; Professor Sweetman had filled out the details of his teams visit. She stared at the names and smiled.

She re-read the entry and realized that something was wrong. She read the entry again; but couldn't figure what was bothering her. Owen returned with more coffee and was chatting with the girls manning the monitor and radio. Alex placed the book on the floor and accepted her coffee from Owen. "Have a look at the Visitors Book. The last entry: can you spot anything wrong with it?"

Owen nodded and picked the book up and stared at it; "Everyone is there, Sibby, Jen, Mouse and Callan." He said and sipped his coffee. Both he and Alex slowly placed their cups down and rose from their seats. The same solution had appeared to both; the professor hadn't signed the damn book.

Alex asked Sibby who had made out the entry in the book. She smiled and said, "Callan. The professor hadn't arrived when he did it. I'll tell him [the professor] to add his name." She smiled and went back to watching the monitor. Alex and Owen excused themselves and headed out, lighting the way with their mirrors.

They could see the car headlights coming from the old stable block. They slipped through the broken doors and stood in front of the big Jaguar car. The professor was in the driver's seat, head in hands. Alex walked up and opened the door; "Do you want to talk about all those deaths Alec?" She walked around to the passenger door and slid in. Owen jumped in the back and checked his mirror.

It was quite a few minutes before Alec lowered his hands and breathed deeply; he was clearly suffering inside. He smiled at Alex and wiped his face with a bright orange hankie. "I arrived late; you see this young student....I forget her name now....she stopped me just as I was leaving. Well. I couldn't...I mean, I had no will power; she was very pretty."

Alex sighed; "You were having sex while your students burnt to death in an old hospital, unaware that they shouldn't have plugged anything in the East Wing sockets. But you knew it was not safe. They should have been in the West Wing; where they are now." Alec nodded and wiped his face again; "Yes, I was told that morning about the change of wings; except I was late, and the team had already left. I should have rushed down there, but the pretty little student distracted me."

"Who's in the graves Alec?" Owen asked, but he already knew. The professor looked up; there were little tears on his face and in his eyes. "My team of very good young people; everyone felt it was proper to bury them here; where they worked and died doing something they loved."

Alex nodded; "Why did you deface the memorial date?" Alec sighed; "I hoped to change all that. I tried year after year and nothing changed. Then I realized something....I realized..." He stopped talking and wiped his face.

"Mobile phone signals don't pick up round here; do they?" Owen asked him and he nodded. "I drove like a madman and arrived just as evening was falling. The west wing was already ablaze. They didn't get out." Alex gripped his arm; "You've carried this guilt for an awful long time Alec, it's time to put it behind you and move on."

Alec nodded slowly; "Sibby had such a bright future. She was my best student by a long way. But all she wanted was a man to call her own and some children. I took all those little dreams from her...and the others ...all their dreams went up in smoke." He groaned and folded his arms, pushing back in the seat. He was in turmoil. A little dribble of tears ran down his cheeks and he brushed them away with some restrained anger.

Alex gripped his hand and turned to Owen; "What have we got on him?" Owen checked his mirror and shook his head; "Nothing that would interest Jericho or the department. He's basically clean." Alex smiled; "I think you should head back to the University and take a few days to get around this. Every time you come back here Alec; they are unable to jump. It's your guilt holding them here and they really need to move on."

He stared at Alex and very slowly nodded. Alex slid from the car followed by Owen. They stood amongst the mud and straw, watching the big car pull away. Owen nodded as the dashing professor Alec Sweetman slowly changed back to his real appearance, an old man. The car disappeared down the hospital lane towards the main road.

"He's been coming back here on the anniversary of the fire for some twenty years and his team have been waiting that long, waiting for him to turn up and save their lives by warning them about being in the wrong wing." Alex said and Owen checked his mirror; the current date was 13th May 2019. Alex took Owens's hand, and they walked back to the foyer; they both hoped Jericho and Wilson would soon join them. They had four lost souls to speak with.

Sibby stared at camera four - the night camera set up over the cemetery - and turned to Jen; "Does the caretaker or his sister have a car?" Jen shrugged her shoulders; "I don't know. I don't think so." Sibby called the professor on the radio and received nothing but static. She called again; nothing. Something told her that he had gone. She sighed and placed the little handset down. Jen was smoking again, standing by the open door. "I think he's gone." Was all she said.

Callan and Mouse wandered in, sipping coffee and looked about. "What's that slight smell? I could smell something earlier." Sibby chuckled, gesturing to Jen; "Battersea Power station is at it again." The boys chuckled and dropped in front of the monitor. Sibby and Jen headed for their makeshift bedroom and Mouse put his feet up; he was knackered. Callan told him to doze and sat reading his book. The hours crept past, and Callan's head was nodding. He never smelt or saw the thin whips of grey smoke. He never felt death slip over him as the hospital wing caught fire with some violence. The smoke had overcome the two boys as they slept. The girls tried to get out the windowless room - screaming hysterically - but couldn't get past the wall of fire. They were burnt to death; mercifully, quite quickly. The fire consumed their bodies - curled up into balls - beneath their beds.

Jericho and Team 74 stood watching the blaze and Jericho checked his mirror; 13th may, 1999. They watched the big jaguar pull into the drive and the professor running up to the doors of the wing. He couldn't get past the flames and collapsed on his knees, screaming, cussing and sobbing. He had arrived too late. In the distance could be heard the sirens and bells of the police and fire brigade. The old caretaker: Mr. Edwin Rush had called them and he ran over the professor, dragging him away from the burning building.

"Where the hell are they?" Wilson said. Herbie the Collector shook his head; he didn't know. He had five names in his Soul ledger for tonight. Jericho sighed and turned to the team; "He still won't let them go," He operated his mirror and the team disappeared. Herbie shrugged and watched as the fire brigade arrived on scene. The old caretaker was shouting to them about the students. Two brave firemen crashed through the front door, under the protection of a spurting hose and wearing breathing apparatus; tried to find the students. Fire Officer Kevin Higgs fell under part of a crumbling blazing wall and didn't make it back out. The fire chief called off any further rescue attempts; he had lost one good man already. That was enough. Young Kevin Higgs and Herbie stood watching for a few minutes and then the pair disappeared.

6. THE FIELD TRIP; DAY ONE. [AGAIN]

The University minibus turned from the road into Tabbert's Lane; "It may get bumpy so hold on!" 'Sibby' shouted [Ms Sylvia Fellows] and the other three occupants gripped seats and arm rests. Sibby kept a tight grip on the wheel and the minibus struggled up the gravel lane; sodden by weeks of rain. "Well, I'm not getting out and bloody pushing." Jen Phillips called out to no one in particular. She drew on her shaking cigarette. She was sitting right next to a large 'NO SMOKING' sign on the window and didn't give a fuck; like she did about most things "You would have thought that old 'Sweetie' [Professor Alec Sweetman] would have bloody warned us about the bloody road." She added and blew little smoke rings about...

Jericho sat in the front passenger seat of their van and turned to Wilson, who was driving the van that Supplies had given them. He checked his mirror; it was 13th may, 2020. "Right on time - again." He muttered. They had passed the professor's old Jaguar car parked in a gravel layby some minutes earlier. The old man had been sobbing into hands - again.

Alex leaned on Jericho's seat and said quietly; "We'll have to confront him. He must know that's he's holding them back." Owen tapped his mirror and looked up; "We have to do something. He won't be back next year. The cancer will finish him off next March. Then what will those poor buggers do?"

Wilson grunted; "Ghosts waiting for a dead man who will never show up. How will that play out?"

Alex leaned forward and stared out the windscreen, the wipers pushing slowly across it. "Something is wrong. They appear to be stuck at the gates." She said softly. Jericho rubbed his chin; "Of course; we've changed things. There is no Gary the caretaker to open the gates for the other lost souls. He's moved on; willingly or not."

Wilson chuckled a little; "If they can't get back in - as they always did - what will they do now?" Jericho smiled and pulled out his mirror; "A call to Herbie may be in order."

But Owen leaned across him and tapped his arm, shaking his head; "I would hold on that, take a look." They watched as the big Jaguar pulled up behind the van; professor Sweetman jumped from the car waving. He was his youthful self again.

Jericho stared at his mirror; "It's May 13th, 1999, for them." The team watched as he held up keys and walked to the gates; ignoring the tumbling rain and unlocked them. The van pulled away and the professor walked back to his car and follow the van in, locking the gates behind him.

Wilson sighed; "Now that's a bloody turn up for the books. Now what do we do?"

Jericho's mirror buzzed and he answered it quickly. The call from the Senior Time Controller was not unexpected. Jericho spoke for a few minutes and when the call had finished, he turned to the team and sighed; "The current human timeline has changed. It appears that Alec has changed his and the students destiny. The wing still catches fire, and the young fireman dies at the scene. But the students had moved to the other wing - the safe one - and so they didn't die." Alex asked; "How did the fire start if they didn't plug anything in?" Jericho almost smiled; "Apparently the professor set up a camera in there and that was enough for the dangerous wiring to start the blaze." Owen was already reading about the new timeline. He really did chuckle.

"You have to admire the fucker. he turned out to be one brave bastard." Owen said and smiled at his puzzled colleagues. "What happened Owen?" Alex asked gripping his arm with a growing smile. Owen stared at the big gates; "Alec turned up alright and moved everyone to the other wing. But he set up a camera in the old wing; knowing full well that it would start the fire. He was the only member of the team that was killed in the blaze. The other's all escaped."

Alex flopped back in her seat and shook her head; "When we were talking in the car that night. He said he had realized something, but never finished what he was saying." She sighed; "He realized that only his bloody death would stop the team living that dreadful, terrible night over and over again."

Jericho nodded; "And it did. Professor Alec Sweetman defaced his own memorial. I bet if we take a look at that now; there's only one well-kept grave there." Owen looked up and smiled; "Here we go." He said simply and the team watched the small convoy of cars approaching the gates, which were being opened by the caretaker, dressed in a bright yellow rain coat. The cars passed through and Jericho patted Wilson's arm; "Shall we go?" Wilson nodded and started the van, following the last car through.

Alex consulted her mirror; it was 13th May 2020. Some twenty-one years after the fatal fire.

Owen tapped his mirror and spoke to her softly; "The firemen went in to save the professor and not the students - they were safe - and so fireman Higgs death, which was scheduled, could take place. That part of the timeline continues normally. He knew he was to die of cancer; an old and distraught man, living a terrible life of bad dreams and regret, this way he could die on his own terms and save his students. His terrible guilt was over." They followed the other cars to the old cemetery and watched them empty out. Wilson stopped the van and the team decamped, they headed for the graveyard in respectful silence.

7. A CEREMONY OF REMEMBRANCE.

They joined the mourners huddled around the little memorial and a strapping young man smiled at Alex; "Sorry, but this is a private service of Remembrance for my mum's old professor. May I ask who invited you please?"

Jericho answered him, shaking his hand; "Professor Tibb's and the paranormal team from Edinburgh University. Being the 21st Anniversary of Professor Sweetman's tragic death, the University thought it would be appropriate for another team of investigators to show their respects." The young man actually smiled and turned to the other mourners; "Mum! You'll love this. A team of paranormal investigators from Edinburgh University have turned up to show their respects to dad." Everyone just stared at the young man; he was Alec's son!

They recognised 'Sibby' at once; she of course didn't recognise them but smiled and shook hands all round. She was still a very beautiful woman. She pushed her arm through her handsome son's and said quietly about how nice it was; that the University had sent someone after all these years. She stared at Alex and really did smile, saying; "I'm sure we've met before. Maybe at a paranormal get together?" Alex just nodded and the two women chatted like old friends. A very small, but smiling Reverend joined them; the team recognised Mouse immediately. He was clutching his bible; "Shall we start Sibby?" He asked.

"I thought that was absolutely lovely." Alex grinned and settled back in her seat. The team was sitting in the van watching the cars depart. They had been invited to the small 'wake' at the local pub but knew they wouldn't attend.

Owen folded his arms; "So Alec had more than one reason to

save his students. Sibby was carrying his baby. I wondered where that pair had disappeared to that first night. She had to tell him that she was pregnant. Little wonder her tragic death cut him up so much. He had killed his own child as well."

Wilson sighed; "He kept going back, each year and every year, trying to change things, then realized that only his death could do that. Bloody human freewill and all that."

Callan's two daughters had represented their father at the ceremony; he had died two years ago, suffering from chronic heart disease. Ann and Sylvia had both liked the look of Owen and Wilson. Jen didn't bother to turn up and no one seemed to mind; that was Jen's way. Apparently, she was a very successful businesswoman - quite ruthless in her deals - she told Sibby that she couldn't find the time; but had sent some flowers; cheap ones.

Jericho's mirror buzzed and he really did sigh. The screen had lit up like Blackpool illuminations; everyone knew that was Angel Margret herself calling. He answered it slowly; unsmiling. It was a brief conversation and Jericho lowered his mirror and shrugged his shoulders. "I have an interview with Margret about this little mess. It appears that dirty old doctor Tabbert lied to us." He pushed his mirror into his jacket pocket and smiled at their inquisitive faces. "It appears that a certain young woman in 1473 gave birth to an unscheduled baby. The dirty doctor's child."

Wilson sighed; "Young Lizzie I assume." Jericho nodded.

Owen chuckled; "Are we going to deal with that?" Jericho folded his arm; "Let's find a pub and have a drink. Not the pub with the bloody wake going on. We're in enough shit already." Then he smiled.

Alex sighed - she didn't look happy - "I bloody hate those medieval clothes and where can I get a maid? No woman of quality travels without one in those times. Ruth is on her Collector's course." Jericho smiled; "Over to you Owen. Do you fancy resurrecting 'Jacqueline' again?"

Owen laughed; "Why not." Wilson groaned; "I bloody knew it. I said he would go strange if he kept dressing in bloody women's clothes!" Everyone laughed at that including a smiling Owen.

THE END

EPILOGUE:

"This mission was not considered a success - despite closing the time portal - and recovering eight lost souls. The changes to the timeline by Professor Sweetman's actions had to be absorbed into the current Timeline. Angel Margret wasn't happy with Team 74 and told them so. They would - of course - shrug that off and continue with their duties."
SJW

CHARCTERS:

Sylvia Fellows married in 2002; a pleasant fellow who was a dentist. She continued to enjoy exploring the paranormal and bring up her son; Alistair [Alec.] Sylvia died in 2033. Her soul was collected and processed. She is now a temporal detective trainee on Team 61. She and Alex are good friends.

Jennifer Phillips became a very successful businesswoman on the internet; selling flowers in frames! She never married but had a son by one of her many partners, over the years. She died in 2042 and her soul was collected and processed.

Callan Carter never finished his university course and joined the British army in 2000. He married a German lady [where he was stationed at the time] Callan had two daughters by her, and they divorced in 2010. Callan died from chronic heart failure in 2018. His soul was collected and processed.

Morris Maxwell completed his degree course and joined the Church of England. He proved to be a popular and much loved 'local vicar'. He never married nor had children. He died in 2031 and his soul was collected and processed. He now works as a Collector; he's very good at it!

Professor Alec [Sweetie] Sweetman changed his own destiny that fateful day; he walked away from the 'pretty little student' and rushed down to Tabbert's Hospital. He saved his students but lost his own life. What he was actually doing in the East Wing the night of the fire remains a mystery. His soul was collected and processed. He gave no explanation to the Collector and was allowed to jump back into the Human Life Cycle immediately.

Gabriele [Gary] London had died in 1845 and like his sister, avoided being collected until 1999. His soul was collected and quarantined for fifty human years. He rejoined the Human Life Cycle in 2049.

Charlotte [Lottie] London had died in 1847 and avoided collection. She finally walked to the light in 1999. Her soul was collected and was given no quarantine by Angel Margret for her actions.

Charles Jobson [the boy] had died at the hospital in 1882 at 13 years of age. He had avoided being collected and remained as an 'Earth bound spirit' until Herbie the Collector took him in 1999. His soul was collected and processed. He didn't receive a sanction for his actions and re-joined the human life cycle immediately.

Edwin Rush [Caretaker 1999] was a former NHS staff nurse. He had taken the 'quiet' job after he retired in 1992. He died in 2006 and his soul was collected and processed.

Kevin Higgs [Fireman] was 22 years old when killed at the fire. He had never married nor had children. He was given an appropriate Service Funeral and a small memorial was erected at the hospital. It was removed when the hospital was demolished. Its current whereabouts are unknown. His soul was collected and processed.

Doctor Xavier Tabbert was returned to his own scheduled time period by Oscar [A Guardian of God] and met his fate in 1861. He died on schedule and his soul was collected and quarantined for a human century. But the child he had by Elizabeth Westhouse [Lizzie] would cause problems later on, down the current Human Timeline. Jericho and Team 74 have been tasked with sorting that one out.

John Farmer [small boy - 1472] never reached adulthood. He died of smallpox in 1476. His soul was collected and processed.

Elizabeth Mary Westhouse [Lizzie - 1472] gave birth in 1473 to an unscheduled baby boy. He grew up quickly - as children did in that harsh time - and worked as a farmer. He married and had three children by two wives. The changes that caused to the current human timeline created problems, several generations later. Inspector Jericho Tibb's and Team 74 have been tasked by

Angel Margret to restore the line. But that is another story and another mission. Lizzie died in 1491 and her soul was collected and processed. She rejoined the Human Life Cycle immediately. The same soul was to be subject of yet another temporal Investigation in 1967!

Alistair Fellows [Sibby's son] became a history teacher and taught in a couple of local schools. He retired in 2057. He was one of the last 'human' teachers working in the profession. He spent his retirement doing charity work. He had two children with his partner Kathleen. He died in 2078 and his soul was collected and processed.

Tabbert's hospital was finally demolished in 2027 and a large supermarket with car park was constructed on the site. There have been no reports of any 'paranormal or supernatural' occurrences at the place where it stood.

EPISODE 8: "HARBINGER."

MI9SSION SUMMARY: "August1959, three teenage students camping in Dalby Forest, North Yorkshire have suddenly gone missing. The Police have searched the woods which cover 8,000 acres and found nothing. Their little campsite appears to have been abandoned in quite a hurry. The locals believe it's the work of 'HARBINGER' a mythical and dangerous 'Tree-Spirit', a legendary figure in these vast woodlands. But Jericho Tibbs and team 74 are on scene because the student's souls have gone missing from the current human time-line."

NOTES: Contains strong language and scenes of mild BDSM and murder.

TRIGGER WARNINGS. ALCOHOL, SMOKING, STRONG LANGUAGE, SEXUAL REFERENCES [including BDSM] AND STRONG VIOLENCE.

AGE 15+ ONLY. **30 Minutes reading time.**

1. THE CLEARING IN THE WOODS.

"Sod bleeding all." The big sergeant fumbled in his pockets and pulled out his cigarettes and lit one. He took a well-earned couple of puffs and stared at the two tents; one had fallen down - well almost - and the other had collapsed completely. The young uniform constable didn't smile; "There no chance of footprints, the bloody ground is too dry. There's been no rain for weeks around here. They probably fucked off to an orgy or something, smoking pot and pissing everywhere."

The sergeant nodded and sighed; "Bloody students. Why couldn't they have gone missing on the Moors, then it wouldn't really concern us; bloody selfish gits."

Inspector Parish walked back to his two colleagues and shook his head; "Sod all sergeant. But it does look like they just abandoned the place. There are dinner plates with sausages and beans still on them. Their coats and other clothes are still around." He held up a wallet; "One of them even left his wallet and watch in the bloody tent."

"So they buggered off in a hurry then Sir." The constable muttered. The Inspector walked back to the big police car and slipped into the front passenger seat and picked up the radio handset. "I'm going to call it in. We are going to need more manpower and someone who actually knows these bloody woods." The sergeant just nodded. Three bloody young students from York University had now been missing for five days. Worried parents and friends had been calling the police station about them for the last two days. Especially the concerned mother of Miss Iris Weeks - the only female of the three - she had arranged with her daughter; that she would call her mother every couple of days. Her mum had even given her a big bag of pennies for the phones.

The constable walked from the small clearing and stared into the dark woods. "They wouldn't be the first bloody people to vanish in this place. People have been going missing in here for years - probably centuries - and now these three have simply disappeared." He spoke softly to himself and then looked down at the small slope that ran down to a gravel path. There were dark twigs and small branches everywhere. He rubbed his chin and pushed up his cap. He looked about and shouted to the sergeant, who wandered over, throwing down his cigarette. "Sarge, how come there's a trail of twigs here. There's no tree's in this clearing."

The sergeant looked down at the trail of twigs and small branches; the young constable was right; there were no trees or even bushes to drop them; never mind that they seemed to form a zig zag line into the woods. "Now that's bloody strange." He said and gestured for the constable to follow him. They walked next to the trail of wood splinters and stopped at the small stream. The tree's on the opposite bank looked dark and forbidding despite the day being sunny and clear. The sergeant wiped his face and neck; "That's bloody queer; it seems to stop at the edge of the woods." They could hear the Inspector shouting for them and they walked back to the police car.

"The bloody Superintendent is on his way back to the station. The name in that wallet is important, the bloody son of an MP. Now the shit has really hit the fan." The Inspector sighed and stared up at the sky. "I've told old Ames [the Station Sergeant] to ensure there's a couple of lads sent up here to preserve the scene. They can use my car tonight. I think the weather is about to break and we could have rain." The sergeant and Constable both looked up at the wonderful blue sky and sighed together.

Inspector John Parish was a keen fisherman and knew about the weather. If he forecast rain; then it would probably piss down. Good bloody luck to the poor bastards who pulled this baby-sitting job tonight.

The three sat in the car and waited for the relief officers to turn up. The sergeant had to chuckle; the incoming night sky looked full of rain. The sergeant sat in the driver's seat and fiddled with the radio set. He picked up BBC light and they listened to some music. The Inspector sat scribbling in his notebook. The first drops of rain splashed upon the windscreen and were quickly followed by more. The young constable chuckled; Jesus, Parish was like a bloody bloodhound when it came to the weather.

The darkness fell slowly, and the sergeant switched on the engine and turned on the sidelights. At least old Robbie [the night shift van driver] would be able to see the big black car in the gathering darkness.

"We'll do a swap; the car can stay, and Robbie can run us back to the nick in the van. It's Saturday night and the van will be needed. Inspector Kelly is covering our district tonight; he has a car and driver already." Inspector Parish told the sergeant who just nodded and lit another cigarette. The young constable stared out the rear windscreen and found he actually shivered; no one in their right mind would be in the forest at night. He settled back in his seat and watched the rain tumbling down the rear screen.

He actually jumped when the police radio burst into life; the station was calling the Inspector. The sergeant quickly turned off the music and Inspector Parish answered the call. Everyone smiled when dispatch told them; the van was on its way.
They didn't smile at the rest of the message; apparently the Chief Constable had been contacted by the Home Secretary himself and the police had - gracefully - accepted assistance from an outside agency. A team of private investigators had been hired by the MP and it had been agreed, to give these 'experts' in tracing missing person's full police co-operation and assistance.

The Inspector hung the radio handset back on its clip with some restrained force. "I don't bloody believe it! Private Investigators; since when did the police hand over their responsibilities to a bunch of bloody amateur detectives?" He sounded annoyed, amazed and surprised - because he was - and slumped back in his seat. "What fucking next? Call in the local peasants with bloodhounds?" He muttered.

The sergeant sat up and pointed to the dirt road that leads into the clearing. "Sir, there's a van coming up the lane and I don't think it's ours. It's bloody white with a big black fella driving it!" Everyone leaned forward as the van pulled up some yards from them and the driver flashed his lights in a sort of 'Hello'.

The Inspector grunted; "Stay put. Let them bastards get wet." His two colleagues chuckled at that. The sergeant flashed the headlights of the police car and sat back. "I bet their all wearing old raincoats, smell of booze and were kicked out of various police forces before they even finished their probation." The sergeant predicted with a chuckle.

The light came on in the van opposite as the doors were opened. "Fuck me, that's some piece of bloody skirt!" The sergeant exclaimed, they could see the young man and woman clearly as they jumped from the van. "What the fuck have they got a tart with them for?" He added; actually, a little amazed. Sheltering under a big black umbrella, the couple approached the front passenger side. "What a fucking pair of tits and legs!" Was all the young constable said and leaned forward to get a better view.

Parish rolled the window down halfway and nodded at the face that appeared under the umbrella. "Inspector Parish Sir?" The young man asked, and Parish just nodded. Jericho pulled an envelope from the pocket of his smart three-piece suit - under his very expensive black raincoat - and handed it to Parish. "Jericho Tibbs Sir; from the Company of Thyme, Tibbs & Trayvel; Private Investigations. That is from your Chief Constable Sir." He smiled and Parish didn't. He tore open the envelope and read the letter; he sighed and nodded. "It appears that the Chief Constable has authorised these people to assist us with finding the three missing students." He pushed the letter into his tunic pocket and stared at the woman; she was a bloody stunner. Dressed like she was about to attend a Buckingham Palace Garden party. She probably couldn't investigate a hole in her bloody stockings! But he kept those thoughts to himself. He told 'Tibbs' that two uniform officers would be here to relieve him and would they kindly keep away from the tents; until scene of crimes officers had attended in the morning.

Mr. Tibbs nodded and asked if they [the policemen] knew of any good B & B's around the place. The young constable said quietly; "Yeah, try York City." His colleagues couldn't restrain their laughter with that quip.

Jericho and Alex slipped back into the van and Wilson just smiled; "I bet they were as helpful as giving a glass of water to a drowning man."

Jericho nodded and turned to Owen; "Who are the missing souls?" Owen stared at his mirror and said quietly; "The oldest student is twenty-year-old John Hammond; likes to hike and fish, studying Political History. The second male is Caleb Mortimer Harding; nineteen years old and studying Modern History. He's father is the MP. Finally, we have Miss Iris Weeks - aged nineteen - and studying Medicine; wants' to be a doctor apparently. All three souls vanished two days ago from the current timeline."

"Looks like their relief has arrived." Alex said and leaned forward, adding; "I wonder if they'll be a bit friendlier?" Jericho smiled; "They may be if you wander across and ask if they want coffee and fish and chips from that chippie we passed in the village." Alex just sighed. The team watched the changeover and the police van pulled away, disappearing down the lane.

Owen looked about and rubbed his chin; "This place is steeped in strange stories and legends. There was a very evil witch's coven here in the 1700's. Old 'Doc' Underhill and his team cleaned that one up. A real nasty bunch into human sacrifice; it's had a couple visits from demons over the years; James and Arthur [Knights of God] cleaned them up. Then, there's the strange legend of the 'HARBINGER'."

Wilson chuckled; "Bloody HARBINGER? What the hell is that?" Owen shrugged his shoulders; "No one really knows, but it's always sighted when strange things happen around here. I think it could be one of those old 'Tree Spirits' that the BOSSES [Owen is talking about GOD] father created, after all, he knocked up the bloody dinosaurs, so anything is possible!" Everyone laughed at that. "Give it another hour and we'll make contact with our new police friends." Jericho said and settled back in his seat, watching the rain falling.

2. THE BIRD WATCHERS HUT.

Owen leaned forward and stared out the windscreen and grumbled about when they would be going for fish and chips; he was going to indulge in a battered sausage as well. Then he went silent for a few seconds; "Am I seeing things or is that a light showing the woods; its faint but its there."

Everyone strained forward and all could see the faint light flickering deep in the wood. Jericho sat up straight and nodded; "It's a light alright. It's not moving." Alex tapped his shoulder; "The two coppers can see it, but they have just turned back to their papers." Jericho pushed open the door and grabbed his umbrella; "Come on Alexandra; let's find out if they know what causes it." He stood in the rain - umbrella up - and gestured for her to follow.

Wilson and Owen watched them talking to the officer through the driver's side window and then jump into the rear seats, Wilson grunted; "That's more like it. Amazing what a decent pair of legs and the offer of hot coffee and fish and chips can do!" Owen smiled - still staring at the light - which remained steady. "I think it could be a house or something. It's not car lights; it's too dim. I didn't know anyone lived in the forest." He consulted his mirror; "Yes, I was right. There's no human habitation for miles."

Jericho and Alex re-joined them, smiling. Jericho eased in and gestured for Wilson to start the van; "It appears that a certain Lionel Tanner has a small hut deep in the woods; the local council allows him because he's an Ornithologist and teaches kids about the bloody birds that infest the place. The two coppers say that he must be after night feeders like Owls and that. He's definitely is worth a visit."

Alex just sighed; "The cheeky buggers wanted my phone number." Wilson pulled the van away, chuckling. "Don't tell me your surprised by that?" He muttered and drove down the gravel lane towards the main road. "They call them 'twitchers'; people who watch birds. They are also called 'Birders'. What the difference is I haven't a clue." Owen said, but no one really listened.

They returned some forty minutes later and dropped the goodies to the very appreciative policemen. Alex politely declined their offer to join them in the police car and have her supper with them. Owen was overjoyed and scoffed his down quickly; cleaning up anyone else's left over's. Wilson just sighed; "Where the hell does he put it all? He eats like a pig and stays skinny as a rake."

Jericho was reading his mirror - in between mouthfuls of chips - and wiped his hands on some paper serviettes. "Let's go people; the hut is some six miles down that gravel path. The van should make it; School buses do." Wilson drove off, following the road carefully into the dark forest.

They had to leave the van - next to a Morris Minor car - some two hundred yards from the hut which was quite large with two big windows. The doorway was lit by two powerful lamps. Jericho knocked and heard a deep voice shout 'Enter; its unlocked!' They wandered in and found a big man standing by a small wooden table; stuffing binoculars, torches and camera's into a canvas sack. He introduced himself, Lionel Tanner. Retired History Teacher and President of the local Ornithologist Society. He matched Wilson in size with a nasty pink scar down his left cheek. He pointed to it and smiled; "Bloody war; caught one at 'Juno' beach. [Part of the D-Day landings in 1944] Could have been worse; the bloke next to me had his head blown right off." He smiled and pointed to the steamy kettle on the small paraffin stove. "Anyone fancy a cuppa?"

They sat on old wooden chairs, sipping hot sweet tea and Jericho - after introducing everyone - asked about the missing students.

Lionel shook his head; "Sadly, they're not the first to disappear in these woods without a trace. Back in '22 [1922] two young hikers went missing; nothing was ever found. My grandfather told me a story that back in the 1890's a family on a picnic disappeared up by 'Angel Ridge'. Shame really, I had only seen the kids arrive a few days ago. I don't know how that rusty old heap of a car made it down Hobbs Lane."

Jericho tapped his chin; "They had a car?" Lionel nodded and offered digestive biscuits all round; Owen took a handful and drew a disapproving look from Wilson; who just sighed. Tanner continued; "Yeah, some right old banger. Bloody pre-war I think; haven't seen a motor like that since I was a teenager." He lifted the huge teapot and poured himself another cup, offering refills to everyone. "The driver was a skinny kid; didn't actually look old enough to drive. But he made it."

Wilson sipped his tea; "Which one of the three missing students was driving Lionel?" The big man shook his head; "None of them. The skinny kid didn't apparently stay. The car was gone the following morning and so was he."

"Did you actually see them around the woods Lionel?" Jericho asked and Lionel sat back and ran a couple of fingers through his neat grey beard. "Come to think of it; no. I never did see them around the woods. But old Gabby - the woodsman - told Marge in the village post office, that he saw them heading towards 'Angel Ridge'. He knew it was them because of the girls flaming red hair. She's a very pretty little thing apparently." He sipped his tea, cradling the cup with both hands. "Now here's the odd bit. Marge - the local Post Mistress - told Gabby that the skinny kid with the car, brought postcards and sweets in her shop. Lots of them; said they were for his friends. He also bought several cans of beans and soup. Oh, and a fresh loaf of bread. The Post office doubles as a local shop."

"Sounds like he was staying." Alex said quietly and turned to Jericho; "You don't think we have four missing people but only three missing souls?" Jericho placed his cup down; "If there is a fourth missing student; then where the hell is he?" Jericho sat thinking while Lionel explained to Owen about the difference between 'twitcher's' and 'Birders'. Owen asked him which he was. Lionel grinned; "Bloody both I think. Just love birds." He shrugged his shoulders.

But Jericho interrupted the pair; "Lionel, can you take us to Angel Ridge'" He nodded but pointed out that they weren't really dressed or equipped to walk in the woods at night. Jericho just smiled; "Give us fifteen minutes and we will be."

The little group assembled, and Lionel was thoroughly impressed. They had walking sticks, back packs and rain proof clothing, including stout hiking boots. Alex had swapped to a pair of trousers and looked the part. He chuckled - a little amazed actually - "Do you always carrying such equipment on your investigations?" Jericho nodded; "Especially when big bloody forests are concerned!" With Lionel in front, torches swinging, the group set off for Angel Ridge.

Wilson asked Lionel what the police had said when they interviewed him. Lionel shrugged his shoulders and wiped rain from his thick spectacles. "Don't know my friend. They haven't spoken to me or even old Gabby." Now that did surprise the detectives.

"Incompetent and bloody rude." Owen muttered to Alex, who had to agree. Lionel was also impressed by the group's stamina; considering they had scoffed down fish and chips, with loads of coffee and tea. He shouldn't have said that; Alex had to find a bush; quickly. They stood around waiting and then heard Alex yelp.

"What's up Alexandra?" Jericho shouted; quite unconcerned. Alex emerged from the big bush and ruefully grinned; "I think, I just peed on a poor bloody badger." Now that did make everyone laugh.

They made Angel Ridge after a couple of hours of gentle walking. Lionel filled the time pointing out the various night birds who were active, especially a couple of Owls. It was quite clear that the big man knew these woods like his own garden. He admitted that Rose - his late wife - had introduced him to bird watching before the war. He clearly missed her and that made Alex a little sad.

But they reached Angel Ridge just before midnight and stooped at the foot of the gentle slope and passed a hip flask around. Lionel was impressed by the quality of the brandy. Suitably reinforced by the drink, they tackled the slope and made the top.

They couldn't see much; it was night after all. But something caught Owens's sharp eyes and he pointed down to a thick clump of ancient trees. "There's something odd about them. Look at the base: it's seems to be shaped like..." He wiped rain from his face and finished; "Looks like the shape of a car!"

3. THE STRANGE SECRETS OF ANGEL RIDGE.

They struggled a bit to reach the small group of very old trees. They stood around shining their torches into the thick undergrowth and everyone agreed; it was shaped like an old car. They managed to push closer and now could see the remains of a car, mingled in with the big trees and bushes. One very old tree had grown through the boot. Lionel shone his torch about and muttered to himself, finally turning to the others - he looked totally puzzled - and said quietly; "This is bloody impossible! These trees are hundreds of years old. But they have apparently grown through the car, which means the damn car had to be here before the bloody tree grew! That's impossible!"

Owen was peering in, what would have been the front passenger side and shouted for the others; they gathered around and stared where his torch was pointing; on the passenger side floor were several rusted tin cans. He held one up and shone his torch close to it; "I can just make out the name - Heinz Baked beans - and there are several cans here." He said and dropped the tin back down.

Lionel was standing staring at the wreckage entangled in the trees and bushes. He spoke quietly - the amazement and bewilderment obvious - "If I really had to make the call; I would have to say that this rusted piece of junk was the car that bloody skinny student was driving." He ran a hand over his face; "But that's bloody impossible. These trees are hundreds of years old and I only saw the car a few days ago; working."

The team exchanged glances and said nothing. Owen and Alex moved to the other side of the trees and Owen operated his mirror discretely. "Body search?" Alex asked in a whisper. He nodded and wiped his face; "There's a set of human remains in there somewhere." He looked up at her and said quietly; "They belong to John Hammond, and he must have died hundreds of years ago; that's how old these trees are and he must have been here before them. No soul was collected; obviously."

Alex nodded; "One down, three to go I think." They re-joined the others and said nothing, but Owen nodded to Jericho, who clearly understand what he was saying, without him saying anything. He walked away and operated his mirror. "I think we should make camp in the shelter of the ridge. Are you staying Lionel?" Jericho informed the team - and Lionel of course - and pulled off his backpack. Lionel actually stared at it. It seemed to have grown since leaving his cozy little hut. He watched the others pulling off theirs and would have sworn on Rose's grave that they were bigger than when they set out, which was impossible of course! He nodded and looked back at the clump of old trees. He had walked this forest since he was boy with his grandfather and couldn't remember this strange little group of trees. The three tents were quickly erected, and everyone settled in. Wilson and Jericho shared, whilst Lionel bunked in with Owen; Alex had her own small tent and looked quite happy in it.

Lionel had - obviously - missed Jericho stopping time and old Joe from Supplies arriving with the new backpacks. He smiled at the still Lionel and said to Owen; "He looks like he knows what he's doing in a forest." Owen just smiled. Alex asked him if there was any way to date trees accurately, short of cutting them down and counting the bloody rings!

Joe nodded and pulled his mirror out; "Trees are living things with a life cycle and with a little adjustment you can..." He stopped talking and tapped at his mirror. Then smiled; "The tree through the boot is 213 years old. This being 1959 means that it started to grow in 1746." He grinned and said his goodbyes and disappeared.

Chuckling to himself; Jericho had restarted time.

Owen shared his hip flask with Lionel and they sat chatting; he asked him about the legend of the HARBINGER and Lionel smiled; "Goes right back in time. Our ancestors worshipped nature then, especially trees, mountains and rivers. The sun and Moon of course. It's said that all this forest - it was much bigger then - was his realm. He was apparently a 'tree spirit' and a force for good in the woods. He was said to have helped the early humans survive around here. But all that changed when Christianity appeared; he was forgotten, and he really didn't like that. So, over the centuries, he changed from a benevolent entity into an evil creature of legend. The witches around here used to call upon him. But I think he always preferred to be helpful to humans. I don't think he deserves being called 'evil'; I think the stories have that wrong." Lionel handed back the hip flask and stared up at the stars; the rain had stopped.

"That's some story Lionel. Do you tell the kids that one, when you take them to chase birds around here?" Owen said, making himself comfortable. Lionel chuckled; turning over to catch some sleep. "It's not a story lad. I've seen him a couple of times myself over the years and he never did me or the missus any harm."

Owen just stared at the big man; "You've actually seen him?" He asked incredulously. Lionel nodded and yawned. "Sure have. You can't really miss him." He drifted off to sleep and Owen quietly slipped from the tent and Joined Alex, Jericho and Wilson who had gathered in Jericho's big tent. He told them what Lionel had said. Wilson just grunted; "Yeah, Goldilocks and three big grizzly bears live two miles down the road. The bloody porridge is really good I understand."

Jericho smiled; "Well, it looks like a rogue time portal operates around here. That may explain all the disappearances over the years. We need to find and close it. So, I think a little trip back to 1746 may be in order. We're going to need to rescue those bloody students before they all end up like Hammond."

Owen and Alex returned to their tents, and everyone was soon asleep. It was Alex screaming that woke everyone up and made them jump from their tents. They found her running back and straight into Wilson's arms.

"What the hell..." He said, but Alex was actually shaking and pointed back to the dark trees of the woodland. Finally, she calmed down and sipped Owens's hipflask. "What the hell happened Alex?" He asked.

"I needed to pee and so I took my torch and found a big tree, I just squatted down and..." He gulped down some more brandy. "I was careful. I didn't want to pee on any more small animals. Then the bloody tree walked away!" Everyone just stared at each other. Lionel just patted her shoulder; "Don't worry. It was only HARBINGER taking a look at us." He walked back to his tent; like they had just received a call from the bloody postman!

Alex shouted after him; "Bloody HARBINGER! Is that it? A bloody tree just walked away!" Owen shoved the hipflask back under her nose. "Come on. I'll explain about the walking tree, and you'll see sense." He took her back to her tent. Jericho and Wilson stared into the forest and exchanged an amused look.

"The BOSSES granddad did have a bloody good imagination and did create some strange bloody things." Jericho said quietly as he and Wilson settled back in their tent. Wilson nodded; "Well, anyone who created the bloody Duckbilled platypus must have a warped sense of humour." They both chuckled at that and settled back down. Owens's head appeared in the tent flap, and he held up his mirror; "Check the date on our mirrors. It's Sunday, 15th June 1567." He whispered and didn't smile.

Wilson confirmed the date; they had been thrown back 392 years in an instant. They quietly walked past the sleeping Lionel and shone their torches at the strange clump of trees; it had gone.

Jericho rubbed his chin; "Now that's bit of a co-incidence. HARBINGER turns up and we're thrown back in time 392 years."

Alex joined them and shook her head; "Never mind the disappearing bloody trees, what going on over there?" She pointed to the forest edge, some miles away. It was large bonfire, and they could make out several dark figures around it. Owen checked his mirror; "Several humans - nine to be exact - five men and three women and a child." He really grimaced; "I think they're witches and the child must be a...."He hesitated and wiped his face; "A child sacrifice."

Alex prodded Jericho's shoulder and said quietly; "What are we going to do about that?" She folded her arms and stared at him. Jericho shrugged his shoulders and sighed; "Your bloody love of living humans, is going to get us in some real shit; sooner or later." She almost smiled; "Well let's make it sooner than latter for the sake of that child."

4. A CHILD OF THE MOON.

They crept through the undergrowth and stared at the scene - illuminated by the bonfire - and Owen did chuckle a little. "All stark naked and dancing; bloody mad bastards."

Alex pointed to a tree stump; the little girl sat clutching a stick doll. Her head covered with a wreath of flowers. The child had a strange look on her face. "I bet they drugged her." Alex whispered angrily. Owen nodded; "They do that to get co-operation, probably told her it would keep the cold night out at the bonfire party; she would trust adults at that age."
Jericho lay quietly in the grass, then suddenly reached into his jacket pocket. He pulled his orb out and everyone could see the red streaks forming around its circumference. "A bloody demon." He said and watched the streaks swirling about the orb. Wilson pulled out his mirror. "A Guardian?" He asked softly and Jericho nodded; "It's a Tier Three. A Guardian will do nicely."

They watched - a little horrified - as a big man walked up to the child and easily picked her up. He held her aloft and the others started to chant. He walked back to the bonfire and shouted - in old English - that the child was a gift to the goddess of the Moon. The flames would consume her, and the rising smoke would send her up to the Goddess.

The coven started to dance again, chanting and singing. Jericho almost jumped when Oscar [a Guardian of God] tapped his shoulder; "Well, the gangs all here now." The little man said with a broad smile. He looked across at the witches and grunted; "Another bloody sacrifice to the moon. Mad bastards."

Owen nodded; "I said that too."

They watched as the flames of the bonfire seemed to part and a dark figure emerged. Oscar sighed; "Bloody Taliss, He's a right twat. I've kicked his arse a couple of times. Really does like child sacrifices. The dirty piece of shit likes to fuck them first." Alex patted his shoulder; "Go get the fucker big man." She whispered.

Jericho rose from the ground and stopped time; his mirror would have no effect on the demon of course. Oscar leapt from the bushes; his Staff of Moses gripped in both hands. "Arse kicking time you mother fucker! Yippee Ki Yay!" He yelled and set about the surprised looking demon. Wilson just sighed; "Bruce bloody Willis has a lot to answer for."

The demon was no match for an enraged Oscar, who beat the shit out of him and the demon fled screaming back into the bonfire. Owen handed Oscar his hipflask and patted his shoulder; "Nice job big man." The dwarf smiled and took a sip. "I do enjoy my work sometimes." Alex gave him a well-earned kiss which made him grin. Wilson gently pulled the child from the arms of the big witch and Alex wrapped her in her coat. "She can't be more than ten." She muttered with great sadness.

Owen coughed; "According to Human Records, young Kathleen - her father is a farmer here - died this very day. No soul collected. That fucking demon would have stolen it. That's changed now." Jericho smiled at that; "Well that gets us off the hook. We recovered a lost soul. Angel Margret won't be able to moan at us; well not too much."

Owen ran his mirror over some of the naked witches and groaned; "For fuck sake" The big man is her father and that skinny woman with the filthy hair and pock marks; is her bloody mother! Now what do we do with her?" He gestured to the still child in Alex arms. Jericho sighed and rubbed his chin; "Well, we can't leave her with those devil worshipping murdering bastards."

Everyone just looked at each other; thinking. Owen smiled; "According to my mirror; there's a convent some seventy miles away. In these times, it may as well be, in a different country. We could drop her off there. They have a good reputation for looking after orphans properly. Kind women by all accounts."

Jericho nodded; "That's the best chance she'll have in these times and circumstances. You and Alex get going." Owen and Alex operated their mirrors and were gone.

Jericho looked at the naked witches and smiled. He stared at the bonfire - frozen in time - and gestured to it. "Shall we move these bastards a little nearer? I'm sure they feel cold." Everyone chuckled at that. Oscar just grinned; "Angel Margret won't be happy about this. But then she's not happy about a lot of things you get up to Jericho! Everyone would love to know how you get away with so much." He gleefully helped move the witches a little closer to the fire, muttering; "You can have a little taste of what that poor bloody kid would have endured; you mad bastards."

They made their way back to the encampment and Jericho restarted time; they all laughed at the distant screaming. Oscar said his farewells and Jericho returned everyone - including the sleeping Lionel - back to 1959. Alex and Owen returned just before sunrise. Alex really did smile; "The nuns were lovely and didn't hesitate to take in little orphan Kate. But they thought we were an odd pair." She chuckled and pointed to Lionel; who was sitting up in the tent; stretching. "What do we do with the twitcher?" Jericho rubbed his chin; "Take him back to his hut I suppose." Owen pointed to the strange clump of trees; "He knows something is not right here. He's bound to tell people about this. That could be a real problem; evidence of time travel and all that."

"We'll deal with that later." Muttered Jericho and they started to fold up their tents. Lionel admitted that was the best sleep he had enjoyed in some time. "I must camp out in the woods more often. HARBINGER won't mind the company." Everyone just stared at him. They headed back to the hut.

Owen insisted they visit the village and find a café; he was starving. The van pulled up outside 'Maggie's Dinner' and the team piled in. The smell of bacon, sausages, black pudding and other breakfast delights filled the place. Owen actually rubbed his hands together and they sat at the table by the window. The middle-aged waitress appeared and took their orders; she peered over the top of her large, black NHS glasses and asked Owen to confirm what he just ordered.

Owen smiled; "Two fried eggs, two sausages, two bacon, mushrooms, beans, black pudding, fried slice and grilled tomatoes. That's it I think." He grinned and she just sighed; "Hungry little soul ain't he." She muttered and wandered off. Wilson just shook his head; "I'd swear the beggar must have hollow legs."

Jericho called the briefing to order and spoke quietly; "We know that John Hammond must have travelled back to 1746 or sometime before that and been killed or died. No soul obviously, so where is the other two souls? We know that the skinny kid, who was driving, must still be around here. No soul collection and no soul missing from the timeline like the other three. So where the hell is he?"

Wilson grunted; "Then we have the problem of the HARBINGER. Does he possess some sort of time portal? It can't be co - incidence that he appeared, and we get thrown back 392 years?"

The discussions were suspended by the waitress bringing the food. She slapped the large plate of breakfast down in front of Owen and almost smiled; "I can ask the chef to shoot a horse if you need a snack." She grunted and walked off. Owen just sighed and set about his breakfast with some relish.

Wilson rubbed his chin, placing down his fork; "We could jump back to 1746 and conduct a body search, but if negative, we would have to jump back each year until we achieved a result. We could end up in the Stone age." Alex was enjoying scrambled eggs on toast, but she suddenly stopped; "A creature like the HARBINGER wouldn't have a bloody time portal; he's basically a bloody tree that can think and walk. What if HARBINGER IS the time portal? That would make sense with people disappearing whenever he is seen." She sprinkled some salt and squeezed a little ketchup on her eggs.

Owen paused his relentless scoffing to agree with her - he chuckled between mouthfuls - "Why not just ask the strange old bugger where he sent them?"

Everyone stared at him and he lowered his knife and fork; "Now what have I said?" He asked softly. But Jericho did smile; "I think our human dustbin has a very good suggestion there. If anyone would know; the HARBINGER would." Alex groaned; "That means spending another bloody night in the forest. There's no proper loo's." She muttered and sipped her coffee. It was agreed that was the plan of action; but first they had to return to the student’s campsite and check it over. They finished their breakfasts and the waitress stood speechless, as Owen ordered two bacon rolls to go!

They climbed in the van and set out for the woods. They drove past the Parish Church of St. John and Jericho shouted 'STOP!' to Wilson, who pulled up by the crumbling brick wall of the church's graveyard. They all jumped from the van and walked back to the churches driveway. Everyone stared at the old car parked on the gravel. Owen checked his mirror; "It's a pre second world war car. A Morris Cowley made in 1932. Now there can't be many of them in this small village."

Jericho walked up and peered in the windows; he gestured for everyone to join him. He pointed to the front passenger foot well. There were several tins of Heinz soups and baked beans on the floor with a newspaper. The date on the paper was the day the students disappeared.

Wilson folded his arms; "How can this car be buried under those ancient trees and still be sitting here? That doesn't make sense." Jericho looked up and smiled; "Just admiring your old car Reverend. A 1932 Morris Cowley unless I'm mistaken." The old man stood in the doorway of the small Parochial House and finally smiled; "Yes, it is young man. You know your pre-war cars. I bought it new back then - in 1932 - and now my grandson Chester drives it. He loves the old girl; calls her Molly."

"Grandson?" Whispered Wilson, adding; "How would he know the students from York University?" Jericho walked up and shook the reverends hand and introduced himself and his team from; 'Thyme, Tibbs & Trayvel' - private Investigators - The reverend just nodded; "I had heard that some amateur detectives had been hired by Caleb's father to help find the missing youngsters."

Jericho smiled; "Is your grandson in sir?" The old reverend nodded. "Can we speak to him?" Jericho asked. It was clear the old reverend wasn't firing on all his cylinders! The reverend sighed and shouted into the house; "Chester! There are some amateur police people here!" He gave the team a little backward wave and disappeared inside, leaving the door open.

Everyone noticed that the old man was wearing different shoes, Alex sighed; "I would say early signs of dementia." Owen shook his head; "Sorry to disagree Doctor Kildare, but isn't dementia a modern disease? Only came about in the early 21st century." Alex shook her head; "In these times it would be called senility, you twerp and don't tell me how to be a doctor." But there was no real censure in her voice. Owen just smiled; that smile that annoyed Wilson so many times.

A scruffy, skinny young man appeared wearing a baggy jumper and dirty trousers. He was eating a sandwich; "Who wants me?" He asked and lowered his sandwich, smiling at Alex. Jericho - again - introduced himself and the team. Chester grunted; "Not this crap again. Like I told the coppers last night, when they stopped me in the old car; I dropped off some stuff to John and his friends and didn't stay." He shrugged his shoulders and turned to walk away, stopping; "Don't bloody annoy me again with this crap." He threw the remains of the sandwich at Jericho's feet and slammed the door shut. "Rude, obnoxious, lying little shit." Was all Owen said. No one disagreed with him.

5. CAMPISTE CLUES.

They sat in the van and Owen ate his bacon rolls; cold. Alex leaned back in her seat; "He's lying because the bloody cans are still in the front passenger foot well. He never dropped them off to John Hammond, so what else is he lying about or what is he hiding?" She asked and had to grimace at Owen, eating stone cold bacon rolls. Jericho nodded and told Wilson to head to the students campsite. "Something is not right here? Lionel believes that Chester dropped off the students and left. The woman in the shop sold Chester canned food, which he said was for his friends, but never delivered them apparently. The only person to see the students here was the character called 'Gabby' the woodsman." Jericho recounted and stared out the windows. They made their way back to the little campsite. It was swarming with police and scenes of crime personnel.

Inspector Parish actually groaned at seeing the van pull up. But the old sergeant tapped his arm; "They did look after our lads last night and they did keep away from the tents; like you told them." Parish shrugged his shoulders; "Always the voice of reason sergeant." Jericho and the team waited by the van until called over by the Inspector. The team bid the two policemen a cheery good morning and only the sergeant replied. "And a good morning to you. Sleep well in the woods with mad old Lionel?" He chuckled.

Jericho smiled; "So you've spoken to Lionel then?" he asked. The sergeant laughed; "Yeah. We heard the tale of Chester Freeman's car - now a wreck and hundreds of years old - the HARBINGER jumping out on your girl taking a pee. Oh, we heard the whole fantastic story. You can see why people call him mad Lionel." The Inspector - smiling now - gestured to the campsite and said, "Help yourself; let me know if our sloppy professionals missed anything." He walked off and the sergeant followed.

It appears the police operation at the camp site was over. The sergeant turned; "We have a team turning up to remove all this. The Council insists it's cleaned up." He nodded and jumped into the big black police car and drove the Inspector away.

Owen sighed; "It appears that old Lionel has no real credibility around here. That makes our job easier; doesn't it?" Jericho didn't answer but walked over to the tents. "Come on people, let's have a look - a good look - and use your mirrors." He shouted and knelt down by one tent. There were footprints everywhere, the rain last night had turned the previously hard ground a little soft. That's when he noticed the little ruts in the grass. Owen peered over his shoulder; "Looks like pram wheels." Jericho nodded and rubbed his chin. "Or a wheelbarrow or something similar."

Wilson shouted to them; he had walked down the small slope that ran down to a gravel path. They joined him and stared at the trail of wood splinters and small branches. "Lovely zig zag pattern and there's no trees to drop them here." He gestured for them to follow, and they did, stopping at the small stream. The tress opposite seemed to move despite there being no wind. "I think the HARBINGER was here." Wilson said softly.

Owen walked the stream's edge for a few yards and stopped. He waved everyone over and they gathered around him. It was a lipstick that looked new. Alex turned it open and smiled; "Cherry red." She said and closed it.

Jericho surprised them by splashing through the shallow stream and stopped amongst some rocks that protruded from the water. He reached down and pulled a woman's powder compact up. "Check the other bank thoroughly." He said and the team - reluctantly - joined him in the stream. They crossed to the other side and looked about. Owen shouted; "By the tree line; there's a pair of eyebrow clippers!" He held them up and stared into the dark trees. "There's a small path in here."

Shaking their wet shoes, they pushed into the trees and Jericho immediately noticed the little wheel ruts. They were spaced and intermittent but could be followed. They had gone some yards when Wilson found a woman's face powder brush. Alex held it and said softly; "Do you think someone is leaving us a trail to follow?"

Jericho nodded; "Miss Iris Weeks, I strongly suspect." They followed the little path for about an hour until it ended where a rough dirt road began.

Owen found a rough wooden sign with metal letters [well rusted] forming; "Copes Farm'. They walked up the road and found the ruins of the old farm building and large yard. The house had little roof left and no glass in any of the remaining windows. The front door was hanging half open and Owen shouted. In the driveway to the yard, he had found a silver cigarette lighter - he held it up - "It's engraved with the name 'Iris'." He said simply.

Wilson already had his mirror out, but Jericho pointed out the little wheel ruts in the gravel. "Our mysterious pram or wheelbarrow pusher was here." Alex stared at the old house; "Yeah, but what did they have in the bloody wheelbarrow?"

Wilson wiped his face; "There's no humans in the house or human bodies present." He lowered his mirror and looked about. "This place hasn't been occupied for years. I didn't think anyone lived in the forest." Jericho was walking the yard; "Maybe not these days, but someone lived here years ago. Owen, check the house's history." Owen stood operating his mirror and sighed; "No one has lived here since 1916. The Cope family owned the place since 1856, but the last member of the family was killed in 1915 at the Battle of Loos. No one has lived here since then. According to Human Records, the local Council now owns it."

"Well, we know that Iris Weeks has been here and possibly someone else; the wheelbarrow pusher." Jericho muttered. Alex was kneeling by the rusted metal gates of the driveway. She looked up; "There's tyre tracks here. Someone has brought a car up here." Jericho looked around and then cursed loudly. Everyone turned to him; "I know it's like slamming the stable door after the horse has bolted, but I think we should have checked Chester's car for a time portal!"

Wilson groaned; "I follow your thinking Jericho; the trail ends here with no bodies, nothing. The last place the students were alive in the current timeline is here. Well, Iris Weeks was here, possibly with someone else. There are no time portals in the house or grounds. I would throw my hat in the ring and say they were transported from here in that bloody car to some other time."

Jericho - now quite grim - pulled out his mirror; "Back to the van - the quick way - and let's check obnoxious Chester's bloody car." They vanished and the house returned to its lonely derelict quietness. The HARBINGER moved slowly from the tree line, shuffling towards the dark interior of the forest that it loved so dearly. If it had a face; then it would be smiling.

6. THE OLD SPIRIT.

The Parochial House was in darkness and Wilson parked opposite. The team was disappointed; the car was gone. Jericho asked Owen to check the house; he did so thoroughly. He sat working his mirror for some minutes. "Parts of it were built in the 1700's, but most of it is middle Victorian; early 1860's. The Church grounds it sits in go way back to Anglo-Saxon times. There was church here first in 953AD." He chuckled; "It [the church] sits right on top of an early pagan temple, that's hundreds of years older. But there are no time portals present. But there is something that may interest us; really interest us." He lowered his mirror and smiled broadly. Alex sighed; "What will bloody really interest us?"

Owen gestured to the old house; "It's haunted. There's an earth-bound spirit in there. From way back, possibly well before even Christianity came on the scene." They all stared at the house. "Do we know who it is?" Jericho asked. Owen shook his head; "Human Records have nothing on the spirit. Which is quite odd?"

Jericho jerked open the van door; "Well, let's have a little chat with it. Shall we?" They all jumped from the van and headed up the driveway. Jericho banged loudly on the door and received no answer. "There's no one in. Well, no one still alive!" Owen muttered, pushing his mirror back in his pocket. Jericho held up his orb; it was clear. "No bloody demon then." He said and nodded to Wilson.

Wilson had the door open in seconds and smiled with satisfaction. Owen grunted; "Are you sure you were in the bloody NYPD?" Wilson just grinned and gestured into the house; "After you baby brother."

They pushed into the dark house and gathered in the messy front room. It was covered with dirty plates, cups, beer tins and bottles. There were clothes thrown about the place and the sofa was threadbare. Alex stepped over a pile of old newspapers and shook her head; "Chester - the little shit - is not looking after his old grandfather very well." Jericho shouted a couple of times for the spirit to show itself. They watched in silence as a little white mist began to form in the fireplace and slowly grow into a human shape.

The young man was dressed in a simple white robe with a hood; he had a gold rope about his waist and bare feet. He was a very handsome young man, well built with stunning blue eyes. Jericho bowed a little; "We are sorry to disturb you sir, but I think you know who we are and who we work for." The spirit nodded and smiled a little. "I know who you are Jericho. I have been expecting you or a colleague to finally arrive." His voice was deep - almost hypnotic - he could make a fortune doing movie voice over's!

Jericho nodded; "You have been expecting us sir?" He asked quietly. The spirit nodded again. "The theft of the young people's souls would bring you on scene. You are clearly well suited to the tasks assigned to you; otherwise, you wouldn't be standing before me. Living humans now only exist in the illusionary world created for them. They have little understanding of their true reality." He clasped his big hands in front of him. "What do you seek Jericho?"

Jericho said simply; "To return the stolen souls to their allocated time sir." The spirit smiled. "A worthy cause Jericho; the HARBINGER has already informed me of your excellent endeavours in that respect. He particularly likes your young woman. She was most generous and watered him, which he greatly appreciated."

Alex went a little red at that revelation. The spirit raised his arms; "Let us travel together. Time is just another illusion of the human mind; it only exists where living humans dwell. They are freed when their bodies fall away. The flesh always fails; the spirit never does. Come with me now." The dingy room was empty. The reverend's old cat crept out from under the sofa and pissed in the fireplace. Then settled back down on the sofa; she had seen the spirit many time over the years; but the humans in the house never did.

They walked through the woods; the weather was glorious with blue sky and warm sunshine. They followed the spirit in silence. Owen tapped Jericho on the sleeve and pointed to his mirror; it was offline. The spirit tuned and smiled; "You have no need of anything whilst with me." He gestured down to the Manner House: its numerous chimneys were smoking. There was a strange burning smell in the air. "Someone's having a bloody bar-be-que." muttered Wilson.

The Spirit didn't smile; "The humans you seek are trapped in the cellars of this house. They are awaiting the same fate that befell the others. Their captors are destroying the evidence of their inhumanity and will take great joy in more savage, earthly pleasure and death. They are full of darkness."

"What human year is this sir?" Jericho asked, staring at the house and wondering what the hell was going on in there. The spirit smiled; "There are many ways to date human progress. But for your connivance it is the year 1715." He gestured to the side of the house, adding: "That is somewhat out of place." Everyone could see the old Morris Cowley car standing near the stable block. The spirit did not smile; "I would have suggested you call a Knight; maybe one of the best. James, Arthur or Lucinda. But whilst I'm here, you have no need of them. The dark demon Kiri has taken up residence and his minions are devoted to him. I will cast him back to his foolish young master."

Owen sighed with relief; his mirror was back online. The spirit gestured to the house; "Go now my friends and fulfill your task." They could hear screaming and chaotic noise from the old house. The spirit did smile; "Kiri is back with his master. Act now Jericho." The team headed quickly for the house and saw young Chester running towards the car, followed by a tall thin man wearing an ill-fitting three-piece suit. He was gripping an axe in one hand. Jericho stopped time and the two running figures froze in time. "Let's find them!" Jericho shouted and the team ran into the house. At the foot of the stairs was a middle-aged woman in a black robe; the hood pulled back; her still face frozen in a shout.
Wilson stopped and stared at the woman; "Isn't that the bloody waitress from the café?" He shouted and they located the hatch to the cellars with their mirrors. Jericho checked his orb; it was clear. Wilson and Owen heaved it up and they shone their mirrors down. It was not a pleasant sight. The two young students were chained against a wall - quite naked - and had bruises and whip marks upon their legs and backs. Alex shone her mirror on Iris and cursed with some anger. The girl's thighs were bloody, and she had probably been raped more than once.

Wilson pulled out his lock picking kit and soon had the chains and collars off. The two students sobbed, and the girl gripped Alex tightly and simply wouldn't let go.

Jericho ran a hand over his face; "Alex and Owen, take them back to the day they arrived in the clearing. That way, they wouldn't have suffered these horrors. Wilson and I will deal with the bastards above." Alex nodded and she and Owen disappeared with the two students.

Wilson and Jericho searched the house and found human remains - partially burnt - in the big fireplace of the main reception room. There was a pentagon painted on the floor, in human blood apparently. Wilson checked the remains in the fireplace and cursed loudly, lowering his mirror; "It's the poor fucking old reverend. Now why did the bastards kill the poor old senile bugger? His soul is lost to the darkness now."

Jericho shook his head; he didn't know. The spirit stood in the doorway and smiled a little; "I will call his soul back from the darkness and you obtain the assistance of a Collector Jericho." The old reverend appeared by the fireplace in a state of confusion.

Herbie the Collector also appeared; checking his soul ledger - he smiled at Jericho and Wilson - and muttered; "That's bloody odd. I have no scheduled collection for this time and place. Then suddenly I get this one!"

Jericho just jerked a thumb at the spirit and Herbie grinned. "Oh. Now I understand." He bowed a little at the spirit. "As you order sir." He said quietly and guided the reverend towards the light.

They were gone.
"What about John Hammond's soul?" Wilson asked; the young man was missing from the cellar. Jericho stared at his mirror; "Why the hell was he in the car? Why did we find the damn thing hundreds of years before it was even built? They are pretty interesting questions."

The spirit chuckled; "The soul known as John Hammond has escaped your clutches and even now is frantically operating the time portal contained in the car. He was part of the devil worshipping sect here and in the future. He and the soul known as Chester Freeman arranged for the other two students to be brought here. But - unfortunately for the evil young man – he failed to operate the time portal properly. He had appeared in 1563, in front of some very unpleasant witches and they used him and the strange vehicle, as the ultimate sacrifice to their master. They burnt him alive. I do love the beautiful irony of that."

The spirit smiled and simply disappeared. Wilson finally had to ask; "Who or what the hell was he?" Jericho checked his mirror and wiped his face; "The BOSSES granddad created humanity and also assigned some of his earlier creations to watch over the fledgling humans. But humans being humans; they soon went their own way, came up with their own religions and Gods. I strongly suspect that creatures like the Spirit and HARBINGER are all that's left of those early babysitters."

Wilson nodded and smiled; "What do we do with these bastards?" Now Jericho really did smile. "Well, they do love devil worship; shouldn't they want to join their friend John? I mean, what if they were stupid enough to appear in the middle of a witch trial in the 1400's? I think they would love that." He said quietly and Wilson just had to grin. They stood outside and saw the car had gone. John Hammond had fled the scene; leaving his two fellow devil worshippers running towards him and simply abandoned them to their fate. He certainly regretted that; he didn't quite understand how the time portal worked and paid for that ignorance with his life and soul.

7. RETURN TO THE WOODS.

They sat in the van and waited; the two students from York University never arrived to set up camp. Chester Freeman and his old car also didn't put in an appearance. Owen sat reading his mirror and chuckled; "The timeline has changed a little; but Angel Margret has apparently authorised the changes. The old reverend and his evil grandson have disappeared from this time and place. They never existed here. There's a young married vicar in the Parochial House with his wife and three kids. 'Maggie's Dinner' is now a bloody kebab shop - can we stop there later? - [Jericho just nodded] and she has been removed from the human timeline. Gabrielle - Gabby - Houseman; the woodsman never existed here and now. Whilst John Hammond, who died in 1563, never existed here and so; the two young students never met him or came on this trip."

"Looks like old mad Lionel will have his hands full." Alex chuckled as a small school bus passed the team's van, heading up the dirt road to Lionel's cabin. "Of course, old Lionel would have never met us; we only met because of the students and that has now changed." Wilson grunted and watched the bus full of happy young children pass. He grinned and waved at them; he received loads of waving back from the clearly excited youngsters. "Must be a lot more fun than sitting in a stuffy classroom on a day like this." He added and sat back in the driver's seat, smiling.

The team would wait in the little clearing until old Joe from Supplies arrived to collect the van and equipment. Then they would jump to the lighthouse for a well-earned dinner and some brandies. Jericho already knew that they had another mission waiting; a trip back to England in 1977 and a dead woman bricked up in bloody Canterbury Cathedral! [See episode: **'The corpse chronicler of Canterbury Cathedral.'**]

Jericho pulled out his mirror which was buzzing; "Bloody Temporal Operations Control, what do they want?" He answered and relaxed back in his seat; then sat up suddenly. He lowered his mirror and really looked grim. "What is it?" Wilson asked. Jericho shook his head in disbelief; "We've been given another assignment here, at this time and place, they passed it to us because it happened right now." Alex leaned forward; "What has happened?"

Jericho stared down the dirt road and sighed; "Two young girls have just vanished from the timeline. Their teacher is presently at a phone box down that very road, reporting them missing from the school group; right now, to the local police." He ran a hand across his face and sighed loudly.
"A time controller flagged the disappearance and the Senior Duty Controller - Janet - knew we were already on scene here; waiting for Supplies to recover the damn van. She passed the call straight to us. A Susan Morris and Clare Roberts; both aged nine have simply vanished from this time and place." Jericho said and gestured for Wilson to start the van; "Let's go people." He added and checked his mirror for updates.

"What the fuck! We've closed the bloody time portals. How is this possible?" Wilson said and started the van. Jericho sighed;

"Maybe they got too close to the bloody HARBINGER and were thrown back in time. Whatever happened; we have to find them." Wilson turned the van around and headed down the road. He had to pull over; a police car passed them at speed, its shrill bell sounding and the headlamps flashing. They followed and found the scene outside Lionel's hut utterly chaotic.

They young teacher - between sobs - was giving a description of the missing girls to the police driver. He wrote everything down and shouted to his colleague to call the station for more men and inform Inspector Parish. The young constable had his hands full; throwing four mischievous boys from the police car. One had already sounded the bells and shouted into the radio handset!

Jericho walked over to him and asked if they could be of assistance. The harassed young copper nodded, giving one boy a gentle slap across the head. The boy was writing with a crayon in the police car's logbook. "Teachers really earn their bloody money; don't they?" He said - quite ruefully - to Jericho, who just smiled.

Lionel sat on the steps of his hut talking softly with two girls. He looked up at Wilson and Alex; "According to Margaret and Lilly. The two missing girls went around the back of the hut: giggling together over something. They never came back." He stared at Alex; "Don't I know you Miss? Are you an actress off the telly or something?" Alex shook her head; "No, I'm a doctor actually." That admission caught the police drivers attention, and he called Alex over; "Can you look after Miss Grimes please Doc? I think she's in shock." Alex nodded and put her arms around the young woman and walked her to the van. They sat in the back chatting.

Owen and Lionel gathered the children together and was explaining about what the police would be doing and why. The Police driver pushed up his cap and smiled; "Thank fuck for that! I'd sooner handle a couple of armed blaggers." [That's armed robbers in police slang] He admitted to Jericho. His young colleague informed him that Inspector Parish was on his way with more men and to get a search party together. "We'll stay and help of course." Jericho told the driver, who nodded then asked who the hell were they!

Jericho kept to the old cover story about being private

investigators, except he changed the crucial part of the story, to the team chasing after a persistent debtor, who owed their client thousands of pounds and had absconded. The copper just smiled and muttered; "Inspector Parish will really welcome your help." Jericho could hear the sarcasm in his voice. The driver joined his colleague by the car and Owen tapped Jericho on the shoulder and gestured for him to follow.

Wilson joined them and they followed the zig zag pattern of small twigs and pieces of wood away from the back of the hut. They stood before the dark forbidding tree's at the edge of the vast woodland. "Well, the bloody HARBINGER was definitely here. I wonder if those two kids got too close to him and zap, they were gone." Owen checked in mirror and grunted with real satisfaction; "The Time Controller has finally traced the breech in the timeline." He looked up and ran a hand across his face; "There was a breach of the time line here at this time and place. Two souls were transported to 698AD."

Jericho nodded and said quietly; "Owen, go get Alex. We're going to defy temporal protocols and jump as we are. There is no time to mess about with Supplies, costumes or such stuff. Two children could be in real danger in this forest in the 7th Century. So we're going right now; as we are." Owen wandered back to the van and spoke with Alex. Wilson stared at the forest and grunted; "I agree with your call Jericho, but Angel Margret may not." But he did smile.

The team climbed into the back of the van and Jericho operated his mirror and the van was empty. They stood in the slight drizzle and shouted for young Susan and Clare. There was no answer. Jericho wiped rain from his face and told his team to split into two. He and Owen would search in the one direction and Wilson, with Alex would search in the opposite.
Owen sighed; "Jericho, nothing is showing on my mirror when I do a body search. That's really odd. The girl's human form should be picked up; but nothing is showing." Alex lowered her mirror and agreed with Owen. "That's not right. We should be picking up their bodies. They can't have gone far; we were too quick on scene and they should be here."

Jericho didn't smile as he gestured very slowly to the forest edge; "Maybe they can help." He said quietly and the team all turned as one and saw the group of men standing together between the dark trees. They were all carrying spears and axes. They really didn't look very hospitable. Jericho held up one hand and shouted - in old English - that they had come to find two young girls; missing from their village. The men spoke amongst themselves, and the team couldn't hear what was said.

I hope their friendly fuckers." Muttered Wilson and the team soon found that they weren't. The group of men charged waving their spears and axes. Jericho cursed loudly and operated his emergency travel app and the strangers were gone, to the utter astonishment of the angry men. The team assembled outside the lighthouse and Jericho ran a hand over his face; now what the hell do they do?

8. THE TOWER OUT OF TIME.

The team moved through the woods quietly with Jericho constantly checking his mirror. They were now appropriately dressed for the period; Supplies had come up trumps - yet again - and they were back in 698AD in Anglo-Saxon England. Alex was moaning - as usual - about her bloody dress; she had pulled the damn thing up to her knees, so that she walked better and with more freedom. Owen chuckled; "That's not how proper ladies behaved, showing an ankle was considered shocking, never mind your bloody knees."

Alex just grunted and the team moved on. Jericho suddenly stopped, hand in air and gestured forwards; "There's a bloody stone tower ahead. It wasn't here in the time we just left." They crept forward and could see the old stone tower in a small clearing. It looked ancient with just slits for windows. A thin grey wisp of smoke arose from the top.

Owen tapped Jericho's shoulder and pointed to the grass around the towers base; it was dead and brown. He pointed to two rabbits lying dead by the edge of the brown grass. "I don't like the look of that." He said quietly and pulled out his mirror. He nodded; "The soil is poisoned with a pretty nasty chemical. Some sort of defense system." Wilson leaned on the big battle axe he carried and rubbed his chin; "Someone could be in; there's smoke rising from the roof, and I can definitely smell something cooking."

An arrow thudded into a tree next him and the team fell back, hiding behind some large trees. "Not a friendly time, is it?" He said and Jericho lowered his mirror; "One human inside with several small animals; cats I think." Owen nodded and rubbed his chin; "Human records report that the soul inside is a William Gates and his from 2108, A bloody unfriendly time traveler."

Jericho sighed; "Let's try and make contact." He shouted out in modern English; the man's name and where he came from. There was no reply and Jericho shouted again. Alex dropped her dress and pointed to the roof. There was a hunched figure now kneeling behind the stone balustrade. It was holding a bow and arrow and Jericho repeated his words and waved a grubby white hankie. The figure stood and threw back the hood on his dark cloak. "Who the fuck are you and from what time?" The young man shouted down to the detectives.

Jericho shouted back; "We're temporal detectives. We work for God. We're looking for two young girls; missing in the woods. They're from 1959 and we need to find them urgently. We think The HARBINGER accidently cast them back here."

The young man lowered his bow and shouted down; "Wait there, don't come near the tower. The bloody grass will kill you in just a few minutes. I'll lower the drawbridge." He turned and was gone. Owen looked at the tower - quite puzzled - and muttered to Alex; "What bloody drawbridge? There's not even a door." Wilson pointed to the grass and said loudly - with amazement in his voice - "The bloody grass is lifting!" And it was, a metal plank slowly emerged from the dead grass, and they all watched as several of the 'ancient' stones also opened. It was a small doorway and the young man stood and gestured to them. "Don't fall off the bloody plank or you'll be back with God in a very short space of time."

In single file, the team crossed the deadly clearing and entered the stone tower. They stood inside and noticed that the place was completely empty, apart from a wooden staircase up to the roof and a small fire basket which was alight and smoking. The young man stood - arms folded - and watched as the stone 'door' closed behind the team. He gestured to the floor, and everyone noticed the slab. He pulled a small remote control from his pocket and pressed a button. The slab rose, revealing a staircase. The metal rails were long lights and he headed down; telling everyone to follow him. Quite impressed they did. Down the small, illuminated staircase was a large room with several doors. It was furnished like a 20th Century front room. It contained a big sofa, fireplace, chairs and a huge TV screen with various black boxes and cables scattered about.

"No TV signals obviously, but the TV is connected to my computer which has thousands of TV shows and films. Everything is powered by a single power cell; from 2099. It lasts forever." He told them and tossed his cloak onto the big table, followed by his bow and arrows, he walked to an ornate cabinet and pulled the doors open. Now that did make the team smile; it was stocked with alcohol from top to bottom shelf. He pulled a bottle of whisky down and said quietly; "Anyone fancy a drink?" Silly question!

Everyone sat around and William Gates poured out generous measures; especially for himself. He slumped on a big chair by the fireplace and almost smiled. "Now, how did old HARBINGER toss the two kids back to here?" Alex sipped her excellent whisky and said quietly; "We think that it was done accidently, but the children are around here someplace, and we need to find and return them. If they die outside their ordained time, their souls will be lost to the darkness of real death."

William nodded; "A risk all time travelers take. Even Temporal detectives I think." He raised the glass and smiled at Alex. "Here's to a real woman. There weren't many of them, where I'm from." Alex raised her glass to return the compliment. "How did you end up here, in this time and place?" Owen asked outright - as usual - and William chuckled; "Good or bad fortune, take your pick. One minute I was a scientist working for the bastards who ran the shitty world and next; I'm sent here with a small team to set up this place. I think the bastards were trying to bail out the mess they made of the world. They never did make it here." Jericho rubbed his chin; "What happened to the others, of your team I mean?" William sighed; "The other three didn't last long. They had no idea about these times, within a year I was all that was left. The bastards never did recall us, and we were stuck here. But - thankfully - we had finished setting up the tower."

Wilson grunted and finished his delightful whisky; "So they abandoned you?" He asked. William shook his head; "I think they had no choice in the matter. The stupid sheep were revolting everywhere; they had suffered enough and turned on the evil, totally controlling, murdering bastards. It was really bad when we [his team] left. Our little institution was already under siege by crazed mobs. I guess they finally got past the killing machines and put an end to the bastards."

"So, the ruling elite [at the time] thought they could hide back in time; clever really." Owen muttered and also finished his drink. William smiled; "If your two kids are still alive, then the only place they would be is at Michaels. The villagers are not friendly. they kill all strangers on sight, even pretty women and young children. I sometimes suspect they may be ancestors of the bastards." He chuckled at that.

Jericho placed his glass down and asked; "Who is Michael?" William smiled; "A crazy, lovely old man without whom I would certainly be dead now. He has a place some miles from here. He is also in regular contact with your HARBINGER. He's what - in the 1960's - would be called a bit of a hippy."

William leaned forward and didn't smile: "Michael told me about you people. That you protect the so called human timeline and who you work for. Well Mister temporal detective; the next time you see God, you tell him to get off his omnipresence arse and help fucking humans out. Oh, and tell him William says hello." He bent down and ran his fingers through the fur of the big black cat that had emerged from under his chair.

Owen had to chuckle; two more cats also crept from under the chair. They sat staring at the visitors. "You like cats then?" Alex said, quite bemused as two smaller cats stuck their heads out from under the big sofa.

William smiled; "Their better company than most bloody humans, Michael has more than me. I got these from him as kittens. Most people who visit him come away with a kitten in their pockets." He laughed and slumped back in his chair.

"Can you take us to him William?" Jericho asked outright and William nodded finishing his whisky. "I can. But the deal is this; I help you and you forget about me. No tricks or sending me back to 2108 or anything like that and I want your word on that mister temporal detective. Man to man."

Jericho nodded and said quietly; "You have my word on that

William." The young man leapt from the chair and grinned; "Well, let's get going. I hope you like cats."

9. DRAGON'S, CASTLES, KITTENS & LOST CHILDREN.

Night was just an hour away as the little group passed through the woods. It was clear that William knew his way around the forest; He stopped suddenly and examined the soft ground. "A group of humans have passed this way, perhaps a couple of hours ago. They appear to be dragging a litter with some weight on it, probably villagers out hunting." He hesitated and didn't smile adding; "But they normally carry their kills over their shoulders on a pole. I wonder what was on the litter?" he stared about and walked on. Owen, just behind, asked him how long he had survived here. William chuckled; "In human years, I suppose I've seen sixty winters here, so about sixty years I suppose."

Owen nodded, humans out of their own time aged very slowly. William was still a young man and would remain so for centuries of human time. Darkness was creeping around them when William stopped the little party beside a large oak tree with an enormous girth. He patted the tree; "This is Modor. She's the oldest tree in the forest." He eased himself down and pulled his cloak around his body; "She'll let Michael know we're here." He said and fumbled in his pocket, producing a small pie - pork - and ate slowly.

Wilson shrugged his shoulders and stared up at the magnificent tree; "I wonder how old the tree is?" He muttered and Owen tapped his mirror; "According to my mirror, she's over two thousand years old. Cut down in Late Medieval times to build fucking warships for Henry the Eighth. Bastards." Alex touched the tree - sadly - and whispered; "She's beautiful. How the fuck could they do that?"

William chuckled; "Because stupid sheep brained people let the bastards run the world. That's how." He said, the anger in his voice really apparent. He rose slowly and smiled; "He's seen us and there's our ride." Everyone turned to the large clearing beyond the trees. To say they [the team] were shocked, amazed and impressed - all at the same time - would be a real understatement. There was silence for a full minute until Owen - as usual - stated the bloody obvious; "It's a fucking dragon! A real, living breathing fucking dragon!"

Wilson slapped his shoulder; "No shit Sherlock." He said quietly. He had never seen anything so fierce or so beautiful. It shimmered in the moonlight, lifting and lowering its multicoloured wings. Its huge head, with rolling red eyes, lifted high. William lifted a hand in welcome; "She's called Eve. Come on, there's room in her basket for all of us."

Jericho rubbed his chin and spoke quietly; "I think I know who 'old Michael' really is. Come on." The team approached 'Eve' slowly and realized that the claw beneath her 'starboard' wing was holding a large wicker basket - similar to what the first big air balloons carried - and Eve watched closely as the group climbed in. Alex pulled up her awkward skirts and dropped in. William did smile at that; "Bloody beautiful. Best thing I've seen in years." and chuckled to himself.

Alex brushed down her skirts and sat on the floor; knees pulled up. "Hang on everyone; she's off!" William grabbed a rope hanging from the wicker wall and the others all did the same. Eve took off and soared into the night sky. Wilson wasn't too impressed by the ride, but Owen loved it. Alex kept her eyes closed and gripped her piece of rope tightly. Jericho held on with one hand and peered through the gapes in the weave of the basket. He was further impressed, when he saw their destination, a small island on a large lake with a dark castle at its centre. "Now that's beautiful." He muttered to himself and gripped the rope as Eve descended.

She landed gently on one of the turrets and slowly lowered the basket into the circular courtyard. The group decamped slowly and Owen was ecstatic and wanted to go again! But Eve folded her wings about her huge body and flicked her tail. She closed her eyes and rested. Light appeared, shining through a large ornate doorway and everyone saw the old man standing there. He held up a hand; "Welcome my friends to Castle Asgard, my very humble home. Come, come and enjoy my hospitality. I hope you like cats." He grinned, his deep blue eyes sparking.

Jericho actually bowed; "Thank you sir, I believe you know why we must disturb you?" The old man chuckled and gestured for them to enter. "Always the bloody diplomat Inspector Tibbs. Come on. Warm your arses and sip some brandy." They followed him in and Owen whispered to Alex; "Who the hell is old Michael?" Alex ruefully smiled; "The BOSSES [God] grandfather.

The one you admire so much for creating the bloody dinosaurs." Owen gulped and pulled off his rough woolen hat. "Oh fucking shit!" Was all he said. The great feasting hall was silent and empty, apart from loads of cats; they were everywhere.

Alex's sharp eyes caught the big cat, sitting by the roaring fireplace that was the size of a small dog and she smiled; "Now that could be Mr. Parker's dad." She whispered to Owen, who nodded. The cat was huge, totally black and sitting next to the big chair that was close to the grate. Michael dropped in the chair and smiled at everyone, who stood around him. There were no other chairs. The old man clapped his hands and a figure from a dark shadow emerged into the room.

He was about nine feet tall and dressed immaculately in an evening suit, complete with a dark bow tie. He appeared to be human, but obviously wasn't. His face resembled that of a very handsome ape. "This is Adam. He's my PA here. He'll get you drinks. Anything you want." The team ordered the same thing; brandy; big ones. That's when they heard the giggling and laughter. Alex really did smile as Susan and Clare rushed into the room, both clutching fat little kittens. They stopped and smiled at everyone. Susan held up her kitten; "I've called him Sooty because he's so black." She grinned from ear to ear with happiness. Clare held her kitten up and stroked its ears; "Mine's called Marmaduke fluff button because he's...well, he's...he's mine!" and cuddled the mewing kitten.

Alex and Owen accepted brandies from Adam and then played with the girls and their kittens. Michael sat on his chair and smiled at Jericho and Wilson. "How's my grandson doing?" He asked simply and smiled broadly. Jericho cleared his throat; "He's fine sir. Doing well." The old man chuckled; "Never ask a bloody diplomat a straight question."

Wilson had finished his brandy and watched with amazed eyes, as the glass refilled itself. He liked this place, he really did.

William sat at the old man's feet and sipped his brandy; "Alright to stay over Michael? I could do with some company, and I'll let you beat me at chess a couple of times." Michael nodded; "You're always welcome young William." He turned back to Jericho and ran a hand across his face. "HARBINGER told me that he had accidently thrown the children back here, so I quickly gathered them up. The villagers in that particular place are not very welcoming. I could do something about them, but human freewill must always take precedence. You of all humans, do understand that."

Jericho nodded. The old man leaned back in the big chair and smiled; "Tell my grandson, that one day, he will have to shift his omnipresence arse [he grinned at William] and actually do something. Humans are abusing the privilege of freewill for power and greed. It will end badly. My Great grandson tried to help and was isolated from the family. But he does like visiting his old great grandfather." He leaned forward in his chair and gestured at Owen who nervously smiled, "I see you are caught between two worlds. Once you've decided, speak with angel Margret – or any angel – and they'll sort it out."

Owen just stared at the floor and Alex tapped his hand with some affection and a big smile. She whispered, "I think we both know what he means." Owen didn't reply, but managed another smile.

Michael sighed and rose from the chair. "Back to their families, I think." He smiled at the giggling little girls, and everyone was gone.

Alex and Owen held the girls hands as they walked through the tree's towards Lionel's hut. Alex smiled at the girls; "Go on, back to your friends. You shouldn't have wandered off like that. You could have got lost in the woods. Now, off you go." The girls grinned and nodded running back to their friends and very relieved teacher.

Owen watched the school children filing into Lionel's hut and the police officers jumping back into their car. "He must have wiped their minds. They think they're only being gone a few minutes." Alex sighed; "He certainly looked after what he created - when he could - you have to admire him for that." She suddenly yelped; something was moving in her coat pocket. She carefully extracted a big black kitten from it and held it gently with both hands. She grinned; "I think I'll call her Isis." She whispered and stroked the kitten.

Owen just sighed; "Do you think Mr. Parker will like a little female company?" Alex grinned; "Oh yes, I really think he will."

They were joined by Wilson and Jericho and headed back to the van. Jericho stared at the little kitten and just smiled.

THE END

EPILOGUE:

"An unusual mission for Jericho and the team, but it was deemed a great success; they had closed a dangerous time portal, broke up an evil group of Devil worshippers and returned two souls back to the human time line. They had met old 'Michael' - the BOSSES grandfather - and taken a flight with a real dragon. They had not met the HARBINGER but, of course, Alexandra received a real cute present; Isis the kitten. It turned out that Mr. Parker actually received a nice present too...."
SJW.

CHARACTERS:

Inspector James Parish finished his career and retired in 1968, He retired to Scarborough and with his wife and daughter; ran a modest B&B. He died in 1978 and his soul was collected and processed.

John Hammond died outside his ordained time period and so, his soul was never collected and remains missing to this day.

Caleb Mortimer Harding followed his father into politics but wasn't very successful; he lost three local elections and turned his hand to farming. He died in 1986 and his soul was collected and processed.

Miss Iris Weeks completed her studies and graduated as a doctor. She worked practices in York and Manchester for some years. Finally, after retiring, she worked in Africa for various medical charities. She was tragically killed on a Kenyan dirt road when her jeep overturned. She had never married nor had children. Her soul was collected and processed.

Margaret Caulder [Maggie the waitress] was a member of the Witches Coven and suffered the same fate as her evil companions; her soul was lost to the darkness and remains missing to this day.

Lionel Tanner continued his 'hobby' - some would say, obsession - and enjoyed showing youngsters the pleasure of the woodlands. He died in 1972 from a stroke. His soul was collected and processed. There is now a little brick-built hut on the site of his old wooden one; called the 'Lionel Tanner Memorial Hut'. He had no idea how many lives he had touched with his love of birds and the forest. The public subscription for the new hut was heavily oversubscribed and several hundred people turned up for his funeral. He is still remembered with love and affection to this day.

Taliss [the demon] defeated by the Guardian Oscar was to make more appearances in the human timeline. But this nasty little demon has disappeared from the scene and Demon Ingress has had no reports about him for some time.

Kathleen Coldstone - who would have been the child sacrifice - lived her life in the Convent as a nun. She was very kind and caring woman and died in 1603. Her soul was collected and processed. She now works as a Collector and is very popular.

Chester Freeman died outside his ordained time period and so his soul was lost. It remains missing to this day.

Reverend Freeman had died outside his ordained time period, but his soul was recalled from the darkness of real death, by 'THE SPIRIT'. His was collected and re-joined the human life cycle. Currently, she lives, as a mother of five in a small Mexican town.

Gabrielle Houseman [Gabby the Woodsman] died outside his ordained time period and so his soul was lost to the darkness of real death. It remains missing to this day.

Susan Morris had no idea of the adventure she was involved in and when she became a woman, worked in the local Tesco's, and married a bus driver. They had two children and Susan died in 2001. Her soul was collected and processed.

Clare Roberts also had no idea about her trip to another time. She did well at school and attended a local college. She finally, became a teacher in 1971. But her career was brief; she was killed in a swimming accident in the Cumbrian lakes in 1973. She left a husband and a son. Her soul was collected and processed.

William Gates continued to live in the forests of Anglo-Saxon England. He has not aged much, being out of his own ordained time period. It is rumoured that he should have died in a hunting accident in 1104AD. But it appears that his friend 'Michael' recalled his soul and William re-joined the human life cycle. He is currently living in Hongkong as a local Taxi driver and is married with three children. He has - of course - no recollection of his adventures in the woods of old England or his dreadful life in 2108. After William had moved on; Michael erased the Tower from human history.

Pamela Grimes [the schoolteacher] only taught class for a couple of years. She married the young constable who had attended the missing girls report [yes, Susan and Clare were bridesmaids!] and then left the profession. She had four children and died in 2019. Her soul was collected and processed.

HARBINGER remains somewhere in the forests and woodlands that he loves. He tries to keep away from living humans now; he doesn't want any more accidents!

Like HARBINGER, the SPIRIT remains watching over humanity and tries to help whenever possible, but [to him] humans appear to be growing darker with each new generation. The influence of the 'The Dark Prince' is slowly overpowering the followers of the 'Light' and the future of humanity does indeed hang in the balance. Worse still, is that the majority of humans have no idea about the dark changes they are experiencing. It really doesn't look good for them.

Special appearance *by* ***MICHAEL;*** *retired* ***GOD II;*** *The current BOSSES grandfather, who is now* ***GOD IV.***

EPISODE 9: "UNKNOWN NUMBER."

MISSION SUMMARY: "Old Lester Lightfoot hears a disturbance outside the front of his house one night and upon investigation finds that someone has thrown a broken mobile phone into his front garden. It has no battery or Sim card, and Lester tosses it on his hall table to dispose of properly in the morning. But at Midnight the phone starts ringing, and the dead are apparently calling!"

NOTES: This mission is considered quite unique amongst the adventures of Jericho Tibbs. Can you spot why?

TRIGGER WARNINGS. STRONG LANGUAGE, SUICIDE REFERENCES AND MILD VIOLENCE.

AGE 12+ ONLY. **30 Minutes reading time.**

1. THE DISCARDED PHONE.

Mr. Lester Lightfoot was a man of habits; he woke every morning at six o'clock, showered and ate breakfast, then at seven o'clock walked his Scottish terrier: Wellington, around Victoria Park for exactly half hour.

He then returned home to his small apartment; Lester had worked for the local council for over forty years and had taken early retirement, just a few months ago – now he struggled to fill his time. He had worked in various departments over the years;

starting at sixteen in the Transport offices, then moving to Property maintenance and finally ending his service collecting Council Tax payments.

Lester was an introvert; he had made few friends over the years and if he was honest with himself, only married his wife by accident! Their only child: a son, lived in Australia with his family and had little time for his aging parents. David Lightfoot was an Accountant with a taste for the expensive lifestyle, which he pretended to live: on other people's money. To quote the old saying: 'he borrowed from Peter to pay Paul'. The Lightfoot's had not heard from their wayward son in over two years and Lester wasn't that unhappy about the situation, but he would have loved to see his Grand-daughter. He sat drinking coffee, watching through the window of his sitting room; at the large wrought iron gates of Victoria Park which lay immediately opposite.

He liked to watch the parade of people passing in and out of that beautiful Victorian gateway – the gates were quite magnificent; with crowned lions and Unicorns holding majestic scepters of state. He remembered how his wife; Irene, loved to walk their dogs in the park over the years. He sipped the coffee and glanced at the calendar/clock upon the wall; she had been gone now for almost six months. Lester eased himself back into the sofa and watched Wellington sleeping under the window ledge.

Irene had not wanted another dog after 'Beckett' died. But Lester had wanted to give a loving home to a deserving canine; he smiled as he recalled the many arguments between them over another dog. But Irene had got her way and Lester never replaced 'Beckett' until after she left.

Lester picked up his mobile phone and saw there were no calls or messages recorded for today, he tapped the screen and noticed that he had received nothing for three days. He sighed and slowly lifted his legs upon the sofa and drifted into a troubled sleep filled with odd dreams about strange people and dark places.

It was someone shouting around the park gates that broke Lester's troubled slumbers and he awoke slowly and noticed that it was already dark; he glanced at his mobile and saw that the time was almost eleven o'clock – he had been asleep for about five hours. He peered through the window, and something caught his eye falling into his small front garden. At first, he thought some drunk had thrown a beer tin or bottle over his fence, so he thought it was safer to let Wellington do his business in the rear garden tonight – it was far too late to walk him through the park. Lester could see no movement in the street outside or hear any more voices.

He let the dog out and collected a small hand torch from a kitchen cupboard; then he watched Wellington in the rear garden for some minutes, giving the dog some food and biscuits when he returned. Lester than headed for the front garden and shone the torch around neat flower beds, grass and pots.

Nothing obvious appeared in the sharp light; but a gust of wind slapped Lester and he shivered, turning around and headed for his front door, that's when he saw the mobile phone a few meters from the doorstep.

He picked it up and held the torch light against the battered object; it had a couple of small cracks on the screen – it wouldn't switch on and Lester turned it over to see the phone had no rear cover, sim card or battery. He sighed and locked the front door behind him, placing the phone upon the hall table – he would dispose of it tomorrow, properly, not slinging the damn thing into someone's bloody gardens.

Lester shuffled into the bedroom and undressed for bed, he watched with a smile as Wellington jumped upon the bedroom chair and curled up for the night. Lester pulled the sheets over and tried to sleep, but he tossed and turned for some minutes before the dreams returned; ugly, vile people and dark towers crowded into his dreams. He groaned loudly in his sleep, waking Wellington who watched as his master moved continuously under the covers; he called out Irene's name several times and fell into a deep sleep.

2. THE MIDNIGHT CALLER.

Through the misty dark dream came a shrill ringing noise and Lester awoke very slowly and his hand pushed around the small bedroom cabinet next to his bed. Grabbing his phone, he said quietly; "Hello." It took a few seconds for Lester to realize that the ringing was continuing, and he switched on the lamp and stared at his phone - there was no call registered.

"Who's bloody calling at Midnight?" Lester muttered and then wondered where the damn ringing was coming from!

That's when he could hear the phone ringing in the hall. Lester rose slowly from the bed and made for the hallway; not even bothering to put on his slippers or dressing gown. He opened the bedroom door and in the semi-darkness of the small hall could see the phone lit up on his hall table, and it was ringing loudly.

He gasped and covered his face with a trembling hand and shuffled very reluctantly towards the noisy device, as he reached to pick it up, he recalled that this was impossible – the damn phone had no battery or sim card – how the hell could it ring?

He hesitated for some seconds, but the ringing appeared to be getting louder and so he lifted the phone and saw it was showing: "UNKNOWN NUMBER." Lester ran a hand over his face in surprise at the date, because it was showing Friday, 1st September 1989 at exactly Midnight: 00.00. - That was some twenty-eight years ago!

The date stirred a dark memory in Lester and with a dry mouth and shaking hands, he answered the caller with a soft spoken; "Hello, Lester here."

A child's voice spoke quietly in reply; "Hello Mr. Lightfoot, its Susan - do you remember me?" The child paused for a few seconds and then added; "All the other children are here too; do you remember them Mr. Lightfoot?"

Lester couldn't speak; fear had taken his voice and made his hand shake violently. A clear vision of the child called 'Susan' appeared; her little broken body with torn and bloodied clothes sprawled before him on the damp grass.

A ghastly sight in the bright warm sunshine; he could see his trembling and bloodied hands gripping her shoulders and the child's bright green eyes now dull with death.

"I'll call again Mr. Lightfoot; we have so much to talk about - especially how you killed us. Goodbye for now." Susan spoke with no emotion in her voice and the phone went dead.

Lester let it fall from his hand onto the floor and he staggered, leaning upon the walls, until falling on his knees and he cried out in sheer, terror filled horror; "God forgive me! God forgive me!" and collapsed in silence upon the carpet - Wellington sat in the doorway and watched; apparently unmoved by his master's distress.

3. MEMORIES IN A SUITCASE.

The sun was filtering through the blinds, casting short shadows about the small kitchen where Lester sat in silence, sipping a mug of coffee and staring at the RSPCA calendar on the wall opposite. He was unwashed and had failed to shave [the first time that has happened in many years] and so Lester just sat in his crumpled dressing gown and continued to stare at the wall.

When he had awoke this morning, he thought it had all been a bad dream - a really terrible nightmare - but then saw the phone on the hall floor where he had thrown it down and young Susan's voice could still be heard in his troubled head. Sighing hard, he eased from the chair and shuffled to the bedroom and from beneath the unmade bed, dragged out a small, battered old suitcase. He knelt on the floor for some minutes before pulling it open and slowly removing the sole item it contained, a bright red scrapbook with yellowing pages. Written across the cover with a black felt pen was just a date; Friday, 1st September 1989.

Lester clutched the book to his chest and wandered back to the kitchen, placing it upon the table. But was distracted by Wellington whining at the back door; he needed to go out. Lester unlocked the door and the small dog leapt through and ran about the grass and slabs with some delight - and relief.

Having refilled his coffee cup, Lester gently ran a hand over the old book and steadied his nerves. He couldn't recall the last time he had opened it; maybe several years ago when he still had problems with alcohol. He watched Wellington in the garden for some minutes, then carefully lifted the front cover and stared at the photographs glued upon the first page.

He turned the pages slowly, staring at the newspaper cuttings and various letters of support, then some of threats. Finally, a simple colour picture of the little memorial in the School grounds with the seven children listed in alphabetical order. Miss Carol Renauld had been placed at the bottom - a little space separated her from the children's names - she had been their class teacher.

Lester remembered her with great affection; a pretty young woman who always seemed to be smiling and was very caring of the children in her care. She had always treated Lester with respect, not like some of the others he had met over the years.

He closed the scrap book and walked slowly to the front door and stepped out into the pale morning sunshine. He shuffled down the path and opened the gate, stopping to smile at the beautiful gates of Victoria Park. Lester stood on the kerbside for a couple of minutes and then stepped into the roadway just as the gravel lorry approached the green traffic lights at some speed.

Lester must have lived for just a few minutes after the lorry hit him, he mouthed words to the gathering group of shocked motorists and passing pedestrians, but no sound emerged. He died quietly on the blood splattered tarmac and Lyle the collector tapped his soul ledger and spoke gently to Lester, the pair standing by the bus stop; "I'm sorry Lester, but this has to be referred to the Duty Death Angel; your scheduled departure date was in six years' time!"

4. Mr. TIBBS IS PLACED ON THE CASE.

Jericho opened the brown paper folder and read about his latest case, particularly the interview with the soul that had belonged to a certain Lester Lightfoot, now placed in quarantine, like all suicides were, until their final fate was decided by Angel Margret [the current Duty death Angel].

Alex sipped her tea and read her copy of the interview with interest, then tapped the file and said quietly; "The mobile phone call is the key to this." She looked up and smiled as Owen sauntered through the study door and flopped into the chair opposite. Jericho nodded his agreement with Alex's comment and spoke to Owen directly; "What does Records have on him?" Owen pulled the mirror from his coat pocket and scratched his chin; "Nothing really stands out, except the accident in 1989 and what subsequently happened to him. It completely changed his life, and his personality. He became a drunk, abused his wife who left him and it distanced him from his only child; a son, now grown up. He was blamed for the school minibus crash that killed the seven children and their teacher. He and three other children survived. Lightfoot was in hospital for two months and was charged with their deaths and received four and a half years in prison. But oddly enough, upon his release was given a job by his old local council employer in their tax office."

Owen fumbled through his pockets and pulled some mints out; he offered them about and then dropped one into his mouth. "The police investigation concluded that Lester had fallen asleep at the wheel and the minibus left the road and took out a large electrical road sign at some speed." Owen smiled a little and pushed the mirror back into his pocket. "The really interesting thing is the postmortem results on the body. It appears Mr. Lightfoot was an undiagnosed epileptic at the time of the accident [with the truck]. Apparently, he told Wilson [who conducted the interview] that he could recall only having three seizures his entire life and the first was behind the wheel of that bus. He had another when Irene left him some years later, and the last one was when he received that call. He was only really guilty of not seeing his doctor regularly!"

Alex sighed quietly and placed the folder upon the coffee table and repeated; "The mobile phone call is the key to this." Owen nodded and leaned back in his chair; "I wonder if Mr. Harris is going to serve afternoon tea soon?”

Jericho eased himself from the chair and picked up his long dark coat; "Wilson is already at the scene and I think we'll join him. The tea can wait." Owen and Alex followed Jericho to the light room and disappeared to 2017.

Wilson grinned broadly as his companions appeared in the small house, he was standing in the hall, examining the discarded mobile phone. He gestured towards the kitchen; "The scrapbook is there. It makes sad reading,"

Jericho picked up the phone and turned it about in his hand, it was exactly as old Lester had said. He shifted it about, feeling the weight, and then pulled his mirror out, reading about the make and model. He almost smiled and looked up at the little group; "It appears to have gained a little weight since having the battery, rear cover and sim card removed!"

Owen took the phone from him and started to prize it apart, they watched in amazement as a hidden sim fell out into the palm of his hand and he pointed out the miniature battery wired very cleverly at the top. "Probably had enough power for just a couple of calls." Owen grunted and handed it to Alex, who shook her head in disbelief. "I wonder what type of call was made on it?"

They stood in silence and Jericho said quietly; "It appears Lester was driven to an unplanned suicide, a suicide not in the current timeline and in our books that's murder."

"Poor bastard." Muttered Owen and turned to Jericho; "Since it's not connected with the 'Dark One's activities, will we be taken off the case now?" Alex shook her head in reply; "I don't think so, Lester still died six years early and that will almost certainly produce minor changes to the Time-Line, that are unwanted."

Jericho rubbed his chin and pulled his mirror from a deep pocket; "I think we'll brief Angel Margret about what we have found and see what the human detectives come up with." They group vanished in an instant, leaving the scene exactly as they found it.

5. ACCIDENTAL DEATH AND Ms ELLEN CABOT'S CAMPAIGN.

Wilson pushed fingers through his hair with both hands and smiled broadly; "Those dumb, so-called coppers, have ruled the death of Lester Lightfoot an accident!" He dropped into the dining room chair and picked up his knife and fork, waving the fork about he added; "Road traffic accident: the murdering bastard will get away it." The smile dropping away; "They didn't even check the old phone, it's bagged up with Lester's possessions awaiting his son's arrival from Australia, to arrange the funeral and collect his father's effects."

Alex leaned over the table a little and placed her cutlery down; "Jericho is with Angel Margret; apparently there's a real problem with Lester's early death that has appeared down the Time-line, involving the money his son inherited upon Lester's death. Had it been ruled as suicide or murder, his son would not have gained a penny."

Wilson carefully dissected his roast potatoes and nodded; "Jericho sent Owen to records; to personally view the Fate Tapes of Lester's life and find out who would have been involved in those six years he should have had."

Alex smiled; "Poor Owen missed afternoon tea and now a wonderful roast dinner; he won't be happy!" Now that made Wilson chuckle and he started to enjoy his mea. Especially when Mr. Harris topped up his wine glass; he was a very happy man.

"Mrs. Harris has kept a hot plate for young Mister Owen, my lady." Mr. Harris refilled Maude's glass and stood quietly by the fireplace until the Dining room door opened and Jericho appeared. Mr. Harris took his coat and disappeared to fetch Jericho's dinner, after pouring him a large glass of wine.

Wilson bought him up to date with the Lightfoot case human outcome and Jericho just nodded, then smiled a little, sipping a most excellent wine. He raised his glass and said quietly; "We're back on the case my friends. It appears that a certain Ms Ellen Cabot, who Lester would have met in seven months had he not jumped in front of that lorry, will save the lives of several people. One of which is vital to the current timeline. You see, old Lester not only donated generously to get the campaign started but would have been mentioned to raise awareness about the dangers of undiagnosed epilepsy and this certain person is so moved by Lester's story that he seeks the medical attention he needs. Lester basically saved his life, and the young man goes on to be Prime minster of Great Britain!"

Alex placed her glass upon the table and stopped smiling; "Now Lester's dead, there's no inspiration for that young man to help himself and I assume dies at some point with no treatment." She shook her head and said softly; "The simple fluttering of Butterfly wings can change the universe."

"Quite so." Jericho whispered and sipped his wine. Owen bounced through the door and jumped into his seat with a big grin upon his face and placed a brown folder upon the table. "I'm looking forward to this!" He exclaimed as Mr. Harris appeared with his dinner.

He took several mouthfuls and then wiped his mouth with the napkin. "The shit really hits the fan some thirty human years down the line. The woman elected as Prime Minster makes a total balls up and everything goes wrong in a big way. But in the original Time-Line the Prime-Minster is hailed as a hero for his handling of the situation." Owen placed his fork down and his usual smile was gone, he spoke directly to Mr. Tibbs; "The Time

Controller can only hold for another 24 hours in human time before the new Time-Line takes over." Everyone sat quietly with little conversation, but Jericho ate in silence until he had finished and pushed his plate to one side. He indicated for Owen to pass his folder over and Jericho read it with great interest. He glanced at the Dining room clock and smiled a little; it was stopped at 7.35pm; as usual. He stood up and said; "The clock is ticking my friends, back to 2017 and let's avert another bloody balls up for humanity!"

6. THE PHONE THROWER UNMASKED.

The team gathered by the ornate gates of Victoria Park as the growing gloom of night descended, Jericho pointed out Lester's house almost immediately opposite the park gates and consulted his mirror. "In a few minutes old Lester should appear in his front garden after hearing the noise of some kind of disturbance out here. Then we should see who threw the damn phone into his garden." Jericho spoke quietly and looked about. But it was Wilson that pointed out the two drunks approaching, arm in arm, talking very loudly about Elvis Presley of all people!

They appeared from the park and wandered across the road; still almost shouting and laughing. That's when Alex pointed to the parked car whose interior light came on as the door opened. A figure pulled himself from the car and threw something into Lester's garden, then started the engine and drove off; passing the two drunks still talking loudly and laughing.

"Did you get who it was?" Jericho asked Owen, who lowered his mirror and nodded; affirmative. Alex pointed out the old man now in the garden and about to find the phone any second now. They watched as Lester retrieved the phone and disappeared inside.

Owen turned to his colleagues, unsmiling he said simply; "David Lightfoot - his son who is supposed to be in Australia."

Wilson, who was already reading his mirror, grunted and said; "David Lightfoot has some serious money worries, but more important than that, he has a young daughter of eight years and he works as an Accountant; but his big hobby is electric's, computers and mobile phones." Jericho nodded; "A young child's voice is just a child's voice; especially if you've not seen your grand-daughter for four years. Susan's voice was he's own granddaughter."

"How do we stop that murdering rat from getting his hands on Lester's money and ensure that Ellen Cabot has it for her campaign; we know she will give full credit to Lester and may even publicise his story?" Owen pushed the mirror back into his pocket and the little group stood in silence for a few seconds.

Then Jericho smiled to himself and pulled his mirror out again and motioned to Wilson; "Do you have the number of that 'magic' phone on record?" Wilson nodded that he did. "Well then; let's make a little phone call just at the right time."

The little group disappeared into the darkness.

7. A SIMPLE PHONE CALL.

Constable Eric Burke eased himself back into his office chair and flicked open the local paper. There was little of interest for him in this week's edition, but the story about the old man killed by the gravel lorry did catch his eye.

He rubbed his chin and sipped his mug of tea; where had he heard that name 'Lightfoot' before? Eric wondered about that; he had seen or heard that name somewhere. He looked about the Police Property office and the big polythene bag laid on the bottom shelf was noticed immediately. The old Policeman wandered over and lifted the tag attached to the bag.

It read; 'Lester Lightfoot'.

He grinned to himself; "The old mind is not ready for retirement yet!" and refilled his mug with fresh tea from the large pot that stood on the small fridge.

"Only another seven weeks and it's off to Spain for three weeks in the sun and then retirement after twenty-seven years' service." Eric muttered and tapped the calendar; he had been counting days now for some nine weeks. He dropped back into his chair and picked the paper up, reading about the accidental death of Lester Lightfoot.

That's when he heard the phone ringing.

Eric walked slowly back to the big polythene bag and stared at the broken phone all lit up and vibrating as well. He tore open the bag and cautiously lifted the phone to his ear; "Hello." He said softly.

Eric sat on his office chair and called the extension of Detective Inspector Reece Norman and waited patiently for the deputy head of CID to answer. The Inspector answered after a few seconds and Eric introduced himself and explained that the 'broken' phone in the property bag of a certain Lester Lightfoot had just received a call about applying for PPI payments compensation - from a very nice women who explained how they could get thousands of pounds for him - for the payments he made, towards an expensive life insurance policy in favour of his only child; David Lightfoot.

He pointed out that someone had deliberately rigged up a broken phone to still actually work and Mr. Lightfoot had it just before he stepped in front of that lorry. He said how sad the scrapbook, mentioned in the paper, must have made the old man. He also wondered what calls were made to the old man on a supposedly broken phone, and more importantly; why?

The Inspector sat in silence for a few seconds then told Eric to bring everything he had for Lester Lightfoot to the CID operations room; this would require looking into.

8. A DIFFERENT VERDICT.

Inspector Reece Norman walked slowly down the steps of the Coroners Court, passing a very disappointed David Lightfoot who pushed through the throng of reporters and curious passerby's, then jumped into a waiting taxi. He was not a very happy man and ignored the reporters who rushed towards him.

The Inspector stopped in front of the group and the reporters crowded about him instead, shouting questions. Mr. Norman stood for a few seconds and then waved the crowd into relative silence. He placed a hand into his pocket and read to the reporters a prepared statement regarding the inquest's verdict into the death of Lester Lightfoot.

Some yards away, a little group stood listening with great interest to Inspector Norman's statement about the verdict of

'Suicide' in the sad case of Lester Lightfoot. He also outlined how the Crown Prosecution Service had recommended charges against David Lightfoot in connection with his father's death.

He also mentioned that Ms Ellen Cabot's campaign to make people aware of the dangers of undiagnosed epilepsy was to use Lester's sad tale, with full permission of Lester's widow; Irene, who now was looking after the dog 'Wellington'. Smiling a little, the Inspector stated that donations in tragic Lester's name had been flooding in, via the internet, for Ms Cabot's campaign, since the story first surfaced.

"He's sad passing will not be in vain, if just one person is motivated to seek medical help for their condition." The Inspector announced solemnly, and the crowd of reporters dispersed to get the story to their papers Editor.

Alex smiled broadly at Jericho and nodded her head in admiration; "That was quite a stroke; getting David Lightfoot investigated, by using the very phone he created to get his hands on his father's insurance money. I particularly liked the touch of using an enquiry about Payment Protection Insurance to set the ball rolling!" Owen chuckled; "David couldn't really explain what he was doing in London, having never visited either his father or worse; his mother and why he never even told them he was here."

Wilson sighed and placed the mirror into his jacket pocket, then smiled; "His fingerprints were on the concealed battery and sim card - the rest of the phone had been cleaned before he threw it - I guess he forgot that someone might just open the damn phone!" Jericho said nothing but pulled his mirror from a pocket and they disappeared.

Walking back to the lighthouse, Wilson turned to Alex, still smiling and pointed to Jericho striding out ahead of the group; "Angel Margret is well impressed with the outcome. The Time Controller has informed her that the current timeline is back on track - that young man who will become Prime Minster in thirty years, will seek help after being inspired and motivated by tragic Lester's story."

Alex slapped Wilson on the back and with a grin, spoke softly; "A case like this will also do your promotion prospects some good.

You'll make Temporal Detective Inspector yet."

Wilson nodded; "Right on baby girl!" He loved the idea of managing his own team: but not quite yet.

THE END

EPILOGUE:

"This particular mission was quite unusual for team 74, in that it involved NO time travelers, demons or any interference from the 'Dark Side.' The restoration of the current human timeline was the sole object achieved. Why David Lightfoot suddenly hatched the plot to kill his father remains a mystery; it did not happen in the original version of his life history!"
SJW

CHARACTERS:

Lester Lightfoot killed himself, filled with remorse for the deaths he had caused many years previously. But this state of mind was bought on deliberately, by his son to gain access to Life Insurance money. Lester's soul was collected and processed. It was quarantined for fifty human years.

Susan Lightfoot [the voice of the child] was coached by her father to play the voice of the dead child from the minibus accident. This was to haunt the girl for remainder of her life which was filled with conflict and drug abuse. She died, aged 24 and her soul was collected and processed.

Miss Carol Renauld was the teacher who was killed in the mini-bus accident. Lester always remembered her with great fondness. She was 26 at the time of the accident and her soul was collected and processed.

David Lightfoot's plan to collect his father's life insurance money failed and he was convicted of attempted fraud at Crown Court, he lost his job and family; his wife kicked him out of their home. He worked various jobs over the years and died in 2032. His soul was collected and processed.

Eric Burke - the police officer - finally retired and moved to Kent with his wife and two dogs. He became a 'lolly-pop' man and spent his final years, happily, outside the local school. He died in

2029 and his soul was collected and processed.

Reece Norman, the CID Inspector became quite ill in the summer of 2020 with cancer of the bowel and subsequently died near Christmas of that year. He was just one of many who were dying because they couldn't receive proper treatment with the 'pan epidemic' in full swing that year. His soul was collected and processed.

Irene Lightfoot never really forgave her son for his part in Lester's suicide. She grieved strongly over the death of her granddaughter and died the year following Susan's death. Her soul was collected and processed.

EPISODE 10: "SNOOKER, STOCKINGS & DEVILSH DECEIT."

MISSION SUMMARY: "Inspector 'Doc' Silas Underhill who heads Team 13 and is Jericho's old Mentor and good friend has visited the Lighthouse with a disturbing story. He has a file which contains a very strange picture and newspaper clipping from England in 1985. Seemingly innocent and just some fun at first, the file contains a picture - apparently of Temporal Constable Alexandra Cappanni - flashing her underwear at the famous final of the World Snooker Championship held that year in Sheffield! But it's the 'man' sitting next to her that sets off alarm bells; it's the 'Dark Prince' himself!"

NOTES: This episode contains references to Demonic activity.

TRIGGER WARNINGS. **ALCOHOL, STRONG LANGUAGE, STRONG SEXUAL REFERENCES [including sexual assault] AND MILD VIOLENCE.**

AGE 15+ ONLY. **30 Minutes reading time.**

1. 'DOC' SILAS UNDERHILL AND TEAM 13.

Old Doc checked his fob watch and watched through the window of his cabin; his sergeant, Isabella Pugg and his Constable, Skyrise Young Mountain were due back from horse riding at any minute. He eased himself back into his rocking chair and picked up the file that young Ivan - the messenger - had delivered from Angel Margret's office. It was the team's latest mission, and it was a strange one. He sighed and re-read the summary. He tapped the enclosed pictures and smiled at one. "Sweet saints, she does have some pair of legs." He muttered, looking up as 'Crabby' appeared through the door. Crabby stood arms folded and didn't smile; "Doc, Ma Washington wants to know when those two white folk are getting back; she wants to dish up supper."

Crabby was a big African male, who had been a house slave to a white family for about thirty years; he had been born and died a slave. He and the Doc had real history and had been together for years - when alive - and were still friends now, many years after passing over. Doc just sighed; "Crabby, do you have to refer to Issy and Skyrise as white folk? You know you like the both of them; just use their damn names once and again." But there was no admonishment in his voice. Crabby just grunted and gestured to the file; "Where you off to now? Anything interesting?"

Doc held the file up and showed him the picture and old Crabby grinned from ear to ear. "Now, that's the kind of white folk I like. Long legs and don't mind showing her drawers." He chuckled and ran a hand over his face. "Ain't that the nice white lady who doesn't mind coloured folk and is some kind of doctor?"

Doc nodded; "Alexandra Cappanni from team 74; she's the mission." Crabby smiled and scratched his arse. "What she been up to? Who's she been showing her crotch off to?" Doc sighed; "This picture was taken from a television still, apparently in 1985, she appears to have attended a big sporting event and was caught on camera, flashing her stocking tops and white panties to a television audience of about 18 million people. But that's not the real problem."

Crabby stared at the picture again and smiled - again. "What's wrong with that Doc? No one could surely object to seeing those legs and knickers. That damn girl is a real beauty. She could show me her parts any time of day...or night!" He laughed and Doc just shook his head; "Crabby, you are a dirty old man; you're old enough to be her grand daddy." Crabby just grinned; "Yeah, but I ain't. So it's fine to stare." He shuffled to the door and turned back; "I'll tell Ma that the white folk ain't back yet, So what's the problem with her showing her crotch on that television thing?"

Doc eased back in his chair and just smiled. Despite being dead for nearly 200 years, Crabby hadn't changed a bit. "It's the man sitting next to her, that's the real problem." Crabby stared back at the picture; "Who's that then?" He asked.

Doc didn't smile and tapped the photograph; "It's the bloody Dark Prince himself." Crabby scratched his arse again and sighed; "That's bad, isn't it?" Doc nodded and closed the file, saying quietly; "It sure is Crabby. It sure is." He could hear horse's and voices outside and Crabby smiled; "I'll tell Ma to dish up, since the white folk are back." He disappeared through the door and Doc shouted after him; "Just call them by their names for heaven's sake!" But he knew that Crabby wouldn't change.

He and Crabby had been born slaves together; Crabby was a house servant and had quite an easy life on the plantation, good food and no hard labour. He really loved his 'posh' servant's livery, even if, it was just dark trousers and frilly white shirt. But Doc had worked the fields under the overseer's whip. Everyone called him 'Doc' because he had a real aptitude for fixing up people; especially after a good whipping or beating. He had gone on the run after the family had sold the young girl he was madly in love with.

Doc had discovered that young Delphi had been sold to a plantation some two hundred miles downriver. He went after her and it was almost a year before he found what had happened to her. She had died in childbirth, giving birth to a daughter by her new owner. She was fifteen. Doc spent the next few months on the run and finally ended up in the North before the civil war and was taken in by a Methodist Reverend and his wife. They paid for his education, and he became a doctor, in all but title. But then, he could only 'practice' on fellow coloured people, Chinese, Mexican or Native Americans.

He had real fond memories of Reverend Joshua Gates and his wife Margaret. "Good people. Damn good people." He muttered to himself. He and Skyrise got on really well, both had become 'Doctors' under extreme circumstances, and both were not from privileged white families. He didn't realise, just how much Skyrise admired the old man; both as his Inspector and as his friend. Jericho could have told him, just what a decent man old Doc was; Jericho valued his opinion above all others and that says a great deal about the man.

Like all team Inspectors, he had the choice of where to place his home and office in any time or place. Doc had chosen a small cabin in the woodlands of North Virginia. The cabin was like Jericho's lighthouse - suspended in time and place - the current date here was August 8th, 1869, and it was 6.25pm on a warm and pleasant summer night. The inside also defied space and time. Everyone in the cabin had their own suite of rooms. The household staff consisted of old Crabby - who didn't like being called a 'Butler' - Ma Washington, a lovely lady in her forties, who could cook anything, but loved dishing up Cajun food. The other member of the staff was young Rosemary Dogwood.

Rose was the maid of all duties, and she loved her new life working for Doc. She had died at just twenty from smallpox in 1791. She really didn't fancy another slice of life, as a living human and so joined Doc's staff. She had been a maid to some rich white people in Boston. But they had treated her really well and actually did mourn the young girl, when she sadly and unexpectedly passed over. Doc could hear her laughing with Crabby in the dining room, setting the places for dinner. But his attention was drawn back to the front door.

Skyrise came through the door and slapped his hat down on the hallway table. He jerked a thumb behind him; "Sweet Jesus Doc, she is impossible!" and headed for the dining room without another word. [For the history of Skyrise Young Mountain: See the episode: **'Doctor Alexander Harris and his battle with God'**] Doc just chuckled to himself; young Issy was one hell of a woman. She was NEVER wrong and would NEVER admit it, even if she was!

But she was a fine Temporal Detective Sergeant. Not quite up to the standard of young Jericho, when he was Doc's Sergeant, but then, who could follow that young man? Doc cleaned his glasses and waited for Issy to storm through the door. He wasn't disappointed; she pushed in and said loudly; "That bloody Indian can never be wrong, can he?" and threw her riding helmet and whip on the same little hallway table.

"Like someone else I can mention." Doc muttered, adding: "What has he done now?" Not really wishing to know about the latest disagreement between the two. Issy stood, hands on hips, and sighed loudly [she did very little quietly!] "I try and tell him, about just how damn lucky his people were to be given the gift of real civilisation, by the settlers to his land and he throws a fit. He simply can't listen to facts. Oh no; he's always bloody right; just another typical, domineering oppressive man!" She walked past and into the dining room.

Doc sighed; the dinner conversation could be lively tonight and grinned. Still, his trainee, Leon Murphy would bring some sanity to the chat around the dinner table; he always did. His real name - in full - was Napoleon Wellington Patrick Murphy! He had been a history teacher in a small Irish village. His father: Patrick had worked the roads, laying tarmac, but was a model war games enthusiast and only played the Napoleonic Period. He had a total fascination with Napoleon Bonaparte and the Duke of Wellington. The attic rooms had no less than four massive layouts of famous battles; Waterloo, Battle of the Pyramids, Marengo and the Battle of Austerlitz.

Little wonder that the boy, who played for ages with his dotting father, became a history teacher. Leon was soft spoken and gentle in his ways; he saw good in everyone; even the rotten bastards, like those that had ended his life at just 27. He was caught up in a Belfast bombing, while shopping with his fiancé, Grace McMurry. She survived the bomb with minor injuries, and he was killed outright. He had worked as a collector for a few human years and had been recommended for Temporal Detective Training because of his sharp mind and dedication to detail. Angel Margret very rarely got her recommendations wrong and even old Doc - who had high standards - was already well satisfied with Leon.

He was the only current member of Doc's team, that Crabby called by his name. That spoke volumes! Doc would outline their latest mission over dinner. Issy would be happy going after Alex and her apparent failings; she couldn't stand her. Alex was everything that Issy detested in another woman. She [Issy] thought she [Alex] was a disgrace to the feminist agenda; wearing expensive clothes, letting men fawn over her, wearing makeup and acting the 'little woman'. She didn't even admit that Alex was quite a beautiful and intelligent woman in her own right. No, Alex was practically a traitor to the cause of feminist change. She would enjoy exposing her and maybe, even getting her thrown out the Department. She ate her meal with a much-revived appetite.

2. A MATTER BETWEEN TWO GOOD FRIENDS.

Mr. Harris had met the team at the door [as usual] and immediately spoke to Jericho; "You have a visitor Sir; I have placed them in the study." He informed Jericho, as he took coats and hats from the team. "Who is it?" asked Jericho - not expecting anyone this evening for dinner - and headed for the study. "Why, it's Inspector Underhill. He is quite anxious to speak with you in private Sir." At that, Wilson ushered Alex and Owen into the Dining Room, where young Ruth was laying down warm plates.

Jericho greeted his old 'Boss' with some warmth and poured the pair a large whisky each. He, of course, invited 'Doc' Underhill to dinner. But the Inspector had to refuse; he was expected elsewhere. "I'll come straight to the point Jericho; how much do you trust Detective Constable Alexandra Cappanni?"

Jericho gestured for him to seat and joined him; the pair sat in the armchairs by the fire and 'Doc' pulled a brown file from under his white linen jacket. He tapped the file gently; "My team has christened this mission; 'Snooker, Stockings and the time cop.' my human agent recognized the girl in the picture; he had met Alex when she was temporarily attached to me. You remember when she was stood down over that damn play that was apparently written about her? You got 'Jumbo' in replacement." Doc sipped his whisky and opened the file. [See episode: '**William Shakespeare's lost play: the Lady of Cappanni'**]

Jericho remembered that mission well; James 'Jumbo' Jolly had replaced Alexandra for part of that mission. He had been genuinely pleased, when he heard that 'Jumbo' had been promoted to Temporal Detective Sergeant on Inspector Stella Longstreet's Team 35. But he had also heard that Doc's new sergeant was a real pistol! He accepted the file slowly and Doc continued; "That's a newspaper cutting from 1985 - the day after an incredible final of the World Snooker Championship - which is still talked about even now. But the papers also ran a story about a young lady who - by accident apparently - flashed her stocking tops and gave everyone a glimpse of her panties on TV. She was in the audience and crossed her legs just as the camera ran over the crowd. This newspaper was famous for topless women and sex scandals. They offered thousands of pounds, if she would come forward and do a topless lingerie shoot for them. She never showed up. Take a look at the picture taken from the evening's television coverage."

Jericho stared at the photograph; it was apparently Alexandra! He handed the file back, but held on to the photograph and studied it carefully; was it really Alexandra? He stared long and hard at the photograph and felt a little knot in his stomach; surely it couldn't be her? and sipped his whisky, slowly.

Doc finished his whisky; "What the hell was Alex doing in Sheffield, in 1985 flashing her knickers to the world? And look at the man, sitting next to her with her hand firmly gripping his knee?" Jericho sat staring at the newspaper clipping and then rubbed his chin. "Your mission wasn't in Sheffield in 1985 then?" He mumbled. Doc shook his head and smiled a little; "We were working on a case during the Miners' strike in 1984. That's how my human agent met Alex. She was temporally on my team." He placed down his glass and dropped the file upon the coffee table and straightened his jacket; "You're a friend Jericho and I think you deserve the first pass over this one."

Doc refilled his own glass; "No one would really care if Alex flashed her underwear. Most men would bloody enjoy that, but it's the man sitting next to her that is the real problem." Jericho stared at the handsome young man and grunted; "Who is he?" Doc sipped his whisky; "The reason for the mission; Operations Control confirm that man is one of the human forms that the Dark Prince uses." Jericho ran a hand over his face. What the fuck was going on?

Doc finished his drink and walked to the door; "I can sit on the mission for a human day or so, then I will have to act. But I'll wait to see what you uncover about it." He smiled and Jericho shook his hand. They walked to the front door together and Mr. Harris showed Doc out. Jericho returned to the study and sat back in the armchair and stared at the picture again. If it wasn't Alexandra; then it was her twin sister. The word 'sister' produced some bad memories for him. He grunted and pushed the file into his jacket pocket and stood, as Mr. Harris stuck his head through the door and announced dinner.

"Thank you Mr. Harris. I'm just coming." He muttered and headed for the Dining Room. Dinner conversation could be quite lively tonight and smiled to himself, he could soon sort this matter out, by simply checking Alex's mirror. All he needed to do was enter his Inspectors Code and he could check where his Detective Constable had been and more importantly; when.

But that little matter could wait - for now - Jericho had other problems to contend with; the whole team was summoned to appear before Angel Margret in the morning. He knew that Alex's resurrection by the Dark Prince would be the major topic of conversation. Despite the incident in the Devil's Garden, the Prince had basically saved her soul from the darkness of real death. [See episodes: **'Ghosts in the Devil's Garden of the damned'** and **'Sister Sarah dreams of demons'**]The young prince still had a real passion for Alex and clearly had forgiven her insults against him.

Jericho sighed; was it co-incidence that such a story [about the snooker final] appears after the prince had basically saved her soul? He stood outside the dining room door and thought about the changing seasons of a woman's heart. He had suffered that at the hands of Elizabeth; it could always go the other way. On that disturbing thought, he pushed open the door and smiled.

Suddenly Jericho had a terrible and clear feeling of Déjà vu. It stopped him in his tracks, and he actually shivered. Something was wrong - but what? He knew that such a strong feeling could indicate that time itself had changed. He leaned against the hall wall with one hand and took a couple of deep breaths - the feeling was almost over whelming. Something had changed with the near past and had altered the future. Something in the past that involved him.

He called the Duty Time Controller on his mirror and was reassured that little changes were happening all the time, but none concerned him yet. He pulled the file from his pocket and stared at the picture again. Had it altered? He sighed; he couldn't tell. Replacing the file and his mirror, he headed for the dining room. Mr. Parker rushed past him from the stairs and disappeared into the kitchens; something must have bugged him or it was dinner time for the big cat. He shrugged his shoulders.

Jericho joined the others in the dining room and Mr. Harris served the soup course. He asked for everyone's attention and the table fell silent as he produced the file and passed it to

Wilson. "Who do you think the woman is in the picture?" He asked and Wilson snapped open the file and really did grin. "Sweet lord Alex, I think I'll keep a copy on my bedroom wall; what the hell were you up too!" He handed the file to Owen who smiled broadly; "That is definitely a keeper; stocking tops and little white panties. I'm in heaven!"

Alex snatched the file and stared at the picture. Jericho watched the expression change on her face. She said nothing for a few seconds and then exploded in denial and a little horror. Jericho calmed her down and asked, quite plainly, if it was her. She slammed the file down; "No it's bloody not! Why the hell would I be watching bloody snooker back in 1985 and showing my underwear to bloody TV cameras? I don't even like ruddy snooker!" Everyone chuckled at that; a little relieved.

"Well, it's really easy to sort out Alexandra; I simply check your mirror and if you were never back in Sheffield, England in 1985. that's the end of the matter." Jericho smiled as Alex quickly dragged her mirror out and pushed it into his hands. "Check away, I've never been there. The nearest I got was the bloody Miners' strike, the year before." She managed a smile and sat back, folding her arms. Wilson chuckled; "That's right, we had to swap you for bloody 'Jumbo' on that case with William - I'm a piss head - Shakespeare." Owen nodded; "I do remember that one, the old boy threw tantrums because Alex wouldn't be his bloody muse; dirty old drunken fucker!"

Jericho accepted her mirror and tapped in his Inspectors Code; "A quick look and we can all enjoy dinner." He smiled at Alex and sat reading her mirror. Alex held up the file and didn't smile; "You don't think old 'Doc' Underhill is pulling a fast one on his old pupil, I mean this is quite funny, I suppose. I wonder who he got to produce the bloody picture...." She stopped in mid-sentence, when she saw that Wilson and Owen were staring at Jericho. The expression on his face was priceless. He slowly handed the mirror back to Alex and said softly; "It confirms that you were in Sheffield, England in 1985."

3. IS THE ACCUSATION PROVED?

There was absolute silence at the table. Needless to say, Alex exploded again. It took a couple of minutes for her to calm down. She jumped up from the table and paced the room; no one had ever seen her so angry and it should be said, confused. Mr. Harris brought everyone a large tray of brandies and Alex downed her first one straight away. No was now thinking of food. That's when Owen picked up the file and opened it. "I wonder if anyone has checked the young man next to the Alex look-a-like." He muttered and ran his mirror over the photograph. Jericho already knew who was in the picture but remained silent for now. He wanted someone else to make that announcement and was actually pleased that young Owen was on the ball; he really could become a good detective, if he matured a bit more.

Wilson had managed to calm Alex down enough for her to sit back down at the table.

Owen looked up from his mirror and ran a hand over his face; "Everyone, Human Records confirm that the woman is Alexandra Mary Cappanni - nee Featherstone - and the man, whose knee she has hold of is....." He hesitated and held up his mirror; "You can see the Warning its flashing - the man is known and is on record, as one of the Human forms that the Dark Prince uses. It's him."

Jericho actually jumped a little as his mirror buzzed and he answered it slowly. It was the Duty Controller with a grim message. Jericho muttered 'yes' a few times and placed his mirror on the table. He was not smiling; "Doc Underhill has been given the official go ahead to investigate this. We're all stood down until it's resolved. Basically, Alexandra, you are under house arrest. I must take your mirror." He held out his hand and Alex just sat staring at him. "I must take it now Alexandra." He said simply and Alex handed him her mirror very slowly.

"Thank fuck they allocated it to old Doc Underhill. He's fair and thorough." Wilson said quietly - everyone's appetite for the excellent cooking of Mrs. Harris was gone. Jericho pushed Alex's mirror into his jacket and clasped his hands together, he spoke softly; "Normally, a Knight would be dispatched to oversee the investigation. But because who may be involved in this, The BOSS [he glanced up at the ceiling to reinforce his words] has decided that someone from the family will babysit Alex - just in case her supposed boyfriend turns up - and that's his sister, Princess Isis. She'll be here asap." He turned to Mr. Harris, who was actually gripping the back of Jericho's seat in mild shock. "The guest suite is up to your usual excellent standards?"

Mr. Harris managed to nod and mumble quietly; "Yes Sir, I'll inform Mrs. Harris of our guest." He walked away very slowly and headed for the kitchens. They all heard the normally reserved man yell; "Yes! Fucking Yes!" and then there was silence for a few seconds, and everyone started to laugh, even Alex had to chuckle as she brushed tears away. "I dread to think what awful waistcoat he'll have on for this one." Wilson said and everyone knew exactly what he meant.

Jericho leaned back in his chair; "I don't even have to ask that everyone WILL be on their best behaviour until this is over." Wilson chuckled; "You know that her grandfather - when designing modern humans - based the female form on her. You would have certainly met your better with this one Alex." Owen just grunted and sat in silence. Wilson slapped him on the back adding; "Best behaviour baby brother!" and laughed some more.

Alex sighed loudly and sat up in her chair; "I want to see the actual film, the part where I supposedly expose my crotch to millions on TV whilst groping the bloody devil!" She turned to Jericho; "I take it we have the bloody game on record?" He nodded and rose from his chair; everyone followed, and the team headed for the study, past a confused looking Ruth holding a silver soup tureen.

"We'll be back." Owen smiled at her, and they all disappeared into the study. He whispered to Wilson; "Even if it's a bloody look-a-like, I'm still going to enjoy this!" Wilson just shook his head in mock despair and muttered; "There is no bloody IF."

Wilson served everyone large brandies and they settled in front of the big ornate mirror above the fireplace and Jericho said quietly; "The world snooker championship final in 1985, just the final frame please." The mirror flickered into life and they sat watching, with very little conversation. After a few minutes Jericho grunted; "The broadcast Director plays the camera upon the crowd to create more atmosphere. It was a male dominated sport and men were clearly the majority and target audience, so any pretty young ladies would have the camera pointed at them." Owen rubbed his chin; "I don't see many in that lot - pretty women I mean - no wonder he zoomed in on Alex...well, the look-a-like I mean."

"That's if he actually did; at the time." Jericho said softly.

4. CHESS WITH BRIGHTLY COLOURED BALLS.

They were disturbed by a beaming Mr. Harris who stood in the doorway and rubbed his hands together; "She is here Sir." Everyone rose from their seats, and all groaned a little inside; their normally exquisitely attired Butler was sporting a bright gold waistcoat, embossed with black and silver....kangaroos! He stepped aside and bowed quite low. Her Highness Princess Isis swept into the room; they really did all stare; she was stunning despite wearing a loose-fitting white jumper and black jeans with tears about the knees!

"Jericho my man, how are you?" She gripped his arm and smiled, broadly. He managed to bow and mumble; "I'm fine you're Grace." Wilson and Owen bowed, well they tried, but it didn't turn out too well. Alex curtsied with some elegance and Florence walked straight up to her and placed a kiss on her cheek. "Hi Alex or do you prefer Alexandra?" Alex whispered that 'Alex' was fine.

Princess Isis turned to Wilson; "Mister Wilson, how are you?" Wilson nodded and said softly; "Very well, thank you, your Grace." Owen just stood with his mouth open. She nodded at him; "Owen, isn't it? I understand you were a monk at some stage." Owen just stood with his mouth open. Wilson smiled; "Yes, that's right you're Grace. He was a novice monk in his last lifetime." She smiled and stared at the paused screen.

"So you're watching snooker, my brother David loves the game, he says its Chess, only its played with bright coloured balls!"

Jericho gestured to the big armchair that he normally relaxed in; "Would you like to sit your Grace...and maybe Mr. Harris could fetch you a drink?" She nodded; "Thank you Jericho; I'll have a large brandy please." And plonked herself down in the chair and smiled at Alex. "Everyone, please sit down." She added and accepted a giant glass of brandy from the shaking hand of Mr. Harris.

"Well, let's see what the fuss is all about. Please play the naughty bit." She grinned and downed the entire glass of brandy in one go. She offered her glass to Mr. Harris for a refill. He poured her another large one and actually wondered if there were enough decent bottles of brandy in the bar stockroom for this visit!

Everyone sat in silence as the screen played on; the camera swept across the audience and stopped suddenly at a very pretty young woman in a stunning business suit with a very short skirt. She was in conversation with the young man next to her and she slowly crossed her legs. Owen actually groaned a little, as her black stocking tops were revealed, and everyone received a view of her tiny white, frilly panties. The camera moved on and the commentator chuckled that she'll be in the news tomorrow.

Wilson and Jericho exchanged a concerned look, both thinking the same thing; if that's not Alex, then they are a pair of monkeys. Everyone was now staring at Alex - well, the Princess wasn't - Mr. Harris was pouring her another refill. "Oh that's definitely David. He often uses that form when visiting humanity. He goes by the wonderful name of 'Adam Anderson'. He says that form is quite popular with human females, and we know how much he likes them!" She actually giggled a little and relaxed back in the chair, cradling her brandy glass with both hands, warming the contents in the traditional way.

She sipped her brandy and peered over the rim of her glass at Alex, whose cheeks had gone a little reddish. "Now Alex, don't be embarrassed, I'm sure a lot of women have a revealed a little too much, when crossing their legs. Just they didn't have a camera peering up their skirt!" She placed the glass down and leaned forward in her seat. "I take it you now realise that it IS YOU in the film. David told me he had quite a date; he was impressed that you love snooker too. Oh yes, he was really impressed with you - really impressed."

Everyone sat in absolute silence until Alex pushed a tear from her cheek; "That can't be me. I think, I would remember going on a date with the 'Dark Prince' and showing my crotch on TV." She whispered and swallowed down her brandy.

Jericho rubbed his face - something wasn't right here. He knew that Alexandra had no real interest in the game of snooker; no interest whatsoever - she would prefer Chess any day of the week. He sighed and picked up his glass. Something was definitely not right here; but that was Alexandra in the film and she was with the Dark Prince. He sipped his brandy and thought hard about what the hell was going on.

In the quietness of the late evening, Jericho was walking alone in the grounds of the lighthouse; the only real noise was the sound of his boots on the gravel. He stood and watched the sea for some time and then headed back. Jericho sat in the study and re-watched the scene on the big mirror; he had already decided that it was indeed Alexandra. But he truly believed that she was being totally honest in her denial; so she believed. That thought made Jericho sit straight up and he thought about the last encounter the team had with the Dark Prince in person.

Boston, 1959 in the car park of the North Boston College of Art and the Dark Prince had intervened with his own minions, to ensure that Alexandra's soul wasn't lost after the demon Phara had killed her. It would have been lost because she was out of her own allocated time period. It was a danger all Temporal detectives faced whilst on duty in a time period that was not their own.

"Why did he do that?" That was the question Wilson had asked Jericho after the incident. Jericho stood staring at the now dead fireplace and ran a hand through his hair. "Why did he do that?" He repeated to himself; they had a Knight of God there; James, who could have easily recalled Alex's soul. Jericho sighed, time was running out; Arch-Angel Michael had convened a special disciplinary hearing against Alex tomorrow and it certainly didn't look good for her - despite her vehement denials - If only he had more time.

It was like a light being switched on his head, Time. He actually laughed out loud and headed up the stairs to Wilson's room and knocked gently upon the door. He could see the lights were on and so the big man was still up. Some very quiet music was playing; probably soul music from the 1970's.

Wilson opened the door and Jericho stepped in. On the small table by the window was a very old fashioned typewriter. There were sheets of paper scattered around the table and on the floor. Jericho smiled; "Writing your memoirs big man?" and was definitely surprised when Wilson nodded; "I put together stuff about the missions we get lumbered with, just an interest, well, hobby really and the latest one is a cracker; first the Dark Prince turns up and saves Alex's soul, then his bloody sister appears and practically condemns Alex's soul for the disciplinary hearing tomorrow."

Jericho nodded and then grinned; "Do you fancy doing something naughty and help Alexandra?" Wilson smiled and picked up his jacket; "I hope by naughty you don't expect me to flash my wedding tackle on prime-time TV?" Jericho chuckled; "No, we would need a special wildlife permit to let that bloody thing escape!"

Wilson stopped; "The team is stood down; the bloody light room won't allow us to travel and; besides, our mirrors are off line." He grimaced and sat back down on the end of the bed. But Jericho smiled; "We don't need either of them, if we have a Knight of God." Wilson nodded his head and grinned; "And boy, do we know one that will do anything for our girl." They both now smiled as the same name came to them, James.

As they sneaked down the stairs, they passed the darkened Guest Suite and stopped suddenly - they really struggled to stop laughing out loud - at the noises coming from the room, which caught their attention. "Sweet Jesus, she snores louder than a pig on bloody steroids!" Whispered Wilson and they crept down the stairs holding back some terrible fits of giggles. They made the study and let it go; both laughed for a few minutes then calmed down. "Oh bollocks! How can we call him without our fucking mirrors?" Groaned Wilson and slumped into his favourite armchair.

But Jericho pulled on his coat and jerked a thumb towards the door; "I think a little visit to our resident recluse will solve that one." Wilson jumped up; "You clever fucker; John of course!" They slipped quietly through the front door and headed for the small cottage at the end of the Island, as they closed the door behind them, Mr. Harris stood in the doorway of the kitchen and sipped his glass of milk and grinned; Mr. Jericho Tibbs could be accused of many things and loyalty was one of them. He made his way to his suite, smiling.

They were pleased to see that the lights were still on in John's small cottage. Jericho tapped on the door, and it was opened by John, who smiled; "Let me guess gentlemen; a very naughty, unauthorised little mission to Sheffield in 1985 to save the reputation and career of our much respected and loved Alexandra?"

Jericho and Wilson exchanged a knowing glance. John may be a reclusive bugger, but he certainly had knowledge about the human condition and rather strangely for a recluse, human friendship.

Jericho just nodded and was about to ask about James, when John picked up his coat and hat, then grinned; "Let's not get a good Knight into trouble with his Arch-Angel. I can help and no-one will call me into question. Let's go." The three disappeared and found themselves standing outside the Crucible Theatre, in Sheffield on the afternoon of April 28th, 1985.

5. THE GAME IS ON!

"Fuck!" Exclaimed Wilson as little snowflakes, tossed by the breeze, fell about his face and shoulders, then added; "I should have grabbed my bloody coat." Jericho pulled his jacket around himself and just had to smile at John, in his heavy black coat and woolen hat. "How the hell did he know what the weather would be doing?" Wilson muttered. Jericho didn't answer and checked his mirror; it was still offline. Then wondered if the Duty Time Controller had picked up their naughty and unauthorized, little time breach?

John rubbed his hands together and seemed quite excited; "I'm a great fan of snooker and this was simply, one of the greatest matches ever played. It went right down to the final ball in the final frame - fantastic!" They watched the crowds forming outside the doors and Wilson stopped smiling; "How the fuck can we get in with no working mirrors and more importantly; no fucking tickets!"

John just smiled and rummaged in his old black coat; he pulled three pieces of paper from his pocket and tapped them; "Three tickets for the final session of the World Snooker Championship Final and we'll be sitting just three rows behind where Alex and her unwanted date will apparently be." Wilson just stared at them, but Jericho chuckled; "He is the BOSSES son, he can do things like that. Come on, let's get our seats." They joined the happy queue and John said quietly; "My uncle told me once, that snooker was basically Chess played with brightly coloured balls. That's a good analogy, isn't it?"

Wilson gave Jericho a strange glance and Jericho held a finger to his lips; "Not the best time to mention how much we dislike his uncle." Wilson just nodded; he had his own thoughts about Prince John but would keep them to himself for now. "Does this place have a decent bloody bar?" He said and pulled his jacket tighter.

The Principle Time Controller; Estelle Lagarde walked slowly into the Duty Time Controllers suite and stared at the mirrors full of flickering images. There were nearly a hundred Controllers working this shift under her Senior Assistant Theodore Rhodes, who greeted her at the door. He gestured to the Special Operations section, located in its own space, in the corner of the room and almost smiled; "First trip he's taken in some time and he's not alone - that's why I called you in."

They walked slowly to the busy room and Lagarde asked quietly; "All the other family members are located and where they should be?" Theo nodded; "Prince David is still cloaked - as usual - Princess Isis is at that bloody lighthouse of Jericho Tibbs - you know - dealing with that classified matter and now Prince John has suddenly stopped being a recluse and jumped to Sheffield, England in 1985. The Heir is still sitting on that bloody mountain in Canada and Prince Alexander has cloaked himself but was last reported in Scotland in 1746. The Princess Mary is...fishing in an Arctic Lake back in 1844 with that useless boyfriend of her's." He saw the look on Lagarde's face and added; "Sorry, with her current best friend." but she just smiled, as a rebuke for his disrespect to a family member.

Princess Mary's latest 'boyfriend' was a Knight who was as useful as a snowball in space. He owed his current position entirely to his 'friendship' with the BOSSES' daughter. He made the 'Three Stooges' look like a trio of Einstein's or Gavel's. Still, the princess must see some good in him, even if no one else could.

Lagarde folded her arms and stared at the screen before her. She sighed; "In the company of Inspector Tibbs and his sergeant - Wilson, isn't it? - looks like they are all snooker fans." Theo smiled at that. Lagarde leaned on the desk and stared at the screen; "The two Detectives are not cleared to be there. The prince can be where he likes and with whoever he likes. But inform Angel Margret about her snooker loving, currently suspended detectives, who apparently, are taking a little sightseeing trip; I don't think." She then chuckled; "I have a pretty good idea what Tibbs is up to there. A clever bugger getting John's help; that is really clever. Best inform Family

Liaison and get some directions about what action we should take - if any is necessary." Theo nodded and watched the screen; "Well, the weather surprised the detectives, but not Prince John." He leaned forward and pointed to the corner of the screen; "Ma'am, isn't that him, in that human form he's so fond of?"

Lagarde ran a hand over her face and nodded; "Yes and I know who the pretty human female is. He has her under control. Inform Family Liaison at once about this." Then she stepped back; "No, inform the Queen directly. She may be needed on this one and get a message to Princess Isis. Then Inform Demon Ingress to get some Knights on standby; if he's there, then he's bound to have some very senior Minions hanging around him. Those two brave, but naïve detectives would be in real danger; if Prince John wasn't with them."

Theo agreed and Lagarde returned to her office, leaving explicit instructions that she would be kept up to date regularly. She was smiling broadly to herself; that young woman certainly has a pair of good friends in those two crazy detectives - they were simply risking everything for her - including their souls!

Jericho eased his way past several people already sitting and joined John and Wilson. He was impressed; they had a good view of the table and the final, evening session was about to start. John tapped his arm; "That's the seats they'll be sitting in." Jericho rubbed his chin; "There are three empty seats, why three seats?" He whispered and Wilson said softly; "I just mentioned that, but we never caught sight of the people sitting next to them, with the bloody camera pointing at Alex's underwear."

Jericho sighed; "And we don't have any bloody mirrors to check now." Wilson shifted his big frame about in the chair - getting comfortable - and stared down towards the aisle which contained the empty seats they were very interested in. He wiped his face; "They're here."

The trio all leaned forward at the same time and saw the Dark Prince - aka 'Adam Anderson' - with 'Alex' on his arm. They took their seats with no conversation. "The dirty bastard has his hand up her fucking skirt!" Wilson said with real anger in his voice. They all noticed that Alex's face was expressionless, and she appeared to make no comment. Jericho rubbed his chin; "There's something very wrong here; Alex wouldn't allow that bastard to take that sort of liberty with her. No, something is very wrong." John agreed and Jericho could see he had formed his right hand into a fist, with the other hand clutching it. "I really don't like the way he's taking advantage of his position with that young woman. He clearly has her under control...he's removed her Free-will, just like he would with every human; if given the opportunity."

The game was now underway and the seat next to the pair remained empty; "No-one will be allowed in now the match is underway." Wilson muttered with real anger growing inside of him, as he watched the Dark Prince push his other hand into Alex's blouse; still without any reaction from her. "Dirty bastard." Was all he managed to add.

John turned to Jericho with a real determined look; "I now see for myself why my...why he must never inherit the throne after his brother. I see and understand it as clear as day." They watched as the Dark Prince stopped molesting the silent Alex and sat back in his seat, he simply waved his hand and Alex started talking and placed her hand upon his knee. "This is it." Jericho said quietly and they watched, as Alex now opened her legs as the ceiling camera passed over the pair. The Dark Prince was actually laughing, and Wilson really wanted to punch him straight in his grinning face.

Jericho stared hard; the outfit Alex had on, was the very one she was wearing on the Boston Mission, where the dark prince had recalled her soul. He wondered about the significance of that. He ran a hand over his face and stared at the couple; how the hell did the Dark prince get control of Alex; he would have to physically touch her to gain that sort of control...He groaned as remembered the Boston incident. He turned to Wilson and was about to speak, but that's when he noticed that everyone was silent, there was no noise from the crowd and the players were like mannequins in a shop window.

The three friends rose from their seats and could see the Dark Prince also slowly standing. John smiled at Jericho and Wilson; "I've stopped time. Let's have a word with the ..." He pushed both hands through his long hair and finished his sentence slowly; "Rat." was all he said and meant it. He rose slowly and headed down the aisle.

Jericho and Wilson followed John down the aisle stairs and saw the expression on the Dark Prince's Face; He was grinning. He had recognised John, his nephew.

6. NOW A DIFFERNET GAME.

Theo stepped back from the screen with a real serious and grim look upon his face and gripped the shoulder of the Senior Controller sitting before the mirror, who also was unsmiling. "Get me the Palace; urgently; the Queen herself - NOW!" The second controller was already calling Lagarde, he didn't have to be told.

John stood in front of David [The Dark Prince] and gestured towards Alex, still sitting with her legs open, having no further orders to move. She stared ahead with no expression. "Sorry Uncle David, but we're here to collect young Alex and take her home. I'm sure you'll find another little plaything to amuse yourself with." He folded his arms. David nodded at Jericho and Wilson; "You really are a clever little human Jericho. You knew that you couldn't come up against me without some real heavy protection. I really have underestimated you. I won't do that again, believe me." Jericho just stood unsmiling and said nothing.

John simply waved his hand across Alex, and she slowly came round; she looked totally confused and jumped from the chair and grabbed John with both arms and gripped him really tightly; she was crying. John put both arms around her and whispered in her ear. He turned to Jericho and Wilson, with a smile; "Take her home please." Alex, Jericho, and Wilson disappeared.

They were outside the lighthouse and Wilson had Alex firmly cradled in his arms; She was now sobbing. She wiped her face with both hands and smoothed her clothes; "That bloody demon Phara, [back in Boston in 1959] had hold of me and there was darkness, I was in total darkness, I could feel nothing....see nothing. There WAS nothing except darkness. I was dead and my soul was...lost."

Wilson embraced her tightly and stroked her hair. "The Dark Prince had you in his clutches, but you're safe now." He whispered and noticed that Mr. Harris had appeared in the doorway, gesturing for them to come.

Jericho wiped his face and muttered; "Now what?" The team made their way into the lighthouse and Mr. Harris opened the study door; "You have a serious visitor Sir and herself has gone [Princess Isis]." He stared at Alex and looked quite relieved; "I was also about to inform you that Lady Alexandra had also disappeared." Jericho smiled; "John dealt with little problem; we can't have two Alexandra's here, can we?"

Jericho just sighed and said to Wilson; "Take Alex into the kitchens. Get Mrs. Harris to look after her." Wilson nodded and took Alex to the kitchens with Mr. Harris following, saying there was a decent bottle of brandy next to the Utility Room door. "Good, because we need a big one." Wilson said and guided Alex through the door.

Jericho took a deep breath and stepped into the study. He knew immediately who was sitting on his sofa, legs crossed and holding large Vodka - neat. It was Adam; yes, that Adam - the First human ever made by the present BOSSES Grandfather - He was himself's personal Servant and Private Secretary. Adam was simply the most important - and powerful - human that existed. He has close up and personal dealings with all members of THE FAMILY each and every day. It was said that Adam was totally trusted by the hierarchy and carried real power in the organisation. Jericho was a little stunned; Adam didn't usually make house calls!

Adam rose and held out his hand; "Hello Jericho, I hope I'm not intruding on your leisure time." Jericho shook his very firm hand and mumbled; "No Sir." Adam gestured for him to sit and dropped back on the sofa. He smiled. "I trust that Miss Alexandra will recover from her ordeal. Queen Mary is quite concerned about what befell the girl. The matter will be taken up by Himself, you can trust me on that." Adam finished his vodka and placed the glass down. He leaned forward and the smile was gone. Jericho had a strange feeling that he really didn't want to know, what Adam was about to tell him.

"Prince John has told me that you can be trusted - completely - I was also told that by Queen Mary. That means, I know I can also trust you and your judgments." He sat back and Jericho refilled his glass from the bottle that Mr. Harris had left.

"Excuse me Sir, I think I may need one of these." Jericho said and filled the second glass [left on the tray with the spirit bottles] with brandy. Adam chuckled; "You and your team have a well-earned reputation for hard work, hard playing and total commitment to your assigned roles, that is how it should be. That's the sort of endeavor that I need."

"What happened to Alexandra would just be the tip of the iceberg should Prince David [The Dark Prince] inherit his brother's throne. Currently, his plans for his grandfather's creation - us humans- do not look good. The Heir appears to have made it quite clear, that's he wants nothing to do with his father or humanity. His brother Prince John displayed no interest in anything to do with humanity and had also refused to take the throne, when the time comes. But that was until the little adventure with you. He now understands what will happen to humanity, should his uncle be placed upon the throne. Those feelings will be encouraged Jericho and I'm sure you can clearly understand why?" Adam ran a hand over his face; "They MUST be encouraged - Yes?"

Jericho swallowed his brandy in one hit and nodded; "I do understand Sir." But thought; what fucking shit have I landed myself in? Adam rose and walked to the door; "I'll be in touch Jericho." He hesitated and turned, unsmiling; "Watch your back Jericho. There are some very powerful forces that would see the Dark Prince on the throne, and they will stop at nothing to see that happen." On that unhappy note, he departed.

Jericho held his head with both hands and muttered; "What the fuck have I got myself into?" He looked up and saw Wilson standing in the doorway; almost smiling; "You mean what the fuck have WE got into." He dropped into his favourite armchair and clasped his big hands together; "Mrs. Harris has sorted our Alex out - she's quite a knowledgeable and caring woman - and now our girl is just plain angry. A bit like our Owen; who is sulking over being left behind; despite me telling him why we did that."

They both turned to the door and watched Alex march in and pour herself a large brandy with some real determination. She took a couple of mouthfuls and placed one hand on her hip; "I going to shove the bastards balls so far up his arse, he'll think he has bloody tonsillitis!" and finished her drink, then poured another one. She was angry and it showed; "Slimy perverted rat!" She added and shook her head in disgust. "Feel me up will he, the bloody creep!" and sipped at her brandy, adding; "What did our Adam want Jericho - if you don't mind letting us into the little secret." She slumped into her armchair by the fire and very slowly and ladylike, crossed her legs. Wilson started to clap, and Jericho joined in; that did surprise Alex, then she realised why they were applauding. She raised her glass; "See, the lady can seat herself comfortably without displaying her panties and stocking tops to the entire world." then actually chuckled.

Wilson stood up and fetched himself a large one from the drinks tray and refilled Jericho's glass, whilst he was at it, he poured a large one for Owen, who he knew wouldn't sulk for long, if there was brandy about. He pretended to grimace; "Tonsillitis!" was all he said and sat back down.

Everyone looked back at the doorway. Owen stood there - arms folded - looking a little angry. He walked over and sat down on the sofa. Wilson passed him the brandy he had poured. Owen took a sip and nodded; "I do understand why you had to leave me behind. New to the Department, a novice, my career as a Temporal Detective would have been over before it really started. But I still feel that I should have made that decision for myself. Nevertheless, I do understand why you made the call Jericho." He raised his glass to his silent colleagues; "I apologise for acting like a spoilt brat. I'm sorry."

Wilson and Jericho exchanged a really surprised look, until finally Wilson smiled and raised his glass too; "I think our boy has finally turned into a young man." Alex nodded; "Bloody amen to that." Jericho just smiled.

7. REVELATIONS.

"Room for one more?" Everyone turned again to the study door and John wandered in and dropped on the sofa next to Owen. Since they all knew, who John was now; they started to stand, but he waved them down; "I normally like a red wine, but a bloody brandy will do me nicely." Alex stood and fetched him a glass and pushed it into his hand, she bent over him and placed a real smacker on his lips. "Thank you so much." Was all she said.

He really did grin at that and to everyone's real surprise knocked the brandy back in one hit. "I suppose you all want to know what happened with my arsehole of an uncle." He walked over to the drinks tray and refilled his glass; "Re-fills anyone?" Everyone was utterly amazed that such a powerful entity would actually perform a service for their minions. But he did and with a big smile.

"What did happen Sir, with the Dark Prince?" Jericho said quietly. John smiled; "It's still John my friend. Uncle Arsehole is not happy. In fact, to quote that wonderful and colourful human expression; His strawberries had been well and truly pissed on." John raised his glass and then took a sip. He grinned and relaxed back on the sofa and patted Owens's arm in friendship.

There was a silence for a few seconds, then a dour faced Wilson asked; "So, officially, we can call him Uncle Arsehole now?" Everyone stared at Wilson in amazement and a little horror. That was some serious breach of protocol. But John just started to laugh, and everyone joined in. Jericho held his hand up; "Come on people, stick to the rules. Prince John can refer to his uncle how he likes, but we'll keep the required respect for a senior family member." that made everyone laugh even more.

Alex grinned; "Spoken like a true diplomat Jericho." and downed her brandy in one hit. John finished his drink and stood. Everyone rose too and John sighed; "Stop that - please." He smiled and headed for the door, then stopped; "Oh, and by the way, that Discipline Hearing called for tomorrow over our Alex's unwilling dating of Uncle Arsehole, will not go ahead. Mother has put a stop to that. But Mickey will probably want to see her." He disappeared and everyone really did relax. Owen scratched his chin in wonderment and muttered; "He calls the Arch-Angel Michael 'Mickey!"

Owen refilled all their glasses, and the conversation was quite lively. The team went to bed a great deal happier. But Jericho remained in the study, sitting by the dying fire and deep in thought. He had checked his mirror - it was back online. He sighed and stared at the smoldering embers of the fire; something still troubled him, and he couldn't fathom out what that was.

Both teams sat outside the Arch-Angel's grand office in relative silence. Only Doc Underhill and Jericho were really chatting.

Owen tapped Wilson and nodded towards Isabella [Issy] Pugg; "If Alex gets away with this, without a warning or official caution, they will have to shoot her with a tranquilizer gun." Wilson chuckled and glanced at the miserable looking Sergeant. "By the look on her face, she already knows the result." It was Owen's turn to chuckle. Skyrise sat arms folded and stared at the floor; even he didn't like to hold a conversation with 'Issy' unless he had too. Being a doctor; he had informed his friends on team 74 that she clearly had suffered a 'personality and humour bypass' at some point. Even old Doc had smiled at that, though he did 'tut tut' a couple of times and wag a disapproving finger.

Everyone stood as Prince John appeared from the office with Madame Eleanor [the angel's private secretary]. He grinned and slapped his hands together; "Mickey wants to see you two for a moment." He gestured to Doc and Jericho and still smiling, walked off down the corridor. Everyone turned to Issy as she groaned and slumped back on the seat and folded her arms; she was not a happy Temporal Detective Sergeant. Now that did make everyone smile.

Madame Eleanor showed Doc and Jericho into the angel's office and everyone sat back down, a lot happier now. Issy couldn't believe that Alex had 'got away with it' again. She stared at Skyrise, Wilson and Owen. "Bloody men. Always fools for a pretty face and pair of long legs." She muttered to herself and searched in her handbag for some mints she had there; she didn't offer them around.

Doc and Jericho emerged from the office - unsmiling - and Doc patted Jericho's arm and smiled. He gestured for his team to follow him, and Team 74 watched their colleagues depart in silence. Jericho jerked a thumb towards the office door and said quietly; "The Arch-Angel will see Team 74 now."

They followed him into the room without comment. Jericho stopped Alex briefly and said softly; "Keep your lips firmly together. I will do all the talking." Alex nodded and refrained from smiling. They lined up in front of the Angel's ornate desk and everyone stared at the sole object upon the beautiful marble desk; it was a miniature guillotine!

The Arch-Angel sat in his chair with both hands clasped in front of him. He nodded to Alex; "Officer Cappanni, you will be pleased to know that no discipline action will be taken against you. The matter is closed and will not appear upon your Personal File." Alex almost smiled but restrained herself; "Thank you Sir." was all she said. He gestured to Owen; "You took no part in this matter and; thus, your record remains clean - as it should for a novice Detective - and I suspect you have your Inspector and Sergeant to thank for that." Owen just nodded and also didn't smile. The angel folded his arms and still unsmiling spoke to Jericho and Wilson; "But you two broke several rules; and you know the very ones I am talking about. You admit that?" Jericho and Wilson nodded.

The Angel tapped his desk gently and said quietly; "I'm afraid that Sergeant Wilson Franklyn is reduced in rank to Constable for an indefinite period. He must receive a disciplinary sanction for what he did. I trust you can all understand that?" No one nodded at that revelation. The Angel continued; "Inspector Tibbs is suspended from duty forthwith for an indefinite period." There was absolute silence from the team; no one expected such a hard punishment. Alex wanted to speak, but the caught the look on Jericho's face and remained silent. Owen just stood with his mouth open.

But Jericho and Wilson said nothing; they had actually expected far worse, for breaking some very serious rules of the Temporal Detectives Department, they had illegally time travelled whilst stood down and interfered with another Teams investigation into a fellow team members Discipline case. They should have been thrown out of the department for that alone; never mind the unauthorized time trip!

Archangel Michael slowly pulled a small fob watch from his pocket and flipped open the lid. He stared at the watch face for a minute or so and looked up at the silent and dour Team 74. He grunted and snapped the lid shut; "Now that the indefinite time period is over. You're restored to the rank of Sergeant, Wilson. Your suspension, Inspector Tibbs is lifted. Now take a seat all of you." He smiled and leaned back in his chair.

The Archangel had done his job; dished out some serious enough punishments to his naughty staff - even if it was for only two minutes! - Temporal Department protocols had been satisfied; well as much as they could for a minute or so!

Everyone slowly sat on the marble bench and a little ripple of laughter passed between them, The Angel clasped his hands together; "Now onto more serious matters." The smile was gone, and everyone sat upright as the angel explained the 'serious matters' happening around them.

It was some minutes later that Team 74 trooped from his office in absolute silence and remained so until they returned to the lighthouse. They gathered in the study and Jericho closed the door and actually turned the key in the lock; no one had ever seen that happen before. He stood in front of the fireplace; grim faced and arms folded. "Well, you heard what the Arch-Angel said. Certain parties within - and outside - the Palace are making moves to have Prince David declared his brother's heir. I certainly don't have to explain what that would mean for us humans. Alex has already had a taste of that. But equally powerful parties are determined to stop that and have Prince John declared the heir. For good or bad, we have chosen to support Prince John and that will put us directly at odds with the Dark Prince and his supporters. To quote Archangel Michael; 'the bloody gloves are off'. We are now in the firing line from some pretty powerful parties."

He walked to the drinks tray and smiled; "Brandies all round, I think." No one argued against that! Owen cradled his brandy glass and said softly; "I think we're really in the shit." No one argued with that too.

THE END

EPILOGUE:

"A very difficult case for the team and especially Alexandra, who was sexually assaulted. It remains to be seen, if Jericho actually tells her what happened, as she currently has no memory of the incident. But the Jericho and the Team need to be very careful with their future dealings with the 'dark Side'.
***SJW**.*

CHARACTERS:

There were no living Human encounters in this particular Episode. But both **Prince David** [the Dark Prince] and **Prince John** had special appearances. There was also a brief appearance by **Princess Isis**.

EPISODE 11: "1914."

MISSION SUMMARY:
"The team is heading back to 1914 on the trail of a very dangerous time traveler who is plotting to change world history. It appears that a certain Katrina Potoski has planned to return to 28th June 1914 and the city of Sarajevo. The Archduke Franz Ferdinand Carl Ludwig Joseph Maria of Austria (18 December 1863 – 28 June 1914) was the heir presumptive to the throne of Austria-Hungary. His assassination in Sarajevo on that day is considered the most immediate cause of World War I. Jericho and his team must prevent the current human timeline from changing."

NOTES:
[1] It is – partly – based on true events.
[2] This is a special **Extended** Edition.

TRIGGER WARNINGS. **ALCOHOL, STRONG LANGUAGE, SEXUAL REFERENCES AND MILD VIOLENCE.**

AGE 15+ ONLY. **45 Minutes reading time.**

1. MOSCOW; 3rd November 1958.

The big black car slid a few times on the ice and snow; but the roads were in quite good condition considering the amount of snow that had fallen in the last few days. The driver slapped the wheel a couple of times and really wanted to cuss - loud and frequently - but held his tongue and his temper in check. He glanced into the mirror and watched District Commander Leon Nebcheski, sitting back and reading his little red notebook. He was the Police Commander of this affluent suburb of Moscow.

The other two passenger were unknown to him; but he knew the pretty young woman was also a Police Officer, he had caught her name; Tatiana Obski, a detective from the same District office. The other man, a tall thin and very unpleasant looking individual; he didn't know, but guessed he was from the KGB. They all seemed to wear the same cheap black suits and hats. Some fucking undercover outfit he thought.

He pulled up at the address he had been given and jumped from the car, opening the door for the Commander, who stepped out and pulled his coat around himself. The KGB man followed and then did Tatiana. They stood on the icy street and stared up at the apartment block. The doorman was waiting to open the building doors, brushing snow from his face and gloved hands. The Commander walked up and nodded; the doorman pulled open the door and saluted like the old soldier he was. Leon just grunted and they made their way to the top floor.

The two young, uniformed police officer heard the lift arriving and quickly threw their cigarettes through the slightly open window and adjusted their jackets and ties. They knew who would be stepping out. The pair came to attention and pushed open the apartment's door for him and his two colleagues. They said nothing. The Commander stared at the younger one and asked; "Is the building empty?" The young man straightened himself, saluted and said, "Yes Comrade Commander; all the residents have been taken for interview at the station Sir." He saluted again. The Commander just grunted again and pushed into the spacious apartment.

The KGB officer wrote down their badge numbers in his notebook and followed the Commander. Tatiana smiled at the pair and also entered. The place was a small palace, the furniture was mostly antique, and the rooms were well heated. She sighed; how the other fucking half lived, whatever happened to the revolution? But she kept those very dangerous thoughts to herself. The missing tenant had some pretty powerful relations in the party. If she hadn't, then a District Commander would certainly not be assigned to her case.

The KGB man gestured to one of the rooms; "It's in here Comrade Commander. It's quite unbelievable, almost like a shrine to the incident." They pushed into the room and Tatiana switched the light on. Leon chuckled; "I know she was a student of history, but why all this, for an Imperialist dog?" They looked about the room; the walls were covered with maps, pictures, drawings, anything relating to the assassination of Archduke Franz Ferdinand in Sarajevo, in 1914.

There was even a full itinerary of his visit, detailed, almost minute by minute. His murderer: 19-year-old Gavrilo Princip, took up one whole wall. The tables and even the chairs were covered with books, newspapers, and magazines on the assassination. Leon stared at the photograph of the Archduke; basically his death had started the glorious revolution of 1917.

Tatiana stood with her notebook open but didn't speak until the Commander gestured her to do so. "She was last seen on Monday afternoon, carrying a large canvas bag into her apartment. Several people saw her enter the building and two cleaners working on this floor actually saw her go into the apartment at about three o'clock. That is the very last time anyone saw her alive, not that she may be dead, Comrade Commander." She didn't smile and closed her notebook. Then added; "She has now been missing for five days. Nothing. No one has seen her, and all shifts of the doormen have been questioned closely. They are all good party men and swear that she never left the building. Nothing appears to have been taken from the apartment including money and clothes. Her cousin confirms this Sir."

The Commander pulled a silver cigarette case from his pocket and lit a smelly yellow cigarette, he smoked slowly; "Any known lovers or really good friends?" He asked Tatiana. She shook her head; "All the students at the university that knew her have been questioned. Apparently, she kept herself to herself. Quite unusual for a young woman at University Sir."

The Commander nodded and stared at the covered walls. He already knew that this 'disappearance' wasn't the usual running off by some love obsessed young woman. There was far more to this and the clues were all over the walls. He had been privy to a very confidential KGB file on the girl and her frequent visits to her university professor, who taught history. The old man also had several reports about straying from official party doctrine; yet no action had been taken against him. Leon guessed that the old professor had very powerful friends in the party elite, as well.

He picked up a silver framed photograph and grunted; young Kaerina Potoski with her mother and her uncle. He smiled to himself. Her uncle was known to have quite a passion for young girls. He replaced the picture and walked to the door. The KGB man asked nervously; "Do I have anything to report...to update the Bureau on this matter Comrade Commander?" The Commander stared at him and almost smiled; "Yes Comrade. That I'm on the case." They headed for the lift in silence.

The two young officers' sighed and relaxed, lighting up more cigarettes. One leaned against the wall and stared out the window. He watched as the big black car pulled away into fresh falling snow. "Do you think the stories are true about her, the uncle and mother?" The taller one asked and turned back to his colleague who shrugged his shoulders; "Who knows, but he really is a kinky bastard." He spat the words out and pushed his cap up; "Anything perverted said about him could be true." He added and blew smoke into the air.

The other one chuckled softly and went back to staring out the window; he would be glad when their shift finished. That's when he heard some noises from the sealed room; he slapped his colleagues arm and threw his half-smoked cigarette down and pushed open the door. His comrade had already pulled out his service revolver and the pair entered the apartment slowly.

Tatiana sat in her drab grey office and shifted in her chair. She had pulled her boots off and sat with her bare feet on the thin carpet. She picked up a couple of pictures that had been spread across her desk. The investigation into Katrina Potoski disappearance had drawn a large blank. No one had seen her leave the apartment; yet she had simply vanished. The grey canvas bag she hauled into her home on that faithful day; what the hell was in it? Her uncle wanted answers and there were - apparently - none to give.

Why the total obsession with the Arch Duke and his wife, who were assassinated in Sarajevo, the capital of the Austro-Hungarian province of Bosnia and Herzegovina, back in 1914? She [Katrina] had covered the bloody day, almost minute by minute; but for what purpose, it was just history now?

Tatiana sighed and picked up the photograph of Gavrilo Princip - the young assassin - sitting on a bench with two other men, outside a big house. There were two well dressed women, with parasols, standing some yards behind them. Tatiana fumbled in her top drawer and produced her large round magnifying glass and held it over the picture.

She stared good and hard for a few minutes and then slowly placed the big magnifying glass down on her desk. That's when she realised her hand was shaking a little. She clasped her hands together and took a couple of deep breaths. She picked up the glass and again studied the women in the picture. She lowered the glass and stared hard at the small, curtain less window; the snow was coming down heavily now. She rubbed her face a little and her mouth was dry; if it wasn't fucking impossible, the younger woman in the picture looked a dead ringer for the missing Katrina Potoski!

2. WALKING ON THIN ICE.

Jericho stared at the file for some minutes before closing it and replacing the brown folder on the coffee table. He leaned back in his well-worn, but very comfortable armchair and folded his arms. The contents of the file had made uncomfortable reading; anything that may change the historical events of 1914 was considered dangerous to the current human timeline.

That year changed human history and culture forever and apparently not for the best. The rise of Nazi Germany and the horrors that inflicted upon the world came directly from that year and the disastrous world war that followed. The outcome of that war started in 1914 had been the rise of Hitler to power. All the rest of human history now followed those two titanic events; the First World War and Adolf Hitler.

There had been other attempts to change that faithful year, but this one was different for one reason; Jericho knew that a History Professor teaching at Moscow University at the time, was none other than his old adversary; Wolfgang Leitcher. See episodes. ***'The man who died in the future to save his past'*** and ***'The Dunmore Witch trials'*** That simple fact made this mission dangerous and complicated. The assassination of Archduke Ferdinand had been a major success for the 'Dark Side'. Why would they wish to change that outcome; now?

He sighed loudly and picked up his coffee cup. Then replaced it and heaved himself from the armchair, snatching back up the file. The coffee would have to wait and headed for the dining room; the dinner would have to wait as well. Jericho knew that Team 74 would be walking on very thin ice with this new assignment.

Radovan the handyman watched from the dining room window - he had been cleaning the ceiling lights since the villa had acquired electricity - as the two cars swept into the drive of Villa Teodora - which had been rented to a mixed party of American & English journalists for two weeks; no doubt here to cover the Archdukes visit. Jana the housekeeper stuck her head around the door and shouted; "They're here! You best get downstairs and collect the bags. Hurry up please!" Radovan nodded and wiped his face and neck; "I'm coming woman." He muttered, straightening his shirt and waistcoat. It was too warm for a damn jacket. He made his way downstairs and into the courtyard.

The young woman stepping from the first big car made he stop in his stride; she was utterly stunning. He removed his greasy hat and bowed a little. Jana was immediately behind him and whispered; "By blessed St. Mary, that is a real beauty." Radovan nodded; he couldn't take his eyes off her, especially when she smiled directly at him. He grabbed her bags with some relish. "I will show you to your suite Ma'am." But Jana slapped his arm - quite hard - and said, "Take the bags upstairs and I will show the lady her rooms; see to the men."

Alex followed the middle-aged woman up the big staircase and into her rooms. Radovan dropped the bags inside the door and bowed; again. Alex gave him some Krone as a tip and he was most happy with that. But Jana was not happy about it; "You do not have to tip household staff Ma'am. That is for waiters and hotels. Radovan will only spend it on drink." She smiled and offered to help unpack Alex's two cases. But Alex declined; saying her maid Ruth would see to that. She removed her hat and stared through the French doors to the little balcony, which overlooked the beautifully kept rear gardens. "Some tea would be most welcome." She told Jana, who hurried away, back to her kitchens.

Ruth appeared in the doorway carrying her own bag and dropped it by the small table and chairs. "Bloody typical, he didn't rush to collect my bags. Owen carried them up." But she grinned and dropped into a chair and gently dabbed her face and neck, adding; "It's bloody hot!" Alex chuckled and joined her at the table. "I don't think we need to unpack much. I believe Jericho won't hang around this time and place too long."

Jericho was standing in the doorway - discretely consulting his mirror - and said quietly; "You've got that right Alexandra. We're here until the assassination and then we're off." He looked about and saw Wilson and Owen at the top of the stairs, Radovan just behind with their bags. Owen stood in the doorway and grinned; "The Housekeeper said you ordered tea, which will be served in the Morning Room apparently." Jericho nodded, his mirror now out of sight, and gestured to the other doors on the small landing; "Take your pick, there's three other bedrooms up here. We have one each, sheer luxury. It's nice to be back when the world was actually civilized."

Radovan couldn't take his eyes of the graceful Alex and stared through the door, wiping his face. He saw Wilson smiling at him and he nodded; "That sir, is real beauty. You could mistake her for a Hapsburg Princess or one of those American actresses." He grinned and walked away. Wilson just sighed and spoke to Jericho; "Do all the staff speak good English?" Jericho nodded; "That's why Operations booked the place." He picked up his suitcase and pushed open a bedroom door and just threw his case in. "Now for a bloody lovely cup of tea." He said and headed down the stairs. Wilson did the same with his bag and followed him. He hoped they had some decent coffee.

They assembled in the 'Morning Room' and Jana served tea and dainty little sandwiches. She bowed and left them to it; after announcing that dinner would be at seven. Alex had told Jana to ensure that her 'maid' Ruth received tea and sandwiches too. She was preparing the rooms and unpacking her 'Ladies' bags. Jana nodded and smiled to herself; the visitor was clearly a great lady and like true 'great ladies' she looked after her personal Maid.

The conversation in the kitchens was all about the great lady. After tea, everyone retired to their rooms - mainly to rest from the heat and change for dinner - Alex enjoyed a warm bath and the admiring servants would have been a little shocked to find that the 'great lady' shared her bath with her maid; to save time and precious hot water! If she hadn't, poor Ruth would have suffered a lukewarm bath. When Owen found out, he actually groaned at the thought of the pair, naked and splashing about in the same bath. Wilson and Jericho just sighed and muttered; "Bloody Monastery."

They were just about to sit for dinner, when Jana appeared - not with the soup - but a message. The woman looked quite concerned; there was a Captain of Police at the door and several police officers on horseback accompanied him. Jericho just smiled; "It's all just routine Madame Jana. He's here to check our papers." But Jana shook her head; "You are supposed to report to them. They don't come to you." Jericho shrugged his shoulders and told Jana to show the officer in.

Captain Advija Kovac strode in the room and stopped. He stared at Alex - standing by the fireplace - waving a silk fan across her face - and slowly started to smile. The young Police Captain simply had not seen a more beautiful woman in his entire life. He stood for a good few seconds before realizing everyone was waiting for him to speak. He politely coughed and smiled; "My English is said to be good. So I will know what you speak about and what I speak about." He finally managed to say; still looking at Alex. She was wearing a formal dinner dress that would not be out of place in London or Paris or the court of the Hapsburgs. She smiled at him, and his heart leapt about his chest. His mouth went dry, and he quickly removed his hat.

He didn't hear Wilson whisper to Owen; "Another bloody moth." Jericho offered the young captain a drink and he accepted quietly. Jana poured him cold lemonade; she knew the captain was a Muslim and certainly wouldn't offer him any form of alcohol. She smiled to herself, as she watched him continuously glancing at the 'great lady' - despite speaking with Jericho - she would wait outside until called and left the room quietly.

Soon as she heard the laughter; she smiled and relaxed. Very few people would laugh before being arrested and dragged away to prison and torture.

The captain quickly accepted Jericho's offer to join them at dinner. He sent word - via his sergeant, who stood in the doorway - staring at Alex - for his men to stand down. Jericho told Jana to give the men some tea. The captain relaxed in his chair and smiled at Alex. Jericho had quite deliberately placed him opposite her. She was the best distraction for any young man. Captain Advija sipped his lemonade and made everyone chuckle as he explained - in quite good English - about the report of desperate looking strangers in the Villa Teodora, who had not reported their presence to the local Police, which was to him, in fact.

Jericho had shown him their passports and journalist credentials. He was really interested when Jericho explained that Alexandra Cappanni was the court reporter for several French and English newspapers; here to cover the Imperial visit. He was both surprised and amazed and just came out with it. "Why would such a beautiful and clearly educated young woman bother to earn a living? She could have her pick of any rich or royal man, who would be more than happy to keep such a wife." And he meant it. Alex just smiled and kept her thoughts to herself on that matter; they would not have been pleasant, out in the open!

The impromptu dinner party broke up and the captain lingered over saying goodnight to Alex; he kissed her hand farewell; twice. The team enjoyed some brandy in the evening sitting room and played cards. But Jericho was concerned; who had informed the police about their arrival? Who would even know that the team was here? He sipped his brandy and didn't smile as one name popped into his head: Wolfgang Leitcher.

3. SARAJEVO; FRIDAY 26th JUNE 1914.

Jericho - chuckling to himself - finally had to swap with Alex and take over the driving. The sight of a well-dressed young woman driving a big car around the streets of Sarajevo had generated far too much interest in the team. Crowds actually blocked their progress on several occasions, simply by standing around the car and staring at Alex behind the wheel.

A couple of times, the crowd turned a little ugly and several rough looking men shouted at the cars; about the 'abomination against God' by a woman driving a car. Alex would normally have complained - loudly - about being replaced for such a sexist reason - but seeing the mob mentality growing right before her eyes, she kept her own thoughts and stayed silent.

Owen was in the first car with Wilson - who was driving - and discretely read, the little map of the Archduke's route on the tragic day, which would be the day after tomorrow. The team were familiarizing themselves with the streets and the place of the assassination. They stopped in the ill-fated road and watched as several carts passed them, pulled by brown and white bullocks. Several men on the various carts all raised their hats to Alex. A couple shouted some dubious 'compliments' and laughed amongst themselves.

Jericho jumped from the car and strode to the corner, followed by Wilson; Owen and Alex remained with the cars, parked outside a small bakery called Schiller's delicatessen. The smell of fresh bread and cakes was far too much for Owen and he was in the shop in an instant. Alex sighed and stretched her legs by walking between the two cars. Jericho and Wilson returned, and Owen emerged from the bakery with a box of assorted cakes. They gathered around the cars and Jericho spoke quietly - in French - about what happened on the dreadful day.

"The bloody driver took the wrong turn and drove right past Gavrilo Princip. He should have taken the other road [Jericho gestured to the other turning] but he turned down here. Had he not taken the wrong turn, Princip would have simply walked home; disappointed and that would have been that. Princip shot the duke and his wife, just about there." Everyone started at the most important piece of roadway in world history.

"Are there any explanation recorded, as to why the driver turned down here?" Alex asked and nibbled at her little chocolate cake, which was quite delicious. Jericho shook his head. "The official record states that the man simply got confused with the streets and Princip got very lucky; very lucky." Wilson grunted; "Lucky is not the word I would use; If I was the Archduke." and ate his little pastry in one hit.

They finished eating their little treats and Owen discretely tapped his mirror; he looked a little amazed. "Do you know that someone threw a bloody bomb before the actual assassination and blew up the following bloody car! And they just carried on after that! I mean, you would have thought that the Archduke would have said *'fuck this for a game of darts; let's get the fuck out of here!'* But they didn't and just carried on. Now that's fucking nuts." The amazement was clear in his voice. "Bloody nutters." He added and jumped in the car with Wilson who chuckled; "Which nutters are you talking about? There were plenty around on that day; on both sides."

Jericho and Alex climbed back into their motor car and the team headed back to Villa Teodora. They were stopped by a crowd of men, some carrying the Serbian Flag. The cars halted and Jericho said quietly; "Let me do the talking and keep calm people." One young man, tall with a small black beard approached Jericho and Alex's car. He stared at Alex, but spoke to Jericho; firstly, in Serbian and when Jericho shrugged his shoulder and replied in English, that he didn't understand the young man [which of course he did] Dragon switched effortlessly to good English; he was clearly an educated man; probably a student. He asked politely what the English party was doing in Sarajevo. Jericho told him their cover story and smiled a little.

Dragon nodded and gestured to Alex; "The dress and coat she wears would feed a starving Serb village for months my friend. That is what you should be reporting about our Austrian allies, who are de-facto our rulers."

Jericho nodded again and explained they were only here to cover the Arch-Duke's visit. But would seriously consider writing about the situation of the people. Dragon rubbed his bearded chin and slowly smiled; "If you really wish to report the truth to your people then allow me to show you the truth." He turned and spoke to his men, who all muttered and nodded. He stepped on to the running plate and another man; a big burly fellow with bad teeth, jumped on the running board next to Alex and grinned at her. He reeked of sweat and strangely enough; horses.

Alex just smiled and held a hankie to her nose, pretending to wipe it. Two other fellows, equally rough looking joined Owen's and Wilson's car.

Jericho followed his directions and found themselves outside the city at a small ramshackle village, filled with equally poor looking people. Alex immediately noticed the sad looking children and couldn't help herself; "Some of those children are malnourished and some need medical care." She said to Jericho. The look

Jericho gave her was priceless. Dragon nodded and jumped from the running board: "The beautiful woman does notice the truth. I hope she has the courage to write about it."

The villagers crowded around the car and stared at the 'foreigners'. He told the team, he would 'show' them around. Jericho slowly eased from the car and walked around to open the door for Alex, but the big man had already pulled it open and took hold of her arm. Alex pulled away, but he dragged her back. Typical of Alex, she slapped his face hard. He just smiled.

Jericho turned to protest and found young Dragon had a very old looking pistol in his hand, he smiled; "You can immediately help the impoverished people of Serbia by donating something to our cause, like your money, watches and cars and of the course, the beautiful lady. She will buy many guns, when sold in turkey; many guns."

The two men on Wilson's and Owens's car had also produced pistols, Jericho shouted for them to remain calm and sit still. He turned to Dragon and shook his head; "An incident like this will show your people in a very bad light. You will gain no sympathy or help by doing this." Dragon sighed and nodded; "But it will fill many empty bellies with real food and not empty promises." He told the big man with bad teeth to take the woman. That's when a deep voice boomed across the village centre and everyone turned.

There was a strapping young man in boots and sheepskin coat. He had a black beret on and a 'Lee Enfield' rifle in his hand. Alex noted that he was ruggedly handsome with a body to match. He smiled broadly and shook his head; "No Dragon. What the English says is true. This will do the cause no good. I'm sure they will donate something to our cause. But it will not be their cars - they can be easily traced and the taking of the beautiful woman would appear as headlines all over Europe and do our cause much harm."

Dragon just stared at him. It was clear by his face that he wouldn't go against the big man. He lowered the pistol, then chuckling, pushed it back into his trousers. "I accept your advice Zoran; on this occasion."

Zoran smiled and slung the rife over his shoulder and smiled at

Alex, now released by the big smelly man. He bowed a little and said; "Please forgive us beautiful lady, but desperate people do desperate things." He waved to the men and said quietly; "Let the English strangers help us as best they can." The men all laughed at that; except Dragon, who just stood with his arms folded, unsmiling.

4. THE RENDEZVOUS; SATURDAY 27th JUNE 1914.

The cars pulled into the driveway of Villa Teodora and the engines were switched off. Radovan stared from an upstairs window and just laughed out loud; "Welcome to Serbia!" He said loudly to himself and headed downstairs; he wouldn't miss this for a fucking gold bed. He stopped and scratched his head; "Well maybe a gold bed." He forced the grin from his face and walked slowly down the stairs.

Jericho sat in his underpants and folded his arms. At least he still had his mirror; the Serbian rebels could find no use or value for that. He turned to Alex, wrapped in a dirty piece of canvas and said quietly; "You did good there. If you had opened your trap, as you usually do, it may have been much worse." Alex just stared at him; "Worse?" She said, then added; "They left me just my bloody panties and bodice. I had to give them my bloody silk stockings and boots. Never mind that gorgeous hat. I loved that hat."

Jericho sighed and eased from the car. He was joined by Owen and Wilson, also in their underpants. Alex glanced at the bulge in Wilson's 'long John's' and that made her smile. A big man in every respect, she thought and stepped from the car, clutching the canvas around her.

They walked to the doors and Owen just had to say it; "That went bloody well, didn't it? Welcome to bloody Serbia!" That made Jericho chuckle and the rest laughed too, even Alex; despite losing that bloody gorgeous hat.

Jana rushed out, more upset than they were. She fussed over Alex, but also stared at Wilson; she wasn't looking at his face. They made for their rooms to acquire some clothes and Jana helped Alex dress, apologizing profusely about the Serbian rebels. Alex waved her apologies away with a smile and asked about Zoran. Jana sighed, buttoning up Alex's dress; "He's the only one with any brains. There is a huge reward for him and yet he walks about untouched. The people love him; they know he's their only hope for freedom from the damn Austrians."

Alex found out that Zoran had managed to keep the Serbian rebel underground together, despite the in-fighting and bitter factions between the groups that made the organization up. Jana was clearly a great admirer of the man. The team ate dinner - which was excellent - and laughed about what had befallen them.

Jana interrupted the meal and whispered into Alex's ear with a big grin. Alex just nodded and Jana disappeared, returning a few moments later with a huge basket of fruit and flowers. On top was Alex's 'gorgeous' hat! Everyone gathered around and Alex unfolded the note that accompanied the basket. It was blank except a large, capital 'Z'.

Wilson sighed and said to Owen; "Chalk up another bloody moth." Owen shrugged; "Well he did get to see her in just her bloody underwear. That alone must be worth some fruit and flowers." The pair laughed and took an apple each.

Jericho stood rubbing his chin; this contact could prove interesting and was potentially useful. He needed to find out more about the man simply known as 'Zoran'. He smiled at Alex and knew the very person who could do that. Alex saw Jericho smiling at her and just sighed; she knew Jericho well and how he thought.

Jana just smiled at Alex's request, as they sipped morning tea together in the music room. You wouldn't be the first woman to fall for his looks and charm. She thought and placed her cup down and nodded at her request. Jana insisted that the meeting should take place somewhere safe for Alex - from the other rebel men, of course - Zoran could be trusted around women. Well, as much as a decent man could be!

Alex had told Jana that she wanted to write about the man and have it published in the European papers; a rebel's view of the Austrians rule of his occupied country. Now that did strike a chord with Jana and sounded excellent for the cause. She agreed to arrange it. Jericho was happy, but Owen and Wilson were not. They insisted that Alex had company when the meeting took place. Jericho finally agreed, but Zoran probably wouldn't appear if they [the men] were there.

It was Alex that solved that one. Her idea was greeted with muted approval. But it was the only solution that they could see. That early afternoon, Alex dressed in a lovely dress and coat, with her gorgeous hat of course. Jana was impressed with her. But she was overwhelmed by the appearance of her companion. She spoke with real disbelief in her voice; "I cannot believe it is the same person. Utterly gorgeous, stunning even." She shook her head in amazement and the two women waited for Alex's new friend to appear.

Alex actually grinned and shook her head too. Owen looked absolutely stunning. He was dressed in a similar fashion to her, including a wonderful hat and white parasol. He actually looked beautiful. Alex still couldn't believe what a stunning young lady Owen made. He smiled at both and did a little twirl and curtsied. "Will this do?" He asked in a soft and very feminine voice. Jana clasped her hands and just smiled in wonderment. "Stunning." She said simply and Alex had to agree.

Ruth stood in the doorway and smiled too; she was well pleased with her efforts to dress Owen as a lady. Jericho had been really firm about not allowing young Ruth to accompany Alex on her mission. Owen would have to become his female 'alter ego' - Jacqueline - for this particular job.

As Alex put it; "He could fool his own bloody mother!" No one disagreed with her. The two ladies pulled away in one of the cars; Alex driving. They took a quiet road out of the city - mainly to avoid the crowds that would gather around the car - and headed for the rendezvous point. Owen - sorry Jackie - checked her mirror; "Just a few miles down this road is a shepherds hut. It’s built of brick with a straw roof. The local shepherds use it in winter." Alex nodded; she loved driving and wasn't really listening.

Alex pulled the big car up and the girls sat waiting. The place looked totally deserted. "You sure we're in the right place?" She asked Jackie after a couple of minutes. Jackie nodded. "We certainly are, I'm great at map reading." She adjusted the wing mirror and checked her makeup and hair. The car had an open top and both 'ladies' had tied their lovely hats down with scarfs. Jackie gently tapped Alex's arm; "I don't want to alarm anyone but there are several men in uniform with guns coming up behind us. I think it's the bloody coppers!" Alex glanced into her wing mirror and saw them; Jackie was right, it was the police. Alex sighed; "I think we've been set up or betrayed."

Several policemen stood around the car - pointing their rifles at the girls - Alex just smiled and slowly opened the door and eased out. Jackie did the same. She asked - in perfect Serbian - if the ladies could assist them. The police all looked at each other and the skinny sergeant walked up to Jackie and grinned. "So, you speak our language woman. I understood that none of the journalists spoke Serbian." Jackie smiled and gestured to Alex; "I'm not with the journalist party. I'm Mademoiselle Alexandra's friend. I'm here to translate." The sergeant scratched his beard, thinking, finally he grinned; "Never mind that. You are all under arrest for helping terrorists and bandits!"

That's when the first bullets struck the ground around the policemen and the car windscreen shattered. Alex and Jackie dived under the car as the policeman scattered, firing their rifles at the surrounding hills. Alex looked out from under the car and tapped Jackie. "There's loads of bullets flying around and not one policeman has been hit. Odd that?" Jackie nodded, keeping a firm grip on her hat. That's when she saw the knelling figure by the door of the shepherds hut; it was Zoran. He was gesturing to them, rifle in hand.

Alex sighed; "Come on. Let's hope the bloody coppers are rotten shooters too." They scrambled from the car and dived through the door of the hut followed by Zoran, who was laughing loudly. "They have no stomach to face real men. They run away. We don't shoot rabbits except for the pot!"

He leaned against the wall, beneath the window and smiled at the girls; "I told my men not to harm any of the pathetic creatures. That would just bring hundreds more and they would be made of sterner stuff than these. Captain Kovac is a different matter in a real fight. He is brave and intelligent; quite a formidable foe." He slapped Alex on the bum and gestured to the open back door; "Come on, before they return with more men, and some may have the stomach to fight."

5. REBELS, BANDITS OR TRAITORS?

The little group made its way up the mountain pass in single file Zoran's men were impressed by the stamina of the two ladies. They seemed to take the hard mountain path in their stride. Franz – Zoran's number 2 – kept a close eye on the young dark-haired beauty and smiled. "Now that is a woman for a mountain man and dedicated traitor to the Austrians. I have never considered marriage, but I think she could change my mind on that."

Zoran nodded his agreement with that; both the women were special. They hadn't moaned once about the hard climb through the ravines and gully's of the mountain. Darkness was coming down when they stopped at the abandoned villa. Jackie stared at the place; "It must have been magnificent in its heyday. How could anyone just abandon such a place?" She asked Alex who shrugged her shoulders; she didn't know.

It was Franz that answered her question; "The family who lived here were all Serbian patriots, Jan who owned the house was known to hate Austria and its influence; he spoke out against them." He gestured towards the ruined stables and grunted; "The Austrian Secret Police came one night. They lined them up against the wall there and shot them; two old men, four women and three children. One of the children – a girl – survived the bullets and so they ran a pitchfork through her. Then the murdering dogs crept away in the dark. They wanted to leave a message for other Serbians who spoke out." He wiped his face and headed for the villa's big doors, followed by a very subdued Jackie who wished she really hadn't asked.

Zoran turned to Alex unsmiling; "This was his father's house, and the little girl was his young sister; she was nine. He hates the Austrians with a passion. This you can understand; Yes?" Alex nodded; she understood all right. Zoran sighed; "Our own people cowering down in fear; frightened of upsetting the Austrians. To some we are nothing but bandits. To others – many others – we are freedom fighters."

The group settled in for the night and Zoran gestured to a room with the door hanging off; "There are good chairs in there and I have this for our little interview." He held up a bottle of brandy and that really did catch the girl's attention!

They sat around a small struggling fire and drank brandy from china cups. Zoran made it clear that he would only discuss the struggle for freedom; he would make no comments about himself except to say that he was Serbian patriot. That puzzled both Alex and Jackie; normally such men would wax lyrical about their lives and adventures. Alex wondered why the big man was so reticent about himself.

But they did discover one very important thing; there was a young Russian woman called 'Katina' assisting the rebels; with money and documents – apparently stolen from the Austrians – that showed the Austrians wanted to crush the upstart Serbians underfoot. Zoran explained that the Tsar and the Russian Empire was considered a 'protector' of all Slav people. He smiled; "The little father [the Tsar] will not stand ideally by why Slav's are butchered. He will come to our aid." Zoran grunted and refilled the cups and lit his pipe. The smell was gorgeous. Jackie took a couple of deep breaths and suddenly realized that she had smelt the strange, sweet aroma before. But when and where?

Jackie complimented Zoran on his delicious smelling pipe tobacco and asked where he obtained it. He just shrugged his big shoulders; "I was given a few good kilo's by an old friend. I think it's American." Jackie nodded and continued to write into her notebook as Zoran spoke about the struggle for his people's freedom.

Alex asked Zoran about the group of patriots called the 'Black Hand'. He laughed with undisguised contempt. "Students, teachers, men of books; not a real fighter amongst them; they do not seem to understand the big picture and I feel their amateur plotting will only bring disaster to the cause."

Alex and Jackie cast a knowing glance at each other, the little group of 'amateurs' will certainly do that; Gavrilo Princip was a member of that group, and his assassination of the Archduke would be the spark that caused a terrible World war.

Franz appeared in the broken doorway and smiled a little – especially at Jackie – He pulled off his rough hat and spoke to Zoran; "Katina is here with donkeys. She has brought food and more ammunition. She has brought several more men and there's some information about our guests friends." Alex interrupted the pair; "What news about our friends?" She asked with some trepidation.

Franz clutched his hat with both hands; "Captain Kovac has taken them into custody, he's questioning them about you [indicating Alex] and your dealings with us. He is a clever man and believes there is more to you journalists than meets the eye." Alex sighed; the captain was right about that!

Zoran jumped to his feet and gestured towards the doorway; "Come on ladies and meet another woman of courage and dedication." Franz stepped forward and offered his arm to Jackie as she rose from the straw covered floor. Jackie gripped it slowly and smiled a little. She caught the big smile on Alex's face despite the news about Jericho and Wilson.

'Katina' was a small blond woman in her late teens, wrapped in fur against the cold of the mountain night. She gripped a mug with both hands and sipped black coffee laced with brandy. She pushed back her dark fur hat and stared at the two strangers. Zoran introduced them to Katina who just nodded; both girls noticed the thick leather belt and holster slung about her hips. She looked like she knew how to use the damn pistol.

The men left the women alone and checked the supplies and equipment on the donkeys. Katina lowered her cup and jerked a thumb towards Zoran; "He's a good man in a fight. But lousy in a ballroom." Alex wrapped her coat about herself and smiled; "I detect a Russian accent, probably Moscow. Am I right?" Katina stepped forward and poured the dregs of her coffee cup at Alex's feet and didn't smile; "I detect an English accent with a slight Italian twist, probably Cappanni. Am I right?" She grinned and walked away.

"Fuck." Was all Jackie said. Alex straightened her hat and tapped Jackie's arm; "Come on. Let's find a quiet place and contact Jericho; he needs to know about this little revelation. She [Katina] knows who we are." Jackie sighed; "This mission is turning shitty by the minute." Alex could only nod her agreement with that. They walked to the derelict stables and found some old chairs by a broken window. Jackie stood watch, keeping an eye on the small camp.

Alex operated her mirror and called Jericho; there was no answer even though her mirror indicated that Jericho's device was 'online'. "He must be unable to answer." She muttered to herself and sent a message. She tried Wilson's with the same result.

Alex searched human records for 'Katina' and 'Zoran'. Just as she expected; Katina was Katrina Potoski; the missing soul from 1958. But a check on Zoran shocked her; there was no trace in human records, which she knew was nearly impossible! "Now that's a bloody turn up for the books." She muttered. Then heard Jackie hiss a little and whisper; "You'll never guess who just rode into camp, bold as brass perched upon a bloody donkey?"

"Well, I bet it's not bloody Jesus Christ." Alex whispered and joined her by the window and stared at the figure being welcomed by the little group; it was Jana! She was wrapped in furs and carrying a rifle slung over her shoulder. Jana slipped from the donkey and pulled her rifle from her back. She was speaking to Zoran and waving an arm about. "I don't like the look of this." Jackie spoke quietly, gripping her mirror.

They watched as Franz gestured to the old stables and several men grabbed up their rifles. "Time to go." Alex said and the pair operated their mirrors as the group approached the stables, rifles at the ready.

The villa was in darkness and Alex slowly pulled the curtains aside and stared down into the courtyard. There was a single motor car parked there and she could see the glow of a cigarette as the occupant smoked. She then saw the other figure standing by the ornate gates; a police officer with his rifle cradled in his arms. She wondered where the hell was Jericho and Wilson.

Jackie crept back into the room and spoke in a low voice; "The place is deserted apart from those coppers guarding the gates. All our bedrooms are a total mess; they even tore open our coats and dresses. What they were looking for is anyone's guess." Alex eased herself down on the bed; "There is still no answer from Jericho or Wilson." She stared at her mirror and called up the Duty Time Controller – it was Janet; Jericho's lady friend – and spoke with her briefly. Finally, Alex smiled a little; "According to Operations, their mirrors are located at Villa Opao just outside the city. That's where we're headed." Both girls operated their mirrors and found themselves in woods, overlooking an impressive three-story house, standing in its own grounds.

Alex sighed loudly; the place was lit up like Blackpool Tower and there were several vehicles parked in the courtyard and on the road leading up to the villa. Two armed policemen stood by the gates. They watched from the trees as, yet another motor car entered the gates with police inside. "Bleeding busy little place ain't it." Jackie whispered.

"Well, we need to get Jericho and Wilson out of there and recover their mirrors. Time – for once – is not on our side. The bloody shooting is tomorrow; Sunday and we still don't know what Katrina has planned." Alex spoke quietly and pulled her coat around; the summer night was quite cold. She heard Jackie chuckle and turned back to the roadway and saw – about a kilometer away – a small black car, jacked up with a lone policeman changing a tyre. "I think I'm about his size, don't you agree?" Jackie said with a small grin.

The girls disappeared back into the woods; heading for the policeman who was just finishing his task. He looked up and actually smiled at the two young women as they approached his car. Alex operated her mirror and he fell silently to the kerbside; she had stunned him. They hid the young policeman – still smiling – in some bushes. Both girls noticed he smelt of alcohol. "The bugger's pissed!" Alex muttered and they stripped his uniform off and it did; indeed, just fit Jackie.

Owen managed to remove most of his makeup and gloves covered the nail polish he couldn't remove. He chuckled; "I bet I'm not the only copper wearing stockings tonight." Alex just sighed and pulled the boot open. She wasn't happy; she just squeezed into the small boot and Owen started the car. He headed for the gates.

6. SURPRISES AT VILLA OPAO.

Owen pulled his cap down and didn't smile; the gates were approaching. The little car reached the gates and the wheel fell off. He just managed to avoid the two shocked guards on the gate and stop several meters inside. "Never trust a piss head." He cussed and jumped out; the two gate guards were laughing and slapping each other. The big sergeant who appeared from a nearby doorway wasn't laughing. He threw down his cigarette and booted Owen up the arse. "Get the bloody thing fixed you moron. I bet your from Cavljak; their all-bloody useless bastards from that station." Owen rubbed his backside and nodded.

The sergeant called over two big men who were smoking and told them to help push the damn heap to the stables [which were used as a garage] he sighed and shouted for them to hurry up; they were going to move the prisoners to Sarajevo. He chuckled; "They will find that our Austrian allies don't ask questions as politely as we do." The two big men nodded and told Owen to steer the damn thing while they pushed.

They managed to get the car inside the garage and walked off; cursing Owen for being an idiot from Cavljak. He checked the garage and found one other car inside: sitting on four bricks with no wheels. He pulled open the boot and a relieved Alex slipped out. She also kicked him up the arse; "You idiot, I thought I was going to bloody die again!"

A disgruntled Owen rubbed his backside – again – and told Alex about the prisoners being moved into the city. Alex brushed herself down and checked her mirror. "A body check tells me, they're on the top floor in a back room." She grunted and almost smiled; "Just one guard sitting on a stool outside. The mirrors are downstairs in a room off the ballroom."

The pair slipped into the kitchens which were strangely deserted and cold. Alex tapped the big stove and whispered; "That's strange Owen; the ovens are not on and there doesn't appear to be any kitchen staff about. With so many men to feed the place should be packed with cooks and staff." Owen nodded and pulled open a door; it was the entrance to the back stairs.

"I'll deal with the guard." Alex muttered – unsmiling – and they reached the top. Owen suddenly gripped her arm and gestured through the dirty small window that allowed a little light onto the dark staircase. He said softly; "That bloke talking with those two coppers; isn't it that Dragon fellow who wanted to sell you to some bloody Turks?" Alex peered over his shoulder and grunted; "Whose side is that bastard really on?"

They heard movement around the corner and Alex lifted her mirror – ready to strike – when Wilson appeared, grinning. "I could hear you two dumbo's from a mile away. At least you've turned up." Jericho appeared at his shoulder and smiled; "The bastards jumped us at the villa. They strip searched us and took everything including our…."

He didn't finish because Alex interrupted him.

"They're in a room downstairs, but all the bloody soldiers and police appear to be down there." She said quietly and Jericho nodded and held out his hand. "I'll enter my Inspector code into yours [her mirror] and stop time; then we'll get the bloody things back."

Alex smiled and handed over her mirror. Owen asked the big man about the guard outside their door. Wilson just grinned and held up a big fist; "You don't need a mirror sometimes when you have one of these. I told the idiot I needed a crap and when he opened the door; bang!" Owen chuckled at that. He also told Jericho about seeing 'Dragon' – the supposed patriot – talking with the police. Jericho operated Alex's mirror and the team ran down the stairs and into the grand hallway of the villa.

Everyone was still; caught in stopped time. Owen – using his mirror – pointed to a small door of the hallway and Wilson pulled it open. It was a small room covered with shelves, hooks and glass cabinets – all empty – and Alex pointed to the small centre table, where an old canvas bag lay. "They must be in there. This was probably the bloody gun room of the villa. Used to store and maintain the shotguns for shooting parties." Owen grabbed the back and pulled out the missing mirrors, handing them to Wilson and Jericho.

"You need to bring us [Wilson and him] up to date with our rebel friends and their plans." Jericho spoke whilst checking his mirror. He had several messages outstanding. Owen – who was rummaging in the old sack – suddenly held up a wad of American banknotes held in a silver note pin. "Are there any other prisoners here?" He asked and then held up a little necklace, a snake and circle of gold. Everyone knew that meant a follower of the 'Dark Prince'.

He emptied the bag onto the table and picked up a small black notebook and flicked through the pages; "Sweet Jesus! It's a complete timetable of the assassination, with times, positions of the cars and even the bloody times! It's written in old hieratic script so that no-one in this era could understand it; well, except a bloody expert Historian I suppose."

Jericho took the book and read a couple of pages; he almost smiled. "Some bugger from the dark side is here. I wonder if they're here to ensure the assassination goes ahead. It was a great day for them; the First World War created Hitler and the Nazi's." He checked his fob watch and cursed quietly; "Come on; we only have ten minutes left before time restarts itself." The team headed out of the villa and walked to the gates. That's when Owens's sharp eyes spotted the figure crouched low in the bushes.

He pulled back the foliage and everyone was surprised to see Zoran staring back at them. "How the hell did he get here so bloody quickly?" Alex said loudly what the others were all thinking. Owen lifted up his mirror and told Jericho that 'Zoran' had no file in Human records – which was almost impossible – so who the hell was he?

Jericho rubbed his chin; "Well, with have no time to find out and time is about to re-start. Let's go." He operated his mirror and the team walked back to the lighthouse. They had been seriously compromised on this mission and Jericho would need to bring the angel up to date on what had happened. Wilson sighed; "How the hell do we return and ensure the assassination is not stopped; everyone back there now knows that we're up to something."

"Now that's a bloody good question big man." Muttered Owen, who was wondering what Mrs. Harris had prepared for dinner. Jericho sighed and held up both hands; "People, we'll be back there after a good dinner and some brandies." He lowered his arms and headed for the big doors of the lighthouse. "How the hell can we return without being spotted?" A puzzled Owen asked Alex, who just shrugged her shoulders.

Wilson couldn't stop laughing; every few minutes he would turn around and just stare at the three nuns sitting in the rear of his car. Sister Geraldine [Jericho] adjusted his wimple and gestured forwards; "Please keep your eyes on the damn road Father." That made Wilson chuckle: he was dressed as a Catholic priest from the Ottoman Empire; strangely enough a black Catholic priest wasn't that unusual! Serbia had once been part of the vast Ottoman Empire and so the locals were used to seeing priests of all colours about the place.

Sister Alex just sighed but had to smile at Sister 'Geraldine'; Jericho did make a good nun – a big ugly nun – but she looked the part, as did Sister Olive [Owen]. The car parked in a quiet side road and Sister Geraldine gave a final briefing before they would join the crowds gathering along the route that the ill-fated Archduke and his wife would traverse this morning.

"Keep an eye out for Katrina; she's not here for sightseeing and we still don't know what the hell the character 'Zoran' is or what's he's up too." Sister Geraldine discretely checked her mirror. "Everything is currently running as previous happened and the royal couple is due to enter the killing zone in about twenty minutes." She added and sat back, staring at the passing crowds of people.

"Come on people; let's mingle." Sister Geraldine pulled open the door and the team decamped onto the busy pavement. Some passerby's lifted their hats to the nuns and Sister's Alex and Olive made for the pavement opposite. In the distance they heard a sharp explosion and Sister Olive pointed to some dark grey smoke rising behind a large office building; "The bomb's been thrown at the car following the Arch-duke!" She spoke quietly, clutching Sister Alex's arm.

Some of the crowd was running towards the noise and smoke from the explosion. Alex nodded; "They will restart the bloody visit and come back along Appel Quay and the first three cars will turn down the wrong bloody street and Gavrilo will be standing right in front of them. We've about twenty minutes before he shoots."

The pair headed for the street corner that would host one of the most important assassinations in human history. The crowds were milling about, talking and shouting amongst themselves. Sister Olive consulted her little fob watch; "We're just minutes away now." She whispered to Sister Alex who wondered where Jericho and Wilson had disappeared too. Several police officers rushed past, pushing and dragging two rough looking peasants, held firmly between them.

Sister Olive stared at one of them and turned away quickly; it was old Radovan from the Villa! They watched the old man dragged away and bundled into a big black police car. Sister Olive also recognized the sergeant driving the car; it was the same one who had kicked him up at the arse at Villa Opao.

"Sweet Jesus! Did you see who that was?" Sister Olive asked Sister Alex who wasn't looking at the arrests.

She had seen their quarry; Katrina Potoski and the man standing with her; it was Dragon Milenković. The pair was staring down a small street. Alex followed their gaze and saw why; it was the young assassin Gavrilo Princip.

7. THE KILLINGS; SUNDAY 28th JUNE 1914.

"He's walking away; he thinks he's missed the bloody car. But he's walking down the very road that the couple's driver will turn down in error." Sister Alex said quietly, and the two nuns' quickly re-crossed the road. They watched as Katrina and Dragon started to follow Gavrilo. "I think they'll try and take him out before he gets to the kerbside as the car passes." Sister Olive whispered, and the pair of nuns speeded up to a fast walk; well, fast for nuns!

Sister Olive could see the remaining cars of the Imperial entourage turning into the roadway ahead. "Come on; their bloody here!" she said, and they quickly came up behind Katrina and Dragon who were both reaching under their coats. The nuns operated their mirrors and the pair collapsed on the pavement. A small crowd gathered about the two and watched – a little amazed – as the two nuns dragged the unconscious pair down a side alley.

The pair were placed against a dirty wall and the good sisters pulled the two pistols from their coats. "Jesus, you could kill an elephant with these buggers." Sister Olive muttered, hiding the guns in her big handbag. That's when the nuns heard the shots ringing out. "And twenty million dead later." Was all Alex said.

But the shooting drew the crowds away from the nuns and their casualties. Sister Alex slapped her friend on the arm; "Come on, let's get this daft bitch back to her own time. We need to find her time controlling device so she can't slip back." Sister Olive nodded; "We can leave dragon here. He won't have a clue what the hell happened to him or Katerina." They checked the entrance to the alley – again – and disappeared, leaving Dragon to awake alone and somewhat confused.

They dumped Katrina on her large bed and stared about the apartment; "How the other half live, some bloody revolution for the poor." Owen muttered as Alex searched the young woman. She carefully pulled a small Icon of Christ from the deep pockets of her coat. "Got it. A bloody time portal." Alex pushed the fragile little painting into her habit's pocket and sat on the bed as Katrina woke. She sat slowly up and stared at the two nuns.

"You stupid bastards! Do you realize what you've done?" She collapsed back on the pillows and sobbed. "Yeah, we know. The bloody Archduke is dead and so will some twenty million other poor sods will die. But that's how human history played out and you had no right to change it." Alex replied and Katrina shook her head and wiped tears away with both hands.

"No, you dumb, stupid bastards; following orders you never even questioned; you're worse than the fucking Gestapo or the guards on the Concentration camps. We were sent to RESTORE the fucking real current human timeline. That little shit Gavrilo missed the Archduke originally and walked home. There was NO assassination and no great war that changed everything and allowed fucking Hitler to seize power!" She collapsed back on the pillows and sobbed some more.

Alex just stared at her; "What do you mean; you were sent back and how the hell do you know what the original timeline was supposed to be?" Katerina sat back up and wiped her face. "Zoran is from the bloody alternative future; the one that was supposed to have existed. He was part of a time travel experiment in the year 2061. He was supposed to go back to 1905 and interview Einstein, but something went wrong, and he realized that the past and the future had changed. That change was someone telling Gavrilo to wait at the crossroads on Appel Quay for a few minutes more. Those extra few minutes changed the entire history of the human race and you two idiots have allowed it to happen all over again."

Owen and Alex stared at each other; little wonder Zoran didn't show up on Human Records; it only covered the current humanity that existed in the current human timeline. Owen headed for the large ornate drinks cabinet and pulled out a decent bottle of brandy and some glasses. Katrina accepted her half-filled glass and had calmed a little. She sipped her brandy and shook her head; "Now millions upon millions will die in wars, humans will use atomic weapons and people will live daily in fear from their fascist controlling governments; all thanks to you two stupid unquestioning buggers."

She placed her glass upon the bedside cabinet and rummaged in her pockets. "Where the fuck is my time device?" She shouted and Alex tapped her dress; "Sorry, but we need to take that." Katrina slumped back and picked up her glass; she actually smiled; "I bet you didn't even bother to look at the painting of our sweet savior; No, you just grab it and carry on following your stupid evil orders. You pair of dumb fucking imbeciles."

Owen held out his hand and Alex slowly pulled the little Icon out and both stared at the painting; they recognized the face immediately. It was Prince John. "Oh, fucking shit!" was all Owen could manage to say. Alex slowly pushed the Icon back into her pocket as the sheer enormity of what Katrina had said, swept over her. John had been the 'Messiah' all along in the original timeline; little wonder he had become a recluse and lived on Jericho's island. She also realized why Prince Jesus was the way he was, with his father and the holy family. He had been the 'changeling' for their plans.

Alex took a big gulp of her brandy and coughed a little. "That's why Zoran didn't register on our mirrors; he shouldn't exist."

Owen nodded; "I wonder what differences there are with his timeline?" Katrina pulled herself up and slapped the glass down on the bedside cabinet. "Everything. Everything is different. There was no poverty, no hungry nations and very few wars; one world government that actually served the people and not just themselves." She stood and laughed, hands on hips; "All gone thanks to you fucking stupid pair of idiots. I hope you sleep well at night now. I'm going to take a shower."

She strode to the bathroom and turned at the doorway; "You can show yourselves out. Best run back to the big puppet master; Mister Jericho fucking Tibbs. He likes to keep his brainless little lap dogs on a tight leash." She disappeared into the bathroom and the somewhat subdued pair operated their mirrors and were gone.

The apartment door creaked open and the two police officer's crept in: their service revolvers in their hands. They could hear the shower running and burst through the door to find a naked Katrina standing in front of them. She sighed and grabbed up a towel. "Here we go again." was all she said.

They walked back to the lighthouse in silence, and both headed for the drinks tray in Jericho's study. Owen poured a couple of large brandies and Alex slumped into her favourite armchair and accepted her glass with a quiet thank you. Owen sprawled on the sofa and sipped his drink slowly. "Do you think there was any truth in what she said?" he finally asked, and Alex shrugged her shoulders; "We're tasked to protect the current human timeline as designed by the BOSS. That's the bottom line really."

Owen nodded and sighed; "What the hell will happen to Zoran's soul; he can't be collected in our existence, and he can't travel back to his own time because it no longer exists. He's lost." Alex eased in her chair and stared at the fireplace; "Maybe Jericho's worked something out." She said quietly. That's when they heard voices in the hallway; Mr. Harris was talking to Jericho and Wilson.

Wilson pushed through the door and smiled. "That went well; did you get that troublesome lady back to where she belongs?" Alex nodded and held up the small icon and tossed it to him. "That was her time portal; except it's not from our version of existence." Wilson caught the object and studied it carefully; "It's our John." he muttered; the surprise in his voice evident. He poured himself a brandy and dropped on the sofa next to Owen. He shook his head and almost smiled; "Sweet Jesus, Jericho was right – yet again – about this job."

Owen sat up; "What did he say about this job?" he asked and rolled the glass around in his hands. Wilson laid the Icon down on the coffee table and sipped his drink. "He said that that there was more to Zoran than meets the eye. Especially his involvement with Katrina; you guessed that the pair was related. She was some sort of distant ancestor of his. Jericho believes it was him that influenced her to jump back in time. He probably gave her the Icon. The time portal it contained would work in our existence, but couldn't take him back to his; that existence was gone with the shooting of the Archduke and the time line that created."

Wilson looked up at the door and said quietly; "Jericho told me that in the original timeline Gravilo walked away, thinking he had missed the royal procession, and that was that. No First or second world wars, no atomic bombs and no revolutions. We all thought that it hinged on Gravilo but it bloody didn't. He didn't actually, change the timeline; someone else did that by exercising human free will in an instant, less than a second."

Both Owen and Alex sat forward; intrigued. Jericho wandered in and clapped his hands together; "Well, that went off all right and curry is on the menu tonight!" He smiled at his team and then just chuckled. "Wilson told you about the big, unexpected twist in all this?"

Jericho walked to the drinks tray and poured himself a large one. He spoke quietly, almost amused. "Everyone thought it was Gavrilo that changed everything using human free will in an instant. But the bugger responsible remains lost and unknown to history. But he changed the world completely in less than a second by pure chance."

Owen actually laughed and shook his head; "The fucking driver of course!" Alex sat back and sipped her drink. The driver in a split second – when he decided which road to take – had changed the course of human history. In the original timeline he always turned left. But with the gift of free will; he had simply changed his mind at the last moment and drove right past Gravilo. It was as simple as that.

"No bloody wonder the Dark Prince wants to remove free will from humans. It even fucks up divine will and plans." Alex said softly and finished her drink. Jericho sighed; "I have reported Zoran's situation to angel Margret. His fate is out of our hands."

Wilson hung back as Jericho headed for the dining room. He gestured for Owen and Alex to do the same. The three waited until Jericho disappeared from the room and Wilson turned to them; unsmiling. "It wasn't quite that simple, Gravilo was about to walk away when a nun stopped him for a few seconds. He turned back and the rest is history as we know it."

Alex ran a hand over her face; "You mean Jericho changed history and not the bloody car driver?" she whispered; a little shocked. Wilson nodded and said softly; "It must have been a terrible decision for him. He always says that real civilization ended in 1914 and that end started with this assassination. But he knew what his duty was and carried it out regardless; you have to respect the man for that, his loyalty to the Temporal Department came before everything he believed in."

The three walked slowly to the dining room; each with a real respect for their Inspector.

Jericho sat at the table sipping his wine as his team took their seats. He placed his glass down and pulled open a brown paper file; "Let's enjoy this dinner." He said, adding: "We're jumping to England in 1977 tomorrow. We really need to look at that strange case of that woman bricked up in Canterbury Cathedral back in medieval times. I can't put it off any longer." [See episode: **'The corpse chronicler of Canterbury Cathedral'.**]

Everyone nodded and set about the soup; they all saw their Inspector in a very different light now.

"All that bloody horror, war and death because someone followed their ordained duty to protect the current timeline." Owen whispered to Alex who just shrugged her shoulders; "The BOSS may have plans, but humans will always throw a spanner into them and sometimes it takes a very brave human to correct things."

Owen nodded his agreement with that. Wilson grinned and held up his glass to her and muttered; "Amen to that."

THE END

EPILOGUE:
"A mission – if a failure – that could have changed everything. But Jericho and Team 74 succeeded in keeping the human timeline on track. The driver of the Arch-Dukes car was Leopold Lojka, but it was a certain Mayor Fehim Efendi Curčić who was actually guiding the convoy at the time. It appears that Lojka simply followed him; so, the error may have been someone else's change of 'free will'? But Jericho stood by his oath and loyalty to the temporal department regardless of his own feelings; little wonder he is highly regarded and trusted within the Department. ***SJW***

CHARACTERS:

Katrina Potoski wasn't able to travel back to 1914 again; her time portal had been taken from her. She graduated from the University and taught History for several years. She married a high ranking member of the Communist party in 1963 and had three children. She died in 2001 and her soul was collected and processed. It received no quarantine for her little time travelling escapade.

Gavrilo Princip was arrested at the scene following the murders. Three weeks too young for the death penalty, Princip was given a 20-year sentence, but contracted tuberculosis and died in jail in April 1918, at the age of just 23. His soul was collected and processed. It was quarantined for half a human century for the two murders.

Detective Tatiana Obski remained in the Moscow Police Service until 1966. That year she – with several friends – took a ski and hiking holiday in the Urals. She had a terrible accident and was seriously injured. She lingered for several months in a Moscow hospital but died of her injuries. Her soul was collected and processed.

Radovan Berković was charged with various acts of 'treason' in autumn 1914 and sentenced to 15 years in jail. He was released in 1919 and simply disappeared. He died in Constantinople in 1924. His soul was collected and processed.

Jana Jacimović was a police informer and had to flee Serbia at the end of the war; she had picked the wrong side and ended up working on a farm in Bulgaria. She died in 1929 and her soul was collected and processed.

Captain Advija Kovac was killed in 1915 fighting for Austro-Hungary. He had never married nor had children. His soul was collected and processed.

Dragon Milenković was killed in 1916 fighting for the Serbian cause against the Austrians. He had been a 'Double Agent' but his true loyalty lay with Serbia. His soul was collected and processed.

Zoran ? – This mysterious character's whereabouts or fate remains unknown to Human Records. But Owen was later to realize where he had smelt the man's strange pipe tobacco before; the elusive McIves smoked the same stuff! That would answer the question about how Katerina knew about the temporal detectives, if McIves was somehow involved in all this.

Jericho never – for whatever reason – didn't report McIves suspected involvement in this particular mission.

Franz Vukomanović survived the war – he fought on the Serbian side – and moved from his beloved Serbia in 1921. Nothing is known about his fate until his soul was collected and processed in 1931. The Collector reported that he had been shot several times and dumped in an alley; in New York City! He made no relevant comments to the Collector, at the time, about his murder. His soul was quarantined for a full human century for three murders he had committed. It appears he had joined a gang of Prohibition 'bootleggers'.

Comrade Commander Leon Nebcheski remained the Police Commander of the affluent Moscow District until he was found dead in his private car, in a quite Moscow Street in the winter of 1964. He had been shot through the back of the head – execution style – and it was believed he had uncovered something big on his current assignment; the brutal rape and murder of two young schoolgirls. His soul was collected and processed. He worked as a collector for a short time before being transferred to the Temporal Detectives Department. He is now a sergeant on Team 49 and is headed for promotion; he is quickly becoming a real asset to the department.

Wolfgang Lietcher - Jericho's old enemy - was believed to have been concerned in this, but no link was actually found. He remains a thorn in the side of Jericho and Team 74.

EPISODE 12: "THE CORPSE CHRONICLER OF CANTERBURY CATHEDRAL."

MISSION SUMMARY: "The ancient English cathedral of Canterbury is undergoing extensive renovation work for its Nine-hundred-year anniversary, since it was dedicated in 1077 AD. There is great excitement when workman find a medieval room bricked up behind an old wall. But the discovery reveals the remains of a woman - apparently bricked up with her books - whilst still alive! But history has no record of her and her newly found chronicles that could change the current timeline. Mr. Tibbs is sent to investigate."

NOTES: Contains strong language and combat violence.

TRIGGER WARNINGS. ALCOHOL, STRONG LANGUAGE, SEXUAL REFERENCES AND MILD VIOLENCE [including battle violence].

AGE 12+ ONLY. **30 Minutes reading time.**

1. THE FORGOTTON WOMAN AND HER DAMN BOOKS.

"What a damn bloody time to uncover something like this. We have the bloody Queen's visit to cope with [as part of her silver Jubilee celebrations] and now the press is all over us because of that damn woman and her damn books!" Lord David Price was not a happy man; he was responsible for overseeing the cathedral's part in the forthcoming National celebrations of her majesty's Queen Elizabeth II's twenty-five years on the throne. Now he had this to deal with. His assistant and Press Officer walked slowly by his side and retrained from smiling. Miss Jenifer Sallies had little time for her 'Boss' and the way he treated women; even one's that had been dead for almost six hundred years. No, that wasn't quite right; she had clearly been murdered almost six hindered years ago.

The pathologist's private & confidential report was quite specific; the woman had starved to death; bricked up behind that wall, left to die horribly in a small room surrounded by her writings and books that condemned her to death some 600 hundred years ago. But why had they done such a dreadful deed in such a holy place; a house of Jesus? To young Jenifer that was the real question to answer. She tried to placate her boss, before he has a nervous breakdown, and she gets lumbered with even more work and problems.

"The archbishop has arranged for a team of experts to look at her [the bricked-up woman] and try and find out what happened and hopefully; why." She spoke quietly to Lord David, who just grunted; "I thought we had enough of them crawling over the bloody woman already."

Jenifer sighed, but managed to smile; "Apparently, they are real experts in medieval times and have a doctor on the team, with an American expert on 'cold case' crime scenes - from New York - and the Professor is an acknowledged expert in medieval crime and justice. He'll be accompanied by his young assistant."

Lord David stopped and folded his arms, staring down the corridor towards the archbishop's small office in the Cathedral that had been set up for the Queen's Visit.

"Well, if it takes some of the bloody heat off me; then I'm fine with that. He [the archbishop] does run the place - well in name - and what he says, goes." He said and almost smiled; but didn't. The pair walked on, and Jenifer knocked on the door and did smile to herself; this could be really interesting. They slowly entered when told to do so.

Jenifer sat in her car and stared at the cleaning team, sprucing up the ancient stonework of the grand doorway. She fumbled in her big bag and pulled out the brown file. She really didn't like viewing the pictures - especially of the long dead woman - but made herself. It was apparent that the 'experts', who had been called initially to the scene, weren't too concerned about the woman's horrific death. They were in a frenzy over her manuscripts and papers; especially the two 'forbidden' books [forbidden by the medieval Catholic Church; the cathedral had been a Catholic place of worship then]. Everyone had long believed that no copies existed anymore; burnt in bonfires by the Holy Inquisition at the time.

In those turbulent times, any book that went against the Bible's explanation of existence was considered heresy and like human heretics; was burnt. She stared at the pictures and flicked through the various reports from the 'experts'. The woman had - apparently - worked out that the planets revolved around the sun; including the Earth. That was heresy back then; the Church taught that the Earth was the centre of the universe, and everything revolved around it and God's supreme creation; man. "Supreme creation my bum." She muttered to herself. That probably went up the Church's nose - at the time - especially that such incredible discoveries had been made by a woman, using mathematics', rational thinking, and logic. Little wonder the ignorant bastards murdered her.

She slowly closed the file and placed it back in her bag. The Church had issued no official statement about what her papers had contained and certainly didn't mention the forbidden books. Jenifer sighed and stared back at the workman, now packing up for the day. The major papers had all concentrated on the sensational finding of the woman's body in the ancient cathedral; few mentioned her books or why she was murdered. The Church still had very powerful friends; even in 1977.

Jenifer had one thing to smile about; she had a quiet drink with John Kennedy last night - he was a reporter for a local paper - about the mysterious woman and the lack of coverage about why she was apparently murdered. He loved the thought of a story about the Church - any story - and agreed to start digging around; about why the Church Authorities were so reticent about the woman. He was a good, dedicated reporter and knew immediately that there was another story behind the bizarre finding. He promised to keep her up to date with his findings and - of course - he would keep her name out of it. He always protected his 'sources'.

She slapped on her seatbelt and started her little Ford Escort car and drove from the private staff car park and headed for home; hoping that the new team of experts had more balls than the others who had looked at the scene. She was really interested in meeting the team's doctor; apparently a hardnosed, sassy, no nonsense woman. She actually grinned; that will get right up Lord Price's nose. She turned into her normally quiet street and found it packed with police and fire engines. She pulled over and jumped from her car.

A young constable was stopping traffic and turning vehicles back, his little 'Panda' car parked across the roadway. She walked straight up and asked what was going on. He sighed and pushed his cap back; "Big fire at a house down there. Went up like a bonfire; it could be arson, so this is now a crime scene Miss. You'll have to move on."

Jenifer stared down the road and could see a huge plume of dark smoke. "Which house was it?" She asked, adding; "I live down there at number 23." The constable stared at her and reached for his radio. "Delta 71 to Incident Control, come in please. Urgent message, over." A voice replied to go ahead. He said; "Incident Control from delta 71. I have the owner of the property with me now. She says she's lives at number 23. Over."

Jenifer just couldn't believe it; her bloody house was ablaze! He held the radio close to his ear and didn't smile; "I'm sorry Miss, but can you stay with me. Some CID officers are on their way to speak to you." Jenifer, still in a state of shock just nodded. The young constable lowered his radio and asked if anyone lived with her. She shook her head and said that she lived alone. The constable sighed and stared back down the road. He turned back to her and didn't smile; "So, whose body was found in the upstairs bedroom?"

Jenifer staggered back; someone had been found dead in her bloody bedroom! Two men approached her and flashed Warrant Cards; they identified themselves as Detective Inspector Gary Meadows and Detective Sergeant William Turner. The Inspector asked Jenifer to confirm her name and address, which she did.

The Inspector didn't smile and took hold of her arm; "Miss Jenifer Sallies, I am arresting you on suspicion of murder and arson. You don't have to say anything, but whatever you say will be taken down in writing and may be used in evidence. Do you understand that and do you have anything to say?"

Jenifer just stared at him and whispered; "Fucking murder and arson. You must be fucking Joking!" The two detectives weren't joking and took an arm each and walked her to their large blue Rover car. With Jenifer secured in the back with the Inspector, the sergeant pulled away heading for the police station.

They stopped at the next turning, which had a police car parked up with two uniform officers sitting in it. The young woman constable walked over and swapped places with the Inspector, who jumped in the front passenger seat. The sergeant set off again. The Inspector picked up the handset of the 'Westminster' radio and called the station; "We're coming in with the suspect now." Was all he said. Jenifer couldn't believe her ears; she was the bloody suspect in an arson and murder inquiry!

2. THE SUSPECT FOR THE NEW MURDER.

Jenifer sat in front of the big, uniformed sergeant and was shaking a little. She had actually never been in a police station; never mind the Charge Room. The sergeant laid out a large sheet and picked up his pen. He started to fill out the large form without comment. The Inspector told her to tell the sergeant her full name, date of birth, place of birth and current address. She whispered and was told to speak up which she did. She was taken to a cell by the young policewoman and searched. The woman officer called out to her Inspector; "House and car keys Guv. She has a car somewhere." She held up the keys and the Inspector - standing in the doorway - asked Jenifer where her vehicle was. Jenifer told him quietly. He took the keys and walked away.

The woman officer packed all she had taken from Jenifer into a large plastic bag and walked to the door. She slowly closed the cell door and locked it. Leaving a little 'wicket gate' open. Her face appeared at it; "I'll fetch you a cup of tea. How do you take it?" Jenifer stared about the dismal little room; bare apart from a wooden bed and toilet. She told the officer how she took her tea and slowly eased herself down on the hard bed. The unsmiling face disappeared. Jenifer sat - head in hands - and cried.

Jericho and Team 74 waited patiently at the small reception area of the Cathedral and watched the middle-aged lady nervously make several phone calls. Finally, she replaced the receiver and almost smiled; "There appears to be a real problem locating Miss Sallies, but Lord Price, her immediate Boss is on his way down." She eased herself down into her seat and almost smiled again. The team gathered together some distance away and waited. Owen discretely checked his mirror behind Wilson's broad back. The other's heard him curse and he placed the mirror back into his coat pocket. He whispered to the others; "It appears that Miss Jenifer Sallies murdered her boyfriend and burnt the body in her own house. Apparently, she even tortured the poor bastard before setting him alight. I've asked the Collector who attended to call us, see what he [the dead man] said about his homicidal girlfriend."

Jericho just nodded; "That's bit of a bloody co-incidence, isn't it? They find the woman bricked up here and suddenly one of the main witnesses to it all gets arrested for murder and arson. You know I don't believe too much in co-incidences. Something is not right here."

Wilson nodded; "I smell a big rat. The papers found around that woman will cause a huge outcry - even 600 years later - and yet, nothing has appeared in any of the papers, or TV stations. They just all cover the current Queen's Silver Jubilee celebrations. Now that is fucking strange."

"The Church in these times still has powerful connections with the 'Dark Side' and what the woman discovered all those years ago couldn't have been revealed then or now. As Wilson said, I smell a big rat. A dark big rat." Jericho spoke softly to the others, and they waited; for some time they waited. Finally, Lord Price arrived, looking grim. He gave Jericho and team no help whatsoever - in fact - he gave them the 'bum's rush' and said their assistance in the matter was no longer required. He didn't even apologise or say 'goodbye', he simply walked away.

They headed back to the van and sat in the car park, watching the preparations for the Queen's visit. They agreed on one thing; they all smelt a 'cover-up.

Owens's mirror buzzed and he answered it quickly; it was Helena, the Collector who had collected the murdered man's soul. Owen listened with some interest and thanked her. He wiped his face and sat back in his seat, clutching his mirror. He sighed; "We were right. The dead man was a journalist who had been contacted by Miss Jenifer Sallies over the lack of coverage over the dead woman. He had made some enquires with his 'contacts' and suddenly, he's bundled off the street by three big men. They beat and tortured him in a derelict garage; even pulling out his toe and fingernails. They 'water boarded' the poor bastard until he told them who had passed the story onto him. They then injected him with something and that was all he remembered until his soul was collected from the blazing house by Helena. He did say that the three men clearly knew what they were doing. Professional hit men."

Jericho nodded; "They're covering everything up again. They obviously mean business. They killed one poor bastard and have 'fitted up' his contact with his murder and as a bonus - for them - burnt her house down to destroy anything she may have hidden there. They are definitely professionals. Probably work for the Government of this time. There are plenty of 'Dark Side' devotee's in both the church and Government here and now."

Wilson turned to Owen; "What happened to Miss Sallies?" Owen checked Human Records on his mirror; he didn't smile. "Poor bloody cow was found guilty of murder and arson at the Old Bailey in January 1978. She served 22 years in prison and was released - on license - in 2000. She seems to have disappeared, but her soul was collected and processed in 2009." He lowered his mirror and shook his head; "Fucking bastards."

There was silence in the van and finally Alex said quietly; "Is that it? Are we going to do fuck all about this?" Jericho ran a hand over his face and stared out the windscreen at the magnificent old building. "You know we're not authorized to interfere with Human miscarriages of justice. She wouldn't be the first person to rot in prison for something she never did." Alex flopped back in her seat; "So that's fucking it. We do sod all!"

Jericho patted her arm; "I said we're not authorized. I didn't say we couldn't interfere a little bit with certain parts of this shitty story." He smiled. The team chuckled and Wilson started the van and they pulled away. He noticed immediately that they were being followed. Owen peered in the drivers wing mirror and grunted; "Three men in a black Rover car and I bet we know who those bastards are."

"They are going to have some fun, checking the plates on our van." Jericho chuckled. Owen looked puzzled; "I always wanted to know who Supplies register the vans to in different time periods?" Jericho turned and smiled; "They have just found out that his Holiness Pope Paul VI owns this particular van." Now that did make everyone laugh. Jericho sighed; "People, we now work for the 'Prayer of Liberty' Department of the Holy Roman Church, and I know just the man, who we can call on for semi-official assistance; Father Paradise Adams." [See episode: **'Sister Sarah dreams of demons.'**]

They booked into a very nice hotel; constantly watched by the men in the black Rover car. The first thing they did was to book dinner and find out if the bar served decent brandy; it did. The team sat by a window table and enjoyed their drinks. The waiter would call them when their table was ready. Owen was really interested in the night's menu - no surprise there - and was impressed. "I'm having the roast lamb, new potatoes and fresh mixed vegetables. Then the chocolate pudding and cream to follow." He looked up from his menu and smiled; "Those three murdering bastards have just sat at the table by the door."

Wilson couldn't help but laugh quietly; he had just noticed that Jericho had suddenly acquired a 'dog' collar. He was now Father Jericho Tibb's of the Vatican's 'Prayer of Liberty' Department. "Let's see how intelligent and subtle our murdering friends are." Jericho said quietly and called the waiter over; he whispered in his ear and the young man disappeared behind the bar.

Alex sipped her most welcome brandy and smiled at Jericho; "What are you up to?" She watched as the young waiter approached the men's table with a tray. He carefully placed three glasses upon the table and lit them with a match. "Fucking Sambuca's! Now that is one fucking subtle message Jericho!" The three men downed their drinks and raised their glasses at Jericho. They slammed them down and walked out.

"We stay together tonight and take turns on watch. I don't think they're very happy that we damn well know who they are and what they did." Jericho muttered and everyone agreed. Alex immediately said; "I'm the only lady here. I should have the bed - if you really are gentlemen - so there!" Owen groaned and smiled; "What bloody lady?" The team laughed and was called for dinner. The meal was excellent.

3. THE CORPSE.

Dr. Frank Gardener peered through the small window of the morgue and stared at the little group sitting in the waiting room. The pathologist turned to his young assistant and sighed; "The bloody Pope still carries weight around here despite old King Henry." The assistant just smiled. Frank walked back to the tray and nodded to the door; "Well, show them in." Peter strolled to the door and pushed it open; he stuck both hands in his white coat and said - without smiling - "This way please; the pathologist is ready for you." Everyone rose and walked in, assembling around the tray. Frank jerked the clean white cloth off to reveal a neat set of old bones.

"Exactly how old are these remains?" Father Adam's asked, pushing a hand through his thick grey hair; the other clutched his notebook and pencil. Frank gestured to them; "Give or take ten or fifteen years, the remains are about six hundred years old; approximately and from the state of the bones, I would say that she probably starved to death."

Owen peered closer and pointed out that the left leg appeared a little smaller than the right. Frank nodded - a little impressed - and said, "She appears to have suffered Polio as a child and would have had a pronounced limp as an adult. It was a common aliment six hundred years ago."

Jericho rubbed his chin; "How old was she when she died?" Frank folded his arms and shrugged his shoulders; "Maybe mid-twenties. But we do know that at some point, she had given birth." Alex looked sadly at the remains; "So she was someone's mother." Frank nodded; "Yes, but I found something that does make her special and probably a little unique." He smiled with a little satisfaction. Father Adam's placed his thin glasses on and took a close look. He nodded, pointing to the larger leg. "You can see where the damn limb healed."

Frank was impressed again; "That's right father; at some point she broke her leg and it healed. Quite incredible for the time she lived in." Father Adam's turned to the others; "Six hundred years ago, if you broke your leg, it was normally, well always, amputated."

Frank shrugged his shoulders; "Medical care wasn't much in those days. If you splintered a bone, it had to come off. Otherwise, you surely died of Sepsis - blood poisoning - they had no antibiotics." He actually chuckled; "They had sod all really; just plants and some magic." He pointed to the skull; "The teeth are in good condition; just two missing. No sugar in the diet." He asked if there were any more questions and Owen held up a hand; "I take it she was white European Sir?" Frank did smile; "You're on the ball young man. I am impressed. She was actually from the Middle East in origin. A chemical analysis of her teeth revealed she had a Middle Eastern diet - since childhood - and this is only speculation, but I would say Egypt or possibly Syria. Around there somewhere."

Alex pushed her mirror back into her coat pocket and smiled at the young assistant who gave her a strange look; he may have seen her mirror. Frank threw the sheet over the remains and that was the end of the session, and everyone gathered outside; talking quietly. Jericho said softly to Alex; "Who was she?" Alex looked about; they were the only people in the waiting room.

"According to Human Records those bones belonged to Ester Clemencies; a woman who was a mix of Jewish and Arab blood. She was born in Jerusalem in 1352 and there is no time of death; she is a Missing Soul. Now that's incredible because she died in her own time period and should have been collected."

"Unless she had sold her soul to the 'Dark Side' and they collected her." Wilson grunted, adding; "There are only two explanations for a missing soul; the 'Dark Side' owned it or you died out of your natural time period." Jericho nodded at that; "So, she died within her scheduled time, which means she was a follower of the 'Dark Prince', That makes this very interesting, especially with the rumours about her manuscripts and books. I smell something wrong here."

Father Adams finished scribbling in his notebook and replaced the thick elastic band that held it together. He removed his glasses and placed them back in his jacket. "I have to agree with Jericho. Something is wrong here. According to the pathologist she died in her mid-twenties, which means being born in 1352, she could have died around 1377 or thereabouts. Now that's some co-incidence; she died on the year that would have been an anniversary of the cathedral's consecration. Then exactly six hundred years later her remains are supposedly found in the Cathedral." He sighed; "Found with her books that call into question the Church's behaviour in those times to science and women. This could be a wonderful little incident for the followers of the Dark Prince to exploit."

Everyone agreed with that assessment; there were too many 'convenient' co-incidences to really be co-incidences. "It was planned to ask serious questions about the Church; back then and possibly now." Jericho muttered and the team headed for their van in the car park. Sure enough; the black Rover was there. Cheekily, Owen and Alex gave the men sitting in it, a cheery wave. Father Adam's admitted that he had been contacted by the Cardinal as soon as his plane landed at London Airport [now Heathrow Airport] demanding updates and assessments of the 'incident'.

"Whatever the reason for this; it has already stirred up a hornet's nest, cost a journalist his life and thrown an innocent woman in prison, so it is serious." Jericho reminded everyone; especially Owen and Alex, who ruefully smiled.

Jericho sat in the front seat and stared at the big black car and turned to Owen; "There must be more to this woman; find out about her family. The pathologist said she had given birth, so find out if there are any descendants and how many are on the Dark Side." Owen nodded and pulled out his mirror; "This may take some time." He said, tapping away. Wilson chuckled; "We're Temporal Detectives, we have all the time in existence!" Now that did make everyone laugh.

Father Adam's turned to Jericho; "What languages were her books in?" Jericho shrugged his shoulders; he didn't know. Owen looked up from his mirror and mumbled something. Father Adam's smiled and asked him to repeat what he said. Owen sighed, lowering his mirror; "They were all written in Latin except one; which was written in hieratic script."

Father Adam's just stared at him, then wiped his face with his hankie; "Are you sure Owen that it was Hieratic Script?" Owen nodded. Father Adam's sat back in his seat and wiped his face again. "That doesn't sound right. Hieratic Script was a simplified version of Ancient Egyptian hieroglyphics. It was dead and forgotten by the First century AD. It was originally used to write letters keep records and accounts. Then suddenly in the 1300's, a woman starts writing a manuscript in it - about scientific and technical subjects apparently - That doesn't make sense. No sense or logic at all."

Jericho rubbed his chin; "It's not the right language a well-educated woman of the Middle Ages would use?" Father Adam's nodded; "Not by a long way. In the thirteen hundreds, she would have written in her native language, old English or Latin. That's it. Writing a single book in Hieratic Script would seem so strange and probably impossible at the time."

Alex leaned forward; "So those books could have been written hundreds of years before the woman was even born?" Father Adam's nodded and whispered; "I wonder if she even knew what those so-called books of hers; actually said. Especially the one in the old Egyptian script." Jericho gestured for Wilson to start the van and head back to the hotel. "I think we may have to pay a visit to Ms Ester Clemencies and take a look at her library."

Owen coughed and lowered his mirror; "According to Human Records she had a son called Adam. His descendants are around today; scattered around Great Britain, America, Australia, Canada, and New Zealand. No one is particularly important to the timeline. But in this time & place, there is just one descendant of any note. A Professor Allan Fordham, he claimed to have discovered the vaccine that would cure both types of Diabetes. He was found hanging in his garage; no suicide note. The interesting thing is that his family claimed he wasn't suicidal but overjoyed at his discovery. But the Coroner at his inquest ruled - death by suicide - and said that all his missing research papers and reports had been destroyed by Fordham, to cover a massive fraud that he was preparing. Well, that's the official story; anyway."

"Wait a minute, his family says he wasn't suicidal, and all his research just disappeared. That sounds a bit strange to me." Wilson shouted back as he turned into the hotel car park.

Alex grunted with some contempt; "Come on people, switch your brains on. Some brilliant scientist says he found a cure for diabetes and is found hanging; all his research gone. He was bloody murdered by the big Pharmacy companies. They make billions every year keeping people alive; but not curing them. It doesn't make economic sense to lose that sort of income by offering a cure. For Christ sake, it's like having the bloody poacher's looking after the rivers and everyone wonders where the bloody fish went!" No one could argue with her.

Owen rubbed his face; he liked the logic and rationale of Alex's deductions and would take a further look at the case, when he had time.

4. PILGRIMS TO CANTERBURY; ENGLAND 1377.

The Supplies truck was waiting in the car park for the team. Old Joe smiled at everyone and gestured towards the big black Rover car; "Friends of your Inspector?" He asked a bemused Jericho, who enquired about what he had brought. They followed him into the truck. Like the lighthouse, it was enormous inside with fitting rooms, props and equipment; including Owens's favourite donkey; 'Freddie.' Jericho smiled at Owen - who was fussing over the donkey - and told Anna [the teams regular Costume Designer] to kit Owen out as Alex's 'Lady Maid'. "No lady of quality would travel without one in the period we're heading for. We can't call on young Ruth; she's on her Collectors Course." He explained to Wilson, who just grunted; "Well, on your head be it. If he goes strange, it's partially your fault." But did smile.

When everyone was dressed, Jericho operated his mirror and they disappeared to England in 1377, some miles from Canterbury cathedral. They gathered in the dark woods - despite the morning being sunny and clear - and Jericho briefed the team. "I'm Lord Tibb's, [no surprises there....] a powerful merchant who is on a pilgrimage to Canterbury, accompanied by his widowed sister and her maid. Wilson is Omar; a Christian Moor from Spain, also on a pilgrimage. Father Adam's is, well, he's Father Adam's! Our spiritual adviser and guide."

Everyone really admired the old man, jumping back in time with the team. As a living human, Jericho had to get special permission from Angel Margret. She didn't hesitate; the priest's qualities were well known to her; she admired the man greatly - as did most people - and told Jericho to look after him.

She was quite specific; "If anything happens to him and his soul is about to be lost to the Darkness; you call for a Knight - immediately - you have my permission to do that." Now that did really impress Jericho; few humans could boast having a Knight of God on standby! But it was very necessary; if the old priest died outside of his ordained time period, then his soul would be lost the darkness of real death. Only A Knight could recall his soul from there and restore him to life. Jericho had explained this very serious danger to Father Adam's and he still volunteered to go. "You and your team take that risk on nearly every mission you carry out for God. So, I think I can just this once." The old priest smiled and that was that.

Their wagon set off for the cathedral; Wilson was driving, with Lady Alexandra Cappanni and her maid bundled in the back. The damn thing had no springs, and they felt every rut and hole on the supposed road. Jericho rode a fine mare and Father Adam's walked with the donkey; feeding him carrots - purple carrots - and 'Freddie' really did like the old priest. They made their way through the forest and were surprised to find another wagon on the edge of the forest. Jericho halted his little convoy and rode over to the others; they were gathered around their wagon; talking quietly amongst themselves.

All their possessions were piled on the grass, chest's blankets, clothes and pottery. There was even a very old suit of armour; but beautifully maintained propped up against a small tree. It was clear that their wagon was stuck in a very deep hole. Jericho introduced himself and asked if he could be of assistance. The old Knight rose from the chest that he was sitting on and wiped his face; "Good Sir, we have emptied the damn thing, but still, it won't budge. I'm afraid we don't have the strength between us to lift it from the damn hole." He cussed the wagon and his old age, in equal measures. Jericho noted that the old Knight's party considered of the knight, a small boy called Simon accompanied by his 'nurse' Alice [a middle-aged woman with a very pock marked face] and the knights young Squire; a thin young man who smiled at everyone and was called Leofric.

Jericho waved his team over, and Wilson jumped down and joined him. Sir Robert De Morse really stared at Wilson and crossed himself. Alice grabbed the boy to her and backed away. The young squire just smiled. Jericho smiled broadly and introduced Omar; the Christian Moor from the Spanish Kingdom of Castile. With the young squire's help; Wilson and Jericho heaved the wagon out as Sir Robert encouraged the horse to pull. They all stood around smiling and were joined by Father Adam's, Lady Alex and her 'maid'. The young squire really did smile at the girls, especially the young maid.

Sir Robert thanked Jericho and insisted that dinner and drinks were on him, when they reached the next tavern. Jericho smiled and whispered to Wilson; "Bloody perfect. Now we are real pilgrims on a Canterbury pilgrimage with a real Knight to accompany us; it's perfect cover." Wilson had to agree with that.

Young Leofric was really impressed with Jacqueline [Alex's maid] - and a little surprised - as she helped lift the heavy chest back into the wagon, with little effort. She smiled at him; "I'm stronger that I look. A farm girl originally, so I'm use to hard work." He just nodded - and smiled of course - he was in love; again. He seemed to fall in love with most pretty young girls he met in the good Knight's service. He wanted to write poetry for her but couldn't afford parchment or a quill. So he would have to recite it; which he promptly did until told to shut up by Sir Robert.

"Bloody young twerp loses his heart every bloody ten minutes." He sighed, but did smile a little, as he spoke to Jericho.
Sir Robert confided to Jericho that Simon [his grandson] was all the family he had left after three wives and five children and three grandchildren. They were all dead except the boy. "That's why I'm on this bloody pilgrimage at my age. My last wife: Gwen had insisted - on her death bed - that I take the boy and together; pray for her soul at the great cathedral. She was most devoted to her devotions to God and Jesus." He just shrugged his shoulders and shouted at Leofric to be careful replacing his armour in the wagon. "I feel sorry for 'Thunder' my old war horse; pulling a bloody wagon at his age and after all the good service given to me on the battlefields of the King." He clearly loved his horse as much as Owen adored 'Freddie' the donkey.

Wilson just grunted at Jericho; "What is it with you English and their bloody animals?" Jericho didn't answer and the convoy headed up the 'Canterbury Road' - slowly - they would have to stop overnight at the Pilgrim Tavern called the 'King's Horn'.

Sir Robert told Jericho that the Innkeeper was an old soldier called Richard Catchpocket and they knew each other well from the Kings wars.

"He's a good man. He was a man to stand with when the fighting was fierce. Really good with an axe; could cleave open a Frenchman's chest with one swing, even if the bastard was wearing armour!" Jericho just smiled; somewhat disturbed by that thought but knew that Medieval battlefields were no playgrounds.

They reached the tavern at dusk; everyone was more than happy to see the tavern appear. Especially Alex and Jackie who moaned constantly about their backsides! Medieval journeys were hard on the arse - by horse or wagon - and the girls were really glad to jump from the wagon and stretch. Young Leofric stood staring at the pair and really needed to write more poetry; well, recite it anyway. He had delicious daydreams of jousting for their honour in the old Knights armour astride 'Thunder'. He grimaced at the thought of trying to mount 'Thunder'; the damn horse didn't like him and always tried to take a bite, even when he fed and groomed him.

Richard the Innkeeper greeted the old knight like a long-lost brother and they embraced warmly. Sir Robert introduced his new friends and Richard welcomed them too, shouting for his serving girl - Mary - to bring ale. They stood and drank from leather jugs; the 'ladies' were given much smaller cups and both Alex and Jackie weren't too happy about that! But they kept those thoughts to themselves. They trooped into the tavern and were immediately served pies, cheese, bread and apples. The old knight and the Innkeeper sat talking about the old days. Mary - the young serving girl - showed Alex and her maid to their bedroom; it had one bed. Both giggled at that. "The bloody big chair for me then." muttered Jackie as Alex bounced upon the bed; well, she didn't bounce – the bed was like a stone. "I think you've the best bed Jackie, should we toss for it?" Jackie just grinned and shook her head and patted the chair.

The evening meal was roast chickens, leeks, carrots, bread and plenty of beer followed by cheese and apples. Everyone ate with their knives and fingers. The entertainment was a scruffy looking 'minstrel' who sang ballads about battles and the gruesome killing of Frenchmen.

"Bloody charming. Does he actually know any happy songs?" Alex asked, sipping her rough beer. Jackie whispered; "There are romantic ballads about in these times, but clearly hadn't reached here yet." She quite enjoyed the beer; but it did remind her of the dark days in the monastery.

A big Welshman sang with a stunning voice and received much applause and some pennies for his efforts. He was on the 'Pilgrimage' too with his family and liked the look of Alex; he was a widower and asked Jericho several times about the status of his 'sister'. At one point he slapped a bag of gold coins upon the table and whispered with Jericho. Alex was not impressed to learn later that he had offered serious money for her hand in marriage.

"I could have bought a decent house and a couple of horses with the coin offered in this time. He appears to own a large chunk of what will become Cardiff. "Jericho told her with a small smile. The big man made sure that Alex knew he had donated his 'earnings' [and a small amount from himself] to the local priest for the orphans of the city. She still wasn't impressed and – politely – told him that she was a wealthy widow in her own right and would decide for herself who her next husband would be.

The fact that she would make her own decision shocked the Welshman deeply; he had never heard of such nonsense! He wandered off a very disappointed man.

The evening finished with a toast to the new king, and everyone headed for their rooms. Jericho and Wilson sat chatting with Richard. Jericho asked if anything important was happening at the Cathedral. The Innkeeper nodded and didn't look happy. He lowered his voice despite the place being empty apart from them three, sitting by the dying fire. He pulled them close and sipped his beer, there was a trial underway of a high born foreign woman; charged with heresy, blasphemy and denying the teachings of the church. Now that really did interest Jericho and Wilson and they encouraged Richard to explain further.

5. THE BOOKS OF ESTER CLEMENCIES.

"Apparently she told the local priest - an ill-educated man for a damn priest - that parts of the bible were wrong. Now that takes real balls; especially for a woman." Richard sipped his ale and wiped his rough face. "She told him that she could prove - with mathematics - that the earth and all the other planets revolved around the Sun and that the earth was just one of many such balls in the darkness; special only by having life on it."

He poured more ale from a huge clay jug and chuckled; "The dumb priest ran to the bishop and told him everything the woman had said. She was arrested by the bishops men the following afternoon. They took all her books and locked her up in a small room in the cathedral." He leaned back and sighed; "The Bishop ordained a trial was necessary and so, two other senior churchman were called. Some justice: having your case heard by three men who apparently believe every word of the bible is absolute truth."

Jericho nodded; "What has happened to her?" Richard poured more ale and folded his arms. "She could find no man willing to defend her or speak for her. So, she wanted to defend herself, but the three apes wouldn't allow a mere woman to address the court."

The entire prosecution evidence of her guilt was the priest producing his bible and reading from it! She kept interrupting him and so the bishop ordered her gagged in court. They wouldn't let her produce any of her papers - they had confiscated them, calling them works of the Devil - and so the farce proceeded.

But they did produce some papers, found in her house that contained writing no one could decipher or understand. The bishop declared that the writing was in the devil's own hand and so unreadable to humans!

"Utter bollocks!" He finished his ale and stood; "The final day of trial is tomorrow; unless she can find some learned man to represent her; she'll burn at the stake."

Richard grunted; "They want to rush the trial through before the celebrations of the new King's Coronation [Richard II]. They don't want any evil lingering about the place. Now that has made me laugh. There is a real stench of evil about the place; the archbishop has stood well back from the trial."

He left Jericho and Wilson finishing their ale and went to bed.

Wilson rubbed his chin; "Well, we know that she was never burnt at the stake for her supposed crimes. So, I wonder what happened at the trial." Jericho emptied his leather tankard and wiped his mouth. "Maybe she found someone to take on the bishop and his cronies?" He really did smile, and Wilson just sighed. He knew that look on Jericho's face well. "I keep forgetting that you were a bloody lawyer." He muttered and the pair retired to their room for the night.

The group of pilgrims arrived in the city the following afternoon. The major topic of conversation was the coming coronation and subsequent celebrations for the new King. Sir Robert managed to secure lodgings in a big tavern by the North Gate. The tavern owner: Percival Parish was also an ex-soldier. He was a big man with no hair, few teeth and one good eye. A jagged scar down his face bore testament to fighting on the old King's battlefields. But there was something about the man that local women liked; it was rumoured that he had several 'bastard' children about the city.

Apparently killing Frenchmen wasn't his only talent!

He welcomed the old knight like another long-lost brother. Percy took an immediate liking to Alex and especially to Jackie. His one eye ran over her, and he smiled broadly. He asked the knight about her on several occasions. His interest caused quite a giggle amongst the team – except Jackie – and the old inn keeper made sure he hung around Jackie. Whatever the young girl wanted she could have; he instructed his servants.

Wilson asked Alex if she was a 'little miffed' by 'Jackie' stealing her thunder; men usually fell about her feet. But Alex just grinned; "No, I'm fine. Jackie can certainly have old Percival. I'm more than happy about that." And she meant it!

Jericho with Wilson in tow made discrete inquiries about Mistress Ester Clemencies and wasn't too happy about what he discovered. Apparently, she had arrived in the city just last year; a widow woman of some means, she had purchased a fine house in the city and employed no less than nine savants. It was rumoured that it had taken a full day to unload her passions from several wagons. The number of books she owned drew real comment. Books were very, very expensive items in medieval times and she appeared to own a King's ransom worth of them.

That fact alone would make the church authorities notice. A woman with books wasn't considered a good thing!

Jericho rubbed his chin as the team sat for their evening meal; "Maybe I'm a cynical old git; but I get the feeling that Mistress Ester wanted to come to the notice of the Church authorities. Now that's not good since we know she's a follower of the Dark One." He spoke quietly to the others and Father Adam's pushed his chicken stew about with a spoon and sighed.

"I still don't understand why they bricked her up in the Cathedral as punishment; normally they would just burn her and her books at the stake, why such a different punishment?" He threw the question out to the group. Wilson broke the crusty bread with his big hands and nodded; "If they had burnt her, then we wouldn't have a mission." Jericho leaned back on his rough chair and smiled; "I think our big friend has hit the nail on the head there."

Jackie dabbed her mouth with a hankie and leaned forward; she spoke quietly. "I think we should really take a look - a close look - at those books of hers. Find out what they really contain and perhaps who actually wrote them." Jericho agreed with that. Alex tapped the table with a slender finger and smiled; "Our Jackie discovered from old Percival that the books are under lock and guard in a small antechamber; near where the trial is taking place. The guard is a bored young fellow who believes he's bit of ladies' man. I think Jackie and I could get a look at them."

Wilson chuckled; "You two together could get the guard on Fort Knox to unlock." Jericho leaned forward and smiled; "Let's have a look at that those forbidden books; over to you ladies."

The boys lay about the big bedroom and Wilson checked his mirror whilst Jericho and Father Adam's played chess with a couple of flickering candles for light. There was a soft knock and Wilson jumped up, pushing his mirror into a pocket. It was a giggling Alex and Jackie. They crept in and Jackie held up her mirror and managed to stop herself smiling.

"It took exactly three minutes to persuade the boy to let us take a look. He actually thinks he's bloody Casanova of the dark ages." She said and tapped her mirror. Alex flopped on the bed and chuckled; "We're supposed to meet him at a wonderfully named tavern; The 'Horse's Rump' tomorrow night for drinks and other things!" Jericho just nodded and gestured to Jackie's mirror; "What have we got?"

Jackie eased herself down on a rough chair and didn't smile; "The covers are wonderful fakes, and the contents are bloody photocopies!" She consulted her mirror; "Copies of 16th and 17th century books about nearly everything; astronomy, witchcraft, medicine, even one about resurrecting the dead and curing plague with boiled dog testicles! But we know that Ester has not time travelled; so, who gave her the damn books?"

Father Adam's tapped Jericho's arm: "That doesn't make sense. The books discovered with her, were the genuine articles, experts took a good look at them, and they would certainly have spotted bloody photocopies!" Jericho nodded; "I'm beginning to think that the little bricked up room didn't originally contain a dead woman. Just books that someone desperately tried to save and preserve."

Father Adam's lowered himself on the bed next to Alex and wiped his face and neck; "I think we need to discover why those books – the original and genuine books – are so important and who hid them away." Wilson looked up from his mirror and said simply; "Someone switched the fake ones for the real things just before the room was discovered. Since the only way into the room had been bricked up for hundreds of years, it was done at the time of the discovery or…." He smiled and added; "Or we have a time traveler who had the ability to jump into that room after the woman died and replace the fakes with the genuine articles. But again; why?"

Alex sat bolt upright; "Now that does make sense. All those original books are rare but known about. Copies have survived down the centuries, so which one was unique and the only copy – apparently – in existence. If there is such a book, then that's the key to all this."

Jackie agreed; "All we have to do is compare the books that were found – all originals – and the fakes we've just seen." She started to tap her mirror with some determination.

"That young man…woman is going to be a fine temporal detective." Father Adam's spoke quietly to Jericho who smiled and replied; "I would have thought you would have disapproved of men dressing and acting as women." Father Adam's grinned and shrugged his shoulders; "We're all God's creatures Jericho." Jericho patted the old priests arm and smiled broadly; now he knew why he really did like and admire this true man of God.

Jackie held up her mirror; "Singulari vitae interdum Anebos Thebarum sacerdos et propheta by the great Josephus, apparently written about 71AD. It's genuine and we all know who bloody Anebos was." [See episode; ***'Tomb ES-42'***] Father Adam's sighed; "And we all know who Titus Flavius Josephus was. He was actually writing just after the death of Jesus Christ. He's works are accepted as some of the best about the first century AD."

Jericho groaned; "Bloody Anebos again. I thought we had laid that bugger to rest. This spells trouble if that book is translated and exposed to the world of 1977." Alex folded her arms; "So it's genuine – the book I mean – about the Christ like prophet from ancient Thebes; a forerunner of Jesus by about a thousand years."

Jackie lowered her mirror; "Probably got the damn story from some old Egyptian priests; there were still some around in the early first century. I wonder why the early Christians didn't comment on it, coming from such a respected writer."

Jericho sat on the bed and didn't smile; "Josephus book was slung out, along with several others at the Conference in 325AD which formed the basis of the modern bible. The strange story of Anebos wasn't wanted; they had Christ. The emperor was a [Constantine I] bloody pagan and yet he had direct input into the books of the Christian faith. Gospels by Judas and Mary Magdalene were also thrown out."

"Owen, sorry Jackie, find out who are the three judges sitting on this case. There's someone of real power operating in the background here and we need to find out who they are." Jackie nodded and returned to her mirror. There was a loud and frantic knocking at the door and Wilson opened it slowly, hand on his sword hilt.

Young Leofric spilled through the door distressed and shouting. Jericho calmed him down and he blurted out his story. Jericho just groaned loudly; this was a turn up for the books. Apparently, the old knight Sir Robert had attended the ongoing trial and had suddenly interrupted proceedings by taking a bloody oath in front of everyone to defend the woman, with trial by combat!

Jericho just shook his head; "The daft old bugger will have to fight another knight – chosen by the church – to the death and if he wins, the church will have to free her. They consider the outcome of such a fight a decision by God." He asked Leofric when all this will happen.

"Tomorrow at noon in the city's main marketplace; my master will face Sir John Gavell, the churches most fanatical knight, who likes to hunt down witches in his spare time." The young man accepted some beer from Alex and sat on a rough chair; he knew that his old master stood no chance against the dark knight.

Jericho folded his arms and said simply; "Oh fuck!"

6. TRIAL BY COMBAT.

The big tavern was packed that night. Jericho got nowhere trying to convince the old knight to drop his insane idea. Sir Robert steadfastly refused and drank his beer and sang songs from his youth. It was Alex talking quietly with Mistress Alice who uncovered the truth about the knight's sudden desire to defend a woman he had never even met.

The team gathered in Jericho's big room just after midnight - once young Jackie had managed to escape the amorous attentions of the tavern owner – and Alex told the whole sorry tale that Alice had confided in her. After several flagons of ale, all purchased by Alex of course.

Alice confided that her master was suffering from a 'blood disorder' and had been told by various 'surgeons' that it would end in death, a very unpleasant death. So, the old knight had decided to go out on his own terms, sword in hand fighting for a good cause. From the details that Alice gave of the actual illness, Alex believed the old man was suffering from bowel cancer, totally untreatable and incurable in the time period. He would die a terrible death with a great deal of pain and suffering.

The team listened in silence until Wilson muttered; "Brave old bugger. I admire a man who intends to go in the way he wants." No-one could disagree with that sentiment. It was a very subdued team that went to their beds that night.

It appeared most of the town had gathered in the small field that warm morning; they stood in little groups and spoke quietly amongst themselves. The trial judges sat on a hastily constructed podium on decorated chairs. They were surrounded by several guards and the three men sat in silence until the prisoner was brought from her cell and held between two burly soldiers with chains about her feet and hands.

She was still gagged to prevent her calling for the Devil's assistance or disrupting the proceedings. Jericho noted that she didn't appear so happy about the mad old knight leaping to her defense. He wondered what the significance of that was. Jackie whispered to him about what the amorous pub owner had told her; he had it on good authority from one of the Church guards that Ester had demanded the court ignore the obviously crazy old man and continue her trial.

Jericho wondered why she had done that. Jackie almost smiled; "Apparently, if the good knight dies in her defense, then the court will know she's guilty and they have to pass the correct sentence required by law; burning at the stake with her cursed books thrown onto the flames to join her in hell." She looked about to make sure she wasn't overheard; "If old Sir Robert hadn't interfered, they would have been merciful – she chuckled at that – and just bricked her up to die. I wonder if Sir Robert has – unwillingly – messed up the Dark Side's plans."

The pair was joined by the rest of the team and Father Adam's told Jericho that the old knight refused to change his mind despite the last-minute plea's by his staff [Alice and Leofric] and himself. "He's set his mind to die with dignity and honour this day." Father Adam's said softly and wiped his face. He had managed to see the book about 'Anebos' and confirmed to Jericho that it was a copy – fake – but a very good fake.

Jericho sighed; "Well that confirms that someone swaps the fakes over after Ester is bricked up; to be found centuries later by experts and scholars who will declare them authentic and that will change history, expose the church to more scandal and judgment. A very clever plan indeed by the Dark Side."

A couple of shabby trumpeters sounded their horns and Sir John

Gavell appeared in full armour; his helmet held in one hand and his sword in the other. He knelt before the three judges and held up his sword, swearing to defend Christ, the Church and Justice. He received little support or applause from the crowd. They knew this evil man by reputation and deeds. When he wasn't defending 'mother church' his was seeking out young girls to rape and burn as witches. He also liked to collect the taxes owed to the church authorities by torture and murder. He was growing wealthier each year and now owed houses and estates in both Kent and Essex.

Most people said his heart was as black as his armour.

The crowd cheered and applauded enthusiastically as Sir Robert appeared. They were ordered to be silent by the leading judge who blessed Sir John. There was no such blessing for a quiet Sir Robert who pulled on his helmet. Alex noted the smile as his face disappeared beneath the iron helmet.

Jackie gripped Jericho by the arm; "The head judge is Bishop William of Winchester and a known supporter of the Dark prince. The two other judges [a rich merchant and a local Baron] are both clean. It's also known that the bishop is a collector of ancient manuscripts. Apparently, it's rumoured that his collection contains several works that the church has outlawed. That's our man, I think."

Jericho nodded and had a pretty good idea where Ester had received her copies from. "Check if there are any breeches of the timeline around him." He said quietly, But Jackie stopped and gestured to the two knights; the fight was on.

Leofric helped his master mount 'Thunder' and handed up his lance. The old knight patted the boy and said something, then slammed down the visor on his helmet. Sir John's squire had done the same for his master. The two knights stood at the edges of the field and waited for the 'Herald' to call for the fighting to start. The Herald rode into the centre of the field carrying a lance with a single black flag attached. He held it up and shouted if both men were ready. Both Sir John and Sir Robert lifted their lances to signal that they were.

The Herald waved his lance up and down, shouting; "By God's grace, let justice be done!" He lowered his lance until the tip touched the grass. Both knights spurred their mounts and thundered towards each other, lances at the ready.

They came together almost exactly in the middle of the field. The crowd screamed and shouted as the lances crashed against the opposite knights small shield. The two passed each other - both apparently unharmed - and the pair turned to face each other again. The pair came together again and there were more screams and shouts as Sir Robert fell from his mount and lay still on the grass. Sir John threw down his broken lance and slipped carefully from his horse; pulling his sword from the saddle.

The crowd almost held its breath but broke into cheers as Sir Robert staggered up and called for his faithful horse to come. Thunder - limping badly - pulled up next to his master and Sir Robert grabbed his sword. Just in time because Sir John was almost upon him. The two swords met in midair and caused little sparks to fly. Sir Robert was forced down on one knee and only just stopped Sir John's sword from crashing down on his exposed shoulder.

He pulled himself up and the two men circled each other; swords at the ready. They came together with real brutality and violence. But young Sir John was the stronger and he managed to catch Sir Robert across the left knee, and everyone could see blood running freely down the his leg. But the old knight struck back with strength found from somewhere and caught Sir John a telling blow across the shoulder. They both staggered away from each other and then Sir John came again. He wouldn't be stopped this time and with his sword gripped in both hands drove the blade down and caught Sir Roberts injured leg.

Sir Robert fell awkwardly on his back and Sir John seized his chance and standing above the prostrate knight brought his sword down on his left shoulder. Everyone could hear the screams across the field as Sir John repeatedly drove the sword through the old knights shoulder and finally just below the neck of the helmet, causing a big spurt of blood to cover the old knight. Sir John stepped away and held his sword aloft shouting his victory.

Few of the crowd applauded his bloody victory. Sir John walked over to Thunder and drove his sword through the horse's neck, the huge blood spurt covered his helmet and chest armour. The horse collapsed next to his dead master. Normally, the vanquished knight's horse would be kept as a prize by the victor. but Sir John had decided that the old - and now lame – horse was of no value to him. Now that did turn the crowd against him. They were booing and screaming with anger. Church soldiers had to confront them with swords draw and spears at the ready. The head judge jumped from his chair and ordered the field cleared.

Jericho wiped his face and stared at his mirror discretely; the fight had taken less than six minutes. Only the Temporal detectives could see Kate the Collector and Sir Robert's soul disappear into the light.

There was now sporadic fighting amongst the town's people and the church soldiers. Percival Parish told the team to follow him – especially young Jackie! – And take cover in his tavern. Everyone pushed into the quiet pub and Percival bolted the doors and covered them with two big wooden seats; aided by Wilson.

Percival asked for silence, and everyone could hear the shouting; "A bloody night curfew until dawn, anyone found outside will be arrested. They're shouting that the witch and her books will burn tomorrow at noon."

Jericho slumped onto a rough seat by the shuttered window and didn't smile; "If Ester and her books burn tomorrow, then that's the end of this mission. If she dies in the flames, then she won't be found bricked up. End of story." Alex sat down slowly next to him and nodded; "That brave old man [Sir Robert] has saved us a lot of trouble."

Jackie had managed to escape old Percival [who went to fetch bread, cheese and beer] and joined them at the table. "Not quite over, I think. All they will burn is fakes; who has the originals and where are they now? Don't we need to find them? Especially that bloody book about Anebos."

Jericho nodded at that and rubbed his chin, smiling as Father Adam's joined them. Wilson was by the door, keeping watch through the gaps in the wood. He shouted over; "The church soldiers have cleared the streets; it appears all quiet now."

Percival had appeared with a tray laden with beer flagons, bread and cheese. He served Jackie first – with a big smile – and told

Jericho that it was on him. He smiled again at Jackie, who just sighed and sipped her beer while Alex managed to restrain some giggles which desperately wanted to escape.

Jericho asked Percival if there were any strangers hanging around the trial who seemed odd or strange. Percival laughed at that and nodded; "Yeah, that's easy; you lot!" he laughed to himself and swilled his beer with some enthusiasm. He then stood slowly and raised his flagon. His was quite solemn. "Here's to gallant Sir Robert, a true Knight." Everyone rose and lifted their tankards in memory of the old man.

They sat in silence for a few minutes and then Percival tapped the rough table with his empty tankard; "You say odd or strange Sir?" Jericho nodded and leaned forward as Percival did the same. "Well, there is one that comes to mind. He turned up the day they dragged Mistress Ester before the magistrate. A big, tall fellow with a scarred face; well dressed, like a merchant but carrying a good quality sword and dagger; he looks like he knows how to use both. Paid for his board and lodging in silver coin, asked old Tom the Blacksmith to re-shoe his big dark horse. Asked lots of questions about Mistress Ester did he."

He rose from the table and went to fetch more ale. Jericho called after him; "Did he give anyone his name and why he was in the town?" Percival stopped in the doorway and nodded; "Said he was called Ralph Coldhands and he trades in books." He disappeared into bar to fetch another tray of beer. Everyone looked at each other and Jericho smiled, saying quietly; "Well, I think we'll have a little chat with this Mister Ralph Coldhands."

7. THE BOOK TRADER AND THE BISHOP.

Just after dawn, the team made its way towards the cathedral [lost amongst the crowds of pilgrims] and they noted the church soldiers out in force, guarding certain points around the town. They stopped in the market square and watched several men driving a big wooden stake into the ground and placing plenty of wood around it. That made Alex shudder a little; Ester may belong to the Dark Side, but no woman should suffer such a horrific fate. The team hurried pass into the cathedral.

There was an early morning mass under way and the team sat right at the back. Father Adam's had disappeared from the cloisters and into the inner sanctum of the cathedral, where only church people went. It was old Percival slipping onto the pew next to Jericho that delivered the news they had been waiting for. In the tavern, 'The Horse's Rump', the bishop and a certain mister Ralph Coldhands were having a full breakfast and clearly enjoying each other's company.

He then whispered to Jericho certain news that he wanted to keep from the ladies; it appears that several of the church soldiers guarding Ester had got drunk and raped her, only stopping when their relief turned up, who were all sober and didn't approve of what was going on. Apparently, the Bishop had forgiven the men and just fined them a few pence for being drunk on duty!

"She was badly injured and will be carried to the flames on a litter. Her books have been bundled into a bag which has been painted with tar to help it burn. When the flames are high enough, the bishop himself will throw the bag of books into the flames." Percival crossed himself – which he didn't do often – and smiled broadly at Jackie.

Jericho whispered his thanks and the team gathered outside. He bought them up to date with Percival's news. "I have a strong suspicion that the bishop and the book trader are discussing who pays what for the books which will never been tossed on the bloody flames. They certainly won't be in that bag he [the bishop] throws into the fire."

They were joined by Father Adam's, wiping his face and neck. "I've found the little antechamber that was bricked up. Take a guess what it's used for at the moment." He muttered with a little smile. No one knew. He smiled broadly; "It's the bloody Arch-Bishop's privy!" That caused a little ripple of laughter amongst the group. The old priest continued; "They're building him a lovely new one in his private apartments here and I expect they will simply brick it up, if they can't think of a new use for such a small room."

Wilson rubbed his face; "Perfect opportunity for someone to place the books in there, so they're found in 1977 when the restoration works are carried out." Jericho nodded; "I suspect it will be our book trader or the bishop that does that. Alex and Jackie; get over to that bloody tavern and find out who the book trader really is." Both girls nodded and were surprised to be joined by Father Adam's. "You two ladies will be much safer if accompanied by a man of God." He waved his wooden crucifix about his neck and added; "This does actually carry real authority in this time and place!" The three set off for the tavern - arm in arm - whilst Jericho and Wilson set off to find Leofric and the others of the old knight's retinue. They found Leofric and the boy Simon heading towards the south gate. It appears that Mistress Alice had disappeared during the night, abandoning the boy to his fate. Leofric told them that several tradesmen and merchants of the town had gathered together and would pay for the old knight to have decent burial in a local parish church.

Jericho asked Leofric about the boy. He sighed and patted the boy on the head; "I'll take him back to my father's farm. He can live with my family until he's grown, then he can decide for himself what he does." Jericho slipped Leofric a small bag of silver coins and thanked him for his kindness and loyalty to his old master. Leofric didn't smile but took the coins slowly. "I know he [the old knight] didn't think much of me as his squire, but I adored the old sod. I'll look after the boy until he's grown, that's my duty now."

Wilson and Jericho watched the pair disappear through the busy south gate onto the London Road. "Now he probably would have made a real knight." Wilson said softly and Jericho could only agree. They headed back to the cathedral, where they had agreed to meet up with Father Adam's and the girls.

They passed a couple of ragged beggars rolling in the mud; apparently fighting over some bones thrown out of nearby kitchen. A couple of equally scruffy dogs joined in; they won. They turned from the strange - and a little humorous sight - and were now facing Mister Ralph Coldhands, standing right in front of them, clutching three or four books. By his shoulders were two burly church guards. Jericho and Wilson bowed a little and stood to one side. Ralph stared long and hard at the pair; especially Wilson and walked away hurriedly, looking behind him several times.

Wilson rubbed his chin and didn't smile; "That bugger looks familiar, but I don't why." Jericho shrugged his shoulders; he had only recognized him by his scar, clothes and books. There couldn't possibly be two men of that odd description in

Canterbury at the same time. But Jericho knew one thing for certain; 'Ralph' had certainly recognized Wilson from somewhere and that could mean he was the time-traveler they were after.

They joined the girls at the strangely named tavern and asked where the good father was. "He was joined by two local priests who insisted he join them for breakfast and mass. He couldn't resist taking part in a bloody medieval mass for some reason." Alex explained and Jackie couldn't wait to inform them about what her mirror had discovered about 'Ralph Coldhands'. Jericho sighed; "What's the real identity of our time travelling friend?" He asked a surprised Jackie.

"I won't even ask how you always know these bloody things, but your right. He's real name is Giovanni Romano, and he was born in 1884, in Naples. My mirror picked up a time portal somewhere on him. He's a missing soul; he missed his dispatch date in 1933."

Wilson sighed; "I remember him now. I was the Detective Constable on Stella Longstreet's team and we dealt with a bunch of Satan worshippers in 1910 that was run by a woman from 2028. He [Giovanni] was a seller of rare books at the time, mostly on the occult and witchcraft. But we got her and most of the Coven, but I know that Giovanni was one of a pair that escaped. He must have jumped, but I'm sure we located the time portal the woman was using and closed it."

Jericho just sighed and folded his arms; "That bloody complicates matters now. We need to close his portal and return him to his own time to meet his departure on time." He stared across the square and saw that little groups of people were gathering to watch the witch burn. "I take it nobody wants to watch the show. Let's go people."

Everyone agreed with that and Jericho slipped the taverns serving girl some pennies to inform the old priest that his friends had returned to their lodgings. That's when Father Adam's appeared - walking quickly – from the cathedral. He gestured from them to follow him and bloody quickly. They did so without questions.

They followed the panting old priest to the huge stable complex at the rear of the cathedral and gathered around him. "You've been exposed by that fellow Coldhands. He's informed the bishop that he recognized Wilson from a previous witch trial and you're here to try and the save the witch. It appears that the bishop is only involved in this to sell Ester's books. He just wants the money. He's ordered your arrest; that's you and Wilson, with the girls of course."

"Fuck!" was all Jericho said and that's when they saw smoke billowing up from the square. Father Adam's crossed himself and gestured to the stable that contained their carriage, horses and of course; Owens's favourite donkey; Freddie. "I think we best get off the streets. There will be church soldiers all over the place once they finish the burning." Everyone disappeared into the stable complex. The place was empty; everyone was at the witch burning.

Jericho pulled open their carriage door and stood on the step; "Right, everyone but me and Jackie will jump back to the lighthouse. Wilson will get Father Adam's home. Now me and Owen will change and tackle that bastard Giovanni and close his time portal. No one will recognize Owen dressed as a young man now. They certainly won't recongnize me; I'm a master of disguise when the time calls for it." Everyone just sighed at that.

They said their goodbyes and vanished. Owen had to chuckle at the disguise that Jericho wore. He was now a travelling minstrel complete with lute and funny hat. Owen was dressed like any young man of the period and carried a small drum and flute. They made their way from the stable and passed several church soldiers: stopping groups of men who had ladies with them. They weren't having much success and fights almost broke out. Jericho actually went up to a couple of soldiers standing by the Baker's and asked directions to Percival's tavern. The solders told him to 'piss off' and went back to talking about the witch and her gang of accomplices. "The big black man will be easy to find; unless he paints himself white!" The older one laughed loudly at his own words. The younger one just grinned and scratched his lice ridden crotch with some vigor.

Jericho and Owen reached Percival's tavern without being stopped by a single church soldier or officer. They passed a couple of town crier's ringing their bells and shouting about a reward of several silver pieces for the gang of warlocks and witches. They sat in the tavern and drank some beer. Little

Helen, the serving girl told them that the landlord [Percival] was always looking for entertainment in his tavern and food was included with the lodging. Jericho strummed his lute and leapt to his feet. Owen could only watch in amazement as the normally restrained Jericho sung and danced on the tabletop!

Owen had to restrain himself from laughing out loud; Jericho was singing the 'Good Ship Venus' – the very naughty version! - The crowd loved it, shouting and applauding. Owen shrugged his shoulders and jumped on the table, joining in with his drum. Percival stood in the doorway grinning; this pair of minstrels were certainly worth their lodging and beer. They would get their hat filled with a few coins tonight.

They lay in front of the small kitchen stove and warmed their feet. Owen held up his hat and giggled a little; "We made four and a half penny's tonight. That is really good money for this time and place; maybe the equivalent of sixty or seventy pounds." He dropped the hat down and wriggled his toes, enjoying the heat. Jericho was consulting his mirror; "The timeline has reverted to its original course. Ester's body was never discovered, but her bloody books were. Our job's still not done yet."

He pushed the mirror into his shabby but colourful jacket and sighed; "Now, how the hell do we get into the cathedral inner sanctum and empty that bloody room of those damn books?"

Owen shrugged his shoulders; he didn't know. That's when the door to the kitchen swung open and both stared at the church officer standing in the doorway. Jericho's finger hovered above the emergency travel icon on his mirror. The big man grinned; "Do you two buggers want to earn a silver thrupence?" Jericho pulled himself up and nodded. The captain of the church guard smiled; "The Bishop is giving a little private party tomorrow night in his chambers at the cathedral. You two seem to know the songs he likes. Be at the kitchens after Evensong. There will be plenty of beer and food." He gave the surprised pair a little wave and was gone. Walking down the small corridor, deep in thought about the failed apprehension of the witches and their evil accomplices; he never heard the pair of minstrels laughing.

8. SHOWTIME.

They stood by the doors of the huge kitchens, packed with cooks and assistants. There was an entire pig roasting on a spit, with several big chickens cooking alongside it. The captain dropped a silver coin into Jericho's outstretched hand and smiled; "You can be rude as you like, sing about anything naughty; this is a stag evening, the only women here are harlots and whores. You're on after the bloody Jester." He slapped Jericho on the shoulder and pointed into the big dining room. "Just behind the statue of St. Peter, you can doss there, watch the show and perform when the Jester has finished." He wandered off, swigging a flagon of beer.

Owen stood with his mouth open as a big girl approached the pair with a tankard in each hand, "Here you are boys. Helen [the girl from Percival's tavern] said you're bloody rude and funny. I can't wait, if you want any more beer or grub just shout." Jericho nodded and his took his tankard. Owen accepted his very slowly and the pair watched the girl walk away. She was completely naked apart from a small black leather apron that covered very little.

Jericho sipped his beer; "Do you know that I always thought senior clergy spent their evenings in quiet contemplation of God and praying a lot. How wrong can you get?" Owen just smiled as another naked serving girl walked pass, carrying four tankards in her hands. "Now that's real skill." Jericho pointed out with a small smile.

Owen just groaned and followed Jericho; they sat on the floor behind the statue of St. Peter and watched the party get underway. A fire-eater received some applause, but only after he had set his beard and shoulders alight; he ran from the room screaming and plunged his head into a bucket of water. He wasn't happy; the bucket was used by kitchen staff to relieve themselves.

The jester was on next, a big fat man with a high squeaky voice. He waved his colourful sticks about and jingled his bells. He told jokes about the King, the Queen, Welsh people, the French and mostly about the Scots. He was as funny as having your penis cut off with a rusty blunt axe. The crowd threw anything they could grab at him. He fled the hall as couple of daggers thudded into the stone floor.

He passed by the two minstrels shouting for God and his mother.

Jericho and Owen leapt to their feet and Jericho strummed his lute while Owen banged his drum. They marched out with Jericho singing 'The Good Ship Venus' again. The crowd loved it. Again. He followed up with several well-known 'Rugby Songs' [well known in another century of course!] and the appreciative audience screamed for more. He finished with 'Lydia the tattooed lady' and there were shouts for more. The pair did two encores before the audience let them go and settled back to watch two young girls rolling about the floor on a rug; having hard lesbian sex with each other and several wooden toys.

The captain staggered past them, and they followed him into the corridor. They watched as he pissed through an open window and then rejoined the party. Jericho was following his mirror's directions and they found the Arch-Bishops little privy. The door was already bricked up half of its length. Jericho shone his torch in; there was nothing but the privy seat and a disgusting looking bundle of cloth.

"Nothing to read?" muttered Owen, then saw the remains of several pages on the floor; he peered closely and grunted; "The Gospel of St. Mark. Charming."

That's when they heard the footsteps in the dark corridor and could see a small light appearing. Jericho operated his mirror, and the pair was cloaked from living humans. They watched as Giovanni, holding a small lamp with a bundle of books under his arm appeared. He looked about and threw the books into the privy, chuckling a little to himself. They watched him carefully as he placed the lamp on the floor and looking about again, pulled a small watch from a pocket.

Jericho checked his mirror and found that it was indicating a free flowing time portal. He raised his mirror and operated the defense app, stunning Giovanni, who collapsed on the floor. "Get those bloody books!" Jericho shouted and Owen climbed over the bricks and pushed the books into his bag. Jericho pulled the watch from Giovanni and stuffed it into his pocket. When Owen re-joined him, they lifted Giovanni up and Jericho operated his mirror. They disappeared just as the captain staggered into the corridor. All he saw was Giovanni apparently floating in mid air then vanish completely. The captain sighed and shook his head; fucking roast pig did it to him every time. He had sworn to give it up, but he loved it dearly. He groaned and stumbled away.

The bishop's party drew him back with the star turn about to perform, Big Kate and her donkey Malcolm.

Jericho and Alex watched from the crowded street as the royal cars passed them, heading for the main doors of the cathedral. They watched as Lord Price welcomed the Queen, next to the Arch-bishop of course. Just behind the pair stood a smiling Jenifer Sailles. "I love the idea that she'll never know how different her fate would have been, had the dark Side succeeded with their little scheme." Alex grinned and waved a small plastic 'union jack' flag.

Jericho just grunted and stood with his arms folded. "Demon Ingress reports that Ester has become a minion of the Dark Prince; he loved her scheme, and we all know that he can spot real dark talent when he finds it." Alex chuckled; "I understand from Owen that you're quite some talent yourself with a lute!"

Jericho almost smiled; "Come on, let's get back to the lighthouse. Mrs. Harris has knocked up a hot beef curry; it's one of my favourites." The pair found a quiet shop doorway and simply vanished.

THE END

EPILOGUE:

"This mission was considered a success for Jericho and Team 74. The original human timeline had been restored and the clever plot by the Dark Prince thwarted. His minion – Ester – was to become a formidable foe against the teams of light."
SJW

CHARACTERS:

Lord David Price had his moment of glory when her majesty Queen Elizabeth II visited the Cathedral during the Jubilee celebrations of 1977. Unfortunately, Lord David was diagnosed with Cancer in 1980 and subsequently died. His soul was collected and processed.

Miss Jenifer Sallies fate was changed by the actions of the temporal detectives and never was imprisoned. She left her job with the Church of England and wrote children's books for a living. She married in 1983 and had three children. She lived to be 97 and died surrounded by her large family in a Kent Hospice. Her soul was collected and processed.

John Kennedy never died in the house fire in 1977 and continued his career as an investigative journalist. He wrote several books about organized crime. He was shot dead on his doorstep as he returned home from the pub. No one has ever been arrested or charged with his murder. It remains unsolved to this day. His soul was collected and processed.

Detective Inspector Gary Meadows accidently drowned whilst on a family holiday in Greece during the summer of 1984. He left a widow and two children. His son [David] was to follow in his father's footsteps and join the Kent Police. Gary's soul was collected and processed.

Detective Sergeant William Turner was involved in an incident with two young women who made serious allegations against him in 1981. Whilst nothing was proved, he left the police and was last heard of driving Lorries around Europe. He died in 2021 and his soul was collected and processed. It was quarantined for 250 human years for abduction, murder and rape of several young women and girls. He may have escaped human justice; but he couldn't escape Divine justice!

Dr. Frank Gardener worked as a Pathologist until his retirement in 1991. He took up gardening and his flowers won several prizes in local shows. He died in 2002 from lung cancer - he was a heavy smoker - and his soul was collected and processed.

Professor Allan Fordham's fate interested Owen. Whilst not connected with this particular mission Owen looked up the Collector who had dealt with the dead man's soul. Owen was shocked to find that Alex had probably been right. The professor claimed he had been strung up by three rough men after they destroyed his papers on his breakthrough vaccine. Diabetes remains uncured to this day and currently costs just the NHS a staggering £10 BILLION each year! It appears Alex was more right than she would ever know.........

Sir Robert De Morse lived up to his title as 'knight' defending a supposed innocent woman against charges of 'Devilry and witchcraft'. His family was disgraced, and his lands confiscated by the Church. He had been killed in very unequal combat and his soul was collected and processed. He now works as a Collector.

Simon De Morse, the old Knight's young grandson lost all his grandfathers lands and titles. He had no other living relatives. Had the boy not been taken in by Leofric, he would probably have starved to death in the hedgerows. He grew into a big strong man and worked his new family's farm. He married and had six children by two wives. He died in 1444 and his soul was collected and processed.

Mistress Alice Field abandoned the boy [young Simon] immediately after his grandfather's death. She worked as a house maid for a local merchant and died of the 'pox' in 1386. Her soul was collected and processed.

Leofric Sailmaker remained loyal to the De Morse family after the knight's death and took the boy Simon into his home. He worked as a farmer and raised the boy like his own son. He died in 1398 and his soul was collected and processed.

Richard Catchpocket [Tavern Owner] died in his sleep after suffering an unspecified fever in 1381. His funeral was attended by several of his old comrades from the former King's wars. He has no less than five hundred descendants living today! His soul was collected and processed. It was quarantined for a full human Century for some serious acts of murder and rape committed whilst a young solder of the old King.

Mistress Ester Clemencies was burnt at the stake and her books were snatched by Jericho. Thus, history never recorded or noted her 'remarkable finds or discoveries'. The current human timeline had been restored by the temporal detectives. She went to her master – the Dark Prince – a failure. But the prince knows dark talent when he sees it. She is currently a Tier Two Demon and is heading for the top. Team 74 will encounter her again.

William Courtenay [Archbishop of Canterbury – 1377] distanced himself from the trial and ensured he wasn't involved. He was a pious man and perhaps didn't have the stomach for a 'show trial'. He died in 1396 and his soul was collected and processed.

Percival Parish died in 1392. He was found face down in a local pond. The magistrate decided he had died – by drowning – after a drinking session. Percival had, in fact, been murdered by his mistress Gwen and her brother Henry. The pair disappeared with his life savings of several pounds and fled to York where they opened a tavern together. Having no family, the tavern was sold to a wealthy merchant from Kent in 1393. It survived until 1658, when it was destroyed by fire. In the modern era, where it stood is now just part of a parade of shops. Percival's soul was collected and processed.

Sir John Gavell was made a Baron in 1380 and married three times - all young girls - and had nine children. He died in 1409 a very rich old man surrounded by his large family. His direct descendants still have power to this day, and most are followers of the Dark Side. Unsurprisingly, no soul was collected. He is now a Senior Minion of the Dark Prince and Demon Ingress believes he could soon be a Tier Two Demon. He's also headed for the top in that organization, he's great friends with the demon Ester; they make a wonderful dark couple!

Ralph Coldhands; aka Giovanni Romano was returned to his own time period by Jericho and Owen. The time portal he used had been closed by Jericho. He died in 1933 and his soul was collected and processed. He received no sanction for his time travelling escapades which surprised Team 74.

The Captain of the Church Guard; Edward Bellman died in 1380 of a strange fever and his soul was collected and processed. He left a wife and seven children. Some of his descendants still live in the area today.

ILLUSTRATION CREDITS.

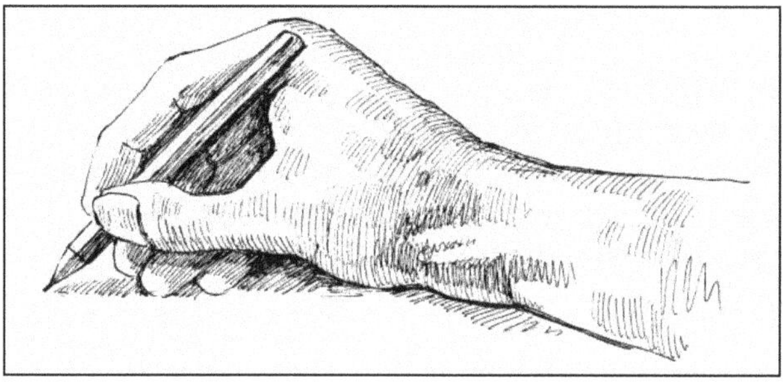

"ILLUSTRATION CREDITS FOR THE TEMPORAL DETECTIVES: SERIES 3. "

"All sketches as noted were created by the author and are copyright. The original images were found in the public domain with obscure or lapsed copyright accreditation. Should you claim current copyright to any please, contact the author immediately at:

stephen.williams24@btinternet.com

ALL original drawings, photographs or other images were found on various websites using 'Google Image Search'. They were found in the Public Domain with no artist details apparent [except where noted] and their copyright status was at the time; obscure or unknown. Where artist details are known; only images released into the Public Domain have been used for the sketches. All the published sketches were created by the author and are *Copyright © 2011-2023 Stephen Williams.*

Illustration credits for this book:

EPISODE 1: "THE JERUSALEM MIRROR."
The original photograph was found in the Public Domain with its copyright status unknown or obscure. The published sketch was created by the author and *Copyright © 2011-2023 Stephen Williams.*

EPISODE 2: "33AD."
The original photograph was found in the Public Domain with its

copyright status unknown or obscure. The published sketch was created by the author and *Copyright © 2011-2023 Stephen Williams.*

EPISODE 3: "THE PREIST."
The original drawing was from a website covering the supernatural and paranormal. It was found in the Public Domain with no artist details and its copyright status is obscure. The published sketch created by the author and *Copyright © 2011-2023 Stephen Williams.*

EPISODE 4: "STRANGER'S MARKET."
The original photograph was found in the Public Domain with its copyright status unknown or obscure. The published sketch was created by the author and *Copyright © 2011-2023 Stephen Williams.*

EPISODE 5: "NAPOLEON'S CHINESE CABINET OF MAGIC – PART 1."
This sketch created by the author from an original Motion Picture Still from the Film: 'Napoleon' a 1927 silent French epic motion picture produced, written and directed by Abel Gance. But the original was found in the 'public domain'. The published sketch created by the author and *Copyright © 2011-2023 Stephen Williams.*

EPISODE 6: "NAPOLEON'S CHINESE CABINET OF MAGIC – PART 2."
This sketch created by the author from a drawing of Napoleon I. The original was found in the 'public domain'. There were no copyrights claimed. The published sketch created by the author and *Copyright © 2011-2023 Stephen Williams.*

EPISODE 7: "XAVIER TABBERT'S HOSPITAL FOR THE DEAD, THE DYING AND THE UNFORGIVEN."
The original photograph was found in the Public Domain with its copyright status unknown or obscure. The published sketch was created by the author and *Copyright © 2011-2023 Stephen Williams.*

EPISODE 8: "HARBRINGER."
This sketch created by the author from an original picture found on a now defunct website: 'Necronomicon'. The book that contains this page is regarded as one of the most evil books in

existence! Copyright status is currently obscure. But the original was found in the 'public domain'. The published sketch created by the author and *Copyright © 2011-2023 Stephen Williams.*

EPISODE 9: "UNKNOWN NUMBER."
The original photograph was found in the Public Domain with its copyright status unknown or obscure. The published sketch was created by the author and *Copyright © 2011-2023 Stephen Williams.*

EPISODE 10: "SNOOKER, STOCKINGS & DEVILISH DECEIT."
The original photograph was found in the Public Domain with its copyright status unknown or obscure. The published sketch was created by the author and *Copyright © 2011-2023 Stephen Williams.*

EPISODE 11: "1914."
This original photograph was found in the Public Domain with its copyright status unknown or obscure.

EPISODE 12: "THE CORPSE CHRONICLER OF CANTERBURY CATHEDRAL."
An illustration of Christine de Pizan writing in her study, from *'The Book of the Queen'* (Harley MS 4431, f. 4r) the published sketch was created by the author and *Copyright © 2011-2023 Stephen Williams.*

IMAGE USED ON PAGE 403.
The 'Pen & hand' sketch was found in the Public Domain and is shown as 'Royalty' free and gave no copyright details.

Ingram Content Group UK Ltd.
Milton Keynes UK
UKHW020044210623
423745UK00014B/441

9 781739 434625